DEAD EUROPE

Christos Tsiolkas is the author of three other novels: *Loaded* (filmed as *Head-On*), *The Jesus Man* and *The Slap*, which won the Commonwealth Writers' Prize 2009, was longlisted for the Man Booker Prize 2010, and was shortlisted for the 2009 Miles Franklin Literary Award and the ALS Gold Medal. Christos Tsiolkas is also a playwright, essayist and screenwriter. He lives in Melbourne.

Also by Christos Tsiolkas

Loaded
The Jesus Man
The Slap

Christos Tsiolkas

DEAD EUROPE

Atlantic Books
London

First published in 2005 in Australia by Random House Australia Pty Ltd

First published in Great Britain in 2011 in paperback by Atlantic Books,
an imprint of Atlantic Books Ltd

1 3 5 7 9 10 8 6 4 2

A CIP catalogue record for this book is available from the British Library.

ISBN: 978-0-85789-1-228

Printed and bound by CPI Group (UK) Ltd, Croydon, CR0 4YY

Atlantic Books
An imprint of Atlantic Books Ltd
Ormond House
26–27 Boswell Street London
WC1N 3JZ

ww.atlantic-books.co.uk

For 'Mitsos' Litras and
Dimitris Tsoilkas, in gratitude

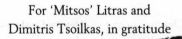

To a saintly man
—So goes an Arab tale—
God said somewhat maliciously:
'Had I revealed to people
How great a sinner you are,
They could not praise you.'
'And I,' answered the pious one,
'Had I unveiled to them
How merciful you are,
They would not care for you.'

Czeslaw Milosz

ANTE-GENESIS

THE FIRST THING I was ever told about the Jews was that every Christmas they would take a Christian toddler, put it screaming in a barrel, run knives between the slats, and drain the child of its blood. While Christians celebrated the birth of Jesus, Jews had a mock ceremony at midnight in their synagogues, before images of their horned God, where they drank the blood of the sacrificed child.

—Is that really true, Mum? I demanded. I could not have been more than five years of age. My mother had been reading to us from an illustrated book of mythology. Her hair in those days was long and raven black; it cascaded down across her shoulders and her breasts. I would weave my fingers through it as I lay between her and my sister as she read to us. Mum had been reading to us about the gods of antiquity and I had demanded to know what had happened to them when Christ was born.

—They all went up in smoke and only God remained.

—And where did God come from?

—He was the Jewish God, she explained, but the Jews refused to accept his Son as their Saviour and for that they turned against him and followed Satan instead. They killed Christ and for that God will never forgive them.

—Is that really true, Mum? I asked again.

She suddenly burst out laughing. I knew then that it was make-believe.

—That is what my father told me and what his mother had told him. Maybe it is true and maybe it isn't. Ask your Papa. He knows about Jews.

—What do you want to ask your Papa?

The three of us looked up as my father entered the bedroom. In all of my childhood memories, my father is a giant, strong and lean and handsome, towering above me. He had just finished showering, and came out buckling the belt on his jeans. His skin gleamed like that of the gods in the plates of the mythology book.

I breathlessly recited what my mother had just told us about the Jews. He frowned and spoke harshly to her in Greek. Her face had crumpled. My hand instinctively reached out to her. My father sat on the bed and patted his thigh and I crawled across my mother and jumped onto his lap. I could smell the poppy-seed oil in his wet hair.

—What's this?

It was a regular test of my knowledge of the Greek language and I was anxious to do well. He was pointing to the centre of his face.

—Nose, I answered in Greek.

—And this?

—Mouth.

—And this?

—Eyes.

—And this?

—Hair.

—And this?

I was confused. I had forgotten the word for 'chin'. He whispered the word and I repeated it to him. He then made a slicing motion across his throat.

—And if I do this, what would you see? What would come out?

I was silent. I had no idea how to answer.

—Blood, my sister yelled out eagerly in Greek.

—That's right, he said, now speaking in English. Jews have my eyes and my nose and my hair and my chin and we may all even share some of the same blood. I grew up with Jews,

I studied with Jews and Jews were my friends. He looked across at my mother.

—Your mother is a peasant. Scared of everything she doesn't know. And she knows nothing about Jews.

Sophie and I were quiet. We knew that for my father the word 'peasant' was one of the worst insults. The word conjured up images of dark, cowed faces, of evil old crones and decrepit, toothless old men.

—I'm sorry. My mother's voice was low, chastened.

My father ignored her. He opened a bureau drawer, pulled out some money and folded the notes into his pocket.

—Where are you going?

—Out.

—When are you coming back?

—When I'm ready.

I understood that he was still angry. He kissed my sister and me and, without looking at my mother, he left the house.

I picked up the mythology book and started flicking through the pages.

—No more, my mother said, shutting the book, I'm tired.

I must have pleaded for one more story. She turned her fury on me and shouted at us both to leave her alone. Scrambling across the bed, my sister and I fled the room, slamming the door behind us. We must have put on the television. The set was new, the black and white images as crisp and sharp as the white shirts my father wore, the black shoes that he shone diligently every morning. We must have watched television till my mother had done what she needed to do to calm herself and then she would have emerged from their room, she would have kissed our brows, and then begun to make us breakfast.

I wasn't to hear about the Jews again until I was eleven and my father started making plans to move us all back to Greece. For a whole summer all he talked about was Europe.

He told us about Paris and Berlin, real cities, he explained, cities in which there were people in the streets day and night. He spoke about his own home, Thessaloniki, how it was the most beautiful city in Greece. His words painted pictures for me: I could see the crowded, dirty port with the ruined castle looking down onto it; I could imagine the tiny alleys and the sloping-roofed stalls of the old Hebrew markets; the crammed terraces of the old city. He said how he would take me on a walk under the Alexandrian Arch that was over two thousand years old. Imagine that, he kept repeating, two thousand years. What does this country have to offer that is that old? Nothing. Fucking nothing. We are going back to real history. Greece is free again.

I knew that my mother did not share his excitement about returning, even to a Greece that had just booted out the Colonels. She had lived most of her life in Australia, and she countered his excitement with concerns about money, about how we children were to cope with learning the language. He brushed her worries aside. He ridiculed her fear of flying.

—There's nothing to fear, he smiled. Aeroplanes are safer than cars.

—They terrify me.

—Peasant, he chided, but there was a smile on his face and he kissed her on her lips. I'll hold your hand the whole time, he promised. He lowered his voice to a whisper. You are so beautiful, I'll have to hold on tight to you in Greece. They're real men there, they'll want you.

I was blushing.

—Shut up, Dad.

My father winked at me as my mother laughed and pulled away from his grip.

—What if we get hijacked?

That summer the news was full of images of military-fatigued Arab men holding hostages to ransom. I found their camouflaged faces, with only their steely black eyes visible, both terrifying and alluring.

—There's nothing to fear from the hijackers, he counselled her. Just remember, if the plane gets hijacked don't say a word in English. Just speak in Greek. They won't harm us then, they'll let us off immediately. They know we Greeks are their friends. Their comrades, he added.

—Why do they hijack planes? I asked him. What do they want?

—What the fuck do they teach you at school? He softened his tone. They want their land back. They're fighting to get their land back. The Jews have stolen their land.

Blood and land. Thus far, this is what I knew about the Jews. Jews were blood and land.

But with the coming of autumn, all talk of Europe ceased and I soon realised that we were not going. It may have been that Dad had lost another job. I can't remember and I didn't mind. The idea of travel had excited me but I did not want to leave either my friends or my home. Mum and Dad took us for a camping holiday to the prehistoric forests of the Grampians; climbing the abrupt ferocious mountains that jutted out of the desert landscape, I forgot all thoughts of Europe, of crowded, never-sleeping cities.

My father died before I reached Europe. We buried him in a civil ceremony; he was adamant he would not be buried as a Christian. My mother pleaded with Sophie and me to agree to an Orthodox funeral but we stood our ground. When I had been just a boy, around the time my mother had told me the heinous lies about the Jews, I remembered a morning when the house seemed to shake from the screams my parents were hurling at one another. Sophie and I peeked into the kitchen to see that, instead of their work uniforms, my father had on a shirt and tie and my mother was wearing her best dress. Dad was drunk, almost paralytic: he was slurring and stumbling. My sister and I clung to each other, terrified. We listened to the argument. Someone had died. The man who had died did not want to be buried by the Church, did not want anything to do with the priests. My father was adamant he would not betray his friend's last wish. He threatened to upset the funeral, to insult the family, the priests, everyone. My mother did not want him to shame her in front of the congregation. You have to have respect, husband, she was crying, you have to show respect. My father was also in tears: They're all fucking hypocrites. Maybe, my mother had answered simply, but your friend is dead, it's the living that now matter. My mother got her way. Dad passed out on a kitchen chair and Mum took us off to school. But I never forgot the force of my father's fury, nor the conviction in his voice when he called them hypocrites.

Sophie and I would not be shaken from our determination to bury my father as he wanted. Please, my mother beseeched us, do it for me. What does it matter? Your father is dead. She was on her knees, she was banging the floor with her fists, she was tearing out her hair. I could tell that Sophie was wavering. I remembered that my mother was a peasant.

—His soul would never forgive you.

We got our way. My father is buried on unconsecrated ground.

For his headstone we ordered a small rectangular stone inscribed with his name and the dates of his birth and death. Underneath, in Greek, we had the words: husband, father, worker. We asked the cheery Croatian stonemason to carve the hammer and sickle into the stone but the burly old man refused. On the day of the burial my sister and I painted the symbol crudely on the stone in her scarlet Max Factor nail polish. Like blood, it washed away in the first rain.

On the third anniversary of my father's death, I took my lover to his gravesite. I crouched and pulled out the weeds around the headstone. I had not long returned from Europe.

On my last night in Thessaloniki, my cousin Giulia, the daughter of my father's brother, had placed a small red pin in my hand. It was my father's Greek Communist Party membership badge, she told me. He never wore it. He didn't dare. It had been hidden behind a portrait of my grandfather and grandmother. My aunt discovered it and was going to throw it away but my cousin saved it. For you, she told me, I saved it for you.

I took that pin with me across Yugoslavia beginning its descent into civil war, through Hungary and Czechoslovakia just emerging back into history. I travelled with it through Italy, Germany and France, flew with it from London to Melbourne.

Colin watched me as I dug a small hole in the ground, placed the badge in the pocket of earth and covered it over with dirt.

—Steve's buried here in this cemetery.

—Who?

—Steve Ringo.

I said nothing.

—I'm going to visit his grave. Do you want to come with me?

—No.

I didn't dare look at him. I was furious. Colin walked away and I sat cross-legged on the ground, took a joint from my shirt pocket and lit it. Steve Ringo had been the first man Colin had ever loved. At nineteen, Steve had been arrested for manufacturing and dealing amphetamines. He emerged from seven years in prison with dual faiths: the teachings of the Christian God, and the doctrines of Aryan Nation. He was the only one of Colin's Mum's lovers to show any interest in her child. He forced the teenager to learn to read. He was adamant, Colin had explained, that the kid wouldn't end up like him.

—He couldn't read, he was fucking illiterate. He made me

read from the Bible for half an hour every evening. He forced me, told me he'd bash my lights out if I didn't do it. So I did, it took me a fucking year but I read the whole thing.

On Colin's fifteenth birthday Steve got him drunk on bourbon and took him to a tattooist mate who carved a swastika on the boy's right arm. Faded to a watery blue, the swastika was still there. I wanted to erase that tattoo. I hated the barrier it placed between myself and Colin. I hated its history, I hated its power.

—You have to get rid of it, you fucking have to get rid of it, I screamed at him when we first got together, I will not go out with you while you still have that evil on your body.

He was pleading with me to stay, crying.

—I can't, he whispered. This is my history and this is my shame.

And I stayed. His shame and his tears made me stay.

Colin believed in the Old Testament God, in punishment and vengeance and sin.

—What happened to Steve Ringo?

—He went back inside and OD'd in jail. I never saw him again.

I finished the joint and was looking at my father's name carved in stone. I suddenly laughed. How did it happen, Dad, I said out loud. How did all this happen? When Colin came back he found me laughing and crying. He offered a hand and pulled me up. Our arms across each other's shoulders, we walked to the car.

That night Sophie asked us to babysit the kids. While I cooked dinner, Zach curled up in the hollow between Colin's armpit and broad chest, and my lover read to him from the old mythology book. He was reading the ancient Egyptian creation myths when Zach interrupted him.

—Uncle Colin, didn't God make the Earth?

—Some people believe that, I hollered from the kitchen. But I don't.

The boy ignored me.

—Is He the same God as Zeus?

—No. He is the Jewish God. Zeus is the ancient Greek god.

I lowered the flame and went into the lounge room. Zach was looking in bewilderment at Colin.

—The Jews created God, he explained. They called Him Jehovah—now he is our God.

—Who are the Jews?

I found that I was holding my breath, waiting for Colin's answer.

—They're God's chosen people, he said simply, and began to read again from the book.

I had promised Zach that he could stay up late and watch *Star Wars*. He was so excited that he had to go and piss twice before we could start it. Lying between Colin and me, his legs were shaking in anticipation as the first bombastic notes of the score thundered through the stereo. Colin read to him as the yellow letters scrolled across the screen.

—A long time ago in a galaxy far, far away . . .

The boy turned to him, his face flushed, his eyes shining. Uncle Colin, he asked, does that mean Europe?

APOCRYPHA

THE MOST BEAUTIFUL WOMAN
IN THE WORLD

HIGH IN THE mountains, where the wind goes home to rest, lived Lucia, the most beautiful woman in all of Europe. Now one must not simply dismiss this claim as an exaggeration, a parochial and ignorant testament from the villagers and Lucia's kin. It is true that most of the village had not travelled far beyond the mountain ridges which formed their world. But the fame of her beauty had spread wide, from village to village, from village to town, from town to city, until carried in whispers through the roaming of commerce and war, it became a legend that began to cross even borders. Word of Lucia's beauty circulated slowly, but it did circulate, and men and women began to swear by the moon-milk complexion of her fair skin, her slender long hands, the coal-black hair that swam down to her waist. By the time of her thirteenth birthday Lucia's myth had spread so wide that travellers would go miles out of their way, circumnavigate the precarious mountain ridge, to stop at Old Nick's cafe, order their coffee or chai, and sit in hope of glimpsing the radiant girl.

But Lucia's father had no intention of allowing any man to covet his daughter. He himself began to be enamoured of the exquisite cast of her delicate face, intoxicated by the emerging abundance of her young flesh. His wife, noticing the stark hunger in her husband's eyes, kept a vigilant watch on her youngest daughter. Between the twin sentries of her father's ravenous desire and her mother's fearful jealousy, Lucia spent most of her days cloistered in silence. She was forbidden to go to school, as were all her sisters, and she was only allowed outside the family courtyard if escorted by her fathers or her brothers. To speak to any man, or even to a boy who was not a relative, was a sin to be punished with the most savage of beatings. She was allowed basic formalities with male relatives but even then she was ordered to not look them directly in the eye and to keep her face lowered at all times. Her mother's eagle gaze immediately noted any indiscretion on Lucia's part, and the punishment that followed was always swift and harsh. Both her eyes were blackened when she had laughed at her cousin Thanassis' impious joke. Her father's belt drew blood from her back when he whipped her on hearing that she had spoken to Baba Soulis' boys after church one Sunday. While thrashing her, Lucia's father would be deaf and blind to her agonies and her laments, exhausting himself with his brutality. Only afterwards, his rage spent, would he crawl on his knees in front of her, kissing her feet, pleading for, demanding apologies, licking clean her bloodied hands or brow or back. Watching all this was his increasingly terrified wife, who silently crossed herself and implored the saints that a suitor would come soon to take away this treacherous daughter. And if the saints won't help, she added, then let Black Death take her.

It should not be thought that Lucia was oblivious to the effects of her beauty. Her sisters, her brothers, her own father had shown enough devotion for her to understand that her looks were indeed powerful. She may have been forbidden to glance at men, but she took any opportunity that arose to break this command. When the priest fed her the communion wine she looked him boldly in the eye, causing his hand to shake; when her older brother hoisted her on his shoulders for a ride, she threw her skirts over his head; when she kissed the cheek of her just-wed brother-in-law before the altar, her whole family was shamed. Fotini, the eldest of the sisters, had been betrothed to Angelos, the oldest son of the widower Kapseli. Fotini's dowry had cost the family dearly—fifteen of their finest nanny goats, their cherished store of carpets and blankets. But the Kapselis family owned vast fields along the valley and it would be a prosperous match. When the marriage vows were completed and the families lined up in the church to kiss and bless the married couple, Lucia kissed Angelos twice chastely on his cheeks, but whispered her blessing close to his ear. The youth blushed and shivered, and almost fainted. And immediately underneath the thick black cloth of his grandfather's Constantinople suit, his erection flared. As the remaining guests kissed him and shook his hand they could not help but notice the awkward lump pressing against them. An initial sniggering, then laughter, and then howls of mirth followed the newlyweds outside the church. That night, on returning home drunk from the celebrations, her father's savagery had been so fierce that Lucia lay bleeding and unconscious for days. She was locked in the cellar, with the wine and the snakes, and only her mother was allowed to see her. And even she was forbidden to speak to her. Silently brushing her blood-matted hair, stroking her bruised face, Lucia's mother nursed her daughter back to life, forcing her to eat wet bread, splashing water on her lips, all the time imploring God and the saints and the Virgin to find a husband for her daughter. And if there were to be no one to the liking of the feverish possessed man who paced the floor above them, contorting in knots of guilt and self-disgust for the damage that he had inflicted on his most prized possession; if there were no acceptable suitor to be found, the mother prayed, let the Devil take her.

—We should marry her to Michaelis Panagis.

Lucia's father snorted, drank from his wine, and climbed into bed next to his wife. She turned her back to him. She smelt alcohol, sweat and sex on him. The embers in the kitchen fire were waning and she could hear her two daughters in the bed next to them quietly snoring. Lucia was still banished beneath the house. The boys were asleep, four of them on the one bed, in the room across the courtyard. Her husband touched her shoulder and she lifted her nightdress and slightly raised her leg. He entered her quickly, fucked her like a hare. He began snoring as soon as he had finished. She shook him awake. Lucia was not responding to her ministrations, was sickening. She must be married.

—We should marry her to Michaelis Panagis, she repeated.

—We have two others to marry off first.

—No, she insisted, Panagis is a good marriage. He'll bring wealth. It will be easier to marry the others after that.

—He's a bastard. I won't give my Lucia to any bastard.

—You won't give Lucia to anyone.

Michaelis Panagis was the child of the idiot Panagis and his Albanian whore, Maritha. It had been assumed that Panagis, who still dribbled and slurped when he spoke, would never find a wife, but his father had returned one morning with a young Albanian girl whom he had purchased across the mountains and whom he offered to his son. Within two years they had three children. As people could not believe that the idiot Panagis had it in him to sire a child, it was assumed that all three offspring were bastards, children of the Albanian whore and her father-in-law. They were all sickly children, living in filth and poverty, but the youngest, Michaelis, had surprised the village by disappearing when little more than a child and emerging years later fat and rich from his travels abroad. He had worked in Egypt and in America and on returning to the village he had paid for a pew and a gold icon for the Church of the Holy Spirit. Now every Sunday the idiot Panagis and the whore Maritha sat in front of the congregation, ignoring the envious glares behind their backs. Michaelis had built a huge house high above the village.

Though he was still insulted behind his back, there was no one in the village who did not greet him with a friendly word, who did not offer him the choice of any of their daughters.

—In the name of God, Husband, he has money.

He was silent.

—She is dying. It's a curse. It's a curse because you want to sin against your daughter.

The force of his fist on her face was so loud in the quiet mountain night that it woke the sleeping girls, who began to cry. He left his wife moaning, pulled on his trousers and descended the cellar stairs.

Lucia was lying still on the solid dirt ground. Her face was pale and her eyes dark hollows. He crouched before her and she hardly stirred from her stupor. He touched first her cheek, then her shoulder. He felt the firm curve of her breast. She did not stir but her frightened eyes looked straight into his soul. He closed his eyes, whispered his love for her and pulled her listless hand towards him. Quickly he stroked himself with her cold velvet hand and he spilt over the black dirt. He was crying.

—If he will take you, Daughter, you are to marry Michaelis Panagis.

He grabbed the child and kissed her harshly on the lips and face. Lucia pulled away.

—You are the most beautiful woman who has ever lived. Satan take you.

He raised himself and pulled up his trousers. Don't forget I am with the saints, Lucia. I am a saint for not raping you.

He climbed the stairs and locked the cellar door.

o O o

What is the use of being the most beautiful woman in the world if I'm barren?

19

The moon was high in the sky, and a slight breeze brought forth a keening from the pine trees that echoed through the mountains. Lucia and Michaelis had been married four years and she had yet to produce a child. The envious whispers and jealous curses that used to follow her along the paths of the village were now replaced by mutterings of pity and self-righteous joy.

Curse the damn lot of you. Lucia found sleep impossible; her dreams were filled with nightmares of demons and dead children. She cursed her father, her mother-in-law. She blamed her sorrow on the evil done to her by years of jealous occult mischief. She cursed her envious sisters and her embittered cousins. Surely it was one of them who had cast a spell on her womb? They were all bitches, jealous ugly bitches.

Every Sunday Lucia offered another promise to God should he make her pregnant, and every Sunday afternoon she and her mother would work together to undo the damage of the Evil Eye. Her mother would drop a touch of oil into the vial of holy water and she would read the villagers' gossip and spite in the dispersion of the oil. Then Lucia would pray in hope of undoing the evil; she would send down her own curses to the women who envied her. But still nothing stirred inside her. And every month when she felt her body flushing out her blood, she cursed the names of every woman in the village, spitting out each one.

But still nothing stirred inside her.

As she lay there, sleepless, there was a scratching on the door and she went cold. She held her breath. From the outbuilding she could hear bleating from one of the goats. Then the scratching continued. She shook Michaelis awake.

—Michaeli, there's something outside.

Her husband jumped out of the bed, reached for his hunting knife and opened the door. Two shivering figures stood under the moonlight.

—What in the devil are you doing here?

Lucia hid under the quilt. She knew one of the men at the door. It was Jacova, who worked as a tanner in Thermos; it was to Jacova that Michaelis sold the skins of the wolves and the minks that he hunted. Beside the Hebrew was a young boy, his eyes large and black. She could not hear the whisperings between her husband and the Hebrew.

Don't let them in, Michaeli, she prayed. Don't you dare let them in. But her husband beckoned her to rise and to bring out some wine. She pulled a shawl across her shoulders and, without looking at the strangers, she made her way into the dark cellar to fetch a pail of wine. She placed two glasses in front of the men and she and the boy sat apart on a bench near the dead fire while the men talked to each other in whispers. They did not dare light the lanterns. Lucia peered through the shutters at her mother-in-law's house across the courtyard. No one stirred. She came and sat back on the bench.

She looked the boy up and down. She had never been so close to a Hebrew and was surprised at how ordinary he seemed. His features were not so different from those of her own brothers. His brow was wet, as indeed it would be if he had just completed the long walk from Thermos up into the mountains. She could smell his fear, and the keen hint of his trade, the bitter reek of pelt and leather. Though still only a child, he was developing the strong forearms of his father. He was destined to be a handsome man. She smiled at him but the boy blushed and immediately looked down at his feet. Lucia smiled to herself. She was still beautiful.

—I will forget him. If you take him he will be as your son.

Lucia strained to hear more of the conversation.

Michaelis shook his head.

—It is too dangerous, Jacova. The Germans are everywhere and all the region knows that Elia is your son. We cannot hide him.

Lucia nodded to herself. Good. Good answer, husband. All the harpies in the village will be lining up to denounce us.

—Michaeli, I have known you a long time. Yes, the Germans are everywhere, that is why my wife and daughters and I must flee. But up here in these mountains there are many hiding places. You can hide the boy. And this war will not last. Once it is over, once the Germans have gone, the boy is yours to keep.

Lucia shook her head in disbelief. The man was a fool if he thought that they would be taken in. Everyone knew that the Hebrews could not be trusted. Even if the Germans were to be conquered, nothing would stop Jacova returning and claiming his son. No, throw him out, Michaeli, throw out the Hebrew and his bastard child.

Michaelis turned to Lucia.

—Up near the summit of the mountain, near where you graze the goats, in what condition is the old church?

—Michaeli, stop this nonsense. Old Voulgaris, Basili Leptomas' youngest, they all graze their herds up there. We could not hide the child.

—We could, beneath the stone. The old monks had a room beneath the church. No one is fool enough to venture there. We could lock the cellar during the day and the child could roam free at night. We could do that.

Lucia stared across the table to where the older Hebrew was sitting. Jacova was looking only at Michaeli, a glimmer of hope shining in his eyes. The boy was staring at her. In the darkness his face was dark and only the white in his eyes was visible. Lucia shuddered.

—We cannot do it, Husband. If they catch us . . .

Michaeli ignored her. He was looking hard at Jacova.

—And what will you pay us if we decide in your favour?

The father nodded to his son. From underneath his tunic Elias took out a small parcel wrapped in black silk. Jacova took it from him, pulled away the silk and opened the lid of a square wood box. In the dark room, the gold and the jewels sparkled like fire. Lucia drew a breath. Michaelis' eyes grew wide and delighted. Lucia rose from the bench and stood beside her husband. The men and the boy had disappeared. From the box she took out a small band, gold and studded with glittering silver stones, which she placed on her finger. She took a ruby brooch and held it close to her lips. All the time the boy's gaze did not leave her enraptured face.

—Ours?

—All of it, yours.

Lucia placed the jewels back into the box. Michaelis closed the lid and placed the box on his lap as if he feared the Hebrew would regret his offer and snatch it back.

—He will work hard for me.

—He works hard for me now.

Jacova placed his arm around his son.

—You will treat him fairly?

—Of course.

Michaelis rose from the table. He gave the box to his wife and beckoned the boy to come with him. The father and son were allowed a moment to say farewell and then Jacova began his trek back down the mountain. Lucia watched as her husband and the boy walked into the black night for their ascent to the summit. She cursed her useless womb, pounding her fists on her stomach, and then fell to the ground and began banging the stone floor. Her anger was so ferocious that on reaching to brush aside a wisp of hair that had fallen loose from her head scarf, she found that she had torn a clutch of hair from her head. In her fury and hatred she had not felt the pain. Her face twisted into a terrible grimace, spit falling from her mouth as she banged her head on the stone, until she finally exhausted herself from curses and lay trembling on the floor. Again she could hear the breeze spinning among the trees. Giving up her curses, her prayers to God spent, she now turned elsewhere.

—Satan, give me my own child. Give me my own child, Lord, and take away the demon Hebrew you've let into my house.

As soon as Lucia uttered her prayer, a peace descended. Slowly she rose from the floor and, gathering her hair tight under her scarf, she dried her eyes. The dawn was beginning. She went to light the fire and prepare herself for the day ahead.

I DID NOT like my hotel room. The bed was too small, the sheets were frayed and the glass window was stained with the dust and the perpetual grey residue of the Athenian air. Not that it really mattered much; the view outside the room was ugly as well. It looked down on a concrete apartment block, a billboard for the Agricultural Bank of Greece, and if I strained my eyes hard enough I could catch a glimpse of the neon from Syntagma Square. The airconditioning hummed at a consistent and annoying low pitch; water dripped dripped dripped in the bathroom. I opened my eyes and nothing had changed. The dull cheap white paint on the wall, the dripping water, the humming machinery.

Beside me, the boy was still asleep. His snores were light and a thin strip of dewy saliva coated his lips. His shoulders and chest were tanned piss-yellow from the Mediterranean sun. Fine blond hairs spread across his belly. He hardly stirred when I got up. I switched on the bathroom light and looked in the mirror. My skin was stretched tight across my face. On the floor, next to the full ashtray, there was still a shot of whisky left. I put the bottle to my mouth and drank.

—I have some too? He spoke to me in his terrible English, and I replied in my inadequate Greek that the bottle was now empty. His eyes were bleary and red. He rose and walked into the bathroom unembarrassed by his nudity. He shut the door and I quickly began to put my clothes back on. I put on my watch and saw that it was close to two o'clock in the morning. I was far from sleep. I waited impatiently for the youth to finish.

I had found him in the park across from the old Olympic Stadium. The day was giving itself over to evening and under the shade of a large English oak a group of young men were playing cards. They were all wearing jeans and most were naked to the waist. Only a couple of them looked Greek. The others could have been Slav. Could have been Russian. Could have been Polish. He had been wearing a singlet, a faded blue sweatshirt with the Adidas stripes. I found myself staring at him, the surprising dark thatch of hair under his arms, his keen concentration on the gambling. One of the other youths noticed me staring, and then so did a pretty transvestite with her arm around one of the younger boys; she winked at me. Embarrassed to be caught out, a little frightened by their youth and poverty, I kept walking.

I heard footsteps behind me.

—Have you cigarette?

I stopped and gave him one.

I didn't want to ask his age. His brow was lined and weary, his posturing was macho and confident, but his eyes and mouth betrayed his youth. As the sun faded and the warm Athenian breeze encircled us, I found myself drawn by the faintly unpleasant but intoxicating odour of sweat on his burnt gold skin. We negotiated prices in the twilight and smoked my cigarettes as we walked back to my hotel.

He had said hardly a word as we were walking, but once inside the room he was cheerful and chatty. He was Russian, he told me, and we spoke a combination of Greek and English in order to understand each other. His cheerfulness increased when I mimed to him that we would not need any condoms as I had no intention of fucking or being fucked. We drank from my bottle, he smoked more of my cigarettes, and he allowed me to shoot my come across his shoulders, his cheeks, his chest. He kept his eyes firmly closed and when I had finished he rubbed his face vigorously with the sheet.

—Your skin very white for a Greek, he told me.

—My family is Greek. But I told you, I am from Australia.

He traced a finger along my shoulder; he smirked as I playfully tugged at his balls.

—But Australia too is plenty sun, no? He moved away from me.

—It is winter there now.

He sniffed, eyed me suspiciously, then got up and went into the bathroom. I heard him pissing and I quickly hid my wallet under the mattress.

—Would you like to stay a little? In this claustrophobic hotel room, with the hot, crowded city outside, I was suddenly childishly lonely: I was scared to be on my own. But no more money, I warned. I don't have much.

He glanced around the hotel room, weighed his options, checked my watch, and nodded. We drank more from the bottle. He had been the first to fall asleep.

Now, he was taking a long time in the toilet. I glanced at my trousers lying on the floor but they were not in the spot I had thrown them when we'd gone to bed. I checked my pockets and discovered that a fifty-dollar Australian note I'd intended to exchange the night before was missing. I smiled to myself. The price did not seem unfair. I quickly checked under the mattress. The wallet was still there.

There was a flush and his steps were slow and hesitant when he emerged. He avoided my eyes. For the first time I noticed that there were tiny red scabs forming a grid along his arms. I felt crushed by my age, my thickening body, the sly strands of grey in my once jet-black hair. I could not wait for him to leave.

—I am going out now. We have to leave this room.

He put on his jeans, slipped on his sandals and rubbed his forehead. He sat on the edge of the bed, silent and sullen. I was afraid of him then.

—Okay, he slurred suddenly. May I have money for taxi? he asked.

—How about the Australian dollars in your pocket?

He grinned and I was struck again by his beauty. I sat next to him and kissed his neck, tasted pungent buttery sweat. He moved away.

—Taxi no take Australian dollar.

I handed him a crisp new euro note and we took the stairs together down to the small lobby. The concierge on duty called me over. He was a man in his mid-fifties, with a thick wide belly and wet moustache. An image of fireworks breaking over the Olympic stadium was dusty and mounted crookedly on the wall. He yelled at me in Greek.

—You've only paid for one person. Yours is a single room.

I blushed.

—I am the only one using my room. This is a friend.

His contempt was clear.

—After midnight, your friends, as you call them, they too will have to pay. He spat out the words.

Still red, not looking at him, not looking at the youth, I slipped another clean euro note across the desk. He glanced at it, then at me, then at the boy. He picked it up, slipped it in his pocket and turned his back to us.

—Fucking cunt! I was humiliated. The boy shrugged.

—He not like what I do. He said it casually, disinterested. It was then I cursed myself: damn, I should have taken his photo. I stretched out my hand and he laughed without taking it.

—I go. Thank you, Mister. His inflection was mocking and I watched him shoot across a crowded avenue and disappear into the shadows of an alley.

The streets of Athens were still choked with cars and people. It was late spring but it felt like high summer. I turned and walked without purpose away from the centre and towards Lecavitos Hill. I passed the main square in

Kolonaki, turned up a small winding lane and climbed the steep stairs that rose towards the peak. The clanking and throbbing of music and conversation, of cars and motorbikes dropped away and I sat on a small concrete wall and looked down to the city below.

I had arrived in Greece aware that I was going to fuck people, eager to engage in a bout of promiscuity, but the memory of the last few hours in the hotel room now shamed me. The experience of paying the youth for sex, while tantalising as fantasy—in fact, a fantasy in which I happily and often indulged in—in reality had proven cliched. It had been sordid and had made me feel old and disappointed. Not even the illicit memory of the boy's tough beauty could lessen my regret. I took off down the hill, past the young Greeks in their synthetic Italian clothes, past the fragile old faggots sitting patiently alone at coffee tables. At a kiosk I asked to use the phone and as the answering machine message began to play I also heard the rapid clicking of the kiosk's meter calculating my toll. It was only then that I asked myself what time it would be in Australia. Would Colin even be home yet?

—It's me, I'm calling from Athens. Are you there? I allowed a short gap of silence and then I continued. I'm safe. Nothing's changed, it's all still beautiful and mad. I'm ringing to say I love you very, very much. I will call again tomorrow. I waited hopefully for another moment, then I put down the phone.

It wasn't true that nothing had changed. It had been over twelve years since I had been in Athens and even after only two days I was aware that this was not quite the same city I had visited when I was twenty-three. The bilingual blue street signs had not changed, nor had the sun and the dust. But the alleys and arcades behind Ommonia had been cleaned up. A giant inflatable corporate clown floated high above the entry to the old market square. Its monstrous grinning face mocked the Greeks smoking and drinking below. The five rings of the Olympic movement were everywhere, as were the red and orange circles of MasterCard. Arabic and Mandarin calligraphy competed with the ubiquitous Cyrillic and Latin scripts. Athens had changed.

I awoke the next morning with a hangover. I had to be at the gallery by ten. What time had I fallen asleep? It must have been well after four. After my phone call to Colin, I had walked around the square, drinking, smoking, listening in to conversations. A young man in tight black pants winked at me. An older woman smiled and stretched out her leg towards me, her partner oblivious to the flirtation as he spoke vehemently into his mobile phone. I drank another whisky and then I walked the streets for kilometres. I walked until I was sure I was lost and when I finally grabbed a taxi to take me back to the hotel, the driver picked me for an Australian, told me I was standing on the wrong side of the road for where he was driving, and took me on a route that seemed tortuous and slow. I didn't care. When I reached the hotel, the man at reception was smoking another cigarette and spat as I walked past. I didn't fucking care. I jumped into bed and fell immediately to sleep.

I was ten minutes late to the gallery and I had to wait another twenty minutes before anyone else showed up. The gallery itself was on a small side street off Panepistimiou and I sat on the stoop chain-smoking cigarettes and making my headache worse. A young woman walking towards me lifted her sunglasses and started shouting.

—Why the hell are you sitting there?

I extended my hand and introduced myself. Immediately her face softened, she kissed me warmly on both cheeks and asked if I wanted a coffee. She took my arm and led me down the street.

—Don't you have to open the gallery?

—We have plenty of time, darling, she told me in her faintly American-tinged English, no one buys art before lunch.

Anastasia had flaming red lipstick, dressed herself in a short tight black skirt that clung to her plump tanned thighs, and spoke as she smoked: incessantly. I drank my sweet Greek coffee, chomped into my rich oily pastries and listened to her talk. She told me that she was born in Kozani but her parents had moved to Athens when she was very young. Of course, she told me, Kozani is the most beautiful part of Greece but what kind of work can I do there? It's provincial, of course, and that is sweet but tiring. She told me how she had travelled to Morocco, to Rome, to Paris, to Sofia and to the United States. She told me that only New York as a city could compare to Athens. I asked her if she had ever been to Australia.

—No, darling, never. It's too far. I detest aeroplanes and you have to fly a ridiculous amount of time to reach Australia, no?

I said she could always stop over in Singapore or Bangkok.

—Not interested. But, yes, China. I would love to see China. Have you been?

I told her no.

I had assumed Anastasia, whose aristocratic manner and decadent sangfroid I found enchanting, to be a spoilt rich kid and I was surprised, later, as we examined my photographs hanging in the gallery, when she told me that her father had tended goats and that she was herself born in a village. She had been looking closely at a photograph of a Greek man in overalls. Stavros had been a friend of my father's and I had photographed him at work, with a grin on his face and the half-assembled bodies of cars behind him. I had taken the photograph during his lunch break; his blue overalls were stained with grease. He was well into his fifties but his round, beaming face was still handsome and his wide-armed embrace of the camera's lens made it appear as if the world behind him—the world of assembly lines, clanking machinery, shadowy workers—all belonged to him.

—*Gamouto ton andra*. This is a real man.

Yes, I agreed, Stavros was indeed a real man.

—How long has he worked there?

—Most of his life. He migrated in the late sixties.

—I have an uncle in Australia.

I waited. This was not an unusual statement in the eastern Mediterranean.

—We have not heard from him in years. My father has attempted to find him, but we have had no luck. Possibly he doesn't want us to find him. She was still staring hard at the photograph.

—I think he might be a *gai*. That or a criminal. Why else would he ignore us?

I was silent and stepped up beside her. She smiled at me and we continued to walk past the photographs. Hanging there, large and colourful on the white walls, I was struck by how inconsequential they seemed. Stray figures, urban landscapes. A miniature Orthodox crucifix magnified to an immense size. Anastasia had not yet commented on my work and I badly wanted to hear her opinion. I was unsure how I fitted into this large, foreign metropolis. I doubted that my work belonged here at all.

She stopped again in front of another portrait, this time of a solid young Australian man in an Akubra hat, holding a blue heeler pup in his arms and wearing an open-necked blue-checked shirt. Fair down coated his pudgy cheeks, his blue eyes were cold and suspicious. I had not been able to make him relax in front of the lens. Instead, I had shot him as he was, tense and distrusting. He was standing against a window and outside was the red Australian desert. Against the wall, to his left, a bank of terminals and keyboards.

—This is very homo-*erotique*.

I was annoyed. I had wanted the photograph to represent something about the discontinuities in the Australia I had lived in. The incongruity of this young man, his appearance and demeanour belonging to the highlands of Scotland, framed against an unyielding ancient red desert, his clothes and attitude no longer suited to a working life spent largely behind a computer. I was also annoyed that she had summed up the photograph so perfectly, perceiving immediately the reasons for the young man's reluctance in front of the lens.

—Just because I am homosexual doesn't mean my work is homosexual.

Anastasia dismissed this statement with a yawn.

—That is a boring conversation and I will not indulge in it. Great art is homosexual. The ancients knew it. Even the Church knows this.

—And how about women? Do they have to be homosexual to be great artists?

—Of course, she snapped angrily, as if I had stated the obvious. And not only artists. We have to be homosexual to be businesswomen, to be anything but a mother or a *hausfrau* in this world.

Her pace increased and it seemed to me that in her rapid glances at my photographs, she was silently rejecting them. When we had completed our circle she drew me close to her and kissed me again on the cheek.

—You are very talented.

—What do you really think of them?

—I am saddened by them. The Australia you represent seems very cold and very empty. Only that man, Stavros, seems happy. No one else smiles in your photographs. She took a cigarette from her bag and lit up. Her unperturbed smoking in a gallery space shocked me. I took one from her and we smoked together.

—It is inevitable, living here in Athens, she continued,

that we meet so many Greeks from Australia. I cannot bear most of them. They are vulgar, ignorant and *très* materialistic. They are what we fear we are becoming. She looked down at her dress, her leather shoes. Eurotrash, she muttered and smiled ruefully. Then there are some Australians who are innocents. Young girls still worried about their virginity, young men who still practise their Orthodoxy as though the twentieth century had never occurred. Them, I like. But I do not understand them. It is as if they have not left the village. We laugh at them but they remind us of the past. And then there are a few who are not like Greeks here, and who are not like the French or the Germans or the English. And, thank God, nothing like the Americans. They are of their own world. Your work reminds me of those Australians. She looked around the gallery, taking in my work.

—*M'aresoune poli*. I like them a lot.

My hangover was cured, my eyes ablaze, I was elated.

The afternoon was spent on lunch, and on two interviews that the gallery owners had organised with magazines. One of the owners, Mrs Antonianidis, was a heavily made-up matron in her mid-fifties who proceeded to tell me how much she had adored my art, though it quickly became obvious that she had no interest in the photographs whatsoever. Her husband was large and stern-faced and spent the whole of the lunch on his mobile phone. The first journalist who interviewed me was a suited young man barely out of his teens who did not take off his Calvin Klein sunglasses throughout lunch and spent the first five minutes complaining about the slack habits of his Albanian maid. He was disappointed in my Greek and when it came time to photograph me he took a few lazy snaps with an instamatic and wished me well. The second journalist was better prepared. She invited me for a coffee in a bar filled with

Miro prints and her first question, when she snapped on the tape recorder, took me by surprise.

—Isn't the theme of homesickness, of exile and return, irrelevant to modern Greece?

It was a good question and it did strike me, as we sat in the stylish bar, indolent dance music throbbing quietly in the background, that the Greece I knew in Australia was indeed largely irrelevant to these modern Europeans. I scrambled for an answer.

—Maybe those themes are no longer relevant to you Greeks, but they are indeed relevant to Australians. In Australia we all ask ourselves where we come from.

—Even the Aborigines?

She was sorting through a series of black and white photocopies Anastasia had gathered of my photographs. She pointed to one of a young Aboriginal boy, a baseball cap on his head, a Tupac t-shirt on his chest. He was standing outside a Greek bomboniere store, scowling at my lens.

—Is he asking himself where he comes from?

—No, he's asking me where I come from. I looked around the bar, at the Athenians elegantly sipping their drinks. What should I say to him? Am I from Greece?

She too looked around the bar.

—Certainly not from this Greece. This is not Greece. This is fucking *marie-claire*. She turned back to me. Do you speak French?

I must have looked surprised because she laughed and told me that she did not feel confident in her English.

—You speak it well.

—No, I do not. My accent is terrible.

We spoke for twenty minutes and then she shut off the tape recorder and asked me if I wanted a drink. She ordered gin and tonic for herself and a whisky for me and proceeded to tell me that she had cousins in Australia. She told me of how much she loved her cousins and how much she wished they would return to Greece. But, of course, she added, they are like you. Not Greek like we are. She then told me that her cousin Thomas had told her of the Aboriginal flying men and asked me if I had ever seen them. I shook my head. It is the desert I would like to see, she said to me. When she finished her drink she shook my hand and I kissed her cheeks and wished I could kiss her eyes. She thanked me for my time and told me that her father had a brother and sister in Australia and that at every wedding, every baptism, every funeral and every celebration her father would prepare his suit, brush his hair, take her mother by the arm and on leaving the house would mutter, I wish my brother and my sister could attend as well.

—How many more interviews do you have to do?

—I just had the two. You are my last.

She shook her head.

—We Greeks have forgotten what we owe to exile. But I will not forget what it has cost my father to lose his brother and sister.

—People have short memories.

—*Pardon?*

—People forget. I spoke in her language.

The last thing she said to me, as she was rising to leave, was that I should improve my Greek.

Only a dozen people turned up for my opening and five of them were staffers from the Ministry of Culture who had paid for my ticket to Europe. I was asked to say a few words and I stumbled through as best I could. As I spoke of migration, the history of the Greeks in Australia, as I watched the happily nodding faces, I realised that nothing I said was of interest to them, that what they were seeing was some nervous young foreigner mangling their language and pretending to speak with commitment on a subject that had long ago become ossified. They were not interested in my return. I was not interested. I dribbled out in English, quoting Cavafy's 'Ithaka'. The applause was slight and polite.

Later, I got drunk on the wine and sold the photograph of Stavros to Anastasia. One of the bureaucrats took us out to a tavern for a meal and for more drinks, and Anastasia and I got very drunk and she apologised for the lack of attendance at my show.

—Australia is very far away. I understand.

—It is not that. We Greeks are insular. We don't believe in the rest of the world.

—You Greeks are arrogant.

She nodded her head in agreement.

—You are not insulted?

She stared at me, perplexed.

—Was that meant to be an insult?

We drank and we drank and I was driven to my hotel, but instead of going to my room I walked a drunken path through the crowded, carousing city and found myself at the park at Thission where I had bought the boy the night before. Many more youths were out that night; there was the potent smell of marijuana in the air. There were men who wandered in the shadows and if I had not been drunk I would have feared for my life. There were plenty of Russians, women and men, girls and boys, there were Greek whores and Albanian whores, there were Romanians and Poles, but I couldn't find the boy. I walked back alone and I fell into bed and when sleep arrived it came quickly to rescue me from exhaustion.

I spent the next two days walking around Athens, drinking the thick black coffee. I rang Colin and when he asked me how the show went I began to cry. I was ashamed of my vanity, ashamed that the poor attendance had humiliated me. Across the world, across time, Colin quietly told me that he loved me. How he desired my return. He told me how he missed my flesh, my smile, my eyes and my arse, my cock and my balls. I stopped crying.

My mother, when I rang her next, was not as sympathetic.

—Why haven't you visited your dad's family yet?

—I've been busy. I've had the show. I'm heading out of Athens tomorrow.

—Well, they've rung. Her voice was terse. She distrusted my father's relatives.

—Did you tell them about the exhibition?

—No. We were both silent. I understood. I was sure we were thinking of the same three photographs. *Tassia and Vivian*, silver gelatin print, 1999. Two women, naked, mouth to mouth, cunt to cunt. *Untitled 15*, c-type print, 1996. A withered Mediterranean man, Karposi's Sarcoma all over his face, dying in a hospital ward in Sydney's south. *Self-Portrait*, c-type print, 1999. Me, naked, with an erection. At the last moment I had decided against taking the self-portrait with me to Greece. I had paranoid visions of disgusted customs officials in Singapore or Dubai. Or Melbourne. But my mother didn't know this.

—You should have invited them.

—You think so?

Fat fucking chance.

I was thirteen when my mother overdosed on heroin. When I was much older I was to discover that it had not been the first time. Luckily my father was between jobs at the time, and my sister and I were at home on summer holidays. Dad had whacked up as well but he was bigger, stronger than Mum. I remember him screaming, attempting to wake her, shouting at me to call the fucking ambulance. I was terrified but I did as I was ordered and when I came back into their bedroom I saw my big strong father crying and praying, shaking my mother's pale listless body. I remember the syringe on the pillow, the spoon on the floor. And then I don't remember much at all except that one of the men in the ambulance was very tall and very blond. My mother survived, obviously, and soon after she gave up smack. My father never did. He died one night, alone, after he'd finished the night shift at the factory. He went into the work toilet and had a hit, a present to himself after a gruelling eight-hour shift in blistering heat. Maybe it was the heat that did it. Maybe it had weakened him. They didn't find the body till morning.

This is why his family hates my mother. We didn't tell anyone in Greece, of course, how their son had died. But word did get out. Word always gets out, words even travel across the bloody ocean. The ocean sent back the word that my father's family blamed my mother for their son's death.

—I love you, Mum.

—Tell it to Colin. He's missing you.

—I know.

I wandered, aimless and homesick, into the early evening and into the night. I walked a large circle from the hotel to the base of Lycavitos, walked through the sweltering concrete maze of Kipseli, turned back to the city, wandered through the green patches of Zographou, ate a hurried plate of tomato and egg at a tavern, and then kept walking. I found myself exhausted at midnight, in Exharheia Square, where I sat across from a boisterous group of young Greeks who were arguing and laughing. I ordered a whisky and soda from an attractive waiter in tight black jeans, and I lay back in my chair and smiled from ear to ear. I was in Europe. Across the road from the square three young men in ragged clothes, their eyebrows and mouths and noses pierced, set up their instruments. Two of them had bongos and one of them carried an acoustic guitar. One of the Greeks yelled out a good-natured insult and the tallest of the buskers thanked him sarcastically, donned an English bowler hat and began to strum the opening chords to Hendrix's 'The Wind Cries Mary'. There were whoops of satisfaction from the tables around the square. I listened half-heartedly to the music, the argument. I watched the endless circuit of cars and bikes and scooters zooming around the square. One of the men across from me leaned over and offered me a cigarette with a dazzling smile. I grinned back at him. I was in Europe. I could do as I pleased. Home was thousands and thousands of miles away.

The next morning, the man at reception did not bother looking at me as I fixed my bill. I paid for the phone calls I had made but I told him, in English, in commanding complex English, in an officious arrogant accent, that the Ministry of Culture was paying for my room. He pretended to not understand me. He demanded money.

I refused.

He said he'd call the police.

I gestured at my crotch. And you can suck my dick.

He threw the receipt after me as I went through the dirty lobby. I was whistling as I sauntered through the doors and hit the thickening Athenian spring heat.

I had nowhere to go except that I knew I had not liked my hotel room. All my belongings fitted snugly in my backpack and I walked away from Syntagma towards the noise and traffic of Ommonia Square. I passed the grand nineteenth-century façades of the embassies and walked into the first hotel I saw that dazzled me with its elegance. The porter waved me through into the cool lobby. At reception a young woman was smoking a cigarette, but she smiled and put it out as I approached. I asked for a room with a balcony and a bath.

—All our rooms have baths, sir.

I insisted on a balcony.

—She checked on her terminal and began to shake her head. I'm sorry, sir. All our balcony rooms are taken. There was barely a hint of Greece in her accent. The disappointment on my face must have been clear because she checked her computer again, and then, slyly winking at me, she asked me to return in a few hours.

—We will have a room then. She quoted me the price and it was so outlandish I had to ask her to repeat it. This was indeed a foolish extravagance I was indulging in, but after the grime and squalor of the room I had been in for the last few nights, I wanted to experience nothing but pleasure. I wanted to retire in a plush bed, to soak in a deep bath, to stand on a balcony in a foreign city with a cigarette in one hand, a drink in the other, and to survey a beautiful avenue, to look across to the lit monastery of Lykavitos Hill. To believe myself favoured in this city.

I left behind my bag and my credit card imprint and I ventured out again. The bus took me through the heart of the city and as it twisted through the congested roads, and the Acropolis stretched up above us, I pressed the button and I got off.

It was not yet noon and instead of half-naked boys and chain-smoking transvestites, the park was full of over-dressed tourists wielding every imaginable type of camera. I walked in the shade, whistling to myself. As I walked I became aware that though it was day, there were still men idling, searching among the trees. I felt a pulse at my crotch and I slowed my pace. A man in his forties, handsome and greying, sweat marks on his shirt, his tie loosely hanging from his neck, began to fall in step behind me. I stopped, lit a cigarette and he overtook me. He turned around and though there was no smile or warmth in his face, his eyes were fervent.

The path he took me on wound up towards the Acropolis. We climbed steadily through bush and over rock and soon I was sweating. He approached a secluded grove of trees— tall sinewy limbs and a dense canopy of emerald-green leaves. As I followed him into shadow, the temperature cooled and I felt sweet relief. He had turned around, his hand already at his zip, when behind us we heard a burst of noise, then short, sharp yelps of pain. The man shot past me, fear on his face. I stood still and waited in the shade. There was more noise, thuds, the unmistakable sound of slapping. It was followed by what sounded like crying. Fear and lust made me curious and reckless; I moved deeper into the grove.

Two youths, both in black t-shirts and ill-fitting jeans, were standing above a small figure curled in the dirt. It was this figure who was crying. One of the youths was holding a knife and he turned to look at me. His face was clear of any aggression or fear; instead he gazed at me calmly and confidently. His companion, younger, was angry on seeing me standing there. I felt—of course of course of course— terror. But I was unable to move. If the knife had approached me, had cut me, had slashed me, I would have still just stood there. Trembling, but incapable of motion.

Then the older boy turned back to his prey and kicked the now motionless body while the other boy stamped his foot on the victim's hand. There was one more pathetic yelp and then silence. The youths laughed and brushed past me insolently, the younger almost nudging me off my feet. Then they ran down the path, speaking in a language I did not recognise.

As soon as they were gone, the first thing I did was turn my back to the figure in the dust, unzip, and piss long and hard into the ground. Only seconds before, I had feared that both my bowel and bladder would fail me.

The figure on the ground was a child. I knelt beside him and lightly touched his shoulder. He whimpered, his body tensed, but I asked him if he could walk, and on hearing my voice he lifted his head and looked at me.

He was very young and grimy, and looked thin and weak. His fair hair stood up in a shocking wave.

—Would you like me to take you to hospital? I spoke in Greek.

On hearing this, the boy shook his head violently. This caused him pain and he grimaced. There was blood on his face, his cheeks were grazed and his left eye was swollen and would soon blacken. His frailty and his youth touched me, and I felt fury at his attackers. Scum. I had cursed out loud and in English.

The boy pushed himself up off the ground. I tried to help him but he would have none of it. He fended me away and began to move slowly along the path. But he staggered as he walked, and then he stumbled and fell once more to the ground. Again I helped him to his feet and again he pushed me away. In this bumbling manner we descended the hill, him walking ahead, refusing to look at me—a humiliating parody of my ascent—and I followed, anxious and still a little frightened. Not of the boy—he could not have been more than eleven or twelve—but the intoxicating brush with violence had made me keenly aware of the strangeness of the world around me. I was in a city I hardly knew at all and I had foolishly allowed a greedy lust to lead me into danger. And whoever the boy limping in front of me was, it was obvious that his world included whores and pickpockets and thieves. My instinct told me to walk away. I had a flash of the man who had led me to the grove; his imposing beauty had been immediately rendered weak and prissy by his undignified flight. But what of my own immobility? My own terror? My almost wetting myself at the age of thirty-six? I followed the boy, not wishing to be thought a coward.

He was determined to escape from me, though unable to make up much distance, until we reached the dense city streets and the chaos of the traffic brought him up short. He wobbled on his feet and for the first time he turned and looked at me. His eyes were resentful but the child-like pleading on his shivering lip was unmistakable. I walked up to him, placed an arm around his shoulder and, though he tensed and turned his face away from me, I also sensed a relief as he rested his body alongside mine. I let him guide me.

The boy headed south of the inner city and into Kalifea. We moved through narrow alleyways, the cement walls covered with tattered posters and blue and red stencils. One stencil, in thick black lines, had Jesus' face imposed over the five Olympic rings. His serene face was smiling and his raised hand held a bomb. The footpaths were narrow and I dodged the cars and motorbikes that were parked haphazardly on the streets, marvelling at the Athenians' ability to use every possible inch of space in their cluttered metropolis. It was the middle of the day and the city was empty, though there were occasional shouts and bursts of music from the balconies above us. I stumbled over the mangled body of a cat on the street and the boy made as if to run away from me, but the sudden movement made him wince and I tightened my grip around his shoulders. His breathing had slowed and was beginning to labour. I was contemplating lifting him in my arms when we stopped in front of a squat apartment building. The glass doors were blackened as if by smoke, but it could simply have been the accumulation of years of pollution. The boy pressed a buzzer and, after a pause, the door snapped open. In the doorway he stopped and turned to look at me. He waved me in.

He started up the stairs and I grabbed his arm and gestured towards the lift. He shook his head and for the first time he spoke to me.

—*Ochi, douleui ochi*. No, works not.

He was not a Greek. He placed his foot on the first step and when he lifted his body he grimaced. I could see he was in pain. I stooped and he gratefully sank into my arms. I walked up the stairs, heaving from the effort. He lived on the second floor, and when we turned into the landing a young man was waiting for us.

I stopped. I recognised him immediately. But he had no idea who I was. He did not make a move as he watched us coming towards him. The boy in my arms struggled to be free but once on his feet, he hung his head and backed into my body as if seeking my protection. Then the older youth lifted his hand and with a thundering smack he sent the boy sprawling to the ground.

The boy did not make a sound. He lifted himself unsteadily to his feet, still grimacing from the pain, and sheepishly brushing past the older youth, he turned into the open doorway. For a moment, with the light flickering from one naked globe, the hall smelling of cooking oil and shit, the youth and I looked at one another. His gaze was impenetrable. I did something that neither my upbringing nor my culture had prepared me for. I bowed. I turned and I walked down the stairs.

The lights in the hall and landing switched off and I was in the dark. I fumbled for a switch but couldn't find one. Though it was still clear open day outside, the apartment block was in shadow. From the first floor I heard the radio blaring recitations from the Qu'ran. On the ground floor the first snatch of sunlight dazzled me. I pushed open the door. My shirt and neck and face were drenched in sweat.

The street I was on wound back towards Sygrou and the turmoil of the city. On the hill above, a sea of concrete boxes was etched jaggedly against the fierce blue sky. For the first time on my journey—no, for the first time in a long time—I really wanted my camera. For the first time in a long time, I was hungry to create something.

I had nearly not taken my camera with me. It was Colin who slammed it into my chest, who told me that I was being a fool. In the end I grudgingly took it along. Colin's fury had decided the matter. I was guilty that I was leaving him back home while I was heading off overseas, I was guilty that I was looking forward to the pleasure of time alone. I was guilty that I was travelling, adventuring, when the last six months it had been his money paying the bills. I swear that I attempted to work. I would take the camera, I would walk streets, enter billiard rooms and train carriages, walk the city and its alleys, along the beach, along fucking freeways and disused hospital sites. I'd attempt to shoot an isolated figure in a platform alcove, the fall of shadows on a smoking woman's face. Portraits and still lives and bloody landscapes. Colour, and black and white. I would walk into the darkroom that Colin had built for me. I would emerge stinking of chemicals, exhausted and empty. And that was the problem with the photographs that would emerge. They were lifeless.

Dead photographs. I was never a technological pedant. Death in a photograph is not merely a matter of focus or of composition. It is not only the light. It is not the subject. There are photographs that are blurred or ugly or too dark or over-exposed, they can be banal or boring or incompetent. But that does not necessarily make them dead. Death is, of course, simply the absence of life, of the heart and the blood and the soul. The absence of fluid and flesh. The eyes that stared back at me from my photos were dead. The trees and asphalt streets, dead. All my subjects were muted and still. Not calm, but inert. The absence of motion. I would emerge from the darkroom every time, and the smell of chemicals was death on my skin, on my hands.

As fortune would have it, just as I stopped my work, stopped believing in myself, the email arrived from Athens.

The Greek Ministry of Culture invites you to participate in a week of activities celebrating the artistic achievements of the Greek diaspora. They would pay for my trip to Athens. I organised my past into a folio, emailed a return acceptance, and I put down my camera.

—Take it, you fucking selfish idiot. Colin thrust the camera against my chest. I put it away, folded it in my favourite dark blue linen jacket, buried it deep in my backpack. I had not unpacked it. But now I wanted the camera in my hand, I wanted to capture, to make concrete an image. I turned back and looked up at the building I had been in. I wanted to frame the older youth, the boy I had paid for nights before, I wanted him shirtless, his golden face against a bare white wall. I wanted him not smiling, not giving anything away. I wanted him resentful and suspicious, I wanted to capture that moment when he looked silently at me, rejecting me, his gaze demanding me to leave. It was that stare I wanted to capture. I wanted to make my memory of him tangible—so solid I would never forget the boy's brutal tenderness.

And as I turned and looked up at the concrete slab of his home, exactly at that moment, I became conscious that there was singing all around me and the words of Mohammed were being flung into the blue sky from a dozen balconies. The sun was high above and bathing me in white. As I made my wish, an old woman emerged on a balcony. She cupped her hands together and called for me. She beckoned me to her. I looked around the street again. It was empty; the Athenians were taking their siesta. The woman gestured to me to come inside.

The apartment smelt of fried vegetables and sweat; its walls were dark and bare except for a corner of the tiny living area that was filled from floor to ceiling with icons representing the Trinity and the saints. The two boys were lying flat on the couch, their legs entwined, watching the television and ignoring me. Soccer was on. The old woman ushered me in and angrily turned off the television. I protested, but she would not hear of it. In rapid Russian she berated the boys and they reluctantly sat upright and looked at me. The old woman finished her harangue, turned to me, and waited.

—She wish to say thank you. For you help my brother.

—My pleasure.

The boy translated for the old woman.

—My grandmother wishes for you to stay and eat.

On the couch the young boy who I had assisted sat stony-faced, ignoring me completely.

—And you, are you alright? I spoke in Greek but I think any language I would have chosen would have startled him. He looked at me hard, a moment of fury, but I winked at him and he suddenly grinned.

—Strong. He offered the one English word as a defence and as a justification.

The old woman had left us. I looked around the room. The weary, ancient saints looked down on me. A badly aligned poster of some soccer player added colour to the walls. The older boy followed my gaze.

—He is a god.

I nodded in agreement.

—Do you remember me from the other night? The question confused him. I repeated it, again in English, this time slowly. He tensed in his seat and then looked me up and down.

—You stole my Australian dollars, I reminded him.

—I do not understand. There was nothing but dismissal in his eyes.

The old woman returned with coffee and with some almond biscuits soaked in syrup. I accepted the food, sat down on the armchair opposite the boys, and she sat on the arm of the sofa. She took out a packet of cigarettes from deep in the pockets of her black dress and the two boys lunged for them. I reached for mine, offered them to the boys, and we all lit up together.

Her name was Elena, the older boy was called Serge and his younger brother was Yuri. We sat in silence, the three of them looking at me sipping my coffee, the boys' attention drifting towards the blank television screen. I looked at Elena and she smiled at me. Though dressed in black, and her mouth lined with the heavy traces of cigarettes and alcohol, she was far from old. Her hair was dyed blonde and though I had first thought her black clothing the mark of a widow, looking at her closely it seemed more likely that the simple dress best suited the suffocating heat. Our conversation proceeded terribly slowly, as we were all inadequate in Greek, our common language, but when I told them I was Australian, Yuri began to giggle. He raised his hands, made them paws and then, placing them each side of his head, he made them ears. I nodded. Yes, kangaroos.

Elena asked me many questions then. About the weather back home, about work, about space and desert and ocean. The boys asked me about snakes and sharks and crocodiles. I answered and then the conversation fell silent again. I looked at them, the grandmother, the two brothers, and again the desire to take a photograph came upon me. I wanted to capture her grim smile, to capture the way the brothers' bodies gently touched one another: loosely, affectionately. I looked at Serge's thin brown legs, the soft sparse tufts of golden hair. I remembered the taste of his skin. I put down the coffee, ashamed, and asked for directions to the toilet.

The bathroom was small and dingy, and the boys' underwear and Elena's bras hung from the shower rail. The toilet bowl was filthy with the stains of shit. Mould caked the walls and the porcelain of the basin. I took a piss and looked down at the small wastepaper basket at my feet. There was a yellow syringe hiding among the shit-stained paper. It was uncapped and it was this more than anything that unnerved me. Not the basket of soiled paper, that reminder of waste and human excretion: so confronting for a visitor such as myself whose whole life had been cushioned from exactly such evidence of human need. I washed my hands, flushed the toilet and turned to open the door.

On the back of the bathroom door someone, presumably one of the boys, had clumsily tacked three images torn from magazines and newspapers. The arrogant sneer of Eminem. A lascivious blonde with the largest silicon tits I had ever seen was stroking her shaved cunt. A black and white portrait of the calm messianic face of Osama bin Laden. The photographs were wrinkled from the humidity in the bathroom.

When I sat down again I noticed that Elena was scratching at her thigh. I looked down at her feet. She was wearing slippers and her ankles and tops of her feet were exposed. There were red sores and faint bluish bruises on her pale skin. I could tell that she shot the heroin into her feet.

—I am a photographer. I mimed the taking of photographs. I would like to take your photographs. Elena laughed and shook her head. Serge and Yuri looked at one another.

—Yes, yes, I insisted. I am a professional photographer. Please, I have an exhibition here in Athens. The words were meaningless to them. I cursed myself for not having the camera with me. The lust to take possession of their image made me reckless. I come back, I come back, I insisted. I will take your photographs. I stood up and made for the door. Elena came after me and started kissing my hands.

—I will return, I promised her, and pulled myself away.

There were no taxis anywhere to be seen in the small street so I headed towards Sygrou, confident of finding a ride there. I heard a yell behind me. Serge had followed me. In the glaring sun, his thin torso naked and frail, he looked closer to a child than a man. He came up to me.

—You take photographs of me, and my brother, yes?

—Yes, I agreed.

—You pay much for porno photographs. It was a demand, not a question.

—Do you remember me, Serge?

He looked confused. He repeated his demand.

—No porno photograph. Real photograph. But I will pay.

Just a little, but no porno. I waved my hands in firm denial. He continued to look up at me, then shrugged, and wordlessly turned his back to me.

I found a taxi and barked instructions to the hotel. I asked the driver to wait and he did reluctantly and only after I left him with some identification. I rushed back to the front desk, rifled through the contents of the pack, unwrapped the camera and held it tight in my grip. All the way back to Kalifea I imagined the photographs I would take. The two boys sprawled on the couch, their limbs entwined. Elena's lined face. The syringe among the shit-stained paper. I kept tapping against the door of the cab, impatient to return. And I tried not to think of the other photographs I could take. Of a naked youth, of a naked boy.

The street had begun to fill with life again. Traders had reopened their doors and old men were playing cards outside a cafe. A weary Chinese woman was sweeping the steps of her apartment block. I pushed the buzzer to the apartment and waited. There was no answer and I kept pushing, madly, desperate. After a few minutes a bearded face appeared over the balcony. His features were dark and he wore a skullcap on his head.

—Who do you want?

—Elena.

—Elena left. Long ago.

I thought I had misunderstood his Greek.

—When will she return?

—Elena go! He had raised his voice. Beside him appeared a young woman draped in a plum-red shawl with a small child in her arms.

—I am a friend, I lied, from far away.

The woman said something to her husband. He disappeared and the woman looked down at me, her face impenetrable. The door clicked open and the man appeared on the street next to me.

—Elena is dead, he told me. He placed a hand on my shoulder.

I pulled away.

—No, I said. She's inside, she's inside her apartment.

—Elena die. Many months, she die. *Pefane*. He kept muttering the Greek word, as if its repetition would force me to believe him.

The camera hung limply from my shoulder. The man turned to walk back into the block of flats.

—And Serge, and Yuri?

He turned around, lifted his shoulders and shook his head. I not know. I followed after him, grabbing his shirt. Tell me what happened, I ordered. He shook himself off me. I pleaded with the now furious Arab man to tell me where Elena and the boys were. His eyes were cold and his mouth vicious. He didn't trust me. I let go of his tunic and he slammed the door in my face. I turned. From across the street the Chinese woman had stopped sweeping and was looking at me, resting on her broom. Her eyes too were cold and distrustful.

I took a bus back to the hotel. It was crowded with passengers and I stood next to a tall young woman in a strapless red top. Her midriff was bare and she was listening to a walkman. As the bus weaved across the congested city, we passed an old Byzantine church. The young woman took off her earphones, made the sign of the Cross and then placed the phones back on her ears. Watching her, I realised that I was nothing but a tourist. I had lost Serge. I had turned down the wrong street, crossed the wrong alley, entered the wrong building. I was a stranger in this city.

In the plush hotel room I ran a bath. I soaked myself in the cool water, washed away the pollution and the day. In the middle of the bed I lay naked and gave myself over to depraved fantasies. I was in the apartment again but Elena was not to be seen. Serge led me into a bedroom where his young brother stripped for me and stood naked for my camera. I took my photographs.

I came imagining capturing his pubescent naked image.

Afterwards, exhausted and guilty, I rang Colin and left a message on our machine. That I loved him very much, that I missed him. Then I rang the bus interchange and found the times for the buses leaving for Karpenissi. I closed my eyes and I willed sleep.

IT WAS SAID of the musician Mulan that the first steps he took as a toddler were to climb down from his mother's knees, crawl across the cold stone floor and topple towards his father who was playing the clarino on the kitchen steps. Absorbed in the music he was making as he looked at the cloud-filled valley spread below, the man did not hear his son approach.

—Look, look at your son, urged the mother, and on turning the man saw the boy's small hand reach for the instrument.

—What do you want, my little man? Mulan's father laughed, but he handed the clarino to the boy. The small child had difficulty at first in finding a firm grasp, but he steadied the instrument on stone, placed his mouth to the reed and began to blow. A sweet, captivating note emerged. At that very moment it was as if the world had stopped and only the note was alive. Mulan's mother and father fell silent and the note danced out of the door and flew across the valley till it reached the village on the other side. It wrapped itself around the women at the well and they put down their vessels and began to sing. On the mountainside the goats stopped grazing and the shepherds sat down beside their animals and closed their eyes to the sun that had suddenly pierced through the clouds. In the village tavern the men placed their cards on the tables and all began to cry. In the mosque, the old cleric dropped his broom, lay down on the hard cement floor and, looking up at the mosaics and tiles, listened to the voice of God. The note swept through the village, into the valley and across the mountain peak, perching above the old Byzantine monastery as the monks bowed their heads, clasped their hands together and listened as their Saviour spoke.

When Mulan stopped blowing, the note slowly died and the wind carried it to Heaven. A thousand birds began to trill, the clouds vanished, and the valley, the mountains, the very world, were filled with the warmth of the sun's golden light.

There were tears in the proud father's eyes.

—Look, Mother, look. Our child is blessed. He speaks in the voice of angels.

o O o

Now Mulan was an old man. Grey flecks studded his beard and deep wrinkles webbed his cheeks. He rested his instrument on the dais and listened to the gypsy Rosa sing. His mind drifted and he willed away the music and singing, the smoke, the shouts and the laughter. He answered his father from long ago.

—Blessed I might have been born, but in a damned place am I cursed to live.

He looked up to find Rosa's fierce face glaring at him. Quickly he brought the reed to his lips and began to play. And as always the chattering and laughter and shouting died away and the crowd turned their faces towards the platform and listened. Tears and smiles appeared. Mulan drew breath from deep within his chest, and it was as if the very soul and blood of the tree that had given birth to the instrument had been renewed, was alive again, and screamed its happiness to be once more among the living. A group of young women rose and formed a circle, slowly swaying into the melody. Their bodies caressed the note as, table after table, in a chain from the old men to the young girls, the village began to clap their hands. At first quietly, so as not to disturb the precious music of the clarino, the rest of the band began to play. The bouzouki, the tambourine, and then, at first hushed, then louder and more confident, Rosa renewed her song. Mulan blew strongly into the reed, encouraging the circle of dancers into increasingly fevered motion. Women had thrown back their heads and were laughing into the moon. Men were dancing and gesticulating wildly. Children were fighting and grabbing each other. Rosa howled her song. The band thrashed their music. The old man Mulan closed his eyes and played. The whole of God's earth seemed to be dancing to his delirious, mad tune.

Madness was indeed being celebrated in the swirling frenzy of the dance. There was also hunger, raw, piercing hunger that was only muted by the sweet bliss of alcohol. Even the children were going up to the barrels, filling flagons with the sour red liquid and swilling it down. There was madness in the screeching old women, wrapped in thick swathes of black, who were singing the songs as if they were young and free again. But always the hunger. The Germans had gone from house to house, field to field, piling their trucks with livestock, wood and trinkets. There had been madness there as well. The war had entered its third year and now, certain that loss and humiliation awaited them, the actions of the German boys were growing ever more savage. The week before, four youths had been executed in front of Baba Yiannikas' coffee shop and the whole village had been forced to watch. With the men's blood not yet dry, the villagers danced on the stone and concrete, believing that the spirits of the youths were taking solace from their frenzy.

—Play, you dirty gypsies, urged Baba Yiannikas, his skin hanging in loose spongy folds, his once-bulging belly having disappeared, his ribs visible again for the first time in forty years.

And the band played. Mulan blew a note of such piercing anguish that the very tables seemed to lift off the ground and begin their own dance. He knew he was not singing in God's voice—he was singing with the Devil. The Devil had proved a more faithful companion than God, and Mulan consented to the demons celebrating on this night. As the music became even more furious, the whole village descended into the madness of the dance, more and more circles formed, the men leading with hollering and strangled cries, the women clapping their hands and shrieking with laughter, the children weaving amongst the adults. Mulan blew hate into his reed. The world sickened him. And the world swirling before him danced the hate right back to him. It seemed a thousand stomping feet, a thousand screeching voices, a thousand clapping hands were singing hate and madness and above all hunger, always hunger, right back to him.

Lucia was not dancing. She was sitting alone at her table watching the village abandon itself to the music. Her husband was leading the main circle, drunk, but still nimble on his feet. Her brother Fotis was holding Michaelis' hand, encouraging him to further spins and leaps. She looked across the swirling bodies and spied her sister, Fotini, sitting alone at their father's table. The young woman was with child and she sat, demure and still, with her hands clasped around her rounding belly. Raising her eyes, Fotini spied Lucia. She smiled at her and Lucia smiled back.

Damn you, Lucia whispered to herself, may God grant you a girl, may God grant you an imbecilic girl. May all your pregnancy and labour be in vain. May you die delivering the animal inside you.

Abruptly she rose from her seat. She could find no solace, no pleasure in the music and in the dance. Michaelis forbade her alcohol, so she was unable to drown her torment. Her sister-in-law Irini had just delivered a son. Fotis' wife, Olga, was pregnant with their third child. Even with sickness and war and hunger, it seemed that new life was everywhere. Only she was condemned to the excruciating shame of being barren. Damn you all.

She grabbed a scrap of bread from her table and walked over to where her Uncle Pericles was stoking the fires of the spit.

Baba Pericles had managed to hide three adult pigs from the Germans by concealing them in the desolate caves on top of the mountain's highest peak. He boasted that his pigs understood him and that he had instructed them to keep quiet at the sound of any approaching footsteps. The Germans had indeed climbed the peak but the pigs had remained silent, obeying their master. It was these three pigs that the village had feasted on that night. The crowd had fallen on the roast flesh; all that remained were the charred bones.

The old man was happily drunk. All through the night, when the musicians rested their instruments and taken refreshments, his grateful neighbours toasted him.

As Lucia approached, Baba Pericles stumbled onto his feet and attempted to lead her into a dance. She pushed him gently aside.

—Come on, child, let me dance with the most beautiful woman here.

—I'm too tired, Uncle.

—Are you finally with child?

How she wished she could nod and have him spread his arms around her, have him lift her into the starry night and twirl her around the square. She could watch the envy in every woman's face. She could laugh, she could sing, she could dance. She could dance all night till her feet bled.

—With God's grace it will not be much longer, Uncle.

His face screwed up into sad, intoxicated pity. She stretched out her hand and ripped a remaining meagre piece of flesh from a pig's carcass.

—It's good to taste meat again, isn't it child?

She didn't answer her uncle.

—It's God's will, he called out to her retreating back.

She did not return to her father-in-law's table, but she stepped into the darkness and walked past the churchyard. Inside, she could hear the priest maintaining his solitary lament for the four assassinated men. You're a fool, she muttered to herself. What good are your prayers to anyone? The men are dead and your stomach will be empty in the morning. Even their families dance and eat, even your wife has had her fill. But she made the sign of the Cross on passing.

Lucia walked up the hill to her home. It was a new moon and there was barely any light. She did not cross the yard into her own cottage, but instead maintained her steady climb.

The smell of pine was sharp in her nostrils as she entered the dark forest; almost immediately a chill descended around her. The forest was never warm: even in high summer, the dense canopy formed a shield against the sun. An owl hooted and she started and willed herself to keep walking. She made her way through the black night by listening for the murmur of the rivulet flowing down the mountain. She prayed as she walked, warding off the demons and the wolves. Her greatest fear was that the wolves would take her. If her blood were to join with theirs, she was condemned to Hell for eternity.

She gave a bitter laugh, loud in the still forest. With a clamorous flapping of its wings, the owl soared into the night. Aren't we in Hell already, dear God? The rare feast had hardly satisfied her hunger. It was as if she had been hungry all her life, and she could now not remember what it was to feel satisfaction after a meal, could not imagine living without the gnawing pain in her belly. She stopped and raised the bread she was carrying to her mouth. But she recalled the desperate eyes of the youth on her last visit and did not take a bite.

I am in Hell, she thought. I am in Hell and I am feeding the demons.

She was breathless when she reached the peak and, even in the cold wind, her face was wet with sweat. She stood at the cliff's edge and looked towards the shrouded villages across the valley. The music from the carnival had died away as soon as she had entered the forest, but now, at the top of the world, she could hear the sweet lament of the gypsy's clarino. Damn them all, she whispered into the night. Damn them all and the devils they are breeding in their wombs. She stood at the edge of the cliff and she jumped.

Falling on her fours like a cat, she straightened herself immediately so as not to tumble into the void before her. Turning, she faced the abandoned church. The Germans had removed the weathered timber doors. They had taken everything; they had razed the church as well as the village.

When she had seen the blue doors loaded onto the grey military truck, she had stopped breathing for a moment. Her heart had faltered. She had known immediately what she would do. She would deny all knowledge of the Christ Killer, she would throw herself at the feet of the enemy and she would betray her husband. Let that bastard son of the imbecile, that son of the Albanian bitch, that impotent eunuch Michaelis that God had sent to punish her, let him take the blame. But the occupiers had asked no questions and the hidden youth had not been discovered.

Lucia crossed herself as she bowed under the low archway and entered the church. The stench of ratshit was overpowering and she clapped her scarf to her mouth. She could hear vermin scurrying in the dark. She was glad for the lack of moonlight. The severe, judging faces of the saints painted on the walls terrified her. Their censure seemed even more intense now that the rain seeped down the walls and stained and deformed their portraits.

Slowly, edging her foot along the dirt floor, she made her way to the old altar. She knelt, scraped away dirt and dung and felt for the groove of the cellar door. With a grunt she pulled at the wooden frame and held her breath as dust and dirt flew around her. She could hear the boy scrabbling in the darkness below, and his frightened whimpering.

—Don't piss yourself. It's only me.

—Have you brought food?

His voice had deepened. It was almost a growl.

—Aren't the rats enough?

—Have you brought food?

Lucia sat on the edge of the opening to the cellar and then dropped herself onto the earth below.

She watched silently as the youth lit a fire. The dry wood crackled, then caught alight and the cave was filled with a warm glow. She thought she would gag: all she was aware of was the putrid stench of excrement. In the first year of his exile, the Hebrew had used the immediate world outside the church as a toilet, but with the coming of the enemy, none of them could afford that risk. Michaelis had ordered the youth to relieve himself in a hole at the end of the cavern. But as the fire began its roar, and smoke slowly filled her nostrils, she found that her stomach had stilled.

—You must take care, she admonished the youth, the smoke will suffocate you.

The boy smiled.

—God protects me. He pointed to the damp clay ceiling above. Don't concern yourself with my wellbeing, the smoke escapes. It always escapes and God ensures that fresh air finds its way even into this prison. Everything is God's will.

—It is the Devil that protects you.

She held out the food and he snatched it from her hands.

His hair, knotted and thick, had grown to his shoulders and his face was now bearded. The bristles, however, were soft, almost a down, and they were fair, not black.

He had not bitten into the morsels immediately, but

instead held them in his hands and chanted over them in a language she could not understand.

—Is that how Satan speaks?

—And God as well.

She sat on her haunches and watched him. He ate the bread ravenously, but hesitated over the meat. He forced it into his mouth and seemed to swallow it without chewing. She feared he would choke.

—Careful, she warned.

He ignored her and swallowed the last mouthfuls of the meal. They sat in silence.

His clothes had become rags and she could see the white skin of his torso through the rips in his shirt. His arms were like twigs. His legs appeared abominably long and slender. It seemed a miracle they could support him. The skin on his face was stretched tight across his hideous skull. You don't know hunger, Lucia, this is what death looks like, this is what hunger truly is. She reached out a hand to caress him.

He recoiled from her as if he was a frightened dog. She smiled to herself. She rarely ventured into the cave—it was Michaelis who usually brought food to the youth—but the few times she had entered, he always avoided her touch. But she was also aware every time of the fierce longing in his eyes. She slowly moved closer to him. He watched her warily.

Nausea overcame her. She smelt the filth on him, she smelt death on him. She fought back her bile and rose to her feet. She moved along the wall and examined the thick lines and hieroglyphics the boy had carved onto its face.

—They are the words of God, he said quietly but emphatically. I have to believe that even in here God is with me.

The surge of tenderness that rushed through her almost made her faint. She turned from him and bit into the flesh of her hand so he would not see her tears. She went to him and again he moved away. As he did so, he clumsily kicked over a small clay pot in which they brought water for him and as the pot tumbled, the spindly, charred remains of a rat fell onto the dirt floor. The boy hid his head in his hands. Lucia rose and, taking the clay pot, pulled herself up through the cellar opening into the church and ran into the world outside. She nearly swooned as she breathed in the sweet, cool air of night.

She did not dare ask herself why she felt such pity for the filthy Hebrew. It was as if her emotions and her very body were no longer her own to will: some spirit was compelling her. Was that spirit evil, or from God? She did not care. She made her way into the forest and listened for the gurgle of the rushing creek. She made her way to the spring, and at its edge she sat and ripped the bottom of her skirt until she had four thin strips of hessian. She dragged them through the freezing water and then, after lightly wringing them, she stuffed them into her skirt pocket. She filled the pot with water to take back to the Hebrew. Her shoes and her skirt now drenched, she made her way back to the cave.

The youth was facing away from her. He was rocking backwards and forwards and she understood he was in prayer.

—Come here.

He fell silent but did not move.

She walked up behind him and grabbed him by the shoulder. He squirmed from her touch but it was as if the spirit that was guiding her was stronger than the boy, that she was made powerful by it. She raised the youth to his feet and turned him to face her. She began by washing his face, his neck, his hands, his terribly thin arms. Throughout he had his eyes closed. She wrung out the first cloth and began with another. She pulled the ragged shirt off his shoulders and let it fall to the dirt floor. She washed his chest, under his arms: each rib was clearly visible. She wiped his pale belly. He shivered at her touch. She wrung out the cloth and pulled another one out of her pocket. She pulled at his belt, heard him groan, and his trousers fell to his feet.

He was erect. The lush clump of hair on his groin shocked her and she moved away from him. The youth's cock was thick and full and alive. She found herself whimpering as the boy took the cloth from her hand. She watched, her breaths short and deep, as he washed his sex. When he was finished he squeezed the cloth over the fire and it sizzled harshly. He dropped the wet cloth into the fire. The flames disappeared and the cave was full of darkness and acrid smoke. She felt his hands on her, then felt him lifting her skirts, pulling her pantaloons to her knees, felt his soft beard on her face as they fell to the floor. As he entered her, their tears were joined. On the dirt floor of the cave, with the sounds of the rats above them scampering on the church floor, they rutted like dogs: quick, ferocious. When he was done he immediately threw himself off her.

—Go, he whispered, crying, leave me.

He was crouching in the far shadows of the cave. She could barely make out his demonic shape in the shadows.

Lucia did not return to the carnival. She ran all the way to her barren cottage, stripped off her skirts and climbed into bed, biting into the corner of her blanket. She wanted to scream. To laugh and cry and scream. She knew that it would be hours before Michaelis returned, and that when he did he would be drunk and would want to mate with her. She wanted to be asleep when he came home—all she could think of was sleep but she was terrified of asking for this from God. Could she ask God for anything ever again? She rocked herself in her bed, wishing for sleep, but all she could hear was the wail of the gypsy's clarino.

Mulan was seized by great joy as he played on the dais. The rest of the musicians laid down their instruments and listened. The crowd cheered him. It was as if his instrument had never before made such a sweet sound. As long as those notes played, everyone's hunger could be forgotten. It was as if they had never known hunger at all. The note that Mulan blew danced through the square and up along the mountains, through the trees, and soared as high as the moon. It was a sound full of ecstasy and promise and eternity. Even deep in his pit, alone in the dark and the stink, even there the boy heard the music. He closed his eyes, wiped the tears from his face and fell asleep smiling.

THE SºLID EARTH
BENEATH MY FEET

THE BUS THAT took me away from the sea and deep into the mountains was decorated with the faces of the Virgin and her Son, the saints of Orthodox Europe, and the football heroes of Olympiakos. As the driver pulled out of the terminal and began the slow, convoluted journey out of Athens, he looked at the saints and crossed himself, his lips moving in a silent prayer. Around me the passengers too began to cross themselves. My still hands betrayed me as a stranger.

The rusting blue vehicle looked as if it belonged in a black and white film from the 1950s. These buses were built to transport Greeks, not tourists, and they were in need of a paint job and repanelling, and spewed out a constant stream of black carbon. The roads we took were skinny and mean, and as we ascended into the hilltops, the bus teetered from side to side, as if eager to leave behind its asphalt routine and dive into the craggy ravines below. The driver sped cheerfully along the precarious terrain, singing to the radio. I spent my time looking outside at the yellowing, dry world. Goats and fields of olives, gypsy encampments and the roadside dotted with memorials to the dead. The bus driver pushed hard on his horn and the automobiles screamed back; but always the bus found a way to navigate the tight lanes and streets, and continued its way up the mountains.

In Agrinion, I was to change to another bus for Karpenissi. Agrinion was flat, dusty, full of identical concrete apartments. The weather was unbearably hot and everything seemed ugly. But I was determined to take a look at it.

Agrinion was where, if you asked her, my mother said she was from. It was a shorthand: her parents' village lay two hours further up the mountains, but the town was the centre for the cluster of mountain communities spread around it. It was also far away enough from her village that the Agrinionites in Melbourne had never heard its name. They always asked her, suspiciously, *But where from in Agrinion?* I had an hour and a half before the next bus left, so I dumped my bag with a surly attendant who told me it might still be there when I returned, slung my camera over my shoulder, and walked out into the heat.

Agrinion is not the Greece of the tourist brochures. There were no ancient ruins and no quaint houses painted blue and white. The city was an endless jumble of ugly yellowing cement apartments. The low mountains that ringed the town were barren and dry. A wind was blowing through the streets and gusted dust into my eyes. No one stirred, but the afternoon shadows were beginning to lengthen and I judged that it would not be long before the townspeople began to wake from their siesta. I walked past the concrete apartment blocks, past car yards and warehouses with peeling paint, and found myself in a small square. One of the coffee shops was open and I walked inside, thankful to be out of the unrelenting heat. An old man was reading a newspaper behind the small laminex counter and he greeted me with a suspicious curt nod. I asked for a coffee, Turkish and strong, and took a table near the dusty window looking out onto the drab and empty square. He brought me my coffee, without looking at me, without saying a word.

Greeks are a distrustful people. It was Colin who told me that. He had travelled through this country, avoiding the big cities and the islands, had travelled into the mainland, through the mountains and over the border to Yugoslavia, and he said everywhere he was greeted with suspicious glances and by little children who wanted only to touch and feel his curly red hair. My short hair was black and my skin was starting to tan after only a few days in this climate, but I too was a stranger to the old man. He had turned on a small radio and the commercial Greek music, synthesisers bleating below the Eastern melodies, blared loudly in the coffee shop. A truck pulled up noisily beside the square, shuddered to a stop, and a young man jumped out of the caboose and walked into our cool shade.

—Make us a coffee, Baba Kosta, roared the truck driver, make it strong and sweet.

The old man grunted, displeased, but started preparing the brew. The young man glanced at me, took a cigarette from his shirt pocket and sat down at the counter.

The truck driver was balding, his skin had blackened in the sun, and his khaki t-shirt was wet with perspiration. He was tall, his belly thickening, and his hard dark face was both ugly and beautiful. A thick pink scar ran down the side of his left cheek. He glanced at me and I found myself blushing. I sipped from my coffee and went back to watching the world outside. Across from us, on the pitted wall opposite, someone had scrawled, in large strokes of blue, the number 666 and a thick cross through it. The Devil's number unnerved me, but then so did the brutish young man, and I had nowhere to look except down at my coffee cup.

—Have you read this, Baba Kosta? The young man threw his newspaper onto the counter. I attempted to follow the men's conversation. A ship had gone down in a storm while crossing into the Mediterranean. Seventy-five illegal immigrants, mostly Kurds and Afghanis, had drowned, locked deep in the ship's bowels.

Across the street a woman was lifting the shutters to her kiosk. Cars, trucks, the voice of a city began to be heard.

—They can all go to Hell.

The young man had raised his voice and I glanced over to him. He was stroking his unshaven chin and smiling at me.

—Do you agree, friend?

I pretended not to understand him.

The old man lit a cigarette, coughed and touched the truck driver on the shoulder.

—He's not a Greek.

—I am, I said, but from Australia.

The young man laughed.

—Ah, one of the lucky ones.

I'm not rich, I wanted to say. I'm not a success story. Instead I smiled and raised my glass to the stranger. He came over, sat down next to me and offered me his hand.

—Takis.

I introduced myself and he ordered both of us another coffee, offered me a cigarette, and stretched his legs wide apart. He pointed to the world outside.

—A shithole, isn't it?

The English obscenity was offered with a Cockney accent and I couldn't help laughing.

—But it is, don't you think? He was grinning but his dark, hooded eyes were gazing intently into my own. I could smell his workman's sweat, taking it in over the taste of coffee and tobacco. I also smelt the faint whiff of marijuana.

—I've been here half an hour. It looks okay to me, I lied. I knew enough about Greeks to not dare an insult to their hometown.

—Are your people from here?

I hesitated. I remembered my mother's fierce determination to chop away at her roots.

—I'm just travelling.

He turned to the counter, laughing.

—Did you hear, Baba Kosta, the poor fool is taking his holiday in Agrinion. Who'd guess? Forget Santorini and Rhodes, we'll be first for tourists soon. His voice was bitter and cold.

The old man snorted and coughed again. He came over

and took a seat beside me. Their attention made me uncomfortable. They in turn were distrustful of me. Takis looked at my camera.

—You take photographs?

—I am a photographer.

—Will you take a photograph of me?

His eyes, his long-lashed hooded eyes, were snake eyes.

—If you want.

—And the old man here?

—If he wants.

—Where are you from?

My mother was not here, she was not asserting herself in the face of two bitter men who were determined to remind me that I was not from here. I made the decision, on the spot, in the moment, to speak.

—My mother is from around here. Not Agrinion. Out there, up in the mountains.

The old man sagged into his seat; he was now relaxed with me.

—Has she ever come back?

I shook my head.

—Never.

The young man pounced on my reply and turned gleefully to the old man.

—Do you see, Baba Kosta, they've forgotten us?

—Bullshit! In my anger I had spoken the obscenity in English. I calmed my voice. It is you who have forgotten *us*.

Takis went to reply but the old man patted my shoulders.

—The child speaks the truth. You have forgotten, Taki. He turned to me his old scarred face, and I saw that his teeth were missing, that cigarettes had slowly chiselled away at his lips.

—We have forgotten, son, but not me. I had my sister in Australia. My only sister. A cry began to escape him, but he choked it back, lifted himself slowly up from the table and walked back to the counter. He turned from us and he busied himself rearranging the tins of coffee, washing the cups and the saucers. When Takis spoke again, his voice, his eyes, had softened.

—His sister died last year. Takis lit another cigarette and watched the smoke curl into the air. Imagine this, friend, old Kosta here had never once travelled further than Athens. He's not seen an island, has rarely seen the bloody sea. His sister dies and he decides to fly to Australia. Imagine? I can't. They tell me it takes one day and one night in an aeroplane. You've got to be joking. I don't even want an hour in one of those damned things.

I waited. The old man had sat down again, behind the counter. He was not looking at us.

—Imagine, the poor old fool makes the journey, goes to bury his sister, meets his brother-in-law, his nieces and nephews for the first time, and then within a fortnight he's back. I said to him, Baba Kosta, what the hell are you doing back? He replied, What could I do, my son, Tasia was dead, who was going to run the *kafenio*, what was I going to do in Australia? Takis clapped his hands together and shook his head. So he comes back.

I looked over at old man Kosta. He was back to reading the newspaper, oblivious now to us. Takis leaned towards me.

—I asked him about Australia, he whispered, do you know what he said?

—What?

—Big houses, my son, they have big houses there and they have very fat cows.

Takis' laughter was long and strong.

—Is it true, friend, he asked me, are your houses big and are your cows well fed?

Colin told me that, when he was fifteen, one of his teachers, new to his vocation, enthusiastic and well-meaning, had tried to gain Colin's trust by asking him where most in the world he would like to visit. Colin had replied that he wanted most to see the Nile. Since he was a young child, he had been fascinated by the monuments of ancient Egypt and wanted to see for himself the desert landscape filled with the ruins of empires. The student teacher, encouraging the youth, had asked him to imagine what steps would be needed in order to make his dream possible.

On a late autumn evening, the sun having gone down and the afternoon abruptly cold from an icy southern wind, Colin told me that all he remembered was feeling overwhelmingly trapped by the teacher's question, that he could not ever see himself travelling, flying, walking through strange places, taking photos as mementos. He told me this as an adult, wrapped in an ill-fitting brown cardigan to protect himself from the wind, looking out onto a garden which his hands had sown and nurtured. He told me that he could remember neither the punch nor any of the violence that followed—that all he did remember was the young student teacher's bleeding face and his own foot sore from the savagery of his kicking. They called the police and as his mother was not home, they kept him in a police cell until late in the night when she arrived, breathless and drunk, and slapped him once, twice around the head. When they arrived home, the man who his mother was seeing at the time, an old bastard called Nick, had packed all of Colin's clothes into a bag. Colin's mother had started screaming but Nick hit her and told her to choose. Nick or Colin. Colin made the choice for his mother. He left, and that night walked into the city where he slept on a bench outside the old Wesley Church in Lonsdale Street. Nick didn't stay around for much longer and Colin eventually moved back home. But he never returned to school. His mother wanted him to stay on: he was smart, he could read anything, he was fucking smart. Stay at school, Col. But he found an apprenticeship and started paying his way. Steve

Ringo had also taught him this. You've got to pay your way.

Colin shivered in the evening chill. I have been paying my way ever since. As he told me this story, I looked at the line of tall beanstalks he had planted. When the night got too cold, I asked him to pick some of the beans and he came into the kitchen with a small wooden bowl filled to the brim with the deep purple beans. I cooked him beans in vinegar and olive oil, I had cheese and bread ready. I cooked him a meal my mother had taught me.

—It's true, I laughed along with Takis, the cows are well fed in Australia.

It was evening when I reached Karpenissi. The yellow moon hung low over the town and people were drinking and laughing in the square. Young men on motor scooters circled around and there was music blaring from all the taverns lining the square. Techno competed with popular Greek tunes and I walked through this cacophony searching for a room. I found a small hotel with a view of the mountains and paid for a night. I laid my head on the pillow intending to rest only for a moment, and then go back into the night and explore the town. But I fell immediately asleep and fell into dreams: dreams of motor scooters and pretty boys smoking cigarettes; dreams of old men and old women, looking at me as if I was dead, looking through me.

In the morning, the first thing I did after splashing my face with water was to walk down to the nearest kiosk and put a call through to Colin. The answering machine kicked in but Colin picked up halfway through my message.

He told me he had been working in the garden. I could see him, weeding, digging, creating.

—Not working today?

—I'm working all weekend. Harry's got lots of jobs on.

I fell silent. I was thinking about my credit card bill from Athens. I vowed to myself I would find a fulltime job when

I returned to Melbourne. It was not fair his supporting the both of us, supporting my photography while I got paid a shit wage to push videos and DVDs across a counter two or three shifts a week. I had to get a real job, put my fair share in; I would do it over any of Colin's protesting. You've got to pay your way.

—Are you alright?

—Yeah. I'm in Karpenissi.

—What's it like?

—I've just got here. I'll tell you next time I ring.

—When are you planning on coming back? I could hear the hope in his voice.

—Not sure. Another month?

He went silent.

—Three weeks, then.

—Don't promise me anything. You never fucking keep them anyway.

—I love you.

—Then just come back quickly.

—I better get going.

He asked me to wait and he put down the phone. The young woman in the kiosk was looking at me. She lit up a cigarette and yawned.

—Your cousin Giulia rang me.

—Bullshit.

—Nah. She rang me up last night. She's in Athens and wants to get in contact with you. You got a pen?

I motioned to the young woman for a pen and she sullenly handed me one. I took down the number, wrote it on the inside flap of my cigarette packet.

—I love you, I told him again.

His voice softened.

—Come back soon, baby. I miss you so much. This is too hard.

I walked the town that day. This place, this small town high in the mountains, was where I came from. It was to this town that my mother had come down from the village for celebration and for dances; this is where she had first tasted ice-cream and bananas and oranges. They were so rare, she once told me. I was a child, lying next to her in bed, and she was in a silky heroin daze. I was wearing blue and white checked pyjamas and I was asking her about Greece. On drugs, she would answer. Fruit was so rare. But I remember my father took me to Karpenissi one morning, we had walked since dawn, and I saw an old man with a stick of bananas over his shoulder. I didn't ask for one, I knew they were expensive, but my Dad saw my hunger and he bought me one. He let me eat it all myself, did not even take a bite. Recalling her father, her face had become sad and old. She kissed me goodnight, grumbled that I did not know how lucky I was to be in a place where everyone ate bananas and peaches, apricots and oranges.

I held my camera tight in my hands and willed myself to see Greece, her home, through her eyes.

I took photographs of shopfronts, bakeries and butcher shops. I took photos of the old wooden walls of the town, of the new concrete apartments. I took photographs of the surrounding peaks and of young children playing soccer in side streets. I took photographs of a drunk old man, his teeth all gone, his eyes bruised. I took as many photographs as I could, switching film after film, so when I returned home I could ask my mother, Do you remember this? Does it still look the same?

Even as I pressed my finger on the shutter I was aware that the places I was framing through my viewfinder had changed unceasingly since my mother was born. I knew as I heard the click of the camera that my mother's hazy memories of this place she left when she was still a girl could not compete with the crisp colours and matt tones of the photographs I was now taking. I didn't care. I wanted her to have something more solid of memory than words. I took photograph after photograph. As this was a foreign light, as I did not know this intense but delicate Mediterranean light, so different from the harsh and boundless sun of my own country, I took shot after shot of the same scene, altering the exposure to ensure that the film would capture the houses, the fields, the narrow lanes, the faces, as I wished to preserve them. I altered the aperture and attempted to capture the soul of the town.

The old men of Karpenissi stared suspiciously at my camera. The old women I did not see, they kept indoors. I took seven rolls of film and I was exhausted by the time I walked back to the bus station. The chain-smoking man behind the counter was rude and unsympathetic to my requests. It seemed that buses to my mother's village only left on Wednesdays and Mondays and when I persisted in my pathetic Greek to discover an alternate route, he told me that the village was a clump of Devil's earth and why the fuck did I want to go there when Karpenissi had everything I needed as a tourist. I realised, when he made a disparaging aside to a bus driver, that he thought of me as a complete stranger, that my accent and manner had obscured all evidence of Greekness. I gave up my efforts and decided to hitch. I paid my bill at the hotel and I rang Giulia in Athens.

—*Gamouto, epitelos*. About fucking time.

It had been twelve years since I had heard her voice but I recognised it immediately, recognised the accent of her stilted English. It sounded like the way Slavic women in Australia tried to fix their lips around the hard Australian accent. Twelve years ago, my father's family had not been kind to me. They had taken me in, they had shown me the tourist sights of Thessaloniki, they had politely paid for my meals and my drinks, but they had not protested when

I declared my intentions to travel on my own and they had been relieved to close the door after me. It had been an uncomfortable two nights I'd spent with my uncles and my aunts, my cousins—they doing their duty, I doing mine—sitting on sofas, listening to them gossip and laugh about people I did not know. It was uncomfortable because we could not talk about the one thing we had in common: my dead junkie father. Even his presence had been erased from their houses. His youthful image did not stare down from any of the old photographs that adorned their immaculate bourgeois homes and apartments.

Giulia, younger than I by a month, had sat across from me on a sofa and her penetrating dark eyes had unnerved me. She had interrogated me. Who did I vote for? Were there Greek members of Cabinet in Australia? What was my perspective on the civil war? Was I a supporter of the Velvet Revolution? Did I agree that Scorsese owed his biggest debt to Rossellini? What was my favourite Dylan, my favourite Tsitsanis? Her sharp slanted eyes had scrutinised me, and I thought I had been a disappointment to her, clumsily answering her questions and making it obvious that Australians were ignorant and naive compared to the hunger of a Europe suddenly churning through the vast ramifications of the fall of the Soviet Bloc. But she had laughed when I told her my favourite Dylan was 'I Want You', and had started singing it, and she clapped her hands and squeezed my knees when I defended *Voyage to Italy* over *The Bicycle Thieves*. My aunt had cooked a large dinner and then I was off to the station to take the train to Belgrade. Giulia had jumped up and offered to drive me. I had said my goodbyes, received my stilted kisses, and thrown my black backpack into her car. She was driving silently, smoking a cigarette, and I remember feeling melancholy and alone. But we never arrived at the station. Instead, she stopped outside a cold grey Balkan apartment block and told me to grab my bag.

—Where are we?

—My friend Elena has an apartment here. She is in Rhodes for the summer. I have the key. You are staying here, she announced.

I laughed.

—Giulia, I have a train to catch.

—Forget it, your travels can wait. Here's my cousin from Australia, damned faraway Australia, and he's not leaving until we have a chance to talk.

We entered the apartment block, took the tiny creaking lift to the third floor and entered a cramped space filled with the fragile soothing smells of women with a balcony looking over the Port of Thessaloniki. I smoked a cigarette, breathing in the sea air and the summer wind, while Giulia fixed us drinks.

—Anyway, you can't leave yet, you've hardly seen anything of this city. She was standing in the doorway and sipping from a gin and tonic. Then, taking a seat beside me, looking out at the sea, she asked me very simply, Tell me, how did my uncle die?

—Where the hell are you?

—Karpenissi.

—Karpy-island, she mocked. *Nissi* was the Greek word for island. I was travelling to an island in the mountains.

—And what the hell are you going to do there?

—I'm going to visit Mum's village.

—Really? Her voice was now warm, soft and warm, and caressing. I'm coming. Where shall we meet?

I looked out of the small hotel window, down into the lazy square, across the rooftops to the mountains.

—At her village?

I thought Giulia was going to choke on her laughter.

—I doubt it will be a popular meeting spot, the Wild Forest.

Agrio Dassos. The Wild Forest. Where my mother really came from.

—Hang on a minute, she said, I'll ask Andreas. I heard rapid Greek being exchanged and then she was back on the phone.

—We'll meet at the Megalo Horio.

—What?

—I'm serious, we'll meet at the Megalo Horio. Andreas says that's the easiest place for you to find. It's only a half-hour from Karpy-Island.

—It's actually called *Megalo Horio*? In English, the name translated to the Big Village. In Australia that could only be a name for a theme park. Where at the Megalo Horio?

—It's not that *megalo*. At the square. I heard her call out to Andreas.

—Tomorrow night. Saturday night in the village. She cackled with laughter. Baby, she hissed in delight, choking on her laughter, her accent Brooklyn via Bucharest, We are going to make some noise.

Megalo Horio turned out to be a little like a theme park. The village itself was perched precariously in the forested chest of the mountain, and its neat cobbled streets ran vertiginously down into the lush green valley below. In France or in Germany I would have seen nothing odd in this picturesque prettiness; but in Greece where I was used to the eroded and stripped sunburnt earth of the mainland, or the salt-drenched sparseness of the islands, this handsome cool village surprised me. I wandered its alleys, going in and out of small shops selling traditional sweets and cheeses; I watched a withered old man in a black beret carve a wooden cane into the shape of an elongated horse's head. Only the Greek language was to be heard. The tourists on the streets of the Megalo Horio were all Greek. The women's fleshy buttocks strained against the thin fabric of their Versace trousers. The men's arses were squeezed tight into Calvin Klein jeans, their bellies bulging obscenely over the waistbands.

I found a room above a shop that sold sweetmeats and I bought myself a flagon of cheap retsina and drank myself sick. This was not the Greece I had thought I would find. When I had first travelled here, I had seen the cities and I had toured the islands, playing the tourist. Back then I had found another country. The streets of Athens were dusty, the walls were covered with slogans, and it was I who was the materialist interloper. Now, outside in the square of the Megalo Horio, it was all Prada, Gucci and Versace, and everyone sat drinking, eating, and speaking loudly and ostentatiously on their mobile phones. I drank, I got blotto, and I stripped myself nude. I took photo after photo, of my shins, my hands, the washbasin, the peeling ochre paint on the wall, my cock, my belly, the hairs on my thigh, the single bed, the quilt on the bed. When I came to the next morning, the camera was by my side, I had vomited all over my chest, and the room was filled with the toxic stench of tobacco, of wine, of stale regurgitated food.

It had been twelve years since I had seen Giulia but as soon as we saw each other, as soon as her arms were tight around my shoulders and her kisses were on my mouth and cheeks, it was as if those twelve years had disappeared, and I was back on the balcony, getting drunk on whisky and stoned on grass, and watching the dawn over the Port of Thessaloniki. Before her arrival I had stilled my hangover with a meal of chips and meat stewed in rich tomato sauce, and I had walked across the valley to the town of Gavros where I had drunk coffee and written letters home. The sun was setting when I found her, smoking a cigarette, standing arm-in-arm with a tall man in a lavender jacket, who smiled at me, winked, and greeted me in perfectly accented English.

Giulia introduced us.

—Andreas Kalifakis. A smart man, but not as smart as he thinks.

He shook my hand and raised an eyebrow.

—Our friend here is mad at me because I refuse to go with her to London. She is unused to not getting her way.

I turned to Giulia, who was shaking her head and flinging the cigarette butt across the valley.

—What are you going to do in London?

—Silly things. You know I work for television, now? I shook my head. At twenty-three, it had been theatre that had been her great passion. She smiled at me and touched my hand. I am working on a documentary about Cypriots in London. Are you proud of me? She hugged me, and Andreas led us to a small table at the edge of the square, where we looked down at the fading forest light, and he ordered wine, bread and fish.

Giulia had changed. Gone were the baggy denim jackets and jeans of a Communist Party cadre, replaced now by a thin silk shirt that revealed her cleavage. Her hair had been cut short and thick gold hoop earrings helped accentuate the angularity of her cheekbones and jaw. She was truly a beautiful woman but age was beginning to creep in: wrinkles, shadows and lines beneath her eyes. But her conversation with Andreas was furious and sophisticated, and reminded me a little of my previous shame all those years ago to be the naive traveller from the bottom of the earth. Andreas too worked for television, a journalist who nonchalantly mentioned his time in Sarajevo, Belgrade and Istanbul, which, in the Greek manner, he insisted on calling Constantinopoli. Giulia too had covered the earthquakes in that city and I listened fascinated to their stories. Andreas asked me questions about my profession and I found myself bullshitting, pretending that my photographic career was far more successful than it was, not mentioning the weekend job in the video shop I still had to make ends meet. Giulia looked on proudly.

—Of course, she insisted to Andreas, my cousin is a success. We are a noble family. She squeezed my fingers tightly and kissed my brow. Then taking my hand she opened it and deposited a gift. A small joint and a coarse yellow tablet lay in my palm. Her loud laughter rang through the square like church bells.

—The E's direct from Amsterdam, we have Andreas to thank for that.

Andreas bowed his head and smiled at me.

—I prefer my Ecstasy from Holland, he explained. People swear by London and Barcelona but in my experience that is not the case at all. I think it is Amsterdam for LSD and for Ecstasy.

—And for hashish?

Andreas smiled wickedly at Giulia's question.

—Ah, hashish is best when it is directly received from the hands of a young Pakistani peasant boy.

I placed the tablet and joint in my pocket and pretended a worldliness I did not feel. They were confusing me. They obviously had money, obviously were doing well, but their conversation was bitter and cynical. Giulia's mobile phone went off during our meal and she spoke rapidly and impatiently. I looked around the square and it hit me that from table to table, dinners, dates, conversations were being interrupted by the persistent clamour of the ringing phones. Giulia switched off her phone and turned to Andreas.

—Now you will suffer, that was Antoni. He has a room for me in High Street, Kensington. Serves you right.

Andreas again arched those long slim eyebrows.

—My Giuliana, how many times must I tell you? I detest London. It is a cold, foolish city.

—Bah! Noticing that I was distracted, Giulia turned to me and again took my hand. I am sorry, my little one, we are boring you with our terrible bourgeois conversation, all about work and silly things like that. I want to hear about you. She was searching my face, looking straight at my eyes. How is Colin? Why is he not here with you?

I tried to explain how Colin was a man uncomfortable with formality and artifice, who wanted a holiday to be time spent lounging on beaches or walking through rainforests, who detested the thought of openings, of exhibitions. My jumbled Greek sounded silly. I turned to Andreas and stated simply, in English, My boyfriend hates artists.

—A wise man.

Giulia crossed her arms in exasperation.

—He wouldn't have had to hang around fucking artists, I would have taken him places. Tell him, tell him that I very much want to meet Colin, the man who has stolen my cousin's heart.

I grinned and nodded.

—Maybe I will visit you both in Australia? Maybe I will come and live there? Yes, she insisted, I will come and live in the desert. I will take an Aboriginal man for a husband. I am bored with Europeans.

Andreas laughed at this.

—You would suffocate if you left Europe. You need this oxygen to survive. Leave the poor Australian men alone, marry a Greek, as your mother insists.

—I don't want to marry an Australian, exclaimed Giulia disdainfully. I said I will marry an old wise Aboriginal man.

—The only true Australians, I interceded.

Giulia's eyes flashed approvingly. Good, she answered, so you have finally realised you are a Greek?

I laughed and shook my head.

Giulia pointed at me and sneered.

—He keeps insisting he is not Greek, he is Australian.

Andreas looked at me and then laughed.

—That's preposterous. You are indeed a Greek. Not only physically but in your soul.

I protested that I did not grow up here, that I could not

pretend to be anything but antipodean. They both looked at me strangely, then Giulia shrugged her shoulders and picked up her handbag. I fingered the tablet in my shirt pocket, eager for the heightening that drugs would bring to this singular summer night. Giulia smiled at me.

—We have a surprise for you.

—What is it?

She glanced at her watch.

—Time we had our sweets. Giulia slid the yellow pill onto her tongue, winked at me, and leaned over and kissed me. Andreas asked for the bill, and when it arrived he slapped my hand away and placed one hundred euros on the table. You are my guest tonight, he told me, interrupting my protests. I am paying for the Australian.

—Your father is from here?

We were driving in Andreas' white BMW. And though we were slicing through forest, the night air was full of the music of voices, laughter and the clinking of glass.

—My mother, I answered. I looked back at Giulia, who was smoking in the back seat. My father and Giulia's father were brothers.

—Andrea is from Thessaloniki as well. Giulia leaned over from the back seat and tweaked my nose. I stilled my impulse to tell her to put on her seatbelt. I had never forgotten her reaction all those years ago when I had first jumped into her car and strapped the belt across my torso. What are you, she had screamed at me, a slave? Only a slave binds himself.

Andreas was looking at my cousin in his rear-view mirror.

—You are wrong, my Giuliana, my family is not from Thessaloniki; they're from Kozani.

—I've been there, I said quietly. Last time I came.

Andreas turned and looked at me. He turned back to the road.

—My family were peasants. Unlike yours, he said.

Giulia groaned. She leaned over and butted out her cigarette angrily.

—Look, Andreas, it's not as if our family were aristocracy. Our grandfather was a successful merchant, that's how he managed to educate his sons. But he himself was a dirt-poor refugee from Anatolia.

—From Trebizon, I finished, remembering Dad's stories. I looked over at my cousin. She smiled at me and nodded.

Andreas offered me his cigarettes and as I took one I touched his fingers. He wrapped one of his fingers tight around one of mine, then quickly glancing in the rear-view mirror at Giulia, he let go.

—Why did your father leave Greece?

I looked out into the darkness. When I was six, my father had given me a map of the world and asked me to find Thessaloniki. He had told me nothing about where it lay on the planet. I had taken the map into my room—it covered the length of my single bed—and I had pored over mountains and oceans, desert and sea, until I found the magic word. I was excited when I took it back to Dad. You see, he told me, it's not hard to find where you come from.

Giulia answered for me. Her voice was sad.

—My uncle was furious when Lambrakis was assassinated. He was involved in the Party, at university, and our grandfather feared for him. Our grandfather sent his son to bloody Australia. And probably a good thing. Her voice was faint. He would have not have survived well under the Colonels.

Andreas had his eyes fixed on the road ahead. His next words surprised me.

—And why did he give you a Jewish name?

Isaac, my father would bellow at me when I had made him angry, interrupted his reading, when I was full of boisterous energy. Isaac, I will sacrifice you to bloody God!

—My father liked the name. He just liked the name.

Giulia turned to me.

—Andreas hates the Jews. She tapped him on the shoulder. Be careful, Andrea, my cousin is a friend of the Jews.

—I don't hate them, he protested to me, I simply distrust them.

I was feeling the drug begin to surge through my body. My belly was fluttering and my voice, when it emerged, was low and soft. I turned to Andreas.

—Why are you anti-Semitic?

He did not respond, he was searching the road. *Gamouto*, he muttered, I think I've missed the turn-off.

—Why are you anti-Semitic? I repeated.

—I told you, he replied, I do not hate Jews, I simply distrust them. For their wealth, their power. That they dropped the bombs on Belgrade, that they are forcing my country to be something it is not. That they want to enslave us.

—I think you are mistaking the Americans for the Jews.

—They are the same thing.

Giulia touched my hand in warning. Andreas, she said carefully, is a fine man in many ways but he is a filthy racist.

—I simply dislike their obsession with the past, their moral righteousness. I was sure he was aiming his words at me, not Giulia. I dislike their masochism.

Giulia laughed.

—Of course, she said, their obsession with the Holocaust is a sickness. I agree. But perfectly understandable.

—Have you read the Protocols of the Elders of Zion? he responded.

I laughed out loud.

—That was Nazi propaganda.

—The Protocols predate the Nazis, he replied.

—Alright, then it was early fascist propaganda! The fact is

that they are not true; the Protocols are fiction.

I was amazed that this educated man was using the Protocols to defend his hatreds. But the insidious chemical was playing in my blood and I could not muster any outrage. I was warm and happy.

—You are both ignorant fools, shouted Giulia from the back seat. It was the Russian czar who published that racist slime. I win, she added, in English.

We were approaching a town floodlit with electric light. The taverns and bars were full of people eating and drinking. The music surged through my body and as Andreas parked the car his hand slid across mine. He squeezed it, then he opened the door for Giulia. I was weak as I slid out of the car. Giulia took my hand and we followed Andreas through the crowds, into the music.

—Come, he said, turning to us and smiling, let me take you to a museum that celebrates *our* sickness.

Giulia squeezed my hand.

—I hope you are still interested in museums, my beautiful cousin.

—I am.

I laughed out loud, remembering.

Andreas looked at us quizzically.

—What is so funny?

—It's our secret, my cousin answered firmly, and pulled at my hand, dragging me ahead of him.

—Take me to the Jewish History Museum.

I had been drinking coffee with Giulia at a small table under an awning across from the Port. It was my first trip to Europe and we had danced till dawn the night before and were fortifying ourselves with caffeine, nicotine and Greek pastries. I was absolutely in love with Europe.

— Why do you want to go there?

—My father used to say that Thessaloniki is a city of Jews.

—Once, she answered. A long long time ago. There are no Jews now.

But there were. There were phantoms, and I had found them in the Jewish History Museum of Thessaloniki. The museum was a cavernous warehouse, with black partitions dividing the space into a maze. As we entered we had nodded to the middle-aged man smoking behind the front desk. Above him, a large dusty window framed the gloomy Salonikan sky. We were the only visitors and we walked slowly and reverentially past walls and walls of photographs. They had not been unfamiliar to me: the stark black and white images of destitution, of misery and death. The gaunt, desperate faces of women and children and men being herded into the death-camp trains. The tortures, the experiments, the annihilation. The history of the Holocaust.

It had been a relief to turn a corner and face life. Old sepia photographs from the *fin de siècle* portrayed the Jewish world of the city that had been erased. Families smiled for the camera, dressed in their best finery, the men in suits, the women in fur coats and hats perched on their carefully arranged hair; they were walking the same city streets that I had just explored. On another wall, there was a large photograph of a group of young men and women lying on grass. They wore army coats and had rifles at their sides. They were smiling, laughing, teasing the cameraman. The caption underneath the photograph said that they were Jews of the Resistance; they had taken to the mountainous border between Greece and Yugoslavia to fight alongside their Gentile partisan comrades. I had taken the camera from around my neck, stood back from the photograph and was ready to shoot.

—No photography. The man had risen from his desk and was walking towards us. He spoke in broken but clear English.

—Why? My cousin asked him in Greek.

—What do you want here? He spoke English again.

—My cousin is from Australia. He is interested in your history.

Every time my cousin had spoken in her own tongue, he had answered in mine. He held his right hand over my lens. Ignoring Giulia, he spoke to me again.

—There will be no photographs.

I could tell that Giulia was about to answer him rudely and I interrupted her.

—My father was from Thessaloniki, I explained. He told me about the Jews who lived here. I had been about to continue, to tell him that I wanted to acknowledge the Hebrew past of this city, to make recompense—I knew it was pitiful, hopeless, that nothing I could say or do could make amends for the terrible history hanging on the walls— but he did not let me finish.

—I am not interested in your father, he said firmly. All I ask is that you take no photographs. And with that, he had turned, sat back at his desk and lit another cigarette. He refused to meet my wounded gaze.

—How did you feel, Colin later asked me. How did you feel when he said that to you?

—Hurt.

—Why?

—Because I thought he was making no distinction between me and an anti-Semite. Jesus, I went to his museum, I wanted to learn, I wanted to ask questions, and he treated me like dirt.

—What did you say to him?

—Nothing.

—Why?

—I didn't think it was my place.

—What would you have liked to say to him?

—I don't know.

—Come on, what did you want to say to him?

—I wanted to say, Fuck off, you paranoid Jew, I have nothing to do with this history.

I put down my camera and indicated to Giulia that we should leave. She'd been loudly whistling a tune and the melody had danced and bounced around the high ceilings and walls of the museum. Just before taking the stairs leading down to the street, I turned back to look at the man. He was still ignoring me. In seconds we encountered the loud traffic and human shouts of a living city.

—What was that you were whistling?

—A Palestinian Resistance song.

—You shouldn't have done that.

She playfully grabbed my nose and tweaked it.

—You are so polite—you Australians have that English politeness. That man was rude and so I was rude to him. You must learn, dear cousin, that politeness will not get you far in Europe. Even in England, she added.

I broke into laughter and held up my camera.

—It doesn't matter. I took the photograph.

She had kissed me then.

—Good, maybe you are a European after all.

The photograph hangs above my computer, on the study wall. In the left corner the man's grey jacket is blurred, it dominates the bottom of the frame. But the smiling Resistance fighters are clearly visible, their grins sharp and joyous.

Ghosts. Blood and land and ghosts.

The bluestone building that Giulia and Andreas were now taking me to stood proudly alone in the middle of the town square. I was to discover that it had functioned as a school for communist guerrilla youth during the Greek Civil War. Andreas led us down a long white corridor and then we entered a gallery whose walls were covered by photographs printed on large square canvases. I dropped Giulia's hand and began to examine the black and white panels. The images were largely of men and women in military uniforms, clutching rifles and staring defiantly at the camera. There were photos of young schoolchildren being taught the rudimentary skills of combat. Then there were images of war: headless corpses roughly bound across a donkey's back; a man's body riddled with bullet holes; emaciated prisoners with ropes bound tightly around their wrists. In one photograph an old man was trying to cover his humiliating nakedness. The rope had been knotted so tightly that his wrists had begun to bleed and the rope had been soaked black. I turned to share my outrage with Giulia, but I was alone.

In a corner of the auditorium an old man was talking to a group standing around an old school desk. Andreas and Giulia were there. I walked over and stood listening at the edge of the group.

—Come closer, the old man urged me.

—He's an Australian, Andreas explained, and everyone turned to look at me. I felt my flesh burning and my legs felt separated from my torso. All I wanted to do was lie on the floor, look up at the high white ceiling, and let the old man talk.

—Does he understand Greek?

I managed to nod. The old man proceeded with his lecture, but he remained focused on me, nodding, inviting me into the conversation. I placed a smile and an expression of interest on my face but his words were all a jumble. I was a foreigner with a stranger's ears and I could not make out a word. But still I kept nodding. Giulia came and stood beside me and I laid my head on her shoulder. It was bliss.

—My love, she whispered, come with me. She took my hand and we walked away from the group.

—Did you understand any of that?

I shook my head.

—What did Andreas mean about this place being our sickness?

—The civil war. For us it was like the Holocaust was for the Jews. When I was a child, Isaac, all that mattered was which side your family fought for in the war. Madness—we were schoolchildren and we were still carrying on our grandfather's crusade.

I balanced myself against the white wall, cooling my cheek on the brick. Above us, I could see faint etchings emerging from the scrubbed plaster.

—What are these?

—Is our friend sick?

Andreas had placed a hand across my shoulder and I wanted to sink my head into his flesh. The old man was still lecturing to the group.

—What are these? I mumbled again.

—They were murals that the Right destroyed after the end of the civil war. The museum is attempting to restore them. He lowered his voice to a whisper. They are not so important, social realism, mostly rubbish.

I shook my head aggressively.

—No, it's good they are restoring them. It's great. We don't have anything like this in Australia. This is great. This is beautiful.

Andreas was laughing. He marched us out of the museum and back into the square. The diners were still arriving and the night seemed alive, sharp as shattered glass. I turned back and looked at the museum. It was framed tall and inspiring against the dark purple sky.

Andreas was looking at me.

—Do not take what the old comrade said too seriously.

His was not a complete history.

Giulia snorted.

—It was complete enough.

Andreas turned to her and I could see he was angry.

—You think the Resistance were fighting for Greece and that it was the West that betrayed us?

Giulia nodded defiantly.

—Half-truth. He turned to me and there was a bitter venomous sting to his words. Yes, the English, and yes, the Americans, they did betray us. But those comrades in there, on the wall, they were not fighting for fucking Greece, they were fighting for fucking Russia.

Giulia stood firm.

—So why didn't you say that to the old guy in there, why were you nodding along with everything he said?

The anger disappeared from Andreas' face.

—Because he is old, Giulia, and he has seen and been through enough. He turned to me. You understood he had been away from Greece for decades?

I shook my head. I understood nothing, I told him.

—He had been living in Budapest since the end of the civil war. He was only thirteen when he joined the Resistance. He has only returned to Greece since the fall of communism. The Hungarians don't want him anymore.

He turned back to my cousin and resumed the argument in Greek.

—What should I have said to him? That it was worth nothing, all those deaths, all those years in exile? He began laughing and I realised that for him, laughing was not joy but it was rancour and confusion. He laughed as the truck driver Takis in Agrinion had laughed when I had attempted to describe another world to him. It was the same laugh.

—Come, continued Andreas, it's all in the fucking past, isn't it? There's no exile any more, no civil war, no blood feuds, no more prisons and even the State builds a monument to the Resistance. We are all democrats, now, aren't we? We followed his laughter to the car.

Near the end of his life, Dad had started going a little mad. He would come home after work, have his hit, and stretch out on the couch watching endless television. He was obsessed by the collapse of history, the disintegration of Soviet Russia. I found him asleep one night, coming back from a friend's house, asleep on the couch, an American morning news program flickering away on the screen. Mum and my sister were in bed. On the coffee table there was a full ashtray and a small plastic envelope. I picked it up, looked at it, at the dull film of powdery residue coating it, and he opened his eyes. There was a small smile on his face. He indicated the screen.

—Turn it off, son. Turn off that propaganda.

—You shouldn't watch it, Dad, it just upsets you.

He offered me his hand.

—Help me up, Isaac, I've got to go to bed.

I pulled him off the couch and he took the empty packet from my hand. He waved it in front of my face.

—Rich man's powder, Isaac, to keep us numb, to keep us under control, do you understand?

—I know, Dad, I know, let's get you to bed.

—Jew powder, Isaac, he whispered, do you understand?

I was stunned. This wasn't Dad, this wasn't my father speaking.

—Dad, where the fuck is that coming from?

Anger fought through his drug haze. He sprayed spittle across my face.

—Fucking Jews, fucking traitors, they betrayed us. After all we did for them, after all the Party did for them. Fucking traitorous cunts, that's what they are. He waved his pouch of heroin in the air. Jew powder, Isaac, don't forget.

I said nothing, stood still and silent, did not dare move until he had closed the bedroom door behind him.

We drove back towards the Megalo Horio but turned off before the village and descended a small dirt road. Car after car was parked by the side of the road and everywhere there were people walking, talking, licking at ice-creams and eating bread and biscuits. Andreas edged his car between a small black convertible Saab and a flashy red Peugeot, and we got out and joined the crowd. Folk music was playing in the chaos, and I held tight to Giulia's arm. A small Mack truck was parked assertively in the middle of the road and two young gypsy men were passing white plastic chairs to the milling crowd.

—Quick, urged Andreas, grab us three seats. I walked over to the truck but every time I thought I had one of the gypsies' attention, someone would elbow my side and grab a chair. Giulia, laughing, came up beside me.

—You're in Greece now, my sweet, she said to me, and with a ferocious lunge she threw herself at the front of the mob.

—*Siga, kopela mou*, shouted a red-faced man, *pari seira*. Take it slow, girlie, wait in line.

—Fuck you, retorted my cousin, and winked at the youngest gypsy. She put up three fingers and the young man on the truck passed three plastic chairs above the heads of the shoving crowd. I took the chairs and made my way back out into the open. Giulia had a conceited smirk on her face.

—Did you see that? He only charged me one euro for all three chairs. I turned back to look at the young gypsy but his attention was on the crowd around him; the sweat on his brow and arms was shining in the moonlight.

—He's very sexy, I replied.

—You think so, retorted Giulia? They're like our fucking fathers. Their attitudes to women are awful.

The Resistance Museum turned out not to be the surprise they had in store for me. A ceremony, a traditional peasant marriage, was to be performed by a troupe of travelling actors. This was the surprise. Around the perimeter of a field, the white chairs formed a circle. In the middle of the field were two long trestle tables piled with cutlery, and jugs of wine. We placed our chairs under a tall pine tree, lit our cigarettes and allowed the music to lead us to euphoria. At our left a small cluster of musicians was playing sweet melodic folk songs. Behind them were two small thatched huts. A group of women in traditional peasant dress was standing before the hut closest to us. A group of men, of identical number, sat in a circle outside the other hut.

—The groom's and the bride's houses, I believe. Andreas had leaned across Giulia to speak to me and I felt his breath, hot and moist, on my cheek.

—This is how our grandmothers would have got married, said Giulia. The poor devils.

I watched the wedding: the laying out of the bride's dowry on the long wooden tables, embroidered mats and blankets, a copper jug; the groom's father accepting the dowry; the groom being shaved and washed by his groomsmen; the bride arriving draped in flowers on a white horse; the blessings, the exchanging of the wedding crowns; the feast and the toasts. The traditional thick red skirts of the women and the long-sleeved white shirts and black vests of the men, the whiplash frenzy of the band, the furious circle of men dancing, the women clapping their hands and stomping their feet: the ceremony unfolded like a movie and I was dazzled by the sounds, by the smells of charred meat and roasting vegetables, and the music that sang with both plaintiveness and joy. And around us the audience, sitting on their hard plastic chairs, in their Athenian summer clothes, were clapping and nodding, enjoying the performance, singing along to the old folk songs, cheering, yes, that's right, that's right, that's how it was. And the Ecstasy was churning in my stomach and in my brain, and there was a broad grin on my face as I watched the show. Then Andreas took my arm, was leading us away, back to the car and I was turning back, always looking back, at the beauty of the young groom, not quite yet a man, his face soft and his body lean and hard. I looked for the bride, and saw that she had removed her veil and was smoking a cigarette at the side of the hut. She was an actress at the end of a gig.

—Welcome to Peasantland, Andreas mocked in a pompous English accent. Did you enjoy seeing us playing at being serfs?

—I enjoyed it, I managed to get out, my voice thick, still looking backwards to catch a glimpse of the handsome groom. Andreas followed my stare.

—My grandmother wasn't that lucky, he said quietly. She got married to a man thirty years older than her and she died in childbirth after delivering him his eighth child.

I could not look at him. My cousin had taken my hand.

—They performed a fairytale for us tonight, Andreas, forget the politics. It was just a fairytale for my cousin. She spoke soothingly. The bride was lovely, the groom handsome. What more could we want?

—Andreas turned on the ignition, pressed a button, and a blast of deep booming house music drowned out the sounds of the clarino and the bouzouki.

Much later, late in the morning, I lay naked next to Andreas, touching the wiry hairs on his belly and chest. Giulia had got filthy drunk after the wedding performance. Back in the Megalo Horio she had switched from wine to ouzo and as she recalled the show that we had just seen, the pristine red folk dresses, the groomed wedding horse, the full banquet, she became loud in her anger. The more she analysed the performance as a fairytale the more incensed she became. She could not forget politics. That was bullshit, she roared, and the Greeks sitting at the tables around us were pointing at her and laughing. She turned to the nearest table, a group of four young men, and proceeded to shout at them in Greek. Did you go to the traditional wedding, she asked, and not waiting for an answer she proceeded to lecture the young men. Our mothers' clothes were not new and clean, she insisted, there were no full tables of food after the war, what we saw was full of lies. They kept laughing at her, and Andreas and I had to carry her back to the car before she hit one of them. Europe is all lies, Europe is all lies, she kept repeating in the back seat. When we put her to sleep in my bed she kissed my mouth, my face, my eyes. All lies, she said softly, her breath full of bile and alcohol. Then she promptly fell asleep.

I was in Andreas' bed, tracing lines across his chest and belly. Tell me about Colin, he said.

—What about him?

—Describe him.

I hesitated, wondered what to say. He is gentle and kind, I answered.

—Describe him.

I touched Andreas' hair.

—His hair is red and curly and he always cuts it short.

—What colour are his eyes?

—They are green.

—And is he small or big?

—He is very tall, very broad shoulders.

—And is he hairy?

—Yes. A little on his belly and a little on his chest. He is getting hairier as he gets older.

—And what is his cock like?

I laughed, laughed at myself for being embarrassed.

—Tell me.

—It's long and it is thick. He has a foreskin.

Andreas shifted his squat cock and I placed my hand over it.

—Does he mind you going with other men?

I took my hand away. I lay back on the bed and looked up at the white ceiling.

—I don't tell him.

—Do you think he goes with other people?

I looked at Andreas, at his thin dark face. His tone was lazy and sleepy, but I distrusted the questions. Of course I did. It was because I did not trust myself.

—Sometimes. Sometimes I smell him when he comes home late and I wonder if he has been with other men.

—So you have, how do the Americans say it, an open marriage.

I jerked my body away from him and groped for the cigarettes.

—Fuck you, I was trying to be honest. I love Colin. I love him very much and we have been together a long time. I wish I was strong enough not to need sex from other people. I smiled and blew lightly on the lit cigarette. I love Colin, I repeated.

Andreas reached over for a cigarette and kissed my shoulder.

—I believe you.

—And you, I asked, do you have a boyfriend?

He shook his head.

—Would you like to?

—No, he answered. He covered his cock with his hand and with the other hand drew the cigarette to his lips. I am marrying next spring. Her name is Diana. She too is a journalist. She is a friend of your cousin.

I got up and hunted for an ashtray.

—Does that shock you? I find that it shocks Americans and I assume you Australians are very similar.

—It doesn't shock me. I sat back in the bed and we lay next to each other.

99

—Do you know Giulia is divorced?

I stared at him.

—I didn't even know she was married.

—Yes, she married. She never believed it to be love. I think it was because she was tired of her mother constantly nagging her to get married. So she married, the big wedding, it was lovely. And now they are divorced.

—What was he like?

Andreas chortled and then let out a big hearty laugh.

—Too nice, too tame for your cousin. He wanted children and a nice apartment in Athens. She wants more from life.

—And you?

—I am forty-four, Isaac, and I want children. Diana is very sweet. She accepts me.

—Do you love her?

—Of course. Tenderly. I don't pretend it is a great passion. But neither does she. He chuckled. It is a little like the wedding we witnessed tonight. Our wedding is mutually financially beneficial.

I lay next to him and we were silent as we smoked our cigarettes.

—Have you ever been in love?

—*Americanaki*, he teased me, then he reached over and kissed me violently on the lips. I drew away. He began to touch my thighs, my balls, and I was aroused.

—I stupidly fell in love with a Serbian soldier. In Bosnia. So yes, I have been in love.

His cock was pressing against my stomach, he was on top of me.

—Do you still see each other?

—He is dead.

He pushed my legs apart and his cock was straining against my arse. I gently pushed him away and he dropped back on his pillow.

—Only Colin fucks me, I explained.

—I see. He scratched at his balls and his cock began to droop. He leaned over, pressed his body against me and closed his eyes. Tell me about your family. Your father was university trained. Did he remain rich?

I shook my head.

—My father worked as a labourer in Australia, in factories, I explained. He was educated in France and in Thessaloniki but he had to leave Greece quickly, in 1964. As Giulia explained to you.

—Ah, that's right. The brave migrant, exiled for his politics. We have all heard these fairytales.

I said nothing.

—And your mother?

—She came to Australia when she was eleven. Her family are from here, and I waved across the room, pointed out to the dark world outside the window. She's from these mountains.

—Where we are going tomorrow?

—Yes.

—Has she been back?

I shook my head.

—And your father?

—He's dead.

Andreas nodded slowly but his arm that was wrapped around my shoulder squeezed me tight.

—How did he die?

The moon, the half-moon, was visible through the window and its pale light glistened silver across Andreas' naked body.

—A heroin overdose.

Andreas was silent. His breathing was even and soft. I thought he might have fallen asleep so I slid myself from under him and searched for another cigarette.

—I understand, he said quietly.

—You understand what?

—Why you distrust us Greeks. We are not very kind.

He raised himself on his elbow and looked over to the wooden chair on which he had thrown his shirt and pants.

—That is a Prada shirt, he told me.

—It's nice.

—Yes. We wear Prada shirts now, Tommy Hilfiger jeans, but we still have our Eastern ways. Does your family know you are visiting the village?

—No.

—No, of course not. His eyes were wet with tears.

—How about you? Tell me about your family.

—Peasants from Kozani. So, like you, I too am *déclassé*.

—I don't understand.

—I am a peasant's son in designer clothes. I too don't quite belong. He stretched his arms and yawned. My father took us to England for ten years and that's where I learnt my proper English and how to scrub tables for fat English women who have no taste for food. My mother worked as a cleaner in a hospital in London and when we returned we had money enough for me to attend university and to bribe someone in Antenna to take me on as a reporter. My parents are very proud of me and are very happy that I am finally to marry.

I shivered, chilled by the bitter unhappiness in his voice. He suddenly jumped out of the bed, and he was standing over me, and his voice was cold and clear and calm. Too calm. I wished he had shouted. His eyes were freezing.

—And so now you know why I hate the Jews. I hate them because they killed Dejan.

I heard him pissing in the toilet and when he came out I pretended to be asleep. He lay next to me and pretended to do the same, till finally, blissfully, near dawn, sleep did come.

I awoke to the sound of a loud argument; two men on the street were disputing each other's version as to how their cars collided. I also awoke to that poisoning combination of guilt, regret and a hangover that can so often be the result of casual sex. My first thought on awakening was that I missed Colin, and then, leaning over and looking at the naked brown back of Andreas, my stomach clenched and my eyes felt bruised. He awoke as I was putting on my shoes and he asked me what time it was. When I replied that it was ten o'clock he groaned and asked irritably why I had woken him so early.

—I want to ring Colin.

His frown vanished.

—*Kala kaneis*. It's good you do this.

He closed his eyes, and then, turning his back to me, he said, I won't tell Giulia.

I leaned over and kissed his shoulder.

Giulia was asleep and snoring as I entered my little room. I took my camera and I clicked and she awoke. Stop it, she squealed, I look terrible. She breathed heavily and groaned. That's it, I am an old woman, she said. I have to give up drugs.

—Good on you, I answered, and leaned over and kissed her. She smelt of sleep.

She kissed me back and took a cigarette from my shirt pocket.

—Did you sleep together?

I was framing the view from the bedroom window. I took the shot.

—Yes.

She got up out of the bed and came and sat beside me. I played with her hair. She was naked except for her black cotton knickers.

—*Eisai entaxi?* Are you all right? She sniffed at my skin.

—Yeah. I'm fine.

—Good, she said, and slapped me hard on the cheek. That slap was from Colin, she said, as she threw her cigarette out of the window and went to have a shower.

The journey to my mum's village was perilous and long. The road had never been asphalted and every fifteen minutes Andreas had to stop the car so we could remove boulders and rocks that had fallen across the narrow path. As we drove higher into the mountains, the lush green fell away to a stark barren landscape of bleached rock and tall lonely pines. The three of us fell silent as we journeyed and Andreas switched off the radio. We passed small villages where old women dressed in black, some of them veiled and scarfed, watched us suspiciously as we rumbled past. The only young people we saw were thin men working shirtless in the fields who Giulia said were Albanian migrants.

Agrio Dassos was perched near the peak of a mountain, the small stone cottages balancing precariously on the cliff's edge. The road continued further up the mountain and disappeared into a dark thatch of forest. Giulia shivered and pulled a thin black jumper around her shoulders.

—*To telos tou kosmou*, she muttered. The end of the world.

Andreas stopped the car. There was no square, no sign of life in the village. We left the car and proceeded past an old cottage which had fallen apart, one good wall remaining, the rest of it rubble. We turned a corner and saw two old men sitting at a table drinking coffee. An old wooden sign, with the word *Kafenio* written on it in hasty black ink, creaked and shuddered in the wind.

Andreas approached the men.

—Can we order some coffees?

One of the men slowly rose to his feet and went inside the shop. The space was small and uninviting but the other man gestured at the table opposite and invited us to sit. I looked at his wrinkled face.

—Where are you from?

—From Athens, replied Andreas, and then he pointed at me. This man is from Australia. The old man searched my face.

—I had brothers in Australia. They're all dead. He took a small clump of tobacco from his jacket pocket and began to roll himself a cigarette. We fell silent as we waited for our coffees.

Silence had descended on us as soon as we entered the village: it lay heavy and oppressive on the rocks and trees, it was thick in the air and on the breeze. It was as if we had left spring behind, and as I looked across the terraced fields sloping down into the vast blue of the sky, I wondered if this place had ever known the warmth of that season. The sun above us was dull and far away. We could not keep our eyes still. I thought I heard a whisper behind me, Andreas jumped at a shadow, and Giulia pulled her jumper tighter across her shoulders. When the old man delivered us our coffees the clink of the porcelain on the table seemed to ring through the mountain air. Then we heard the bells.

A woman wearing a thick black dress, a dark blue scarf covering her white hair, was leading three goats along a path. As they clattered across the path the small bells on their necks clanged harshly. She stopped on seeing us, squinted, and yelled up to the old men.

—*Poi einai autoi oi ksenei?* Who are these strangers?

We were all foreigners.

From Australia, one of the old men answered and Andreas did not bother to correct him. Instead he turned to me and asked me what I wanted to do. I shrugged and wondered if my eyes were playing tricks on me or whether there were eyes spying at us from the treetops. The shadows danced everywhere. He spoke to me in English.

—We cannot stay here. There are no hotels or *pensiones* or anything like that here, Isaac. This is a dying Greece. Take your photographs; when you come back next time all of this will be gone.

Giulia turned on him and her eyes were moist. Bullshit, she said, this place has been here for thousands of years and it will be here when your euro and your EU and your fucking NATO will be just memories.

Andreas laughed.

—Do you see young people? No. Look at the old houses abandoned and fallen down. Look at the dry earth with nothing growing on it. This place is dead.

Giulia took a sip from her coffee and then without looking at me she leaned over and touched one of the men on his shoulder.

—Excuse me, Uncle, she asked, do any of you know a Reveka Panagis?

I shivered, and held my breath for an answer.

—Who? inquired the other man.

—Reveka Panagis. She was a neighbour of mine in Australia.

The two old men looked over at each other and began to whisper. I looked again at the old men, at their faces, into their eyes, wondering if I could find a glimpse of my mother in them. Or of myself. I gulped at the coffee, slammed the cup on the table and grabbed my camera. I'm taking photographs, I barked, and without waiting for a response, I left the table.

The silence followed me as I took the path that wound past the ploughed terraces. I walked alongside heavy squat cottages and again I thought I could hear whispers following me. Shadows danced and twitched all around me, but every time I stopped, the silence would descend. The path, full of wild nettles, began a steep ascent and on turning a corner I saw a tiny church. I opened the black wrought-iron gate and walked past the building to the small cemetery beyond. Tall yellowed grass ran wild across the greying cement crucifixes and the cracking white stone. I began to take pictures. I focused on the weather-beaten carvings on the stone. I took photographs of the church wall. I was framing the small bell tower, hoping to catch a shot of the white stone against the blue sky, when I heard a laugh behind me. I turned around and a young boy, his face dirty and his feet bare, was laughing behind the gate. His ragged clothes were thin and filthy and I wondered if he was a gypsy. I looked up at the sky, judging the light, then fiddled with my lens, and raised my camera to take a shot of the boy.

But he had disappeared. I swung around and looked at the path, I walked to the gate and peered below. The ground sloped down to a precarious drop. The cemetery was perched on the cliff's edge. I drew back and looked behind me but the gypsy child had disappeared completely. And then for the first time in years, as I walked out of the church grounds I found my hand had flown to my forehead and to my heart. I had made the sign of the Cross. And again I heard laughter.

I took the path back to the shop and Giulia was waiting for me, smoking a cigarette.

—Where's Andreas?

—Gone for a walk. She took my hand. Are you angry with me?

—My mother doesn't want anyone here to know about her.

Giulia squeezed my hand tight. Her eyes were bright.

—Yes, I know, but listen to me.

I interrupted her.

—No, you listen to me. This is my family business.

She let go of my hand.

—And what are you going to find out on your own, she mocked me, with your terrible Greek?

I started walking away from her, past the coffee shop, past Andreas' BMW now coated with fine coppery dust. I was walking away from the village.

—Wait, she called after me, and I heard her steps running towards me. I did not look around.

—Wait, she repeated, and my anger dissipated on hearing the whine of her tortured English. I turned to her, all smiles, I was going to ridicule her accent. She was breathless as she took my hand. I was about to speak, to tease her, when she placed a hand over my mouth and I choked back my words.

—Will you just listen to me for a second? she pleaded. Just listen. I spoke to those old men.

Her breathing was slow and heavy, she was searching for words. She took her hand away from my mouth and stroked my cheek.

—My darling Isaac, my darling cousin, did you know your mother's family is cursed?

MICHAELIS PANAGIS HAD not liked America. He had not liked the crowds and the sprawling city of New York, he had not liked the tiny rooms in which he had to live, he did not like the bosses who ordered him to do this and to do that. He did not like it that Americans spoke fast and that they travelled even faster: he feared automobiles and electric underground trains. He did not like the thick sound of the American accent, did not like what these strange foreign words were doing to his own tongue. Speak English, wop, speak English. Even the Greeks there cursed him like this. No, Michaelis had not liked America.

But America had been good to him, though it had not been without effort and had not been without sweat. Michaelis' nightmares were still full of the deep black caverns of the ironworks in which he had found himself at fourteen. The dark pits with their charred walls and roaring furnaces had seemed like Hell and he was to spend thirteen years stoking those furnaces, shovelling coal into their ravening mouths. Countless times the flames had snatched at his skin, and his body was full of the marks of the devil fire. But he had money, he had a cheap corner in a room which he shared with a silent Armenian called Essaman and a Persian Hebrew called Samouli, and he was determined to not let the temptations of the city seduce him. From morning, when he arose and began his prayers, to the evening when he threw his exhausted body onto the mattress, Michaelis asked God that he would return to his village rich enough to silence once and for all the insults against his parents. He asked that he be allowed to marry the beautiful Lucia. And with those two prayers on his lips, he would fall asleep until his nightmare began again the following day.

Even when the factories closed at the height of the Depression, Michaelis managed to find employment. Samouli had married into a large New York family who supplied lace and fine textiles, fabrics and cotton, to the American aristocracy: Hollywood. Bergman and Sons supplied the cream chiffons that swathed Garbo in *Camille*; the sleek silk tunics that Valentino wore were made of fabrics smuggled into America by the senior Bergman himself. Samouli had organised work for Michaeli after-hours in the dank warehouse cellar underneath the Bergman store on Broadway. Samouli had also loaned him a sum of money to tide him through the harrowing weeks of unemployment, and to last through the fortnight's trial period that old man Bergman had demanded. Ashamed but desperate, Michaelis had accepted the loan.

The one motion picture he had seen had frightened him and given him a headache, so Michaelis had little idea of the luminaries who wore the silks and cottons that he spent hours dyeing, cutting and sewing in the basement of the Bergmans' shop. The stench of the dyes was so strong that he would sometimes faint and awaken in a panic, with threads of vomit stringing his lips, and stains spread across his work tunic. But Michaelis never complained. He was grateful that the Hebrews had given him work. The warehouse was busy day and night with desperate hungry women and men who also grew sick from their work. They were mostly Hebrews, from Russia and Germany, and other countries that Michaelis had never heard of. The women never spoke to him, refused to meet his eye. Out of respect to the older Bergman he made sure that he never spoke to any of the daughters who worked in the store upstairs. The wife he never saw. She lived high up on the other side of the city, far from the harassed bustle of the store; a million miles from the stench and heat of the basement. The sons he detested. They took every opportunity to make it known to Michaelis that his employment was a favour of which they did not approve. They ordered him around disdainfully, shouted at him that he was lazy and a fool, complained every time they had to pay him, but Michaelis accepted it all. Yes, sir, he would answer and they would take the opportunity to laugh at his accented English. He would bow his head and continue with his work.

All the time he kept himself separate from the Hebrews. He made certain to never touch their food, believing it contaminated with Christian blood. He feared the old bearded men: they indeed looked like devils. Even Samouli, or Sam as he now preferred to be called, he kept at a distance.

When work was again plentiful Michaelis returned to the ironworks and for close to a year he kept a small amount of his earnings under his mattress in order to repay his debt to the Hebrew.

When he had saved enough to return to Greece a rich man, he placed the money he owed to Samouli in a small envelope and he walked the long distance to the Hebrew's house. Since his marriage Samouli had rarely spoken with him and Michaelis had never been invited to the house. He knew that the wife was a strict Hebrew and he understood that his being a Christian, and therefore a reminder of their damnation, made the Hebrews fear him.

Samouli's house was small but it was built from new bricks and situated in a neighbourhood where the streets were wide and clean. Michaelis had knocked twice on the door and waited. The woman who answered wore a soft blue scarf around her hair. The locks that strayed from beneath the fabric were the colour of honey. Her eyes were round and bright, the light in them as fierce as the furnaces he had worked in New York and Pittsburgh. Michaelis blushed, bowed, and asked for Sam. At first the woman seemed to hesitate, as if she was going to slam the door in his face, but then she turned around and called out.

—Samuel! There's someone here for you.

—Who is it?

Samouli came to the door dressed in a suit jacket and a crisp white shirt. Michaelis looked down at his own dusty shoes and frayed pants and could not stop himself from blushing.

—Got something for you, he barked, refusing to look at the woman. He handed over the envelope to Samouli and turned to leave. The Hebrew glanced at the contents.

—What is this?

—The money I owe you.

—You owe me no money, Mikey. Take this back.

Michaelis refused. The woman took the envelope from her husband's hand and looked inside.

—Is this a debt?

—Yes.

Samouli shook his head.

—No, Rebecca. I find him job. That's all, at your uncle's shop.

The woman, still holding the envelope, smiled. She said something in the Hebrew tongue and Michaelis glanced at Samouli, who was shaking his head.

—He is not a Jew.

Her eyes searched the Greek man's face.

—Would you like to come in?

Samouli nodded his head in agreement.

—I have much to do. My ship leaves for Greece next Saturday. Michaelis again made a move to walk away.

—Please, the woman said, please come in. We are fasting but I can prepare you a small supper if you like.

She named the fast: *yam kippa*? Michaelis knew that the

American Hebrews said that the names of all their festivals were announced by God in the Bible but Michaelis had never believed this Hebrew lie. He could not read but he knew the thick strange words the woman had uttered could not possibly be inscribed within the Holy Book.

—No. Michaelis took Samouli's hand and shook it vigorously. Thank you, friend, he said.

He bowed again, then turned and made his way back down the street. His mind was feverish. She was very lovely, still a girl really, her body slender but her breasts and face full. Rebecca, he whispered her name and felt lust surge through his body. Rebecca. She even had a Greek name. Reveka. He cursed Samouli's luck. A pretty and wealthy wife, a soft, easy job in the store, an assured inheritance, a small but comfortable house in the world's greatest city. He was not aware of the streets he was walking down, the neighbourhoods he passed. Even in the New York cold he began to perspire profusely and his clothes felt wet and heavy on his body. On reaching home he threw himself on the mattress and began to weep into his pillow. He was ashamed of his emotions, his rage and envy, but the howls would not stop and when Essaman arrived to share their bed, Michaelis was still sobbing.

—What happened?

—Nothing.

The Armenian laughed.

—You Greeks, crazy.

His face still half-hidden in his pillow, Michaelis blurted out his sin.

—I am jealous of Sammy. He has big house, beautiful wife.

—The Devil protects the Jews. Here on earth, but only here on earth.

—Tell me, you Armenian bastard, you can read: is Reveka a Christian name?

—Yes. It is in the Holy Book. She is a saint.

—Not a Jew?

—No.

—Sammy's wife is name Reveka.

—In America, Jews, Greeks, Anatolians, all of us lose our traditions. That's why you Mikey, me Max and bloody Samouli is Sammy. Names no matter in America.

Michaelis dried his tears. The Armenian had thrown off his shoes and slipped into bed. He had been drinking and soon his loud snoring filled the room. Slowly Michaelis thrust his body into the mattress. Reveka, Reveka, he intoned silently. He spilt himself into his trousers and fell asleep.

His parents had arranged a feast for his return and all the village had turned out to welcome back Michaelis. He had been a child when he had left and he returned a tall and imposing adult. He had always been handsome but the long years at the furnaces had weathered his skin to make him appear older than he was, and he was balding. America had proved a lucrative place for him but he allowed his parents to exaggerate his wealth. He did not have a house in New York, he was not a partner in a cotton mill, he had not met the president. But Maritha Panagis had told all her neighbours that her son was indeed a rich and powerful man in America and Michaelis allowed her to boast. His father had not said much at all but his eyes shone with pride and gratitude and he would not leave his son's side. Michaelis had brought his mother and sisters the finest cloth and prettily laced shawls and squares of fabrics, stolen from the Bergmans over time, which he had kept faithfully stored for his return. He had a suit made especially for his father and he pledged money for the Church of the Holy Spirit. At the feast, for which a dozen goats were slaughtered and barrels of wine ordered from town, Michaelis sat his father and mother at the head of the table, next to the priest, and they wore the splendid clothes he had brought them. The village drank to their health, celebrated their son, wished them the continuation of their good fortune, and though Michaelis knew that they gagged on every word, he knew too that his wealth now meant that not one of the cowards sitting at the tables around his parents would dare to insult them to their faces again. Every door would be open to them, every feast and every religious ceremony would have old Panagis at its head.

He drank copiously that night, celebrating the wide wild sky above him, inhaling the cool pine breeze of the mountains, raising his hand to trace the luminous stars. The years of coal and fire and sweat and cramped rooms washed off him that night and every time he looked back to earth, at the crowd toasting his health, he thanked God for making his dreams possible.

—Why did you return?

His brother had walked with him to the edge of the village, where they sat on a rock and chewed tobacco, looking down at the lights of the village of Klimoni, and up towards the jagged peaks of Mount Ouranos.

—You should have stayed, there is only hunger here. And they say there will be war.

His older brother Stavros was shockingly thin, and his young face was bitter and dark. Michaelis knew that Stavros might never forgive him for returning from America, that he had hoped to one day join his brother in the New World. He tried to explain what it had cost him to live as an exile.

—This is my home. Michaelis stretched his arms out to the sky above, to the world below. This is where I belong. And if I die in war, at least I die here. And if I die hungry, at least I die here. Who would have buried me in America?

And who will bury you here? For close to two years he had thought that God was playing a cruel joke on him. He was childless. All the money he had made, all his boasting, had come to nothing now that he had married a beautiful but barren wife. He knew that this was what the village said of him and of Lucia, that she had been too proud of her beauty, he too proud of his wealth, and God had punished them. He had almost begun to believe it. His mother told him not to listen to their gossip and curses, that it was only envy that made their neighbours so spiteful and it would be they whom God would eventually punish. But as they grew more hungry under the Occupation, as Lucia's womb remained empty, as the summer turned to winter and then to summer once more, Michaelis wondered if his brother had not been right. The Germans would never dare attack America itself, and by God, there was food in the New World. Maybe he should have stayed.

He should never have doubted God. Michaelis awoke one morning to find that Lucia was not by his side. He assumed that she had ventured down to the valley to see if anything could be scrounged from the earth, or that she had wandered over to her sister's home, but on going to the outhouse he noticed her staff was still lying against the cottage wall. He poured water on his face and returned to the house to light the fire. She returned soon after, her face red and her eyes bright.

—Where have you been?

—To Old Woman Nassoula.

He sat beside her. The old woman was a midwife.

—And?

Lucia's smile was frigid.

—I am with child.

He had meant to sing, to swoop his wife into his arms and to dance with her, to shout out across the valley, to every house. I am to be a father. But her cold smile stopped him. Lucia suddenly burst into tears.

—Don't be foolish, woman, this is great news.

—We have no food, we have nothing. This is not a time to be with child.

He stormed out of the cottage and made his way behind the small field of nettles to the shed where they had tended the goats. The animals were gone now, killed to feed the enemy, but the shed still smelt powerfully of them. He fell to his knees, prised a rock out of the ground and removed a handful of notes from the hole it had been covering.

He returned to the house and threw them at his wife.

—Dollars, he yelled. I will pay what it costs to feed my wife and my child. You will not go hungry.

Lucia fell on the money.

—And what about the Hebrew?

Michaelis was silent.

—We have a child now, Michaeli, we are risking him as well as ourselves.

—The Germans are losing.

—They have not lost yet.

—We gave our word.

—To a damn Hebrew! Devil take them all!

She banged her fist on the table, lashed her feet out at the empty air. Her fury was monstrous. As if possessed by Satan himself, her mouth and eyes narrowed till they were lost in a hideous mask of pale skin that stretched across her face.

Michaelis shrank back from her and closed his eyes. There was silence and then only the heavy breathing of his wife.

—And what life is there left for the little bastard? She had gone quiet, her eyes now sad and sombre, her voice pleading. His parents will be dead. Have we heard from them? Nothing. She rose, and by the kitchen hearth, she knelt and lifted the dagger. She offered it to her husband, her other hand cradling her belly. We have our own son to protect now.

Michaelis trembled, not at her words, but at the delight and hope in her demon eyes.

—I will not do it. I will not murder the boy. How can I do such a thing? I would condemn my soul.

Lucia's eyes were ablaze with fire.

—It is by protecting that bastard Hebrew that you are condemning your soul. Why do you think I have been barren for so long?

Sitting beside him, she lowered her voice and put her lips close to his ears. He felt the jolt of lust convulse his body.

—Our child is a child of God. The Hebrew belongs to the Devil. Don't you see, Husband? God has given us an opportunity to redeem ourselves for our sin. You must murder that fiend we have been protecting. Her hand had crept to his groin. It is God's will.

He shoved her hand aside, rose, his back turned to her. He was praying.

—Michaelis? Her voice was still a whisper.

His hands trembled but inside he felt calm and peace. Yes, God was a mystery and God was absurd. Was it a crime to protect the Christ Killer? Was it a crime to murder him? Only God himself knows the answer, he said to himself, and if the priests are telling the truth you will know it as well on the Day of Judgment. You made your promise to Jacova here on earth. Here on earth you will not be dishonoured. He turned and looked down at his wife. Her body was upright, she was smiling.

—I have promised to protect the boy. I will not dishonour myself.

—Then I will inform on you. Her frigid smile was steel on her lips. I will go to the Germans, Husband, and I will prostrate myself on the ground before them and confess. I will tell them how you forced me to feed and protect the Hebrew. I will tell them that you beat me if I protested. Her eyes were daring his. How many nights, how many months, how long have I lived in fear because of this crime you have committed? Do you think I will allow one of those harpies or drunkards from the village to stumble across the Hebrew bastard and run to the Germans to betray us? They're all jealous of me, every single one of them. I will have this child. On my own if I have to.

Michaelis clenched his fist. Whore, you will do as I say. I am your husband.

Lucia's laugh rang through the cottage. Do you think you are a man? You are not a man. You are a fool. You know what the village says of you, what my brothers say of you? That fool, Michaelis Panagis, he didn't have enough sense to stay in America. The fool comes back to famine and war. That faggot, Panagis, we give him the most beautiful woman in Greece and he does not know what to do with her. She spat at his feet. And now you think you can order me to place the life of my unborn child at risk? Who do you think you are? You are not a man. I will be glad to see you hang.

—I am a man. You are the Devil. His clenched fist struck Lucia with such force that she flew from the bed and crumpled on the dirt floor. But she did not cry. As she got to her knees, she was still smiling, a trickle of blood from her bottom lip running down her chin. She licked at it and struggled to her feet.

—You kill me or you kill the Hebrew. What choice will you make, Michaeli?

She offered the dagger to him again. This time he took it and raised it to her throat. She did not shudder; she did not blink. Slowly he lowered the blade. Lucia's smile was warm.

—The crime will be on you. He felt as though he were looking down on his wife, their cottage; it was as if his soul had left his body and it was flying up high into his beloved mountain sky. His hand was still clutching the dagger and he felt its weight; it was ice in his grip, but he was far away from the man who held it. And when the man spoke, he could hear every word clearly, but the words too were coming from somewhere far away from him.

—The crime will be on you, he repeated, still above her; he was speaking to eternity. God will judge you, not I. She was stroking his cheek, kissing his brow.

—Yes, let his blood be on me. But you will do it?

Michaelis slowly nodded.

—You are a man, Michaeli, you are a man. She was clutching his hands now. Don't you feel relief, Husband, don't you feel happiness?

His soul had descended back to earth. He pushed Lucia away in disgust. But the bitch was right; she knew his mind. He did feel relief. Soon fear would be banished, soon the Hebrew would no longer be his concern. And it was not his fault. It would not be his crime.

—I will do it tonight. Let night fall, and I will do it.

Lucia's eyes were closed and her face was upturned. She was praying. Her smile was satisfaction.

A strong will had been God's gift to Michaelis. To escape the derision poured on his family's circumstances, from a young age he would flee the village and spend his days on the summit, watching the sun and earth, tending herds of goats for wealthier farmers. His parents' holdings were sparse: the tiny stone cottage, three goats, a small patch of earth in the valley.

His mother had no dowry, and, worse, she was from far away. Though Maritha now spoke only Greek, though she was the most pious woman in the village when it came to the rites of the Church, everyone persisted in calling her a stranger. And as her child, he too was called names and heard the whispers behind his back. The other boys beat him mercilessly, and he in turn tried to dislike them. But Michaelis did not have the temperament or the cruelty in his character for aloofness. He wanted to laugh and play tricks, he wanted to tease and pull the hair of the pretty girls. Knowing that his attempts at friendship would always be resisted, he chose instead to be a friend to the goats and mules, descending to the village square only when the demands of religion could not be forsaken. He had been shocked, terrified, the morning his mother had awoken him with a rough blade in her hands to shave his head, and said to him that every morning was now to be spent in the school with the other children.

He had kept his fist tightly clenched over the hard chunk of bread his father had given to him that first morning. The school was a small room at the back of the Teacher's house. Michaelis liked the Teacher. Unlike the other men in the village, Teacher never yelled at him, always stopped to greet him and his family if their paths should meet. The small room was fitted with two long tables. That first day there had been sixteen children crammed together on two pews, facing Teacher, who wore a stiff white shirt and a black bow tie. Not all the children were from the village. There were the Litras twins, Christo and Pano from Serita, which meant that their walk to school would have taken them two hours. There was Maria, Thimia and Kostas Mangis from Frousini. And there were the children who Michaelis knew. It was one of them, Nikos Hondros, who began the fight.

Nikos was older than Michaelis, and his father owned three large plots of land in the most fertile, lush fields in the valley. Nikos was tall and strong and he sat in the pew beside Michaelis. All the boys sat in the second pew; the young girls sat demurely in front of the Teacher in the first pew. The morning had been confusing and difficult. Michaelis was used to roaming the mountains in the morning, following the path of the goats. But Teacher was commanding him to stay still, to listen while he pointed to strange pieces of paper on the wall behind him. Michaelis could not stop fidgeting, could not stop tapping his foot, stretching his arms, yawning. But Teacher had instructed him to stay still, to keep quiet, and his father had warned him before sending him off to school that morning, that if he heard that Michaelis had not obeyed the Teacher he would be thrashed when he returned home in the afternoon. So even when his bladder began to ache, even when his mind seemed as if it would fall out of his head, so weary was he of concentrating on the wall in front of him, Michaelis tried to remain as still as possible. But he could not help moving: his hands, his feet, his very toes and fingers seemed to take on a life of their own. The Teacher was now irritated.

—Panagi, what's wrong with you?

—I want to piss, sir.

—Then go and piss, my child. Or would you prefer to do it here on the floor in front of us?

The whole class tittered.

Nikos Hondros piped up.

—It's because he's an Albanian, sir. They all piss in their own houses.

Michaelis ignored the laughter and made his way to the back of the school. He heard Teacher punishing Nikos Hondros and he was glad. He squatted over the hole in the ground, pissed into the earth, and smiled as he looked up into the sky. There were birds flying, he could hear shouts from the men and women working in the fields. He did not want to return inside, to be imprisoned again by the walls of the schoolroom. Reluctantly he hitched up his pants, wiped his hand on the grass and went back inside.

His bread was missing. He had kept hold of it all through the morning but had left it on the table when he had gone outside. Teacher was still talking and the children were all quiet. Michaelis looked all around the table, checked the floor, but he could not see the bread anywhere. He heard a smothered giggle.

—Who's taken my bread? he whispered to Nikos.

The older boy shrugged his shoulders, then smiled and opened his mouth. Crumbs lined his tongue; wet chunks of chewed bread filled the gaps between his teeth. Michaelis was outraged.

—You stole it!

His shout was so loud that Teacher jumped, and dropped his ruler.

—Panagis! What the hell is happening?

Michaelis ignored the man. His face flushed, his hands became two coiled balls; he stood and looked down fiercely at Nikos Hondros. Then he dropped his fists onto the older boy's head. The fight was short. Like feral dogs they bit and scratched and tore at each other. Nikos was older and bigger but Michaelis' frenzy was such that he did not feel the blows on his flesh and he was determined to be the victor in the struggle. The older boy was equally determined not to be beaten by his weaker foe and it was only the wild kicking of Teacher that ended the duel. The man was furious. He gave them a couple of extra blows on the head. The other children were laughing and encouraging Nikos. The teacher held the boys apart.

—I'm going to tell each of your fathers to give you the thrashing of your lives.

Michaelis squirmed away from the teacher.

—He stole my bread.

—He's lying, sir. He's just an animal.

The younger boy stopped still. He was enraged by the lie.

—It's true, sir. I was sitting listening to you and he just started hitting me.

Michaelis found a word.

—Thief! he accused Nikos.

Nikos' eyes narrowed.

—Who do you think you are? Your mother's a slut foreigner and your father's an imbecile.

Two things happened. The whole class erupted into

laughter. And the teacher gave Nikos such a blow that the child lost balance and fell to the floor, smashing his head across the pew as he collapsed. The collision made a sickening thud and the class went silent.

No more argument or fighting occurred that morning but in the hushed schoolroom Michaelis heard the whispers circulate. *Poutana. Poutana. Poutana. Xeni xeni xeni.* He would quickly look up when the words glided past him but each head was lowered obediently to the desk, the children faithfully copying the strange notations the Teacher was making on the board. But still the word persisted. Throughout the day, Michaelis sat, his face red, his eyes wet, listening to the children call him the son of a whore.

That afternoon he returned to his house and told his mother and father that he was not meant for school. His mother fell to her knees, pleaded with him to reconsider, his father thrashed him then and again during the night and again the next morning, but Michaelis would not change his mind. Finally, his body bleeding from his father's blows, his mind slowly drifting back to consciousness, he made his promise to God. That one day his mother would hold her head up high in the village and that all the children who had mocked him would be made to bow to her. From that day he did not waver in pursuing his promise.

In the same way, in the bowels of night, terrified every time he heard the hungry howls of the wolves on the mountains, certain that the shadows that fell upon him from the trees were the shadowy limbs of demons, he did not falter from following the path to the summit. Summer had long left the village and he could feel the first bitter sting of winter. He pulled his jacket tight around his shoulders and proceeded up the slope. With every step he felt the leather sheath of the dagger slap his thigh. It only made his steps more determined. Determination had been God's gift to him.

o O o

The boy was praying. He was on his knees, rocking back and forth, his eyes closed, his hands held out. Michaelis dropped into the cellar and the boy sprang back. The eyes that turned to Michaelis were animal and desperate.

On recognising the man the boy's breathing calmed. He still sat crouched in the corner of the dark but there was something close to a smile now on his lips. He stretched out his hands and begged for food.

Michaelis, recoiling from the foul stench of the cellar, all shit and piss and sweat, seeing the boy's skeletal body, was suddenly aware that murder was the most decent act he could perform. He too smiled, crouched next to the boy, and slowly brushed the Hebrew's hair from his eyes.

—I have no food for you tonight, said Michaelis. But I have good news: the war is over.

The boy shrank back from the man's touch, his eyes wary.

—I tell you, the Germans have surrendered. You are free.

The boy looked down at his emaciated frame, at the rags that clothed his body.

—I tell you, continued Michaelis, your father is with us at the house. He has returned. Your family is waiting for you.

The boy began to cry. His hands fell across his crotch and he looked down at the dirt.

—What is it, you bloody fool Hebrew?

Michaelis rose and looked around the cellar. The boy had scratched Hebrew letters on the stone walls. Reminding himself that the stones above him were once part of Christ's church, Michaelis made a vow that he would return to remove the evil scribblings. Damn this, thought the man, let's get it over with. The boy had still not moved.

—Have you clothes for me?

Michaelis laughed.

—Aren't you the aristocrat? No, my boy, there's nothing for you. The Germans took everything from us. There's precious few clothes in your future.

Then, as he realised the truth within his lie, Michaelis hung his head low. Steel yourself, Panagis, he ordered himself, and lifting his head he demanded the boy come with him. The youth shook his head.

—I cannot see my family like this. He pointed to the rags he was wearing.

—Don't be an idiot, yelled the man, what the hell does it matter what you look like? You've been damn lucky holed up in here throughout the war. You haven't seen anything. And we fed you, didn't we? We fed you when even we did not have a thing to eat. You lousy Hebrew.

The boy began to cry.

Michaelis softened.

—Come, I'll take you home.

The boy came over to the man, and softly kissed Michaelis on the lips. The touch was only momentary, but the youth's lips were full and wet and it had been such a kiss that the man had been waiting for all his life. Lucia would never kiss him like this. The face she turned to him in the evenings was hard. The boy's eyes were open wide and the man took a step back.

—You are the Devil, he whispered, and he made the sign of the Cross. He pushed the boy roughly towards the hole in the ceiling.

Climb, he ordered.

But the boy was weak, and Michaelis had to push him up through the hole.

Once in the shell of the church the boy clung close to the man and when they entered the night the boy began to shiver. His wide eyes took in the black sky, the pearly stars, the world below: he moved closer to Michaelis.

—The world has changed, he whispered.

Michaelis looked out across the mountains and valleys, he looked across the dark.

—The world never changes, he answered.

They descended wordlessly. Michaelis urged the boy ahead and they made their way along the small thin rivulet, following the sound of the water upon the rocks. The lights of the village came into view and the boy's pace began to quicken. Michaelis grabbed him.

—Let's drink first, he whispered, and he took hold of the boy's arm and pushed him towards a small grove in the forest. The creek widened in the grove, and the trees provided shelter from the wind. The boy knelt, cupped his hands, and drank from the cold water. He drank and drank, and when finished he washed his face, his arms, his neck. He turned his face to Michaelis and his smile was rapturous and as large as the earth.

The dagger plunged deep into the boy's throat. There was a muffled scream of pain and the boy fell to the ground. Michaelis searched the boy's still breathing chest and when he found the beat of the heart he screwed the dagger hard into the body. The boy shook, a gurgle escaped his lips and then he fell still and quiet. The now empty eyes stared out at Michaelis from the hollow sockets. He moved his hands across the boy's face and shut out the night. But as he did so, the boy's face grimaced and shook and Michaelis shrank back in horror. Then he smelt the urine and the excrement. The body was again still. Michaelis made the sign of the Cross. Even if he were a filthy Hebrew, the body had once housed a human soul.

Michaelis knew that the wolves would soon smell the blood so he smashed the boy's face with a rock, smashed it repeatedly so the face was unrecognisable. Then he stripped away the boy's clothes, washed his own hands and face in the water, and then ran all the way home. Lucia was awaiting him in the cold, her arms wrapped tight around her body. When she saw her husband enter she sprang up and moved towards him. There was hunger in her eyes.

—Is he dead?

When Michaelis nodded, the joy in her was unmistakable. She clutched at her husband, kissed his neck and his face, his eyes and his mouth. She brought his hands to her lips and smothered them in kisses of gratitude.

—We are free, she whispered.

Lucia made a fire and threw the boy's clothes upon it. She took down a small vial of holy water from the mantelpiece and splashed her hands with it, and ordered her husband to do the same. Then when the clothes had been reduced to ash, she collected the remains and threw them deep into the shithole outside. As some of the ash caught in the wind and danced in the night air, she remembered the boy's skin upon hers, and she shuddered. She returned to her house and fell exhausted into bed. Michaelis soon heard her light snores beside him.

Sleep did not come easily for him. The moon's silver light played on the walls of the cottage, forming the strange signs of the Hebrew. It is only the moonlight, it is only your imagination, he told himself, but he had to keep his eyes shut tight in order to banish the evil hallucinations. Sleep did come, but when it arrived it was full of nightmares. He dreamt that he was a wolf, running in a pack, his body slick and grey. At first the dream was pleasing and arousing. But soon the pack came across the Hebrew boy's bloodied corpse and they attacked the boy with a ravenous ferocious lust. Michaelis awoke screaming, the taste of blood and meat and flesh still in his mouth, on his lips, on his breath. He looked down at his wife but she had not awoken. He forced himself back to his nightmares.

Lucia was not asleep. She had heard her husband's yells and she too awoke frightened. In her dream there had been no wolves, no spirits, no demons. Instead there had only been Elias' eyes, staring at her, watching her sleep. There had only been his eyes. There was no face, no body, no skin. Only his eyes watching her. The eyes and his smell. When she woke, she could still smell him. She recognised his stench, the smell of him after he had finished, after he had been inside her. It was a smell that had always disgusted her. And as always, her eyes closed tight and ignoring her husband's screams beside her, it was a smell that aroused her.

Sleep did not return to Lucia. She spent the night staring into the dying fire, watching a final red ember slowly burn itself out. When the sun came at last, its glow was warm and reassuring. She jumped out of bed and walked outside, looking down on the green fertile valley below. There were wisps of smoky white cloud on the mountain, there was a farewell lament from the last of the nightingales. She breathed in the morning, she breathed in the fresh sun and air.

THE COFFEE SHE made for me tasted far too syrupy, but she assured me that was how Lebanese coffee should taste; unlike Turkish coffee, it should be honeyed and sweet. The cafe was called Beirut; her hands were old but her face was young. Her husband wore a crisp white shirt and wiped down the tables while she brewed the coffee. My photographs were spread across the table; I'd had them developed quickly, but certainly not cheaply, in a Kodak shop off the Piazza San Marco. As the woman brought me the coffee, she pointed to a photograph.

—Sicilia?

—Greece.

She put down the coffee and glanced up at the television screen above the bar. Three elderly Italian men were watching young men playing soccer. The men looked as if they belonged to the sea, with fishermen's caps and thick shirts bleached by the weather. Their bare arms were strong and tattooed. I felt relief that they were not in expensive business suits and more so that they were not tourists with backpacks like me. They shouted at the tiny men kicking the ball across the field; the sound was turned down on the television, and instead, Arabic music came from a tinny radio hooked precariously to the top shelf next to the bottles of spirits.

I had always assumed that Venice would be a modern metropolis grafted onto a Renaissance skeleton, that the medieval palazzi and sculptures would be dwarfed by shiny steel edifices and modern skyscrapers. So when I first walked out of the train station and saw the ferries on the Grand Canal, I was taken aback by how small the city appeared. I climbed onto the first ferry I saw and began my journey through the guts of the city. The sun was shining and cast a clear brilliant light on the tiled walls on the canals. I dismounted at the Piazza San Marco, and began to knock on hotel doors. The prices were exorbitant, so even with the backpack getting heavier on my shoulders, I walked further, determined to find a manageable price. I crossed the Rialto Bridge and moving further away from the tourists and shops I found a small hostel in the north of the city, close to the markets where the Venetians shopped for their vegetables and toilet paper. The *pensione* was small, there was a shared bathroom in which the water was never better than lukewarm, and a midnight curfew; but it was affordable, and I figured as I didn't know anyone here to go out drinking with, the curfew wouldn't be a problem. I was not intending to stay. I was making a mad dash from the southern tip of this immense continent to the west, but I broke my train journey in Venice for it had always been a romance, a city I'd always wanted to see. I had no guidebook with me, and after the bouts of savage drinking in Greece, a midnight curfew was welcome.

I doubt I would have found the Café Beirut in a guidebook. It was a coffee shop a few hundred metres from the *pensione*, tucked between a butcher shop and a tobacconist. The seating was uncomfortable but the tables were large enough to spread my photographs over them. It was usual for me, when examining my own photographs, to concentrate first on perspective, then tone, rejecting immediately the shots which struck me as clumsy or cluttered. But it wasn't anything technical I first noticed when I studied the photographs spread before me. What I first noticed were the ghosts.

I picked up a photograph. It was of my mother's village. I had used a wide-angle lens, wanting a panoramic view of the largely abandoned fields that criss-crossed the steep descent into the valley. I had judged the light well. Even the hasty processing had not dulled the rich greens of the valley, the cool azure of the sky, and the stark, stripped whiteness of the cottages. What I could not understand were the shadows that dotted my landscape. In one of the fields, a thin strip of roughly ploughed land, a figure crouched and stared furiously at the camera. The boy's face was haggard and lean, and even though he was simply an element in the background, his eyes shone brightly. I peered closely at the black ink of his eyes. Everything about him—his body, his face—was blurred and faint, except for that violence in his eyes. As the valley receded, a clearing of poplar trees became visible in the photo and underneath the wooded shelter, tall thin figures congregated. Of them, I could make out nothing at all: they could have been wisps of smoke. All I knew was that they had not been there when I had clicked the shutter for that shot.

Another photograph. Giulia and Andreas standing arm-in-arm in front of the coffee shop in the village. Behind them sit the old men at the table. But behind my cousin and her friend there is the boy again. He is mocking me behind the cemetery gates, his eyes again luminous, fierce and dark.

Cursed. Giulia had said to me, Did you know that your mother's family is cursed? I had attempted a laugh but she was serious, searching my face. There's no one remaining, did you know that? she continued. Everyone in your mother's family has disappeared. The old men say that it is as if they were never in the village.

I felt a weight on me then; I felt that the whole village—the heat, the dust, the mountain air and the stark sky above—were all weighing on me. Cursed. Your whole family is cursed. I had tried to shake that word from me.

Fairytales, I had dismissed. There's no one left because they've all migrated from this shithole. That's why no one's left here. I walked away from her, my camera swinging alongside me, determined to bring this place to clear rational modern life with my flash and camera, through film and chemicals.

Cursed? What the fuck did that mean? That wasn't in my language, that wasn't part of my world. Fucking peasant shit. Not my world, not my clean rational world. I started, looked up; the men at the bar were shouting and screaming, laughing and yelling at the silent screen. Juventus had a goal.

I examined the negatives by holding them up against the light streaming in from the cafe window. The boy's face was there as well. I shivered, ice fingers down my spine. Then I let out a slow, relieved laugh. Not a curse, not magic: a technical error. Superimposed. They fucked up my bloody film. They fucked up my mother's memories. I'd got somebody else's memories superimposed on my film. I silently cursed the sullen bitch at the kiosk off the Piazza San Marco. Then I laughed again, and forgave her. I thought of the millions of snapshots she had to process, had to see, endless identical shots of pigeons, wet stone, the same fucking cathedral again and again and again. I'd fuck up as many as I could get away with as well. I gathered up the photographs and stuffed them into the envelope. This was a technical, scientific world. There was no evil eye. I was not cursed.

I hadn't slept much since leaving Greece. Giulia had wanted me to travel with her to Thessaloniki but I had declined. On returning to Athens I had found myself restless and increasingly irritated by the Greeks. I was angered by their indifference to the sight of beggars and gypsies on the streets; I detested their sour disapproval of the new immigrants in their country.

I could not bear their obsession with the accrual of possessions: Prada, Gucci and Versace. I could not get settled back in the city. It was as if my time in the village had unclogged my senses, had cleansed my perceptions. I felt

I was sensing the world through another's skin. The noise and dirt and dust of the city all seemed amplified: I could not find peace.

On my first night back in Athens, trying to fall asleep on Giulia's narrow sofa, I had closed my eyes and felt a touch on my face. I'd opened my eyes sharply to find myself alone in the room. I hadn't been able to sleep after that; instead I sat near-naked on the cement balcony and listened to the incessant traffic and belligerent exuberance of Athens below. I smoked cigarette after cigarette on the balcony, furious at myself for fearing returning to bed but too scared to lie back on the sofa. I watched dawn arrive and only with the refreshing spring sun streaming into the room did I allow myself to sleep again.

The following night I told Giulia I was leaving Greece and resisted all her objections. She understood that something had changed for me and when I attempted to explain my feelings she grew angry.

—Fuck you, she thundered. We finally have some money in our pockets and the bloody immigrant cousin from the New World comes back to tell us how he regrets the changes. What's wrong with fine clothes, fine food, a decent living?

—Nothing, I yelled back, but there's nothing fine about dressing up like some *nouveau riche* trash.

I stopped then, ashamed. I apologised. She softened and caressed my cheeks. Greece is dying, she whispered to me, this is Europe now. Then she snapped back to anger and slapped me hard on the cheek. We were hungry, for years we were hungry. Even those of us who were lucky went hungry. Do you understand? Her eyes flashed and I nodded my head in contrition. She smiled ruefully.

Pouring an ouzo, she handed it to me, and kissed me on my lips.

—Drink, cousin, who knows if we'll still be drinking ouzo when you next return.

Before I left, Giulia gave me a small gold crucifix on a chain and put it around my neck. I spent the long hours the ferry took to get from Patra to Kerkira, and from Kerkira to Brindisi gazing on the smooth blond-haired legs and arms of young Danish and Swedish tourists. I listened to music on my walkman, I caught snatches of sleep underneath the ferry stairs, but even then I was certain that someone or something was lying next to me, caressing my cheeks, kissing my eyes, but when I opened my eyes it was only the sharp sea breeze. The crucifix hung heavy on my chest. I thought I'd remove it as soon as the ferry left the dock. I hated jewellery on me. But I kept it on. Even though it was only superstition, I was glad for it.

I ate very little, even when the ferry stopped at the port at Kerkira. The harbour was dotted with little cafes and restaurants for tourists and even though the fresh fish and produce looked inviting, I found that I could eat little of it. Some distasteful residue, coarse and thick, seemed to coat every morsel of octopus and every strand of salad that I had chosen for lunch. I was hungry but everything tasted of this sour fluid. It had the consistency of phlegm, of blood. It had a human stink. I hardly touched the meal. I was getting sick.

I kept boredom and hunger at bay by taking more photographs. I had only two rolls of cheap film I'd bought at a kiosk in Patra and so instead of snapping the attractive blond tourists or taking pictures of the sky and the sea, I took photos of the white-uniformed staff on the ferry. I was not interested in taking photographs of horizons and clouds that had been shot at a billion times. I wanted to capture faces. The seamen were initially suspicious but I spoke to one of the stewards and explained I was a student of photography, and he spread the word that I was an Australian Greek and that I should be supported. I took a photograph of him: his black hairy arms. I snapped the deep white grin of a porter. I shot the squatting man who was cleaning the toilets and who, on hearing the click of the camera, spun around, stood up, and smiled obscenely, grabbing his thick crotch and asking me if I wanted to film it. I photographed that pose as well. I took a photograph of an aged sailor, his body sinewy and strong, his hair grey and thick, who was smoking a cigarette on deck and watching a gypsy family spread a meal across a blanket, a meal of sausage and olives, tomato and egg. The gypsies would not let me photograph them. They cursed at the camera. The old man turned to me and I caught him against the sky, just as he was about to speak. I snapped.

—You're the Australian photographer?

—Yes.

—How old are you?

—Thirty-six.

—You are like them, he said, pointing to the gypsies, the old women napping in the sun, their children draped over the adults, sitting on their mothers' thick woollen skirts, grabbing at the food. At thirty-six a man must be a sailor or a gypsy or an artist to journey on a ferry alone.

I am still not sure if he was insulting me.

Within an hour of landing in Brindisi I saw a boatload of Albanian men being shipped back across the Adriatic, their pleas and insults ignored by the impassive young Italian soldiers. I saw a barely teenage girl giving a blowjob to a sailor in an alley; I saw a young boy shooting heroin on the docks who then threw his bloody syringe deep into the Mediterranean waters; I watched a man pick the pocket of another. Soldiers and police, their rifles splayed against their chests, their enormous pistols in black holsters, wandered lazily up and down the dusty salt-drenched streets. They ignored the junkies and the whores, they ignored the drugs and the sex, and eyeing me quickly and contemptuously, working out I was neither refugee nor terrorist, they ignored me. The train north was not due till late in the evening so I rented a room in the Hotel d'Amour for which you could pay for by the hour. Climbing the stairs I saw a Russian whore leading a priest to a room and I was accosted by a Greek sailor who clutched at my balls. I took him to my room and he sniffed at me, then ordered me to wash. There was no shower or bath, only a small basin in the hall with cold running water, and I washed under my arms and scrubbed off the flecks of white grit from underneath my foreskin. When I returned to the room the sailor had squashed a small mouse with his boot. We both stared at the bloody flesh.

—*Broma Itali*. Dirty Italians. I wouldn't let him fuck me or come in my mouth and he left as soon as he had finished. I wiped the semen off my shoulders and pulled up my trousers and discovered that I had run out of cigarettes. I went out on the street, lugging the backpack as I feared it might be stolen if I left it in the room. Three whores, who might have been Romanian, who might have been Albanian or Macedonian, niggers from the Balkans and the East, rushed at me and in English and Greek and French and Italian, asked me if I wanted sex. When I refused, the youngest woman wrapped her arms around me and felt up and down my arse, looked for the zips on my backpack, searching for my wallet, searching for anything. I attempted to be polite, then I snarled and told her to fuck off, and finally I pushed her against the wall. They yelled insults after me as I entered a small grocery shop, they yelled insults when I emerged, they screamed insults as I stepped up to the Hotel d'Amour. Another Greek sailor came through the glass door, more attractive than the man I had just been with, but he did not look at me and the three whores rushed towards him. The youngest one again placed her arms around his neck but he was much more experienced than I. He slammed his palm so hard across her face that she fell to the ground on all fours, gagging. The other women went silent. The sailor seemed to be skipping as he sauntered down the street.

I returned to my room and smoked my cigarettes staring up at the cracked plaster on the ceiling. Through the thin walls I could hear the grind of sex.

It was an Italian who was my first fuck and it was an Italian who was my first love, but they were not the same man. I grew up in a suburb of Melbourne bordered on either side by creeks and bushland; at its southern end, where the city began, the sludge of the Yarra River ran across its border. It was only when I first travelled to Europe that I realised how rare was the profusion of space so close to my city. But as a youth I had no idea of my fortune. I was a loner as an adolescent, and after school and on weekends I would wander the creeks, climb the hilltops that overlooked Melbourne, meander along the cycle tracks that ran along the river.

It was there that I met Signor Bruno. I was thirteen and he had just turned sixty. If that difference in age now seems fantastic, at the time it was of little consequence to me. At thirteen, with thin, sparse hairs I detested curling on my top lip, with my voice breaking and my balls beginning to drop, anyone over eighteen was an adult, and that promise of maturity was what was desirable. More desirable than the football-obsessed boys at school who resented my reading and my love of cinema. More trustworthy than the girls who mocked my gangly limbs and pimpled skin. Signor Bruno, who told me he was retired, lived in a small house close to the river and was not at all like those boys and girls at school.

It was summer when I met him, a summer in which Mum and Dad were always at each other's throats. They would argue about anything. Work, money, Sophie and me, drugs, politics, music. Anything. Mum would scream at Dad that she hated him but I knew this was not true. She loved him. She loved him madly and obsessively. And he? His anger was of a different nature. He'd tease her, mock her, call her a peasant and a fool. He'd laugh at her. It scared me, his laughter, more than her shouts, for there was emptiness in his sarcasm and mockery. She hated him and loved him. He always kept a part of himself shut off from her. So in desperation her fury became venomous and finally, one day, after one petty insult, he simply got up and left. Mum wouldn't cook, wouldn't eat, wouldn't bathe, wouldn't go to work. That summer, Mum stopped being.

So that summer was when I took any chance I had to escape the house and go to the river, taking endless walks along the same paths and bike tracks, pretending it was the solitude and greenery I was seeking. In truth, I would have hooked up with any man who would have taught me truths about my body. It was Signor Bruno who was my first teacher. He saw past the flab of my chest, the embarrassing titties I hated exposing in the showers after Phys. Ed. He did not think me disfigured by acne, or clumsy and foolish in my body. He taught me pleasure, how my cock worked, my balls, my skin and hair, how to play with myself and how to pleasure another man. Beyond sex, he began to instruct me in music and etiquette, introduced me to what he called fine literature—which, for him, meant British and French literature, never anything American—and he encouraged my resentment of and antipathy to the world I came from. Without knowing it, even though our meetings were very short—an hour after school, an hour on the weekend—he transformed me into a coquettish snob. One day, he promised, you will leave high school and the suburbs far behind.

So the damage done was in no way sexual. The little tricks he taught me, his determination to get my adolescent hands off my prick and show me that the arse, the neck, the stomach, the thighs, could also generate pleasure, were lessons that made me confident as a lover. That I was not attracted to him was something we did not talk about. He would have been a good-looking man, even handsome, in his youth, but age had weakened him and he was now ashamed of his body. He would never force me into an act and I learnt the power of being a flirt, a vamp. Just as he had taught me the brutal snobberies of the bourgeoisie, he taught me how ridicule could be a weapon. I won't pretend that words can answer fists. My smart-aleck remarks were often answered by backhanders from the boys at school. But they stopped teasing me, worried that I would respond with some humiliating barb that would diminish them in front of their girls and their mates.

Dad finally did return. One afternoon when Sophie and I came back from school, there he was, in a singlet and shorts, my mother giggling and cooking a meal, a crumpled foil of aluminium on the kitchen table. He kicked my arse for my prissiness.

—What's happened to that kid? he asked my mother.

—Where were you to look after him? Eh? Tell me that, you fucking *malaka*. That's what happens when a father walks out on a son!

My father asked around. It didn't take long for him to hear the gossip. One evening he took me driving in his car. He showed me the factory he first worked in when he arrived in Melbourne, he took me to the beach and we sat beside each other on the Valiant's immense vinyl bench seat and watched small waves run across the stretch of St Kilda Beach. I remember that he had Savopoulos in the cassette player and that he smelt of marijuana.

—How often do you see Signor Bruno Parlovecchio?

I remember I asked him for a cigarette.

—Do you like sex with him or are you doing it for money?

I don't quite remember my answer.

—Are you a faggot?

—Yes. I certainly answered yes.

I remember that he lit a cigarette then, placed his arm

across the steering wheel, and peered out into the sea.

—Never do it for money, alright? You promise me that?

I must have nodded.

—Once you have a reputation as a whore, you're lost. Do you understand?

I must have nodded again.

—I envy you, Isaac. I wish God had granted me a love for cock instead of damning me with the desire for cunt. I envy you. Freedom, no family to think of. You can do anything— remember that, you can do anything you like.

And he got me raging drunk that night.

It was my father who introduced me to my first love. Paul Ricco was forty-one, and he had a wife and two children, one not far behind me in school. But, unlike Signor Bruno, Paul Ricco was handsome and strong; his was a body that I could wrap myself around and disappear into. I thought him the most virile man I had ever seen. His skin was hard, his face was long and thin, and his legs were thick and hairy. I have no photograph of him, so I am reliant on memory. His stubby cock was dark and his foreskin was long and rubbery. He had a mole on his left shoulder, a gold front tooth. He smoked Benson and Hedges cigarettes and drank Melbourne Bitter. And at one point I would have done anything for Paul Ricco. I would have cut off my sex and become a girl if he'd asked me to.

My father and Paul were friendly with a man, Tassio, and his wife, Athina, who owned an emporium on High Street that sold doilies, manchester and bric-a-brac for weddings. The shelves were dusty and the shop always smelt of cigarettes. My sister swore that she had seen a rat run across the dirty wooden floor and she and my mother refused to walk into it from that day on. Tassio and Athina lived a few blocks south from us and on Sundays Dad would take Sophie and me to play with Tassio's kids. We'd play cricket or footy or Monopoly or Twister while in the garage a group of men were involved in secret work. I spied on them once. Through a gap in the filthy louvres, I watched the men dismantle clocks. The clocks had large faces and baroque plastic casings which were moulded and painted to resemble red wood. The men were removing small packages from the body of the clocks, screwing back the faces, screwing back the casings, drinking wine, smoking and laughing. It must have been summer. Paul was sitting on a stool, his back to me, a tight white Bonds singlet stretched across his back. I noticed the shock of dark hair coming from beneath his wet armpits. My father, who was sitting across from Paul, looked up and spied my enraptured face.

—What are you looking at, you devil?

Paul had turned. He was smiling. I still dream that smile.

For three years we were lovers. Paul worked as a market wholesaler, and he often smelt of fresh vegetables and ripe fruit. We fucked in the back of his van, which he would park by the river. He gambled with the Greeks in a little coffee shop in Victoria Street, and often I would meet him there. Did they know, these other migrant tough men, cigarettes always hanging from their lips, their stares cold and impenetrable but their actions often generous, did they know about Paul and me? I would sit at the edge of the table, reading, and when one of the men got up to leave, if he had won, he would buy me a cola, or give me some cash, or stroke the back of my head and in Greek or Italian or broken English, he'd say, Such a nice kid. They must have known, these men, who worked in factories and smelt of tobacco and grease, they must have known what was going on between myself and Paul. But they never asked and they never assumed a liberty with me. In fact, they treated me with great affection, as if I were a nephew, as if I belonged to a family of men, as if by extending friendship to me in the coffee shop they could make up for their wives never letting my family cross the doorway into their homes. My father knew so many of these men. He drank with them, gambled with them, probably went whoring with them. But our family was rarely invited over to their houses for lunch or dinner, or to celebrate weddings and baptisms. When their women would come across us on the street, their faces would tighten. Cold, disapproving, contemptuous. They must have known, these men.

For three years we were lovers and for three years Paul attempted to knock out of me all the manners and values Signor Bruno had instilled in me. He wanted me to toughen up, he thought the English inflections I tried to place onto my accent were foolish and dangerous. Be a man, he warned me. I tried. But Jesus, none of it was easy. In the coffee shop he would flinch at any sign of effeminacy, but when I was in his arms, lying belly down on the towels in the van, smelling the rich gross pong of the oranges or the peaches as he fucked me, he would caress me softly, whisper in Italian and call me his *bella ragazza*. After the sex, refusing to look at me while I cleaned myself up, he would ask me about the football and I would try as best I could to reply enthusiastically. I would have done anything for Paul Ricco.

He dropped me at sixteen, when hair began to sprout from my chest, when I started to regularly shave. It had become habit that he would park the van close to one of the soccer ovals near school and we would meet there. For a week I heard nothing from him. I visited the coffee shop and found him gambling. As always, I grabbed a chair, took out a book and began reading. He had not even looked at me when I came in and the other men too refused to catch my eye. He lost a hand at poker and threw the cards down on the table.

—*Fangoulo*, he yelled, do we have to put up with this little bastard reading all the time? He's putting me off my game.

Tassio dropped a five-dollar note in my hand.

—Pay for your coffee and go, he said to me, don't come back. None of the others looked at me. Paul ignored me. Silently I put my book in my bag, placed the chair where I found it, paid for my coffees, and handed Tassio back the five-dollar note. He refused it but I insisted he take it. I would not be paid for. Without looking at Paul Ricco, I left.

—You're too old for him now, Signor Bruno explained. You are losing your boyish charm.

I had dropped Mr Parlovecchio as soon as Paul had come into my life. Don't hang around with that pederast, Paul ordered me, he will corrupt you. I refused to see the old man, refused to go back to his house. Truthfully, I did not think of him once all the time I was with Paul. I dumped him as brutally as Paul had got rid of me. But as soon as I myself was rejected I ran to the old man and he welcomed me back. He poured me a wine, got me drunk, and then, sliding to his knees, he tried to take my flaccid cock into his mouth. I kicked at him. I could not bear sex with the corrupt old faggot after being with Paul. He did not argue with me, did not anger. Instead, holding his silk handkerchief to his split lip, he rose and went into his bedroom. He returned with books.

—I was hoping you would come back, he said, his voice shaking. I have these books for you. There was Stendhal, and there was Flaubert and a cheap dog-eared copy of Joyce's *Dubliners*. I did not want his books: stories of spoilt aristocrats and bourgeois weaklings. I wanted stories about men with broad shoulders, men who worked and smoked and fucked and knew nothing of the salons and ballrooms of an ancient Europe.

But I dutifully accepted the books Signor Bruno had put aside for me, and then I ran to the creek and cried. I cried so much that I was sure I heard my soul tearing.

—Did he fuck you?

—Yes.

—Did it hurt?

—Yes.

—And you loved him?

—Yes.

Colin had his arms around me. I closed my eyes and could still smell Paul Ricco, smell the sweat of him, the tang of citrus in the van. I can remember the small scar on his left arm and how it felt rough on my tongue when I licked it. If I closed my eyes tight it was as if I could recall the sensation of him above me, breathing heavily on my face, recall the wet of his lips, could remember him calling me his pretty girl. *Bella ragazza.*

I opened my eyes wide from a dream and I was in the hotel room in Brindisi. Paul Ricco was not above me. I had been dreaming of him. But it was as if there was someone hovering above me in the dingy smelly room. I could feel a breath on my lips, faint and moist. I had been dreaming it was Paul Ricco's kiss. I opened my eyes. I was alone in the room and all I could hear was the sound of a man moaning from somewhere down the hall.

—You must go to Venice, Signor Bruno always said to me. Signor Bruno was from Veneto and he told me how as a young teenager he would borrow his oldest brother's wedding ring and travel on the back of a cart into the city of Venice. With the wedding ring on his finger he was no longer a poor peasant boy but a man of the world. He would wander into coffee shops, roll a newspaper across the table and while pretending to read the news he would listen in to conversations about music, politics and art.

—I first heard jazz in Venice, he told me. Isaac, you must go to Venice.

I remember it was raining hard, that it had been a wet and awful winter, and I was anxious to return home where my mother had baked a cake and my family were waiting to celebrate my birthday. My school jumper was clinging to me and smelling of damp and tobacco. I was still miserable and missing Paul. Signor Parlovecchio handed me a box wrapped in gold-tinted paper and tied with a red ribbon. I opened it. It was my first camera, a Pentax, bulky and black.

That spring I was still miserable. But I had begun to take photographs.

The woman came over with a coffee. Well, Signor Bruno Parlovecchio, I finally made it. I am in Venice. But the music on the radio was Arabic, not jazz, and the skies above me were dark and low and Venetians were crowding the bar watching soccer beamed in from a satellite above. The city felt cramped and small. There was a crack of lightning and then thunder rumbled and a surge of harsh rain began to fall. The woman turned on a switch and electric light illuminated the cafe.

—You've picked an awful week to be in Venice, the woman said to me, smiling, as she headed back to the bar. Her husband was cleaning glasses by the sink and increased the volume on the radio to drown out the clattering sound of the rain. A young woman wearing a leather coat rushed in, dripping wet. Behind her shuffled a stooping old man in a long black coat; the rain had plastered his still-thick brush of white hair across his skull. He hung his soaked coat on a hook near the doorway, took a seat across from me, unfolded a large handkerchief and wiped his face and neck dry. When he finished, he clicked his fingers. There was nothing super-cilious in his seemingly arrogant gesture. In fact, the woman at the bar looked up at him and responded by smiling and saying something polite to him in Arabic. He nodded, also with a smile. Something in his obvious happiness—he took a newspaper from his pocket, he was smiling as he rubbed his hands together for warmth—reminded me of Signor Bruno. This man was content to be here, in the Café Beirut, in Venice, awaiting his coffee and his opportunity to read the paper. I was aware for the first time of something that I had no chance of perceiving in my cruelly indifferent adolescence: that every day of his life, Signor Bruno must have missed Venice. And that Signor Bruno Parlovecchio was not an aristocrat. If he had been, he would had never needed to leave Venice.

—It's a spooky place.

Colin was sitting on the edge of the bed, watching me pack. He was still in his dark blue overalls, and our cat Stanley was sitting on his lap. Colin was holding my airline ticket.

—How long did you stay there? I asked.

He laughed loudly.

—Fuck, mate, Venice costs the bloody earth. The whole bloody north of Italy does. I was there for a few hours, then I took the train back out. He stroked underneath Stanley's black and white chin. I couldn't afford Venice, he said.

I stopped packing and sat next to him, lifted the sleeve of his t-shirt and traced my finger along the lines of the fading swastika. Stanley lifted his head, circled once, twice on Colin's lap, then jumped onto me and promptly fell asleep. I leaned my head on Colin's shoulder.

—Did you wear long sleeves in Europe, I asked him, even though it was summer?

—All through fucking Europe, mate. All through fucking Europe in the fucking heat.

—Did you feel guilty? You should feel fucking guilty.

He stood up then.

—I'll take a shower. He kissed me on the lips, then tussled a moment with the cat. Did that Mister Old Talk tell you about the ghetto in Venice?

I shook my head.

—I bet he didn't. He told you about art and music and bloody jazz, told you about Harry's Bar, but he didn't talk about the ghetto, did he?

Across the canal from the Café Beirut there is an old yellowing building. A carved stone doorway leads into a small square. I will drink my coffee, I will settle my bill, and I will walk across into the Jews' Venice.

In the Café Beirut the fluorescent lights were flickering and outside the rain was still falling. The old man was smoking a cigarette. I noticed that the bold black headlines across his newspaper were in the Hebrew script. The woman brought him a small glass filled with thick, dark spirit. Then suddenly, as quickly as it had come, the rain stopped, the clouds parted and light filled the world outside. The electric lights were switched off again and through the glass I could see that the bridge across the narrow canal was glistening. Across from me the old man downed his burnt amber liquid in one, two swift gulps. The woman refilled his glass. I threw the envelope of photographs into my bag and paid for my drinks. Across the bridge I stooped to enter through the low narrow gate and walked into the world's first ghetto.

The wet cobbled stones and the dark brick walls sparkled in the sun. In the far corner was a small shop with Hebrew script on the awning. Against one wall, plastered posters announced political meetings and the tour of Blur. On the far wall was a sculptured relief. I walked over to examine the spidery steel structure. Embossed human forms, shadowy and elongated, looked despairingly down at me. The metallic mural showed the shipping of the Jews to the death camps in the Second World War. In Italian, in English and in Hebrew, a memorial plaque gave written testament to the scene. I closed my eyes and attempted to muster compassion. Or grief. Or shame. Anything, some damn emotion.

I felt nothing. I began to take my photographs. I took photo after photo of the stricken figures, of the plaque, of the wet stones. I took close-ups of the posters: the one word, Blur, the hammer and sickle, the rotund face of the Prime Minister. I took shot after shot of the shop awning, clicked every individual letter. I took a shot of a puddle and took a shot of the sky above. Even as I was shooting I knew what I would do with these photographs. I would have them printed on large white canvases and exhibited in a vast gallery space. I would attempt to replicate the ghetto, and hope to move people in a way that I found I could not be moved at the site. I exhausted my supply of film, and walked back to the memorial, trying one last time to feel remorse or guilt, shame or humility, but instead there was the warm sun on my skin, the murmuring of rainwater in the drains, and I could not stop myself from smiling.

I closed my eyes for a moment, and when I opened them again, the old man from the Café Beirut was beside me, watching me. He was wearing his long black coat. Then silently he raised a finger to his pursed lips and with his other hand motioned me to follow him. I watched him walk away, drunk and clumsy in his movements. Turning around, he frowned on seeing that I had not followed him. He violently waved his hand at me and I decided to follow. He was old, pissed and not at all threatening. He led me through the square and into a large dank corridor flooded by the rain. The man snorted in anger, then grabbed a long plank sitting upright against the wall and splashed it onto the ground. We stepped along the plank; I was holding onto the old man, to ensure that he did not fall. Then he led me through the corridor, out to an alley: I could hear water splashing against the side of a canal. He pointed to the alley wall. A black swastika was scrawled in thick brushstrokes on a peeling whitewashed wall. He pointed at my camera. He wanted me to take the photograph.

I shot the photograph. He took me through the ghetto, all the while pointing at graffiti and wordlessly commanding me to take photographs of it. It was mostly swastikas, the menacing crossed arms sprayed in aerosol on an awning outside a bakery, daubed quickly on the bricks underneath the street sign to the ghetto. But he pointed out other signs to me as well. *Forza Italia*, always painted in black, *USA Out*. A crude sketch of the three interlocking *fasces* of the old fascist party. He led me his dance until we were again inside the square of the ghetto.

Suddenly the old man gave a deep sigh and staggered. I took his arm and led him to the bridge. He took a cigarette case from his pocket. He offered me one as well and we smoked together on the bridge. A mangy white cat leapt off a roof and turned and screeched at us. Below us, an empty rowboat bobbed in the water.

—Are you alright, sir?

The old man ignored me and looked out into the water. His eyes were forlorn and I could smell the alcohol. I looked around, back towards the ghetto, and I tried to imagine what this man might have seen. His insistence on me photographing the crude symbols of continuing racism had touched me. This desperate need to confirm the relevance of history made me melancholy. He was living, he was alive. He moved me. He was a last, dying connection between life and the grotesque sculptural reliefs on the Holocaust Memorial. He, at last, he moved me.

I asked him again, Are you alright, sir? He touched my sleeve, threw his cigarette in the canal, and beckoned me.

He was surprisingly quick for someone old and frail and drunk as he made his way through twisting alleys. We reached a narrow street of tall imposing apartments and I followed him through a low corridor. We climbed a staircase to the third level. At the top of the stairs I turned and looked down at the old city on the water. I could see spires and golden crucifixes. I walked through a heavy wooden door into the old man's apartment.

It was tiny. The room we stood in was cluttered with furniture and its walls were covered by prints of pyramids and fauns, of old temples and grinning gods: the whole of the ancient world covered the walls. The space was crammed with books: heaped against a small statue of the Sphinx, teetering in piles to the ceiling, covering the small coffee table in the middle of the room. A book lay open on the arm of the old sofa. He took me through into a small back room that served as both kitchen and bathroom, the two rooms divided by a stained yellow sheet. There were books lying on the tiny table in the kitchen, and on two small chairs. He threw the books on the floor and indicated that I should take a seat. A small window was open to the sour sea breeze, and from it I could glimpse the scalloped red tiles of the rooftops of Venice. The old man disappeared and I glanced at the spines of the books around me.

Arabic, Hebrew, Italian, German, English, French. Jude. Juif. Juden. Jew. Each seemed to have as its subject the history of the Jews. I rose and walked over to the window, and picked up a book from a pile lying face-down on the sill. I flicked through the pages. The photos were familiar. The death chambers, the dying prisoners in their striped uniforms, the fields of massacred civilians. A mass of arms raised in Nazi salute.

The old man came over to me and looked down at the book. He nodded, agreeing with something in his own head. He stooped and searched a cupboard beneath the small kitchen sink, then smiled and triumphantly hefted a bottle of brandy. He poured two glasses. I was still holding the book. He took a seat and picked up my camera. He was now grunting furiously. He skolled his drink and poured another. He pointed at the camera, then to me and to the book, making odd, rasping, grunting sounds. Again he pointed to the camera, and then to me and to the book.

It was then I realised that he could not speak. I realised too, with embarrassment, that the old man thought I was a Jew. Though I also knew I had not pretended to give this impression, part of me also felt inexplicable guilt. It was as if the old man had assumed a sacred trust, mistaken though it might have been, that I did not wish to break. But inadvertently I was shaking my head, and as if to answer for me—or possibly to betray me—the crucifix that Giulia had given me slipped out of my shirt. I closed the book I was holding.

Signor Parlovecchio, I am in Venice.

His grunting stopped. He stared at the gold of my crucifix as if transfixed by it. Then a shadow passed across his face. He skolled his drink again and poured another. His hand was tightening around my camera. He pulled it close to him, under his arm and glared at me defiantly.

I reached out my hand.

—Give me my camera. Please.

He smiled, enjoying the hint of panic in my voice, and tightening his hold on my camera.

—Give it to me.

He smiled and shook his head. I rose from the chair, and as if mocking my actions, he rose as well. I lunged and he jumped back. I was astounded by how sprightly he was. I grabbed after him but he had dashed into the next room. I stumbled and kicked over piles of books as I followed him. He led me around and around the small central room, crashing against books, making bizarre squawking sounds as he ran. His grip on my camera never loosened. At one point I grabbed him and he turned around and viciously bit my hand. I shouted, pulled back, and looked down at my hand. The teeth marks were clearly visible, deep in my flesh, and I waited for the blood to appear. But there was no blood. I was transfixed by the raw pink wounds. There was no blood.

I was alone in the room. I went back to the kitchen. The old man was by the sink. He was examining my camera.

—Give it to me. My order was loud.

His back was to me. I heard a click. He had pulled out the canister of film. He began to unwind it from the spool, exposing the negative to the dying light streaming through the kitchen window. I moved towards him but I was too late: he flung the ribbon of film out of the narrow window. It billowed and curled in the wind, a frenzied serpent; it glided for a moment, then fluttered and spun quickly onto the rooftops below.

He turned to me then, his breathing long and hoarse, his body shaking. He was still holding my camera. I walked up to him, looked down at his old wrinkled face, his decaying, dying face.

—Give me back my camera.

He spat at me. *He spat at me.* The phlegm smacked my cheek. I wiped it from my face and stared murderously at him. He was hissing, a continuous low sound that cautioned and threatened like a snake.

—Give me back my camera, you fucking Jew.

I had never uttered this curse before. A rush of power surged through every particle of me. It was as if I had been yearning to utter that curse since the beginning of time.

The eyes that stared back at mine were not those of an old man. They were black and luminous. They were mocking me. He was nodding in happiness. I had made him happy. The power I had felt just a moment before drained from me. Standing in front of this pitiful old man I could only feel despair and shame—bitter, stinging shame. He was laughing now. From his throat the sound was a combination of hissing and of groaning, but I knew it was laughter.

Mister Old Talk, I'm in Venice. I'm in fucking Venice now. I'm in fucking Europe.

There came the sound of a key twisting in the latch and I

heard the door opening. I walked into the main room. The old man was sitting primly on the sofa, my camera on his knees. An elderly woman, wearing dark glasses and with her white hair in a bun beneath a black scarf, was standing in the doorway, a shopping bag and a green umbrella in her hand. The old man was smiling towards her. She said something sharply to me in Italian.

—*Scusi*, I answered, *no parlo d'Italiano*.

Then, fear in her voice, she barked out something in Arabic. The old man responded by calling out a series of soothing calm grunts. She turned towards me and spoke in accented clear English.

—What has happened here today? What do you want with my husband?

—I'm sorry. I think there has been a misunderstanding.

The old man's grunts were getting louder and more agitated.

—You must leave, she continued.

I looked over at the old man.

—I'm sorry, he still has my camera.

She was blind. Hands outstretched, she made her way slowly to her husband and searched for my camera. He touched her hand, stroked her face. She found the camera, slowly took it off his lap and held it out for me. I walked over and took it. It felt alien in my hands. I could hardly bear to touch it.

—Thank you.

I looked down at her husband. He did not look at me. It was as if I had disappeared completely from the room. I wanted to say something to him, but no words came. The old woman ushered me to the door. Her movements were brisk and before I knew it she was about to shut the door in my face. I had to say something.

—I am so sorry, I said weakly, I meant no disrespect to you and your husband.

She hesitated, and then whispered to me.

—My husband was made sick by what they did to us. He has never recovered from what they did to us.

—The Germans?

An astonished smile spread across her face.

—No, she answered. We are not from here. She was indicating the earth below her feet but I understood that she did not just mean this city, this fantastical disintegrating city, but the whole world around it.

—They tore out my husband's tongue for marrying an Arab. They blinded me for marrying a Jew. This is what they did.

—Who?

—Our families. She stated this simply and quietly.

—Where?

She shook her head.

—It does not matter.

—Where? I was insistent, I wanted to know.

It was as if she was gazing at my crucifix; it was as if she could see it. For a moment I thought she was about to answer.

It was as if she was about to raise her finger to the Cross itself, to plead with it, to ask something of it, or to accuse it of something. I would never know. She closed the door in my face.

The rain had again begun to fall and dark clouds covered the city. I turned through alleys and narrow streets, crossed bridges, and I realised I was lost. Finally, sweating, I found myself on a promenade at the edge of the city where blue plastic trashcans were lined up in a neat file outside a row of apartment blocks. I sat on the stone wall; the sea was black and the sun was dropping, and a mist was rolling across the water. The long wooden poles of the buoys formed thin sentinels across the horizon. I waited till night, till I could see the lights spread slowly across the mainland and then wearily I asked directions and walked back to the *pensione*.

When I got back to my room I collapsed fully clothed onto the bed, did not even take off my shoes, and fell into weary sleep. I dreamt. I dreamt that I was in the back of Paul Ricco's van. In my dream I smelt the mouldy perfume of the fruit. Paul was driving. I knew this even though I could only see the back of his head. He drove me to a grove in a tall forest. Signor Bruno Parlovecchio opened the doors to the van and beckoned me to follow. We walked further and further into the forest until we reached Colin, who was digging in a garden in a wide clearing. A brook cut through the clearing. Colin's shirtsleeves were rolled up and he was wearing an old pair of trackpants. I ran to him and he looked up and smiled. But as I approached I heard a hissing sound. I turned around and where Signor Parlovecchio had been standing, there coiled and hissed a tremendous black snake. It raised its thick head, its coal-black eyes piercing into me. It hated me, that creature hated me. I turned to look for the comfort of Colin but he was gone. His spade lay across the newly dug ground. I reached for it. The snake hissed fiercely, aware of my intent. I went to grab the spade but the creature leapt for me, its fangs white, gleaming, sharp and wet, its eyes burning, fixed on my throat. There was childish laughter ringing all around me. I awoke, screaming, alone in the dark room, clutching at my throat. The laughter continued. I slapped at my ears until I could hear nothing more than the echoes of my slaps. I switched on the light.

I spread my photographs on the bed and again examined the photograph of Giulia and Andreas standing stiffly on the narrow path leading up to the coffee shop at my mother's village. The pale thin face of the boy was still laughing behind them, his thin, poisonous face mocking and malevolent. I pored over the photograph, searched all three faces, and figured out where the sun had been when I had pressed on the shutter. With my finger, I traced Giulia's and Andreas' shadows, then traced the reflection the boy threw on the dusty dirt road. The elongated shadow was broken, scattered by a clump of rocks and a bunching of camomile grass growing on the bleak road. But his shadow matched those of my cousin and of Andreas perfectly. He had been there; and looking into his eyes, I saw then that he was indeed looking straight at me, confidently, triumphantly. I threw the photographs across the room. The marks on my wrist were burning. I scratched at the toothmarks left behind by the old man but I could not draw blood. I lay down in bed and shut my eyes to get some sleep. I did not dare turn out the lights.

In my time in Venice I did not watch the sunset from Harry's Bar, I did not visit the Guggenheim, I did not have tea at a palazzo or take a ferry to the Lido. I did not feed the pigeons at San Marco's Square, nor did I travel on a gondola. I did not eat seafood in a restaurant overlooking the Grand Canal, I did not step inside any basilicas or cathedrals. I saw no great paintings by Titian and Tiepolo. Instead I visited the ghetto and I drank coffee at the Café Beirut. I saw swastikas washed by the rain. And I looked into the wretched face of a despairing man, and saw the ceaseless misery in his eyes, and yes, an eternal exhausting vengeance. The hatred in his eyes was fierce and passionate. They demanded something of me and they promised no forgiveness. I wanted to forget those eyes, to never ever look into such eyes again. For one deranged, terrified moment—I promise, only a moment; it passed, I willed it away immediately—I wished that not one Jew had ever walked on the face of this earth.

MARITHA PANAGIS HAD stoked the fire all night and when the first light of dawn filtered through the open shutters she crossed herself, rose to her feet and tossed bark and twigs into the flames. The child, still feverish, had fallen asleep but even in its dreams its body moved towards the surge of warmth that erupted as the flames leapt to devour the wood. The boy's breaths were forced and spent, as if in exhaling the poisoned air, he was straining his thin body to breaking point. In the corner of the room, his mother sat silently, watching her son, her eyes now dry but still blood-red from the exhaustion of her tears. The sun's early light fell on the child. Every thin snaking vein was visible on his shivering body. Maritha sighed with relief as the sun banished the night, and indeed, the boy's breathing had seemed to calm with the arrival of dawn. Whatever demon had been with them all of the night had now disappeared.

All her life, Maritha had been able to see the spirit world. She saw the sad young girls who twisted their melancholy locks of hair on the banks of rivers. She saw the men in their ragged uniforms still searching for the battles of long-forgotten wars. She knew which corners housed affectionate spirits, and she avoided the cellars and fields in which banshees and malevolent ghosts shrieked against their human masters. Her own mother had noticed the girl's talents, and fearing that she would be accused of gypsy blood, she forbade Maritha to make her gift public. But there would be no village they entered, no house they passed, no road they took, when her mother would not turn to her, and whisper,

Maritha, what do you see? Tell me. Are we safe? The young girl would search the woods, the rooms of a house, the path ahead, and she would describe all that was visible to her. She often did not understand what she was seeing. A youth in shepherd's attire would be before her eyes and she would think his smile kindly and innocent. But her mother would make the sign of the Cross and lead her onto another path. An ogre of an old woman would be rocking her monstrous body in a corner of the house, and though Maritha would be filled with terror at the sight, her mother would nod to the fierce apparition, smile, and take a seat beside it.

The ghoul that had sat beside the boy all night was far from hideous in appearance. His body was naked and his skin was chalk-white, as pale as the sick child in the bed. All through the night he did not move from the sick boy's side, at times stroking the boy's skin and forehead, at times getting into bed next to him and tightening his spectral arms around him. The sick child's fever would rage in those moments, his body would twist and shudder in pain, and his mother would groan out her despair. Early in the night the child's father had attempted to come into the room, to stay and comfort his son, but the spirit would lash out cruelly if the man was in the room. It would pinch and bite at the boy, kick at him, scratch along his legs and arms and chest, as the horrified parents stared insensibly at the streaks of torn flesh appearing on their child's dying body. They could not see the demon, and Maritha believed it best to neither describe it nor attempt to make it manifest to the grieving parents. She had ushered the father out of the room, forbade him to enter till morning. The spirit stopped its thrashings. Again he had put his arms around the frail sick child and, as if making amends for its behaviour, had licked at the blood and the torn skin. All through the night Maritha prayed.

o O o

—How is he?

Maritha looked across at tall, strong Stavros, at his grim face.

—He is better, now that it is morning.

—Will he live, Kiria Panagis?

Stavros wore a plain black shirt and held his cap rolled tight in his fist. He had entered the room quietly and had knelt down before his son's bed. Even though the sickness had ravaged his small body, Kyriakos shared his father's large honey-coloured eyes, the man's thick brow and full mouth. If he lived, he too would be a good-looking man. Stavros turned to his wife.

—Yiannoula, bring the child some food.

Yiannoula's scared eyes darted to Maritha. Stavros followed her look. His smile was bitter.

—We can trust her.

Yiannoula fell to her knees, lifted a stone from the floor, and beneath it Maritha could see a bundle of dried wheat and a few scrawny cobs of corn. Her stomach knotted and she exhaled slowly, praying for the hunger to leave her. Yiannoula stripped one of the cobs of its kernels and threw them into a small black pan over the fire. She turned to the old woman.

—Are you hungry, Kiria Maritha?

The old woman shook her head. The couple had two other sons and four daughters, and they all needed to be fed. She could not take their food. Instead, she came and stood before the man and whispered to him, Make sure your wife eats as well. Stavros took the old woman's hand and squeezed it tight. She and the children will eat, he promised her.

Stavros had already lost a son in the war. A year ago the English had dropped a load of provisions from their machines that flew in the air—he crossed himself—and the crates of food had been stored in the town hall in Thermos to be divided among the King's soldiers. The news had flown quickly through the villages. It had been expected that the guerrillas would come down from the mountains and storm the building. A garrison of troops had been installed in the town to ensure the food was kept safe. In the end, it had not been the guerrillas who had attempted to steal the food. Four of the oldest boys in the village had hatched a plan together, and one of them had been Stavros' Emmanuel. The idea had been to have the two oldest boys start a mock fight, hoping to draw the guards' attention, and then the two youngest boys would climb through one of the small louvres in the back of the hall and cram as much of the food as they possibly could into their pockets. Afterwards, everyone agreed that it had been a ridiculous and incompetent plan. The youngest boys had not even managed to squeeze through the window before a soldier raised the alarm. On hearing the shouts of their friends, the two boys engaged in the diversion had set off at a run that was halted by swift bullets. The four corpses had been returned to the village, their heads severed from their bodies in retribution. It had been assumed that the boys had been guerrillas. The guerrillas had exacted their own revenge within a week. It had indeed been their plan to storm the hall and to take the provisions. But the military presence had increased after the failed attempt by the boys, and so, instead, the guerrillas swooped on the families of the dead youth and requisitioned any grain or food remaining in their houses.

Is it my son, Yiannoula had asked Maritha the night before. Has he come back to haunt our village?

—Quiet. Maritha had been stern. It is not Emmanuel. But he's not in peace, wailed the dead boy's mother, How can he be in peace with his body so desecrated?

—It is not Emmanuel, I promise you. It is not Emmanuel.

Maritha opened the gate to her own cottage, and on entering the courtyard, she unravelled her long black scarf. Her hair fell thickly around her shoulders; it was as white as the asbestos with which her son had dusted the courtyard trees. She shivered in the darkness and moved to the kitchen to light the fire. From across the courtyard she could hear her daughter-in-law singing. Maritha crossed herself and set the kindling alight.

Her own home had been stripped nearly bare. As the wealthiest family and landowners in the village, they had been the first target of the guerrillas. The bearded men had fallen like furies upon the house, the cellar, the fields, taking livestock, grain, bread and wine. They had not looked like heroes, these gaunt ghosts wrapped in their grey overcoats that had become rags after the long winter in the mountains. Some of the men wore pants and coats they had stripped from dead Germans. Lucia and her Michaelis had cursed the guerrillas but Maritha had let them take what they wanted, watching them silently as they searched the cottage. She had been born in a room with no floors, only the dirt cold ground. Her whole family had slept in one bed. She did not fear poverty for herself. God had graced her with many years. The only words she spoke to the guerrillas were to implore them to leave enough rations for her grandson. Look, she had pleaded with the leader of the men, pointing to her daughter-in-law's distended belly. We have another child coming. He had been kind, that man, for he had indeed ordered his men to return some of the provisions. Maritha doubted that he would be as kind if they returned this winter. If he were still alive.

She tended the fire, then crossed the courtyard and entered Michaelis' house. Maritha shivered and rubbed her hands together even though a fire blazed in the kitchen hearth. She went into the bedroom and found Lucia sitting on the bed, the boy large and obscene in her arms, suckling at her plump breast. On the bed the baby was crying, her bedclothes soiled. Maritha picked up her grand-daughter.

—The baby is dirty.

Lucia laughed. She threw an old cloth at Maritha.

—Wipe her arse, then. She turned back to her son, touched his dark thick hair, and began to sing. They were words of love. Maritha carefully scrubbed at Reveka's tender red arse. She then held the baby close to her chest and the crying subsided. She looked across at her daughter-in-law, whose eyes were closed, who held her son tight into her chest. The demon was wrapped tight around Lucia's feet, his grey dead cheek brushing against her legs.

—Flee, Devil, Maritha snapped.

Lucia opened her eyes.

—Who are you talking to?

Maritha said nothing.

Lucia laughed.

—You are going mad, Mother.

—I am tired.

—Has that bastard Kyriakos died yet?

The old woman slapped Lucia harshly and the child in her arms awoke from his sleep and began to howl.

—Look what you've done, you've woken him.

—Lucia, leave Christo be. He's too old now to be always suckling at your tit. Leave him be.

Lucia ignored her mother-in-law, and instead, she returned her son's mouth to her nipple. Maritha turned away. She dressed the baby, and ignoring Lucia, she took Reveka into the kitchen. She turned in the doorway and looked back. The fiend was still asleep at Lucia's feet. Every night his spirit raged across the village, but every morning he came to rest with Lucia. Maritha raised her eyes and saw that her daughter-in-law was looking straight at her. Christos was still suckling; his mother was stroking his fat long body. Lucia's eyes were shining, afire with insolence, and as Maritha watched her, Lucia's long slender arm dropped and began to softly play with the hair of the ghoul stretched at her feet. The demon sprite stirred, smiled, and wrapped itself tighter around her feet.

—We need to begin preparations for Christmas night, Mother.

Maritha slammed the door behind her.

She bundled the baby tight in a small blanket, and took her into the village. She found her son getting drunk, alone at a table, the old men ridiculing him.

—What do you want, old woman? he roared.

—I am going to church, she whispered, ashamed that all the men's eyes were on her.

—You should have left Reveka with her mother.

The old woman looked at him, and Michaelis dropped his head. He watched as his mother, holding tight to his child, walked under the thin iron arches and into the church courtyard. The men had all fallen silent and when the old woman had disappeared into the church, they began to mumble and whisper to one another. When Michaelis looked up not one of them caught his eyes.

—Go to the Devil, all of you. He rose and spilt his drink across the wooden table.

—It's you who will get to Hell first, cried out a voice.

—It won't be him, it'll be his sow of a wife.

—Then it's his mother's turn.

The men started cackling, like geese. Michaelis staggered after his mother into the church.

He crossed himself and stayed by the last pew, watching his mother pray. She had placed the baby at her side and was on her knees before the altar, was almost chanting her lamentations. Michaelis had never learnt her tongue. His father had forbidden her use of it but she had staunchly continued to pray with the words her own mother had taught her. The Old Man had relented: it was only in her prayers and in her dreams that his mother could speak freely. But my father was a kind man, Michaelis reminded himself, and he crossed himself once more on thinking of the dead. And my mother, she is a good woman.

Not like my wife, that whore, the whore of the Devil himself. In his stupor he had spoken aloud. His mother swiftly raised herself and looked around. On seeing him she started to wail and shake her head. Out, out, she admonished him, how dare you come in that drunken state to God's house. Flee, flee. You should be ashamed.

—God's is the only house that welcomes me.

Maritha swooped the baby into her arms. She grabbed her son's hand and led him out into the courtyard.

—You should be ashamed of yourself.

—Mother, how is Stavros' boy?

Her silence confirmed his fears.

—What can you do for him?

His mother's face seemed to age before his very eyes. The sadness wept from her eyes and seemed to seep across her ravaged face.

—There's nothing I can do for them. She looked up in the darkening swirling grey and black sky. Only God can help us now.

Michaelis glanced over her shoulder to the graveyard that lay beyond the church. In the last year, seven boys had been buried in the cemetery. None had reached the age of four. Another three, who had not been baptised in time, lay in unconsecrated ground. The whole village had learnt from their neighbours' misfortunes. Now, on the birth of a son, the baptism was arranged immediately.

—It's a demon who is taking them. I have seen it.

Michaelis groaned.

—What is it, son? Maritha took him by the arm and led him to the cemetery. Son, tell me what you know, she demanded. She was convinced that Lucia had created this pestilence. It was as if her own grandson was growing fat and healthy on the misfortune and tragedy of the village. She remembered her daughter-in-law's vengeful, gloating face when she'd asked after the young Kyriakos.

—Son, what do you know?

—Nothing, Mama.

He pulled away from her and clumsily fell onto the wet grass. He lay there, dribbling. He is killing himself, thought the old woman, God save him, he is killing himself. Slowly he staggered onto his feet.

—You do know something. She indicated out across the graveyard. She could smell death all around. Do you want more little souls crowding this forsaken clump of earth?

He did not answer. She turned away from him.

—Your wife is behind this. And maybe you are as well. Maybe both of you have cursed us.

—It's her, he blurted out. Her.

—What has she done?

—She sheltered a betrayer of Christ.

—What are you talking about?

—The boy's corpse we buried three summers past, he was a Hebrew. Lucia was protecting him.

Maritha glanced swiftly across the burial yard. They had buried him on Christian earth. They had desecrated the holy ground.

—Why did she do this?

—For money.

—Where is the money now?

—It is all spent.

—What happened to the boy?

Michaelis was silent. He shook his head.

—I don't know. I was fearful, because of the Germans. Lucia told him to flee. That's when the wolves must have taken him. It serves him right. Her son was now shouting. He was a betrayer, a Judas—his spirit is doing this. He's a demon, like all his filthy kind.

—Was she given anything else?

—No. Her son was adamant. He was shaking his head back and forth, like an imbecile. Maritha placed the baby into his arms. Don't drop her, she scolded.

—Where are you going?

His mother did not answer.

She was going to see Papa Nicholas. The priest had to be told of what she had heard. It had crossed her mind when she had heard that a stranger had been mauled by wolves that this could explain the terror that had visited the village. It was an obscenity in the eyes of the Lord for a hound of the Devil to partake of human blood, her mother had taught her this. But the boys who had died had not been taken by hounds, or even attacked by the spirit of such a hound. Maritha knew, however, that the Hebrews had their own spirits and their own magic. There had been Hebrews on her mother's mountains and she had been taught to be as wary of them as she was of gypsies. Their demons do not speak our tongue, her grandmother had taught her, so they aren't frightened of our prayers. Like the gypsies, the Hebrews kept to themselves. But unlike the gypsies, they had their own Church and, again, unlike the gyspies, they worked. They too were tillers of land. Maritha herself had never spoken to one, but her father, who knew the Turkman's tongue, knew something about their ways. She remembered he had told her that for a Hebrew to even be touched by the skin of someone who was not of their kind was a defilement. It must certainly be an abomination for the soul of a Hebrew child to lie in eternity next to Christians. As for her own God, she could only imagine His fury that one of his murderers was lying in ground consecrated to His name.

Her knock was answered by Angela, the priest's wife, whose welcome was cool and distant. He's busy, she said, when Maritha inquired after her husband. Maritha bit her tongue. Now was not a time to insult this fool woman. Angela had been a plump, attractive girl when the adolescent

Nicholas had been betrothed to her. But when he returned from the seminary he found her to have become a fat and ugly woman who allowed him little peace. In turn, Angela begrudged her misfortune in marrying a priest who was indeed a good Christian. Papa Nicholas' simple cottage had not been extended in over twenty years, even though he had sired seven children. All I need, he was heard to remark, is a shelf for the Good Book, and a fireplace in winter. As a younger man, his disappointment in his wife had led him to often commit indiscretions with many of the young girls of the village. It was the one thing that had made people hesitate in proclaiming the priest a saint. But now, an old man, wrinkled and slow on his feet, the last temptation of lust had also been largely conquered. Papa Nicholas was one of the few men in the village who had welcomed Maritha as a young foreign bride, and he condemned any evil talk he heard about her.

—I can wait.

Angela snorted and slammed the door in her face. It was soon opened by the beaming, wrinkled face of the priest.

—Welcome Kyria Panagis, come in, come in.

Maritha hesitated.

—I would like to speak alone.

—Is it a confession, my dear?

—No.

Maritha did not want Angela eavesdropping. The news would travel the village by the morning if that sow heard. The priest suddenly nodded and winked. Come, he said, taking hold of Maritha's arm, I need to stretch my legs.

As soon as they had walked out of the courtyard, Maritha told her tale. The priest listened to her without interruption. When she had finished, he asked, What is it you wish for me to do?

—Raise him. It is a sin he is in the churchyard.

—And how are you sure that he is a Hebrew?

Maritha had not involved her own son or her daughter-in-law in what she had told the priest. One loose word from the man's lips and the whole village would know her family had brought a Judas into their homes. The tragedies of the last few years would be certainly laid at their feet. She did not want this burden for her grandchildren.

—I tell you, Father, my son has heard the men talk. Maritha was blushing, for the lie she had constructed involved a suggestion of such shame that she did not even have the words for it. There was evidence, Father, by the boy's body. She drew her headscarf over her face to hide herself from the priest's face, and she chortled loudly into it. By his thing, Father, his little zucchini was not eaten by the wolves. They knew by his thing that he was a Hebrew. The priest walked silently beside her until her giggling had stopped.

—He could have been a Mohammedan.

Maritha let out an exasperated cry.

—Father, what does it matter? We have to exhume the body. It does not belong in a Christian burial ground. This is why our sons are dying. She raised her eyes to the sky. It would soon darken. She had to reach home and then make her way up the mountain. Stavros and Yiannoula could not be left alone with the demon.

—And we must hurry, Father. Kyriakos is dying.

The priest was suddenly angry.

—This is a blasphemy, Kyria Maritha. Our children are dying of hunger and of war. When this damn war is over, then we will have an end to calamity.

—Will you exhume the grave, Father?

Slowly, hesitantly, the priest nodded.

The demon was still at Lucia's feet when she entered the cottage. Michaelis had left his baby daughter by the hearth and she was screaming. Lucia was oblivious to the screams. Christos was suckling at her breasts.

—For God's sake, Daughter, your baby is hungry.

—Let her drunkard of a father feed her.

Maritha grabbed the boy from his mother's arms. He immediately set to wailing but she planted him by the hearth, grabbed little Reveka and forced her onto her Lucia's teat. The demon was snarling and scratching at Maritha, but the old woman kicked at him. We'll be soon rid of you, she said to herself, and the demon flashed her a look of fear and bewilderment. Maritha stared back at the ghoul's face and she trembled. His thick-lidded almond eyes. She turned back to look at her grandson, at his eyes. It cannot be, she prayed, Lord, it cannot be. I am just a frightened old woman. Christos is Michaelis' son. Christos must be Michaelis' son.

—Are you going to minister to that bastard of Yiannoula's?

Without daring to glance again at her grandson, the old woman tightened her shawl around her shoulders and walked out of the cottage.

On her way up the path to Stavros' house she came across Baba Grigoris' grandson making his way down the mountain.

—Greeting Giagia Panagis, the boy chimed. Two large bronze hooped rings dangled from his ears and his hair was sheafed in a girl's headscarf. The villagers had taken to dressing their young sons as girls, hoping in this way to escape Charos, death. But Stavros and Yiannoula had done the same with Kyriakos and Charos had not been fooled.

—Rush home, counselled Maritha, escape the dark.

—I will, promised the child, and he began to run down the mountain.

She was awoken in the middle of the night by the whimpering of the child, by Yiannoula's tears, and the stench of sulphur and burning flesh.

—Can you smell that?

The young woman shook her head. Maritha could smell

nothing else. The priest must have found the body. The demon was nowhere to be seen and she felt a great relief and joy. Lord, you have saved us, murmured the old woman. But when she had opened her eyes again the demon was crouched over the dying boy and a gleaming triumphant grin was on his face. You mock me, Devil. You are mocking me.

The next morning, on entering her own home, she found the priest waiting for her. Lucia was brewing coffee and when it was done, the priest and the old woman sat in the courtyard and sipped slowly from their cups. The skies above were dark and streaked with ashen wisps of clouds.

—You raised the body?

—Yes, answered the priest.

—He was as he had been buried, intact?

The priest shuddered. The Hebrew youth had not rotted at all. His savaged body was repulsive; the gashes ripped in it by the wolves were still clearly visible. The gravedigger had immediately fallen to his knees and crossed himself.

—There was not even a stench to it, Kyria Panagis.

—And you burnt the body last night? All of it?

The priest nodded and his weariness and sadness made the old woman's chest ache. How do you comfort a man? she wondered. She grabbed his hand and kissed it.

—Thank your daughter-in-law for the coffee, said the priest quietly, and he limped through the courtyard gate. Maritha knew his fatigue was due to the exertions of the previous night. What she was not to know was that for a man who all his life had attempted to live the simplicity and love of the Gospels, the fantastic rituals in the night had shaken his beliefs to the core. He had been terrified on seeing the stranger's undecomposed corpse. He now could not trust that faith and prayer were enough. Burn it, burn it, he had screamed at Stellios Leptoulis. The gravedigger had become almost insensible from his own fear. The priest had to sit with him throughout the long night as they watched the burning body. The smell had been abominable and it still clung to the priest. He had breathed it in, and he feared that it would forever be a part of him, that he would never be able to escape the satanic odour. For eternity. Lord, prayed the priest, may our village be delivered from evil.

But the following night, Charos entered the village and the young Kyriakos died. His body was wasted, his bones nearly pushing through the translucent scarred skin. Maritha sat silent as the boy's parents bashed their own exhausted bodies on the cold stone floor. The old woman looked at the satisfied face of the grinning demon. She understood now what she alone must do.

Michaelis Panagis did not attend the young boy's wake. He was too drunk. Instead, knowing the whole village would be at the church, he had made his way up to the mountain and descended into the basement of the old abandoned church. He had tried to eradicate all evidence of the Hebrew. He had scraped away the evil hieroglyphics the boy had carved into the rock, then he set a fire and cleansed the cave. He never spent nights there. He attempted to do so one summer and the nightmares had been so vivid he never dared do so again. From his years in America he had learnt to be ashamed of lying with animals as one did with women. He had promised God to never do so again. But he kept an old bitch of his father's in the hole, and the dog obediently if reluctantly allowed the man to mount her. He could not keep his vow. It had been a long time since Michaelis could have such relations with his wife. Every time he attempted to be with her as a husband, the face of the child he had murdered would be before him, he could hear the beast's final pitiful breaths, and his ardour would vanish. He had been insensible from alcohol when he sired Reveka. Thank God he knew her to be his child. She had his own mother's features, his father's eyes. But even when she had been born he could not trust that she was of his seed. He had refused to give her his own mother's name. But thank the Lord, the child was indeed his. It had been the last time he had been able to mount his wife. I have a eunuch for a husband, Lucia now sneered.

And I have a witch for a wife. Michaelis had lit a candle and was making his way to the sunken pit in which he relieved himself when in the cave. The stink had first sickened him, it was almost unbearable, but now he was used to it. He dug his hands deep into the hardened layers of excrement and lifted the box from underneath. I want to look at them, he argued with his God, they are mine. The jewels sparkled and threw dancing beams of light around the dark gloomy hole. Slowly he shut the lid, placed the box back in the earth, and made his way out into the open air. He washed his filthy arms in the cold clear water of the stream. He sat on the ground and from his pocket he took out his map.

It had been in America that he had first seen a map of the world. The paper was now browned and torn but he would look at the rainbow colours of nations and dream about journeys across the sea. The Hebrew Samouli had pointed out Greece to him; he now knew where the Turks lived and, of course, he knew where America was. He should have stayed in America, married a Greek there, but the bitch, Lucia, had bewitched him from a young age, and all his hard work had been to no avail. The wars had taken everything. He would have to start again. He looked at the island at the bottom of the world. The Hebrew had told him that no one lived there, it was all jungles and desert, and only black savages inhabited it. But it could not be true. It was the New World. Even some of the village men had begun to talk about going to this strange pink place in the middle of the ocean, at the end of the world. He would take Christos and Reveka. He smiled to himself as he thought of his still helpless baby daughter. His little Reveka, his beautiful child. His child. His thoughts quickly returned to the jewels. It was good he had said nothing of them to his mother. He would only tell her of them when he brought her and his children over to the New World. Let Lucia rot here in Hell. With these dreams he fell asleep on the cold filthy ground.

When Maritha Panagis walked back to their house with her daughter-in-law after the funeral service, she immediately ordered Lucia to feed the baby. The young woman grumbled but she did as she was told. I'll put the boy in my bed, the old woman said. He is tired, he needs to sleep. Lucia nodded. Maritha took the boy in her arms and she kissed his brow, his cheeks. There had never been a healthier child, she thought to herself, and her resolve nearly left her. Then she reminded herself of the dead Kyriakos—this monster in her arms had fed on that poor child's blood. He is not Michaelis' son, she reminded herself, he is not your blood. She crossed the courtyard and a snowflake fell on her shoulder. In the dark room she laid the boy carefully on her bed, tears now streaming down her face. The demon had crouched next to the child, had wrapped its thin arms around it. Maritha placed a hand over Christos' mouth and with her other hand she pinched his nostrils shut. The demon awoke and his shrieks were deafening. He bit into her hands, scratched at her arms, but Maritha implored her Lord to hold her hands fast. The shrieks were thunder in her ears but she did not let go. It seemed to her that she lived infinite time in that room, in that moment, the demon attacking her, she murdering her grandson. She felt the boy's last breath, his last struggles, and then she felt his spirit rise. And then it was gone. The fiend had begun a piteous lament.

Maritha's heart was beating faster than she had ever known it to. There was a pain in her chest and she could hardly breathe. She swathed herself in layers of animal pelts, pulled her white thick hair tight beneath her headscarf. Her arms and her face were bleeding. She threw the shawl across her head and shoulders. Lucia must not see, Lucia must not suspect.

—Is he asleep?

—He fell asleep immediately.

—And where are you going, Mother? It's snowing outside.

—I'm going to church.

Lucia laughed.

—You must have committed many sins, Mother; you are always needing to go to church. Or is it Papa Nicholas you really wish to see?

Lucia's grin was mean.

Maritha walked slowly in the cold. She wanted to lie down on the whitening ground. She was tired. She had been tired all her life. But she forced her feet to make the long walk down the path to the village. A few of the old women were in the church praying. They did not deign to look at her. She crossed herself, kissed the icon of the Virgin, and sat in the last pew. Papa Nicholas was in the vestry, she could see him reading from the Good Book. She looked up at the forbidding portraits of the saints. The Lord's unsmiling face looked down at her.

I have sinned, Lord, I have committed a great evil. Christ was silent. Maritha closed her eyes. She had vanquished Charos but he now had a greater revenge: she was beyond grace. And there, among women who had always distrusted her, in a church that was not hers, in a land that was not hers, under the vigilant gaze of her stern, unforgiving God, Maritha Panagis died.

THE BROTHEL OF PRAGUE

I ONCE HAD a teacher from Prague: I was a most fortunate student. I believe that he sought me out for instruction because when he looked at me, at my dark ashamed body, into my respectful olive eyes, he saw reflected back at him the image of his own children. Or at least, his hopes for his own children. Whatever the differences between my mother and my father—she of the mountain and he of the city, she of the land and he educated—they united to instil in my sister and me an unwavering belief in the importance of education; and, as a consequence of that faith, a respect for those who taught and who made it their vocation. When the teacher from Prague looked over to me, I was always listening patiently and keenly. The other kids were bored, they did not want to learn. They did not have my faith. I listened.

My teacher was alive to the pleasures of art, of reading. He believed in the importance of knowledge and this was indeed a rare thing, a startlingly rare and precious thing in Melbourne in the late nineteen-seventies. He was a brilliant man teaching at a suburban high school, trying to imbue a love of Shakespeare and philosophy in unruly adolescents who mocked his unfamiliar accent and who thought his scholastic ideals effete and irrelevant. But Mr Parlovecchio's teachings had already opened my eyes and ears to the music of literature. I was eager to learn more, hear more, be encouraged to see more.

But soon the teacher's smile left his face, his instructions became harsh and barking just like all the other teachers, and he challenged the boisterous hostility of the classroom with his own furious contempt. *Stupid* became his most common insult, *You're all so damn stupid*. The class would break into titters and someone would mock his middle-European inflections. He gave up, I guess, but I am thankful that for a few of us he still blew magic into language and words. While paper planes flew across the classroom, while Wendy the Slut gave handjobs to Mano the Stud in the back of the room, while Costa beat up on Felix and while the girls discussed soap opera and the boys talked football, my teacher would stand before me and transform himself into Lear and Othello, Iago and Lady Macbeth. My rapt attention only increased my alienation from the rest of my peers. I had to agree with him. They were all so damn stupid. Along with my father's insistence that we as a family were urbane and sophisticated, not peasant and materialistic like other migrants, along with Mr Parlovecchio's elite instructions, along with the fact I was in love with a man nearly three times my age, it was no wonder that the teacher's encouragement took me further away from the concerns of the soccer oval and the mating rituals being played out at the Northland shopping mall. I was a snob, which for my peers was an insufferable affliction, but for my European teacher it was something he saw as natural, as obvious, as bloody necessary. *Your friends, Isaac,* he would tell me, *they are Neanderthals*.

He often invited me to his house where he and his chain-smoking wife fed me books and thick Eastern-European stews of dumplings and sausage, and I would listen as they debated politics and film and the history of the Enlightenment. Outside their cramped, messy lounge room, the neighbourhood bus would roar down a sleepy suburban street, old Australian women would wheel shopping trolleys, and young men in Chrysler two-doors would burn wheelies on the asphalt. They did their best to shut out this world.

Thick red brocade curtains covered the windows and were never drawn. The house was dark and only lit by lamplight. There was always opera on the turntable. The world came in, nevertheless. Their daughter fell pregnant to an Australian; their son, forced to hide his knowledge and love of argument, attempted to assimilate to the dogged, proud ignorance of the Australian working class. That assimilation—it reminded me of my father's—took the form of narcotics. A conscious sleep. His parents took every blow with stoic resignation. The teacher taught me patience. One day, he said, I would move far away from the rumblings and exhaust of the 208 bus. He also, perhaps unwittingly, gave me the taste for a mythical city called Prague. He took me through its history, walked me through its streets. He told me what it was like to rush against the tanks in 1968. There was once hope in my city, he told me, and there will be hope again.

When I first got to Czechoslovakia, the Velvet Revolutions had just spread through Eastern Europe. There was music and dialogue on every street corner, and a young girl kissed me on the mouth as the train entered the central station and said, in bright, broken English, *Welcome to our country—can you taste the freedom on my lips?* I stayed in a hostel at the edge of the city and every morning I would take the slow tram ride through the blanket of cold grey housing estates, cross the muddy polluted river, and spend hours simply walking through the narrow streets of the idyllic inner city. I fell in love with Prague. In the New World we had no layers of history to our architecture, no beauty in our concrete, steel and cement. Beauty was only in our skies and horizons. In the Czech capital I fell in love with a European city that had just emerged from a fairytale: Sleeping Beauty awoken from a nightmare of forty years. So smitten was I that I walked along alleys and through squares for hours and hours, trying to understand every part of the city, to know its guts and its heart, its shadows and its glories. In a bank across from the gilded immense façade of the Opera, queuing behind bollards detailing the victories and memories of the Revolution, I waited patiently in line while behind me five American students, in Nike shorts and Gap t-shirts, debated the backwardness of the former communist states. Warsaw, they were braying loudly, was decidedly much more advanced than Prague for it had three McDonald's restaurants and they had found no difficulty in using their Visa card. Prague, they continued, was undoubtedly beautiful but service was deplorable. I bit my lip and felt smug. Fuck you, Yanks, I remember thinking to myself. This place will be the new way forward. Commerce to serve culture, a democratic socialism without totalitarianism and a liberal acceptance that would be the envy of all Europe. There was hope again in my teacher's city.

Now, ten years later, Czechoslovakia had been reduced to one syllable, there were McDonald's restaurants all over Wenceslas Square, the whores lined up outside the casinos and there were no Czech girls to greet me with kisses at the train station. The first thing I noticed on disembarking was that no one was looking anyone in the eye.

Sal Mineo was waiting for me, dressed in a singlet and jeans, his arms pale and thick with hair, a cigarette drooping from his lips and his hair shorn to a buzzcut. A taxi driver tried to grab my pack and Sal Mineo came running towards me. Fuck off, he yelled, his accent still thick with a Melbourne suburban drawl. He pulled me into his body and kissed me on the mouth and on my cheeks. Holding me tight, he dragged me through the station doors. The air smelt of stale tobacco. He pushed me towards a long red sports car, the roof down, the body elongated and curved, the scarlet paint as garish as a Eurotrash girl's bright red lipstick. I started laughing.

—That's not yours?

—Fuck no, it's the pimp's.

—Who?

—My boss.

—Your boss is a pimp?

—My boss is a cunt. A big fat Jew cunt.

He had slung my pack on the back seat, and with his hand at the driver's door, he was staring at me, challenging me to take offence. I was strangely elated. I was not home. I was far away, in cold harsh Europe. I breathed in the anonymity.

—At least he's not a big fat nigger cunt.

Sal Mineo started to laugh. He charged the ignition.

—At least he's not a big fat nigger Jew cunt.

—Or a big fat retarded nigger Jew cunt.

His small car weaved in and out of the traffic and came to rest outside a dark apartment building that overlooked the river and faced the elegant rising boulevards of the old city on the other bank. He pressed a remote and an old aluminium door began to rattle, shudder, and then rise. Sal Mineo was impatient. He cursed the door, then the remote, then the city and all its folk.

—You'll see, Isaac. Nothing fucking works in this hellhole.

With a skid of the tyres, a spray of exhaust and the stink of petrol, he parked the car. The door rattled shut behind us. He shook his head on seeing me lug my backpack over my shoulder. He winked at me.

—Isaac, baby, just a word of advice, don't walk around this town with a backpack.

—Why?

—You'll be less conspicuous. They've had enough of backpackers. He rolled his eyes. Can you believe it, the fucking gall of them? The only thing they've got going for them is bloody tourism, and they get all high and mighty about that. The fucking Czechs, they think their shit don't stink. He spat on the concrete and led me to the lift. He turned around to me.

—And fucking, they're good at that. Tourism and fucking. That's the Czech Republic for ya.

Sal Mineo and I had met in my first-year photography class. There were seventeen of us, all under twenty-one except for Sal, who was twenty-three and had ditched his job as a mechanic to become a photographer. He'd introduced himself as Steven. A group of us had sat on a long white table in the Royal Melbourne Institute of Technology cafeteria and were introducing ourselves to each other with the mixture of bravado and nervousness which is part of the first day of any school. The table was crowded and he came up to us, a tray loaded with hot chips in his hands. G'day, he said, I'm Steven, I'm in your class. A blond sitting beside me, with chiselled cheekbones and wearing boardshorts, looked up at him.

—Hey, he said, do you know you look exactly like Sal Mineo?

The truth is he did. Steve was short, dark and had thick, coiffed hair that shone from poppy oil. But Steve frowned at the blond. Later I was to find out that he was terrified that first day. He had spent the last seven years of his life rising at six, working on cars with gruff, tough men who teased him for his youth, his love of art and his inability to give a damn about football. In those seven years he had nurtured a dream to become a photographer, a desire he had expressed to no one. He was terrified of the young blond kids, scared that he would not be smart enough, good enough, talented enough to compete with us. But I only realised all this much later. When he was staring down at the blond, his frown creasing his forehead, his eyes dark and angry, he looked fucking scary.

—You mean like the actor?

The table had gone quiet. The sounds of the other students laughing and arguing through the cafeteria seemed to come to us as if through glass. The blond slowly nodded.

—You mean the actor who was the fag in *Rebel Without a Cause*?

The blond was now squirming; I could feel his thigh shaking next to mine. I stifled an urge to laugh.

—Do you mean the fag wog actor? Steve's voice was cold and insistent.

The blond coughed, then nodded again.

Steve placed the tray on the table. A young woman quickly shifted her seat to make room for him but Steve did not sit down. Instead he touched the skin on his cheeks.

—I guess I am a greasy wog, he said.

Someone stifled a giggle. Steve looked around at us. He winked at me.

—You know, he continued, they say Sal Mineo had one of the biggest cocks in Hollywood. Did you know that?

The blond was looking down at his coffee.

—Did you *know* that?

The blond shook his head.

Then very slowly Steve dropped the zipper of his jeans, fumbled in the cotton of his white y-fronts and pulled out a very impressive, long, thick member. The blond's thigh had stopped shaking. Steve was silent, looking down at his prick.

I extended my hand.

—Well, I guess you're Sal Mineo then, I said. How the fuck are ya? I'm Isaac.

Steve started laughing, the blond let out a relieved groan and one of the girls ordered Sal Mineo to put it away, just put it away. Sal Mineo and I were the best of friends after that.

His apartment was on the top floor. Two plain white double doors opened up to a room that looked over the river and city. Evening was falling and I gasped at the sight of the castle on the hill opposite silhouetted against the smoky orange sky. Sal Mineo's bed, his stereo, his television and his bookcases were crammed tight against the window. A small kitchen area was on the right. He had turned half of it into a darkroom. The bathroom extended beyond it. To our right was a small room, a cavity, in which I spied a single mattress on the floor. I walked towards it.

Sal Mineo stopped me and pointed to the double bed flush against the long scenic window.

—No, mate. You sleep here.

That was Sal Mineo. Generous. I shook my head.

—Nah, I'll sleep in there.

—Fuck you, Isaac. Sal Mineo put a cigarette to his mouth. I have this bloody view every night. You're sleeping here. He threw my pack on the double bed, clicked on a switch to the stereo and Run DMC's 'It's Tricky' came thundering out of the speakers. Shower, Sal Mineo yelled at me. Then I'll show you Praga.

He took me to a small pub on the other side of the King Charles Bridge, a basement club filled with assorted punks, hippies and ravers, and he ordered me absinthe. By the second swig I was high. At some point he shoved a small vial of white powder under my nose.

—Slowly, slowly, he urged me, the shit they put in their speed in the Eastern Bloc can fry your brains.

I took a small dash of powder and sniffed. Not the Eastern Bloc, I called out to him, the Eastern Bloc doesn't exist anymore. This is all Europe. I stretched out my hands.

Yeah, yeah, nodded Sal Mineo, pocketing the vial and watching a young woman twist her body to the slushy music that sounded frighteningly close to Supertramp.

—Is that Supertramp?

—What I tell you? It's still the fucking Eastern Bloc.

The music segued into techno. I sat back, relieved. That's better, I said. Sal Mineo was laughing. You reckon? I watched him make his way to the bar, pushing aside bodies, and ordering us another round of the luscious jade liquid.

Sal Mineo was approaching forty and it showed. He had a

belly now. When he was a young man, I used to laugh at his fastidious waxing: now thick swells of black hair poked out from beneath the yellow singlet covering his back. The stubble on his face was shaded with grey. I was thankful that he had not once asked me whether I was hungry; he'd just assumed that all I needed was grog and drugs. I had not been able to eat for what seemed like days. There was hunger—a roaring, voracious hunger that screamed through my body— but it seemed no food could satisfy it and I could hardly keep anything down. I wanted to be with Sal Mineo, out of it, in a city of my dreams. He thrust another absinthe on me and I gulped it down gratefully. Maybe drugs and alcohol could kill my insistent hunger. Let's go, he motioned, and finished his drink.

I remember little of the night. The stars in the dense sky seemed to be close to my face as we stumbled across the bridge. We walked in and out of basement clubs. I remember laughing hysterically, sitting lengthwise across a pink plastic sofa in a club decked out in futuristic geometric shapes. The lithe waitress at the bar was enclosed in a silver space suit. Sal Mineo looked over at her and groaned. You have no fucking idea, do you? he yelled out in the basement club. You're all rank amateurs. The bored adolescents, sipping champagne from tall thin flutes, ignored him. Sal Mineo took a seat across from me, on a small stool covered in aluminium foil. He looked bored and uncomfortable. Above him hung a small painting of three cubist men, staring out at the club below. I remember I crawled to the painting and stared up at it. A small white sticker beneath the painting gave the title. 3 *Cizinec*.

I pointed to it and turned to Sal Mineo.

—What's that mean?

The three men were rotund and surly, as if they had been forced against their will to sit for the artist. Sal Mineo looked up at it.

—What's it mean?

He shook his head.

—I've got no fucking idea.

—Come on, I insisted, you've been here for five years. You must know.

—I don't speak fucking Czech.

I was appalled. He did not notice. Instead he sat upright on the stool and was looking out into the space. I fell across a young man and spilt his champagne. He cursed me. I grabbed his arm and pointed at the painting. What's it mean? He shook himself off me and turned away. I grabbed his arm again. What's it mean?

He turned his eyes to me for the first time. I was an insect. I let go of his hand.

—Three Niggers, he said calmly, his English perfect. It is a painting of three niggers.

Sal Mineo came up beside me, and pulled me up. We walked out of the club. The morning air was cold and I was shivering. That was the last thing I remembered and then I awoke in a bed, with the sun streaming through the window and slamming into my eyes, and a kettle whistling on the stove. A young boy, naked except for his tight white briefs, was standing over me.

—Café?

I nodded.

The boy brought a tray over to the bed, on it a small cup of thick black coffee, two dry biscuits and a large mug filled with pulpy orange juice. He sat on the edge of the bed and looked up and down my exposed body. I slid the sheet to my chest.

Sal Mineo roared from the next room.

—Milos, where's my bloody coffee?

The boy raised his eyebrows, smiled at me, and went back to the alcove. I looked into the spare room and caught a glimpse of Sal Mineo's big hairy arse rising to greet the morning. The boy's own pert, pimply arse wobbled as he crossed the room, and even with a hangover I felt my cock make an involuntary jump. Sal Mineo stumbled into the room, pulling on a pair of boxer shorts. Lenin's profile stretched across the bumpy contours of his crotch. The boy followed, a coffee mug in his hand.

—How are you?

I closed my eyes and did not answer my friend. Sal Mineo headed to the kitchen, started banging plates and cutlery, and I swigged at my orange juice. It tasted poisonous but I forced myself to drink. Milos had sat down next to me again, his legs crossed. Sal Mineo brought two tumblers filled with whisky to the bed. He tipped one into the mug the boy was holding and he handed the second one to me. I groaned.

—I can't.

—Bullshit. Best thing for a hangover. Anyway, you fuck, you're on holiday. I have to work. Sal Mineo placed the mug on the window sill and got into bed next to me. He pulled my arm under his neck and sank his head into my chest. We lay in silence for a moment and then Milos switched on the radio.

—Turn that fucking Eurotrash shit off. Milos scowled but obeyed. He dropped back on the bed and smiled at me. His shaggy mop of dirty blond hair, mussed up and stiff from sleep, half-hid his round blue eyes. He was short, not pretty—his features were awkward, his eyes too large, his mouth too small—but I wanted to reach out and touch his slender neck, softly pinch the layers of pubescent fat that creased around his belly. Beside me, Sal Mineo had started snoring. On hearing him, Milos pushed me over, jumped under the sheet and lay down next to me.

—Good café? His accent was rough and hesitant.

—Very good, thank you.

—You no sugar? You should sugar. No good when no sugar.

—I prefer it like this.

Sal Mineo had stopped snoring. I could tell he was listening. Milos' hand had found my thigh. I sipped on my whisky and pushed his hand away.

—You look very nice.

Sal Mineo laughed. He rose on his elbow and looked across at the boy. His hooded eyes were half-awake and his breath stank of alcohol, his body of dry sweat and sex.

—Milos, the dirty little fag, he wants to have sex with you.

—You make me shamed, scowled the boy, and he turned his back to both of us. I too was embarrassed. All I wished to do was slip into the shower but I did not want Milos to see my nakedness. I was furious at Sal Mineo.

—I have to shower. I stumbled across Milos, fell off the bed, and headed for the kitchen. I could feel both pairs of eyes bore into my backside.

—No hot water.

—Well, turn on the thermostat for him, ordered Sal Mineo.

—Where is it? I can do it myself. But Milos had obediently risen and was making his way to the bathroom. I stood in the middle of the room, naked, my hands covering my crotch as Milos slid past me.

—It'll take a while to heat up, yawned Sal Mineo. He threw me my underwear and t-shirt.

—Who is he?

—Milos?

—Yes. Who is he?

—Don't you like him?

—How old is he?

Sal Mineo grimaced, got up from bed, sat on the sill and lit himself a cigarette. He took a swig of whisky and looked down at Prague below.

—Relax, he said, turning back to me, he's seventeen.

—Is that legal?

—Fuck off. Sal Mineo threw the cigarette packet at me.

I lit one and the first rush of smoke banged harshly against my forehead.

—And for your information, yes it is legal. He turned back to look at the city on the river. They like whoring them young here in the Czech Republic. It's another of their hard-won freedoms.

I sat down next to him.

—Are you lovers?

—For Christ's sake, Isaac, he's seventeen. I'm as old as his fucking father. We've fucked. Don't you remember, we met up with him in the city last night? His boyfriend chucked him out. He needed a place to stay.

I shook my head.

—You remember you fucked him, don't you?

I stared into Sal Mineo's cold green eyes. He burst out laughing.

—Relax, Tiger. You were too far gone to fuck anyone or anything last night. He slapped my shoulder and jumped off the sill. Don't worry about little Milos, that cunt knows how to look after himself.

He found his jeans, which had been thrown over the books and camera equipment on the floor, and he pulled a card from the trouser pocket. He handed it to me.

—That's where I'm working. Meet me at three, alright? I'll show you where my art has taken me.

—Do you want the first shower?

Sal Mineo shook his head.

—That's right, you're from the rich New World. No, mate, we don't shower every day here in the Wild East.

The barb stung.

—I've just come from Greece, remember.

—Sure, agreed Sal Mineo, pulling a t-shirt over his belly, kicking into his jeans. But you're not Greek, are you, you're a fucking Aussie. Go and have your precious shower.

o O o

On leaving for Prague, Sal Mineo had bought himself a cowboy hat. I'm off to the Wild East, he had claimed. I was too much my father's son not to have been dismayed at his merciless enthusiasm to exploit the newly created capitalist states. He laughed at my concerns, and one evening he and Colin had almost come to blows. It was not that Sal Mineo was in any way a propagandist for the free market: he had an unrelenting cynicism about the rhetoric of global democratic peace. But he was keen to mine the opportunity of the collapse of communism, an opportunity he believed was sanctioned by the Eastern Europeans themselves. He had given up fulltime work to pursue his passion for photography and it had cost him the savings of seven years to put himself through college. At the end of the course he found himself working late shifts in a bar and spending the days touting his folio from gallery to gallery.

His work was the one thing Sal Mineo was not cynical about. His work was, I believed, sublime. He photographed the men with whom he had worked, the men with whom he had gone to school, the men he had known all his life. His large black and white prints of working men were distinguished by the unforced freedom of his camera to witness intimate moments of tenderness, whether it be a man laughing at a friend's joke, a youth calling out to his mate through the passenger window to pick up a packet of fags at a servo, or a young boy watching his uncle clean the rusty bumper of a grand 1968 Valiant charger. Colin and I had one of Sal Mineo's photographs hanging above our bed. A group of men watching the final moments of a tense amateur football game. Sal Mineo had waited patiently for light to fall gracefully across a man's rough pockmarked face; he searched out the contrast between the rough creases and the stiff smooth planes of the overalls covering a tight chest.

But no gallery wanted his work. Too prosaic, he was told. They disliked his naturalism, they wanted him to make a fetish of his subjects. This was precisely what Sal Mineo refused to do. His subject was friendship, not sexuality, and his passion was for recording beauty, not defining it. Five months after his move overseas, a much-celebrated exhibition travelled to Australia from Britain, the centrepiece of it being a series of massively enlarged polaroids which portrayed men living on a Manchester council estate. I thought the British photographer's work was good, but not anywhere as beautiful—by which I also mean honest—as Sal Mineo's. For the next year after the British exhibition, the Melbourne galleries went mad for realism. By then Sal Mineo was already in Prague.

I barely put my head under the shower. I switched off the thermostat and dried myself and dressed in the darkroom. I looked over the photographs that Sal Mineo was working on. He had been taking pictures of surly young men with cracked teeth, broken noses and pallid, acned skin. The framing of each photo was simple and identical. The subject would face the camera, the shot would be a close-up from the neck up, the lighting of such a harshness that every blemish and tone was visible. As was every aspect of their beauty. A skinny boy's dark long lashes, the glint of mischief in a young man's sleepy eyes. I recognised Milos, the too-big ears, the crooked nose. But Sal Mineo had also captured a feature I had failed to notice: the boy's firm taut neck, a man's neck. I got dressed and fought off envy.

I was also fighting off my hunger. It was as if the hangover from last night's debauchery had settled not in my head but in my stomach. I was scared that my bowels would loosen, but my attempts to shit out the pain had no effect. There was nothing inside me. I was ravenous, but I could not even contemplate food. The thought brought bile to my throat.

Milos was lying on the bed, the sheet covering the lower part of his body. He was masturbating. He looked over at me, his hidden hand vigorously jerking the sheet. With his free hand he pulled away the coverings. He gestured for me to join him. In the bright morning light I could see the sweat sparkling on the golden down of his belly. I turned, my cock hard against denim, and noisily began brewing more coffee. Liquid. If I couldn't have food, I'd have liquid. Drugs I could keep down. I heard him orgasm.

—You not like Milos?

I handed him a coffee.

—I like you.

He had not bothered to wipe the semen that had fallen on his stomach, his chest and neck. Instead he kept clenching and unclenching his fist.

—You're very young, I continued, offering what I assumed was a valid explanation for my reticence. But on hearing me answer Milos poked out his tongue angrily. He got dressed without looking at me. I was relieved. I wanted him out of the apartment, I was craving to be alone. I was sure that if he stayed for much longer I would turn him on his stomach, grab his boyish shoulders, and fuck him. I badly wanted to fuck him. He left and slammed the door.

I lay on the bed, I unzipped, my cock was rock hard. When I closed my eyes I saw myself ripping into his taut, sweet buttocks, jamming into him. I could hear his pained squeals and groans. I worked mechanically at my cock, thinking it had been so long since I had experienced sensual pleasure that I would come instantly. But I could not climax. I thought of the boy and I pushed my nose into the pillowcase. I smelt his youthful pungent sweat, the bitterness of semen. I closed my eyes and now I was fucking him harder, he was bleeding. And as I imagined blood I felt waves of excitement and my thrashings became delirious as I imagined his face, bloodied and bruised. I could lick the blood, taste the blood, eat the blood, and as I imagined this, I roared out my orgasm. I shuddered and a thought sprang to mind, just a thought but it had the surety and inevitability of truth. Milos was soon to die.

I walked as fast and as far as I could to escape the tourists, to escape Milos. The smell of him, the flesh of him, the future of him. I thought of Colin, and I was ashamed. I thought of Colin and I pictured him smiling his rueful shaggy grin, smiling at my attempt to put distance between myself and the American college students with their perfect teeth, their inviolate enthusiasm, their insistent loud voices and gawky movements which seemed to say to all of us, myself included, all of us who were not American, that they could take up space, they could walk these streets freely, for they were freedom, were they not? The Stars and Stripes were all over Prague. They flew from backpacks and from the fast-food cafeterias that fed the tourist hordes. The ubiquity of the Stars and Stripes was a dare, a defiant fuck-you to the rest of the world. I trekked and trekked, fast and confident, like an American. I walked past the casinos and porn shops, past the fast food stalls and the old men selling sausages. I trekked past the gothic bulk of the museum. I walked until the beautiful medieval buildings gave way to draughty, corroded apartment buildings. Czech graffiti was sprayed against the crumbling walls. A three-word English phrase in bold, black letters: *Yankee Go Home*. A cool wind blew garbage through the bleak streets where street peddlers were selling lottery tickets. I came to a bend in the river, I took a deep breath, wiped sweat from my forehead and stopped.

The river water was turd-brown. Across on the other bank grey laundry fluttered on the narrow balconies. Swastikas, the Anarchist symbol, the peace symbol and the moon and crescent were scrawled across the buildings in bold black or red strokes. Hip-hop tags exploded across the walls in glorious colour. A young woman in a hijab wheeled a pram down a gravel track and disappeared around the bend. A young dark-skinned man passed something into the palm of a thin blond boy and I thought I saw money exchanged. They glanced towards me but I did not exist. I was only a tourist. I walked further towards the bank. Plastic bags and broken toys swirled in the water. Further downriver I saw the woman kneeling at the pram's side. She was carefully arranging the long black sleeve of her dress to fall away from her exposed arm. She shook, stirred, then carefully lifted herself to her feet and continued wheeling her child. She threw an object into the dark waters. I walked alongside the river and saw a syringe float past.

I retraced my steps. I saw young girls with heroin eyes, young men taunting each other, their jaws locked in amphetamine grimaces. There were old men soused on alcohol. I walked past the barbiturated bag lady hawking old radio parts and found myself back in Wenceslas Square. Prague had drugs. Prague was fucking off its face.

I rang Colin.

—Baby, I miss you.

—You've got a fucking nerve.

—Am I ringing too early?

Colin exploded.

—You fucking selfish cunt! You call me, drunk, God knows on what drugs, and then you scream abuse at me for not sounding happy to hear from you. Happy? I'm lonely, Isaac. It's winter here and I want you back home. His voice cracked. When are you coming home, baby?

I was quiet.

—When are you coming home?

—In two weeks. It'll go soon, I promise, baby, I'll be back very soon. We made up and said goodbye. I had no memory of ringing him the night before, of shouting at him. I was ashamed. I wondered what else I had forgotten.

o O o

The apartment building in which Sal Mineo worked was tucked between two gothic blocks. The foyer smelt bad. I took the slow, chugging lift to the third floor. It too smelt of piss. The lift door opened out to a dark, narrow corridor and I searched to my left till I located a switch. I pushed on the button and the fluorescent lights began their flicker. I rang the bell to the apartment. A small window in the door opened and two stoned impatient blue eyes stared out at me.

—Is Stephen D'Arrici here?

An effete soprano voice answered me in a swift alien tongue.

—Stephen D'Arrici, I repeated.

A bolt screamed, the door opened.

I was in a porn shop. The tiny room had shelves along its four walls. Naked youths stared down at me, their cocks pointing towards the centre of the room. Against the far wall the young man with the blue eyes was positioning himself back behind a desk. I smiled but he did not respond. I turned and perused the DVD slicks. One of the racks of shelves shook, tilted, then thrust forward and out came Sal Mineo. His t-shirt was soaked through under his armpits and across his back. He waved me through.

The studio was low and not very wide but it was a much longer room than the shopfront. The walls were covered with dark green plastic, and the room was sweltering. Two redhead lights glared down at us, the source of the heat. A blue mattress half-covered in a dirty pink sheet lay against one wall. On the mattress two youths were munching on McDonald's burgers, nude except for matching blue Adidas shorts. A bearded man, fast swallowing fries, was standing beside a compact digital camera mounted onto a tripod, one hand grabbing at the chips, the other fiddling with the camera. A younger man, with a shaven head, leaned against a wall, a small microphone boom in his hand. He looked asleep. One of the boys on the mattress burped and the other giggled. The bearded man turned to Sal Mineo.

—We'll be finished within the hour. Do you want me to keep the lights up? His accent, muffled by the chips he was still chewing, sounded Scottish.

Sal Mineo ignored him and instead guided me through the bodies and machinery to the far wall, and pulled back a strip of plastic. He waved his hand and I walked through.

Milos was propped against a stepladder. He was naked and casually scratching at his shoulder. He smiled on seeing me and raised his right hand in a mock salute. Under the harsh glare of the lights he looked older, harder. Sal Mineo walked up to the tripod and gestured to me to sit in a corner. I sat cross-legged on the floor, wiped my sweaty face, and watched my friend work.

Milos squeezed lubricant out of a tube and wiped the slippery gel across his genitals. His cock became fully erect. He nodded at Sal Mineo and my friend started taking photographs. Milos stood with his foot on the first rung of the ladder. Sal Mineo took a shot. Milos raised his arms and smiled into the camera. Sal Mineo's camera went click click click: staccato gunfire. The flash fired continuously, Sal Mineo ejected the bulb and planted another on the camera. Milos bent over, a slash of thick dark hair ran along his bum crack. Flash flash flash. Sal Mineo adjusted the lens and shot. Milos started masturbating. The camera whirred into activity. At one point the boy stopped, grabbed a bottle off the floor, and sprayed water on his face and upper torso. His cock flipped up and down as he resumed his position. He looked ridiculous, plastic. There was nothing erotic in this room. I wanted to bash his mouth in. I was hungry for him but it didn't feel like lust. It was more like the instinct of hunger. I wanted him annihilated. I was sweating, I was hard. I focused on the scene ahead of me. When the boy was close to coming he muttered a word in Czech. Sal Mineo unscrewed the camera from the tripod and moved closer to

Milos. The boy's ejaculate was thin, small quick sprays across his thigh, and Sal Mineo was done. Milos wiped himself with a ragged green towel, picked up his shorts and shirt from the floor and began to get dressed.

I stubbed my cigarette in the overflowing ashtray and helped Sal Mineo pack away the lights. My throat was dry, tight. A rivulet of sweat ran down my back. When we had finished, the lights packed away in a corner, the camera slotted into its case, the stepladder filed against a wall, Sal Mineo sat cross-legged in the middle of the room. I sat beside him. He took a vial from his jeans pocket, and picked a porn magazine off the floor. Sal Mineo poured powder over the magazine cover. Milos fell to his knees beside us. We each snorted two lines of the cocaine and in a moment my lips went numb.

—I shower, said Milos, rubbing his nose. When he was gone I looked over to Sal Mineo, who, still cross-legged, was staring at the floor. I touched his shoulder and he jerked away.

—I'm fucked. He jumped to his feet.

I sniffed hard and felt chemicals itch the back of my throat.

—It's good coke.

—No shortage of that, Issey. Sal Mineo spoke rapidly. I lay back, looked up at the cracking ceiling, and listened.

—This is just what I do for money, mate, alright? This is how I make a living. Every guy I shoot, every single one of them, I take other photographs. Not porn. Real photographs. I make them real and I make them beautiful. I still do my job, I'm still an artist, does that make sense?

The room was unbearably hot, the sweat was dripping off me.

—Let's go somewhere.

—There's someone I want you to meet. My boss, Sal Mineo added ruefully. Come and meet King Kike. He laughed ferociously, a drug laugh. He pulled me to my feet.

We stopped in the next room to watch the video being shot. The room now stank of junk food and chemicals. One of the boys had his face deep in the other's crotch. The boy getting sucked lay back on the mattress, his eyes rolling back in his head. His dick remained limp. Sal Mineo laughed and the bearded man with the video camera turned around and scowled. He was chugging from a large bottle of Pepsi and the younger boy stopped performing oral sex to ask for a drink. The bearded man cursed in English, but paused the camera and handed the youth the bottle. The boy handed its back with a surly short retort in Czech. No one looked at us, no one asked who I was. As we left, the boys resumed pawing away at each other.

We took the slow lift to the top floor. The lift doors opened directly onto a plush office with black leather couches on one side and a poster for *All About Eve* on the wall. A young Czech man in a shirt and tie sat behind a polished wood desk, staring listlessly into the computer. A Magritte reproduction of shrouded lovers kissing hung on the wall behind him. He raised his eyes for a fraction, then returned to contemplating the computer screen. Sal Mineo knocked on double French doors panelled in blue velvet.

Behind a mahogany desk sat the fattest man I have ever seen. Behind him the city of Prague stretched to meet the smoggy opaque horizon. The airconditioning sang right into my brain. The man was suited, his hair shorn tight to the scalp. Flab folded over his shirt collar, and his pin eyes were set deep into blubbery cheeks. He munched on a cigar. The room was adorned with framed enlarged photographs of pretty boys with vacant, airbrushed smiles. The boys were framed amidst a green and rustic countryside. No turds floated in these rivers, no syringes.

—Hi, Syd, this is my friend Isaac Raftis. He's visiting from Australia.

The fat man nodded a welcome and I notice the yarmulke sitting on his bald head.

I stepped forward to shake his hand. His handshake was firm.

—Isaac? You a Jew?

—Goyim, I'm afraid.

—Not your fault, he laughed. Then he turned abruptly to Sal Mineo.

—How'd it go?

—Good, answered my friend, that Milos is a good kid. No trouble at all.

—He's a fucking spoilt cunt. Syd contemplated the city below, then sat back at his desk.

—Is he still whoring?

—No.

—You sure?

Sal Mineo nodded. I stayed silent. I would have liked to grab the thick jowls of the man and shake him, slap him around: a movie star moment with me the tough guy protecting Milos, the whore with the heart of gold. But I didn't. The man's bulk, his throaty deep voice intimidated the shit out of me.

Syd pointed to me.

—Where do you know him from?

—College. We studied together.

—Is he any good?

—He's terrific.

The fat man looked over at me.

—You want a job?

Sal Mineo half-turned towards me. His mouth was twisted in a hopeful grin.

I thought of making money shooting beautiful boys fucking rather than serving behind a counter at a video store. Then I thought of the two boys with the smack eyes. I thought of Colin in our garden. I shook my head.

—I'm leaving tomorrow. I'm just passing through.

Sal Mineo's eyes fell back to boredom.

—Suit yourself, said the fat man. His phone rang, but he ignored it. Instead he pulled an envelope from his desk drawer and threw it across the desk to Sal Mineo.

—Drinks. My place. Nine o'clock. Bring your friend.

We were silent for ages. As soon as we hit the street, the sea of tourists, the lazy breeze, I felt the coke buzz intensify. The gnawing hunger had dissipated. It hadn't gone away, I could feel it perched, ready, waiting deep inside my bowels, but the cocaine had muted its call. I was smiling as Sal Mineo took me along a roofless corridor. On a balcony, I saw an African woman hanging out sheets. At the end of a passageway we climbed some wooden steps which led into a small dark cavern. At the bar, moustached older men sat drinking beer and we walked all the way to the back where we sat at an empty booth. Supertramp was on the stereo again.

Sal Mineo finally spoke.

—Will this do?

—Sure. Atmosphere, authentic Prague. Italian television played silently on the screen above the bar. I looked towards the men but they averted their eyes. Sal Mineo pulled the envelope out of his pocket and counted the American currency. I watched the men, their thick moustaches, their pulpy, beefy bodies. I wanted to erase the memory of the naked boys, to erase the fantasy of the bloodied Milos. I heard Sal Mineo say something in a foreign tongue and my reverie broke. A woman in her late forties, in a tight white sweater and a short denim skirt, was asking for our orders. Her hair was dyed blonde, her skin wrinkled from too many cigarettes and drinks. She made me feel surprisingly homesick.

—What do want?

—A pot. I mean a glass of beer.

Sal Mineo gave our order.

When the woman was gone, I leaned over and whispered, So you do speak Czech?

—I can order a beer.

We drank fast and had another round. Sal Mineo was chain-smoking. The Mediterranean boyishness that made sense of his nickname had gone. His skin was flushed, rough, older. I hesitated in taking a cigarette, saw my thick thighs stretching my jeans. Too much alcohol and sedentary travel this trip. I decided to take up swimming when I got home. To give up the cigarettes. To change my life.

—How long are you going to do this?

—What?

—Work here.

—You got a problem with it?

I tried to put words to my feelings. He jumped in.

—Look, Isaac. This isn't Australia. I couldn't even get fucking social security in Italy, let alone here. It's been tough. I've begged, you know that? I've begged on the streets of Naples. King Kike pays me in American dollars so don't fucking get moralistic on me.

Stung by his words, I prissily chastised him for his racism. Sal Mineo roared his laughter.

—You think that Syd gives a fuck being called a kike? You think that Syd is anything like those faggot Jew boys we knew back at college? Syd never went to fucking college. His old man's still in jail for murdering a man. Syd's probably done a few hits himself. You got a problem with that? You got a problem with Syd? Or is it you got a problem with me?

I was about to answer that maybe it was Sal Mineo himself who had a problem with what he was doing. I was about to say, you're drinking too much, you're smoking too much, you're fucking teenagers. I was about to say that we were approaching our middle age and that I was worried for our health. But I remembered his generosity to me, I remembered the calmness I felt when his head rested on my chest that morning.

—I don't have a problem with it.

—Fuck off, of course you do. I'm taking sex photos of kids. You've got to have a problem with it.

He looked around the bar.

—I wish your dad could have seen all this. He'd reckon he had been proved right.

—In what way?

He pointed to the men at the bar.

—They're all unemployed and drunk and their kids and grandkids are making money by selling their fucking arses.

Dad OD'd just after the Wall fell, just before the Soviet Union cracked apart.

—Dad would just want to know how much you get paid.

—What about you, Isaac?

—What about me?

—What the fuck are you doing? Why is Colin not with you? Why are you travelling with a bloody backpack at thirty-five? His questions were cruel, insistent. They came at me fast. And how's *your* work? How much are you earning? Are you still working a grade up from a checkout chick?

—I still work part-time, sure. That's how I finance my photography.

—How much are you selling for?

I was ashamed. I was ashamed to be thirty-five and to not be making a decent living. Travelling with a fucking pack on my back.

—Jesus, Sal, we never expected to make money out of our art, did we?

Sal Mineo was staring hard at me.

—So you're still hoping to subvert the racist represent-ations of colonial iconography?

I laughed. But he wasn't laughing. His next words were vicious.

—Look around you, Isaac. Look where you are. Do you know what contempt these blokes have for you, with your headstart in capitalism and you're still fucking mouthing off about silly ideas you learnt at college. Beauty and art and fucking politics. They'd sell their fucking children for a buck. And you want to talk about fucking aesthetics and ethics.

He stopped. He took my hand and he slowly touched each of my fingers.

—You've got a child's hand, Isaac. Even the most hardened Aussie has these hands. You know that's what they call Australians here? Children. Even Milos senses that, that you're more innocent than anyone he's ever met.

He dropped my hand.

—You'll get a fuck tonight if you want it, they'll all be hanging for you. You want to fuck Milos tonight?

I lit a cigarette. The coke high was subsiding but I was back in Sal Mineo's apartment looking down at his photographs. His real photography, the photos he is not paid to take. There is clarity.

—Then why are you still taking your photographs, Sal? Why do you care to make them beautiful and real? What are you hoping to redeem? Their souls?

In a dingy dark bar in Prague, Sal Mineo punched me. The men stopped their conversations, looked over, then their eyes darted away, as one of them mocked, *puftah*, and there was laughter.

I wiped the tears from Sal Mineo's cheeks. He gently took my chin and looked at my mouth.

—It's the same word, he said to me, the word for faggot in Czech and Aussie is the same.

There was a puzzled wariness in his eyes.

—What is it?

—I split your lip, but there's no blood.

I pulled away from his touch. We finished our drinks and left.

On the way to his apartment we went past a small shrine in which a picture of the Catholic Madonna sat atop a bunch of dried yellow flowers. A small bouquet had been kicked into the gutter.

Sal Mineo stopped.

—A gypsy girl was murdered here, murdered and raped. Her family keep putting the flowers there.

There was black graffiti on the footpath, a rush of scrawled Czech.

—And what's that say?

—That's old. That's from the Velvet Revolution. That's history.

Sal Mineo took a siesta but I couldn't sleep. I snorted more coke, sat on the sill, and looked out on Prague. From these heavens, the city seemed tranquil and beautiful. I watched white pigeons circle the spires of the cathedral and settle on the tiled roofs. A billboard advertising washing machines—a young woman's features frozen in ecstatic gratitude—and the darting cars on the narrow streets were the only evidence of the last century.

From this height I had another hit of cocaine and sat myself on the bed with Sal Mineo's photographs. There was no evidence of the lewd grins or faggy poses of Milos on the stepladder or the bored automation of the two boys fornicating on the mattress. Instead the boys and young men gazing out at me were diffident, gentle, hard, cold, laughing, arrogant, shy, brutal, tender, handsome, ugly, thin, yawning, fat, happy, sad; and every single one of them retained, at least under Sal Mineo's scrutiny, the ease and confidence of youth. Every pore seemed visible on their skin. Scars, residue of snot in a nostril. A young man's unshaven face, his growth not quite covering his soft cheeks.

I went to my pack and rummaged inside for the camera. I sat on the sill and scrutinised my sleeping friend. His arms were above his head, the sheet forming a diagonal across his back. I raised the camera. A cloud drifted across the sun and the room darkened. I waited, I thought I was holding my breath. The sun emerged and I snapped him. I found myself praying. Please, I implored some version of God, please let this be a photograph of friendship. Just a photograph of my mate. When I finished I took off my clothes, climbed into bed next to Sal Mineo, and whispered, I like your work. He hugged me and I fell into sleep.

Twilight was coming through the window when we awoke. Sal Mineo put on a burnt CD which jumped a few times but I didn't mind because it contained horny illegal remixes of Prince and Eminem that I'd never heard before, and with a stamp of our dancing feet the CD always righted itself. We played it over and over as we showered and got dressed. We were camp and bitchy, sarcastic and nihilistic and we fell about giggling. I found an old CD mix of Sal Mineo's titled *Totally Summer Hitz 1993* which was full of half-forgotten pop memories for us. We were dressing up, preening, getting ourselves to look our best but with a determined effort on both our parts to not only look attractive, but also laid-back and straight. Just like in the old days, when we were younger and arrogant and vain, when we'd prize ourselves on looking both masculine and heterosexual. Never too try-hard. We were having fun. We had not been friends like this for a long, long time.

—What's this dinner going to be like?

Sal Mineo offered me a beer, lined up some more coke and did not answer me. He skipped the CD to a madding and infectious fluff of pop and I turned down the volume.

—What's it going to be like?

—King Kike doesn't have dinners. There'll be lots of alcohol and rabbit food.

—*I've got the the Key, I've got the Secret.*

He looked at me contemptuously.

—I can't believe you're singing to that shit.

I just sang louder. Then abruptly stopped, bored with the song myself.

—Are you with anyone? Here in Prague?

I knew that intimate questions could often annoy Sal Mineo but though he warned me with a look, he relaxed and nodded his head.

—Pano. I'm in love with a man called Pano.

I snorted the coke, my mind travelling fast. Sal Mineo never used the word love much. In fact, I'd never heard him use the word before.

—Who is he?

—Married.

—Are you sleeping together?

—Sometimes.

—How often?

—Sometimes.

—Does his wife know?

Sal Mineo had had enough. He jumped to his feet, turned off the CD and began switching off the lights.

But returning from the toilet, he had three black and white photographs in his hand. He showed me then. The man's face was scarred above the left eye and there was also a gash across his chin. He had dirty blond hair, cut close to the scalp in a military style. His mouth was big, his eyes set close together. He looked sad; the half-smile sitting on his lips did not travel to his eyes. He was staring somewhere beyond the camera. A thatch of tightly coiling hair escaped from his shirt collar. Sal Mineo put the photographs back into their clear plastic sheath and tossed them on the bed.

In the street he walked with his hands in the pockets of his denim jacket, and his gait was sure and energetic. I followed a little behind him. When he turned around he was smiling. The metro station was largely empty except for an old woman repeatedly running her fingers along her varicose veins. Billboards for soft drink and a Hugh Grant movie were ludicrous plastered across the stark Soviet-era design of the platform. The train arrived on time.

We ascended into the night. In the distance I could see Prague Castle illuminated by the half-moon's feeble rays. We were in a dark boulevard flanked by imposing nineteenth-century mansions. I had no idea that such space existed in this city, that there were people who did not live in cramped squares on top of each other. We crossed the boulevard and approached one of the dark buildings. An iron gate locked us out. Sal Mineo pressed an intercom and a sharp voice in accented English asked for our names. Sal answered. There was a buzz, and the gate slowly opened.

Discreet yellow globes, a row of flickering glow-worms that jutted out from the balconies, lit the courtyard. A fountain fluttered in the middle of the square and I could hear the faint murmur of classical music.

—Who lives here? I wondered out loud.

—Once the aristocrats did, then it housed top commie bureaucrats and now rich ex-pats live here.

Sal Mineo's tone was bored as he monotonously listed the ironies of history. He rang a doorbell and it was answered by a tall young man, his hair gelled up in a ridiculous rocker quiff. Silently he waved us into the apartment.

A cavernous living space contained ottoman sofas, footstools and rugs. A large poster for Billy Wilder's *A Foreign Affair*, Marlene Dietrich looking seductively over a naked shoulder at the ruins of postwar Berlin, dominated the room. A preposterous wooden spiral staircase rose up from the far end of the room to a dome high in the ornate ceiling. The young man asked us what we wanted to drink. I said a whisky and he asked what kind. Sal Mineo chose a vodka and lime, Absolut he demanded, and my friend drinks Chivas. Make sure it's fresh lime with the vodka.

—So you made it, you ugly wop putz.

Syd's body was so large he could barely descend the staircase. He grabbed Sal by the neck and planted a wet kiss on his cheek. He then grabbed me in a bearhug. I could smell his expensive cologne, the vodka on his breath, the fierce overwhelming sweat of the man. He gripped me for a moment too long. I had to get my breath when he released me.

—So where's the fucking party, Jew-boy?

Syd scratched at his front teeth, put the cigar back in his mouth and pointed to the ceiling.

Sal Mineo groaned.

—It's too cold for a roof party, Syd.

—Shut up, you wop bastard, laughed the older man, his flab shaking. It's a decent night, or what passes for a decent night in this fucked place. Come up, I want to show your friend the view.

The young man handed us our drinks and quickly disappeared.

—Who's that?

—He's new. You like him?

—He's pretty. Sal Mineo's tone was disparaging. Syd laughed, again his whole body trembled.

—He's a Croat. He has an enormous schlong.

He turned to me and winked.

—I have a friend in Paris, she's a doctor, works with venereal disease. Been doing it for years. She reckons of all the races, of all the ethnic groups, Croatians have the biggest dicks. Do you think she's right?

I thought back to high school. Grigor and Mattias in the showers after P.E.

—She may be right.

—Then who's got the smallest dicks? Sal Mineo's grin was broad and malignant. I bet it's you Jew boys.

—No, Syd retorted, the Arabs have the smallest cocks in the world. Then it's us fucking Jews.

We went up the staircase behind Syd, his enormous weight obscuring our view till we climbed out onto an open-air patio with a small glassed observatory along one side. Through the panes we could see half a dozen people sipping drinks.

Syd opened the glass door and introduced us to the guests.

An American couple wearing matching Ralph Lauren polo shirts—one yellow, one red—and sporting matching tans and goatees. I immediately forgot their names. Red was already drunk and Yellow ignored me. A tall, bearded man called Yves who worked for the French embassy. A Czech man with luminous pale skin who was called, incongruously, Jake. Later in the evening he would tell me that he was hoping to be a model in Los Angeles and would ask me to comment on his biceps and triceps. There was a much older man in a suit, whose name I didn't quite catch, with a thick boxer's neck and a gold watch chain on his lapel. And there was Maria. She was smoking long thin black cigarettes and wore a tight red strapless dress that revealed bony porcelain shoulders and an ample bosom. Under the layer of thick make-up there was a ravaged face. Her eyes were sharp, her nose was long and ancient and she was clutching a long-stemmed champagne flute with elegant red-tipped fingers. When we were first introduced she was arguing with Yves. She turned, kissed Sal Mineo quickly on the lips, shook my hand, and returned to the argument. Everyone was sitting on two settees at opposite ends of a round glass table covered with bottles, a loaded ashtray and a platter of antipasto. Syd sank down next to Maria and the settee rocked wildly: champagne splashed from Maria's glass onto Syd's thigh. He brushed it into the fabric of his pants, took a vial from his shirt pocket and spread a thin square of white powder on the glass tabletop.

—Careful, warned Maria, her Russian accent making the English word hard and sensual, there is the wind.

—Don't worry, countered Sal Mineo. Syd's bulk works as a buttress. There were titters from Red and Yellow, and Syd slapped Sal Mineo playfully across his chest.

Maria snorted quickly and turned back to Yves.

—It is bread, darling, she continued, all revolutions start with bread. You should know this, being a Frenchman. Supply bread and you will have all the democracy you want. Without the bread, fuck your democracy.

Yves shook his head. He had a small diamond stud in his ear.

—Maria, I don't agree. First you must have the foundations of a liberal legal system, you must have open markets and a free media. Yours is the traditional socialist mistake. First supply the free market and the liberal media and then you will see the bread follow.

I was offered a line. I knelt beside Maria's legs.

—And is this your job, Yves, to supply us with democracy? Syd leaned towards me.

—Yves is currently a spy for the government in Yemen.

Yves turned to me. I cleared my nose.

—That is not the case. I am working on social security policy for the government of Yemen. I'm part of a consultative committee for the EU. I am no spy.

Yves proceeded to lecture us on the important work he had to accomplish in the Arabian peninsula. I interrupted.

—What's your interest in the Middle East?

Syd laughed loudly.

—Arab ass is his interest.

Yves scowled.

—I have studied Middle Eastern politics for a long time, he insisted. I have been invited by the government there to assist in their country's liberalisation.

Sal Mineo let out a loud snort.

—By fucking Yemenite boys?

—No, retorted Yves, by aiding in creating a market

economy. And ensuring that we develop initiative and competition, not terrorism and poverty.

—Tell the boys your theory on the family, insisted Maria. She touched my shoulder. Yves was just preaching to us on the limitations of the collective family.

—Not the collective family, Maria, the extended family. That is the correct English word. Your vocabulary betrays your socialist past. The extended family, Yves continued to lecture, inhibits the economy; resources are shared and therefore consumption is limited. It is a patriarchal traditional economic mode. We seek to replace it with a modern individualistic ethos. Demand increases, industry increases, wealth is generated, women are liberated.

He smiled at us and snorted some cocaine.

Red had raised his eyes to the heavens. I saw him mouth the word *boring* to Yellow.

Maria's foot was tapping impatiently on the balcony's stone floor.

—And pray tell, what industry will you encourage in Yemen?

—That is not my role.

—Give them fucking bread.

—That is a servile attitude to the economy. You expect the state to supply you with everything.

—And your markets supply us with nothing.

Yves shook his head, as if Maria was nothing more than an obstinate child. There was a patronising sneer across his top lip.

—*Toutes les choses, Madame. Pour tout le monde.*

With a lunge across the table, Maria grabbed a handful of Yves' hair and forced his face towards hers.

—Careful, hissed Red, the cocaine!

—And what about the boys in the streets below? What about the boys you're going to fuck tonight? What does the market give *them*?

Yves pulled back from her. He straightened his shirt collar.

—*L'argent, Madame. L'argent, les opportunités.* More than just fucking bread.

Maria darted up from her seat, a snake's sudden move, and slapped Yves once, twice across the face. Her dress scattered the cocaine to the wind.

—Fuck, shrieked Red. Look what you've done, you stupid Russian bitch. His accent, New Englander and pompous the moment before, had transformed into a shrill mid-western twang.

Syd was holding onto Maria. She was still glaring at Yves, who was calmly rubbing his cheeks. He grinned like the victor.

—It's okay, Syd said to Red, his hand still tight around Maria's arm, there's plenty more. Maria, he whispered, his voice surprisingly tender, would you like some more cocaine?

Maria suddenly laughed, a long ringing laugh, full of mourning. She sat down next to Syd, kissing his face, his hand, his fingers. Yes, yes, she laughed. More cocaine. Fuck democracy, more cocaine.

She's crazy, I heard Yellow whisper to Red.

Red nodded in agreement.

Maria nestled her head into Syd's girth. More cocaine, please, she whispered, more cocaine.

Fuck democracy. My father had said this to me all his life. Colin said it to me when we first met. Confident of the value of my college education, trying to form a coherent faith out of the remnants of my father's politics, my mother's cynicism, my youthful idealism and the demands of my prick, I had chosen for my second-year assignment to photograph unionists. My second-year lecturer was a wiry Jew with Streisand curls and a melodic voice we all had to strain to hear. In private she was shy, nervous and flighty, and until she knew you well, seemingly unable to look you straight in the eye. But once she stepped up to the lectern she became passionate and stirring. Her skill was her knowledge, her craft her preparation, her passion the drive to convince her students of the humanitarian basis of art. She even managed to convince Sal Mineo that, if art should not have a purpose, then at least there was beauty to be found in art and work inspired by ethics. She saw liberty in Mapplethorpe's composition of a thick black cock emerging triumphantly out of an unzipped business suit. She insisted that it was fraternity that was being celebrated in Dupain's young bathers, and yes, even in Larry Clarke's skinny teens shooting up heroin. And everywhere, in Dorothea Lange, in Ansel Adams, Caryl Jerrems, Walker Evans and Cartier-Bresson, she saw the impulse towards equality. For her, art could only be democratic.

What about horror? we'd counter.

She would flash images of Dachau and Vietnam on the overhead projector. Horror without compassion was exploitation, she argued. A hand would rise: what belongs to journalism, what belongs to art? Another hand would rise. Yes, she was confusing the secular vocation of the artist with the spiritual commitment of the philosopher or monk. She made our classroom democratic. We argued and fought and got drunk together and even Sal Mineo, even Sal Mineo overcame his resistance to her bourgeois demeanour and shyness and took part in the debates. And even if he, and some others—if not for the same reasons—remained unconvinced by her argument, they celebrated her teaching. I myself was convinced. I approached her with my idea to photograph unionised workers. She arranged for me to meet a friend of hers who worked for the building and construction union. He made it possible for me to gain access to worksites and introduced me to an organiser of the nurses' union who got me access to her members working nightshift in a large inner-city hospital. And my mum talked to her manager, who shrugged his shoulders and allowed me to wander the textile factory where she worked.

Fuck democracy!

It was smoko. I was standing on a large thick beam seventeen stories above ground level, explaining to thirteen suspicious building workers the purpose of my photography assignment. My voice squeaked as I explained my desire to make art reflective of democracy and labour in both its content and its accessibility. I wanted these men to collaborate in what I was doing.

—Shut up, Colin, interjected a stocky Maltese man who was the eldest of the group. He smiled at me. Go on, son, speak, continue.

—Fuck democracy, Colin yelled again. We'll end up on some yuppie gallery wall, people will comment on how worthy it all is, and then they'll forget it all and still complain next time they have some work done on their place of how fucking tradies and builders get paid too much and have too good conditions. Fuck your photography. Fuck your democracy.

He turned his back to me. Of course, it made me want to photograph him.

I spent ten days on the site. The men never quite lost their suspicion of me, but they tolerated my presence; and by the third day I was simply ignored: they stopped making faces or showing me their arses every time I pointed the camera. I'd sit on the edge of the bench at lunchtime, munching on sandwiches, watching the city streets below criss-crossed by the metallic lines of gables and beams. I didn't join in the conversations and I wondered sometimes how much of what they said was intended to insult and bait me.

They should shoot fucking boat people, shoot any cunt illegally trying to get into this country. Too easy. We've made it too easy for them.

I'd go straight to college from the building site, develop the negatives I had shot that day and emerge stinking of sweat and chemicals.

My son reckons he can't get into his course because they've got to take a percentage of fucking Aboriginals. I should paint my fucking face black. If you're an Abo they give you everything.

I'd take the developed proofs out onto the roof of the college and under the night sky I would examine my images of strong-armed, strong-willed men.

Hey, Isaac? You got a girlfriend?

Bet he takes it up the arse.

You take it up the arse, Isaac? Watch it boys, he's got fucking AIDS.

Colin sat down next to me. His red curls were plastered tight and close across his sweaty brow. He was eating a salad roll and his arm was warm where it touched my own.

—There's your democracy, mate. He pointed to his workmates. Inspiring, aren't they? God bless the people. His hand touched my thigh. I didn't dare believe it was anything more than an accident.

I photographed the nurses and the seamstresses. They too had their suspicions of me. But from time to time, a quiet moment late in the morning in the ward, they would share food and conversation with me. I printed my photographs of the women on large white canvases and I chose photographs that made the women strong but also beautiful.

When it came to the photographs of the men I fitted them into slim frames, under which were simple captions in thin black sans serif lettering. Beneath a photograph of Yianni showing me his muscles I had the sharp obscene phrase, *Asians Out.* Underneath Steve and Mick jackhammering, *That One Deserves To Get Raped.* Slavko and Greg, smoking while sitting above the city on a beam: *Six Million Was Not Enough.* My lecturer was appalled. She argued that if I exhibited the photographs as I intended to, her friends in the labour movement would never support her work or her students again. I would have to remove the captions. I was disappointed and hurt by her but I did as she asked and participated in the final group show with the photographs minus the captions. But I organised with a friend of Dad's who ran a gambling den off Smith Street to let me exhibit on the walls for just one afternoon. I invited all the subjects of the photographs but only my classmates, my mum and her friends and a couple of nurses turned up. And Colin. He came in an uncomfortable suit and a polyester black shiny tie.

Later he would tell me that he had wanted to impress me, had been concerned that as I had only seen him in dirty overalls and shirts, he would seem foolish and out of place at a gallery show. I was kissing the coarse red hairs on his chest, and I laughed.

—I reckon you would have impressed my classmates more if you had turned up in your overalls or Yakka shorts.

—I didn't want to impress them. I wanted to impress you.

He had liked what I had done with the photographs. There was one of him in the show. He is smoking a cigarette at the end of the work day, and he is leaning over a balcony rail, looking down into the city. I had stolen up quietly behind him and then coughed. He had turned and seen me and in that split-second, I took the shot. There is puzzlement and I think there is desire in the startled eyes and tanned face. Underneath this photograph, in the thin type, I had printed only two words. *Fuck democracy*.

—Do you like Prague?

Syd had come up beside me. Earlier I had excused myself and walked out of the observatory to stand on the balcony and watch the speckled yellow reflections of the city on the black surface of the Vltava. The breeze was biting and I wrapped my arms around myself. Syd was standing looking down below into the city and again I marvelled at the size of him: it was overwhelming, ferocious. He was tall, his brow wide, his neck thick, his shoulders massive and his belly obscene. His legs, too, seemed thick and long. It struck me that Syd looked like a giant from one of the old fairytales. I looked down at Prague.

—It's almost a different city from when I was here last.

I glanced into the observatory. Maria had descended into a foetal crouch on the settee. Sal Mineo had disappeared. The men were standing over the prostrate woman, sipping their wines and champagnes. They all looked clean and fastidious and tidy. Their skins were clear, their skins were tanned. They disgusted me. I turned back to Syd, glad for his bulk, his solidity. Glad for his dirt and sweat and grime.

—Maybe Prague is too beautiful, too pretty.

—When were you last here?

—Over ten years ago. A decade is a long time ago in Europe.

—Bullshit. It ain't a thing. A decade ain't a thing.

Syd sniffed loudly. He spat out across the balcony rail and onto the yard below. I could almost sense Red and Yellow stiffen.

—Do you like Prague?

He laughed. A rumble from the gut, his whole body quivering; a growl from the back of the throat.

—I can't stand it.

—Then why are you here? I thought of the young boys fucking in the boiling studio, I pictured Syd's large mahogany desk.

His answer surprised me.

—My family is from here. Well, not from Prague. From Pilsen. From little old Pilsen. My mother's family.

—Are they still there?

He turned to me then and there was a darkness on his

face; I noticed for the first time that there was a small, almost imperceptible scar across his right eyelid. I noticed it as he blinked and turned his face to the moonlight.

—Dead. Assassinated. Murdered. Maria's vowels were thick; she elongated and made harsh and beautiful the clumsy English consonants. She staggered as she got to us and Syd carefully wrapped an arm around her naked shoulders to steady her.

—Yes, my darling. Syd clicked his two fingers lightly. They went up in smoke.

Maria's perfume was sweet; it smelt of honey. She leaned against Syd and lightly brushed a finger across his thick bottom lip.

—Have you seen Pano? Is he downstairs?

Syd ignored Maria. He was searching my face.

—Are you sure you are not a Jew, Isaac?

—Have you seen Pano? She was insistent.

—No, I am not a Jew.

He peered closer, grabbed the back of my head, and pulled me towards him.

—Have you seen my Pano? Maria was shaking his arm. Her slight wrist against his immense bulk seemed comical. It was as if he didn't even feel her touch.

He yawned and gently pushed my face away.

—Have you seen Pano?

—No! It was a shout. Maria jumped back, shocked, as the rest of the party fell silent. Syd tilted Maria's chin towards him.

—He's on a job. He touched her lips tenderly. You should get ready. I don't pay you for nothing.

Maria smiled. Her eyes glistened. She pulled back her hair, wriggled her body. And even though it was a body growing old and wrinkling and falling to gravity, it was still also strong, defiant: a sensual, real, robust body. Maria turned to me and kissed me on the cheek. She did the same to Syd.

—Of course, darling, I am the proletariat. There is work
to be done. She kissed Syd and walked away.

—She's lovely.

—She is indeed.

Syd lit a cigarette.

—Then why are you such a cunt to her?

He barked a laugh.

—You're just like your mate Steve. There's nothing aristocratic about you Aussies, is there?

I repeated my question.

He was facing me but looking elsewhere, beside me and
behind me and above me. He was looking everywhere but at
me.

—Imagine this city covered with my shit. This city of
spires and cathedrals and testimonials, imagine it covered in
my shit. Imagine them all choking from my shit. That's what
I would like to do to Prague.

I remembered what my friend had told me the previous
day.

—But Syd, Czech shit don't stink.

He laughed again. But he did not look at me.

—That's true. That's what they'd like you to believe.
They are always the little innocent in the middle, our darling
Czechs. They're never responsible for anything.

—So, why are you such a cunt to her?

—Syd, are we going?

Both of us turned to Yves. He was pointing to the slim
gold watch on his wrist.

Syd pulled me into his weight. It was warm. But one snap,
I thought, one snap and I'd be gone.

—Yes. It is time to go to the club.

He was looking straight into my eyes. I am the real Jew,
mate. Your friend's smarter than that Russian *zoine*, he'll
never trust me. Spittle landed on my lobe. You don't know
Jews, do you? You think we should be the nice old fella in the

back of the store, wouldn't hurt a fucking fly. Salt of the earth and God's chosen people. I'm not that kind of Jew, cunt. That kind of *mumza* Jew is finished. I hope that mumza has gone forever.

His grip was tight as he walked me down the stairs and ordered the taxis. His grip hurt and I had to pull away. I had to pull away.

The door was opened by a man with a boxer's physique and a peasant's face. He nodded at us and we descended stone stairs into a basement cavern. There were empty tables, each with a candelabrum on a lace white tablecloth. Thick curtains of red velvet hung from the walls. A woman was sweeping the polished wood floor, her hair covered by a scarf. Two young men, dressed only in tight black trousers with dark blue suspenders over their smooth naked chests, were sitting drinking at the small semicircular bar.

Syd was already behind the cash register counting money. He smiled at us. Take a seat, he ordered.

I looked longingly at the alcohol bottles on the shelves. He followed my gaze and smiled. Take a seat, he repeated, I'll get someone to look after you. The rest of our party was at a table at the front of the room, before a small podium empty but for a black microphone. I took a seat next to Red.

—Where's Steve? I asked.

Red pointed beyond the podium. He's there, with that Russian bitch.

—What would you like to drink? Syd called after me.

—A whisky.

One of the boys came over with a full glass. The suspenders bit into his flesh and left a clear pink mark. I smiled up at him. He placed the glass on the white cloth without looking at me. I had an urge to stand then, to stand and fling the glass straight into his hostile young face. I could smell his blood. My hunger was an instinct. I excused myself, jumped on the podium, pulled back the curtain and walked through.

I was in a small dusty corridor. Brooms and mops hung from the wall. It smelt of stale cigarettes. I heard noises behind a door and I knocked and entered. A group of youths, in various stages of undress, were giggling and laughing. I smelt marijuana; the laughter immediately stopped.

—Is Maria here?

One of the youths, his arms crossed, dressed only in white cotton shorts, his wiry legs pale and hairy, threw some Czech at me. I blushed.

—Is Maria here?

Another boy, with a shock of greasy black hair, took my arm and pointed to the end of the corridor. There, he said sharply, and shut the door behind me.

Maria was getting dressed behind a curtain swirling with pale yellow flowers. Sal Mineo sat on a dresser watching a man affix a thin black moustache to his lean, tough face. I recognised Pano from the photographs. Sal Mineo introduced us, and then, pointing behind me, said, This is Mathilde.

I turned around. A thin young woman was sitting on a plastic chair; I must have almost knocked her over when I opened the door. But the face she turned to me for a moment before dropping it again was apologetic and meek.

Pano said something to Sal Mineo, who laughed.

Mathilde said something quietly, and Maria in turn retorted angrily in Russian. The girl stood and offered me her chair. I refused it.

—Please. The one English word was soft and awkward.

I shook my head. Pano yelled at her and she quickly sat down again.

I looked over at my friend. He was watching Pano in the mirror. Sal Mineo's face was softened by desire, a sad, forlorn desire. Pano was dressed in absurd formal clothes: a black suit, a frilled white chemise and black bow tie pulled tight around his throat. I sat down beside Sal Mineo on the dresser, offered him and Pano a cigarette, but when I turned to Mathilde, Pano held out a large calloused hand and stopped me.

—My wife does not smoke.

Maria emerged from behind the curtain. She was dressed in a voluptuous ruby dress, all lace and silk, all folds and pleats, cut low at the front. She twirled around.

—How do I look?

—Beautiful, I answered. I saw Pano frown. Maria sat next to him, grabbed a cigarette from me and began to arrange her hair. Mathilde rose from her seat to help the older woman. Maria stared at my reflection in the mirror. Pano said something in Russian that made her laugh. She took my hand.

—He asks if you are a faggot. There was defiance in her eyes. Are you a faggot?

I nodded. She dropped my hand.

Pano rose from his seat, pretending to hold a gun in a gangster pose. He shot at the mirror. One day, bang bang, all faggots dead. Bang bang. He laughed again. Sal Mineo's face was severe, impenetrable. Pano was tall, nearly seven feet tall. He dominated the room. He turned to me now, pointing his fingers like a gun to my head. All faggots, bang bang, dead? It was a question. I made no reply. He dropped his hand and with a contemptuous roll of his eyes, turned away, dismissing me. I felt slapped. He kissed Maria softly on her shoulder and hugged his wife. He ignored me and Sal Mineo.

—I have some cocaine, offered Sal.

—You have? Pano had stopped, his hand on the doorknob. I wanted him to keep walking, to shut the door on all of us. Instead his broad back heaved, his shoulders slouched, and something in that vulnerable gesture of defeat reminded me of boyhood.

Sal Mineo followed him out.

—Your friend is in love with Pano.

I looked sharply over at Mathilde, who was combing Maria's lank hair.

—It is alright. Mathilde knows no English.

—Yes. He is.

Mathilde had swiftly crafted Maria's hair into a neat bun. Maria rose from her chair, turned, and smiled.

—How do I look?

—Beautiful, I said again.

—Thank you. She brushed her lips softly on my cheek. You must come to the show.

I nodded. She butted out her cigarette and left. Mathilde and I sat quietly for a moment and I could hear the soft call of music, the sounds of feet, a trace of applause. I turned to the younger woman, who was again sitting down. I pointed to the door. Will you escort me, I gestured.

She smiled, but shook her head. I turned back, wanting to convince her, extending my arm out in an invitation, but she had her hands in her lap, her gaze firmly on the concrete floor. There was quiet strength in her silent refusal. I did not ask her again.

You are in Hell. There were voices from the room next door, there was giggling and then there was a rushing of feet. I closed the door behind me and walked down the empty corridor. You are in Hell, the voice repeated, and I was sure that it spoke in Greek. My belly was on fire, as if a ghostly iron fist was at work, slowly, methodically grinding my intestines and belly to fine dust. I looked down at my feet, one following the other, and found myself surprised at their confident rhythm, at their ability to act, to walk. I did not wish them to go forward, I wanted to return back to the little room, sit beside Mathilde, hide myself from what lay beyond the red velvet curtain. Hell lay behind it, I was sure of that. But my feet, my will, were not my own. I breathed deeply, and thrust a hand through the curtain opening.

Maria was in front of the microphone. The club was full, all men, all well-dressed, all European. There were more young men in black trousers and blue suspenders, carrying trays of drinks to the tables which were illuminated by the soft light of the candles. The CD that had been playing Puccini arias sung by Maria Callas faded and there was more applause. A gold spotlight hit Maria. She bowed and held out her hand to still the audience. The club fell to silence.

—I will tell you, began Maria, about the day I first lost my virginity. Her voice was soft and melodic, her accent giving the obscene English words a gravity and charm they did not deserve. As her tale continued I realised that she was speaking in the character of an eleven-year old boy who was at the wedding of a favourite uncle. Something brushed my shoulder. Pano stood beside me. Next to him was the young boy who'd refused to answer my English. He too now wore a formal suit; his hair was slicked back, his arms crossed. Ignoring me, they waited in the wings.

Maria continued. She described the day of the wedding, the preparations, the exchange of gifts, the shaving and dressing of the groom. She then told how the boy was taken by the uncle to his bedroom and how the uncle explained that even though he loved the boy, that a man must marry, must produce a family, that this was the way of the world. Then, whispered Maria, My uncle laid his hand on my shoulder, pulled me towards him and kissed me on the lips.

Pano and the boy emerged from the wings. There was more applause. I scanned the audience. There was one lecherous smile on its face.

Maria continued the story of the boy's deflowering. She made no attempt to hide her accent or her age. The words came out stamped with her smoky inflections. The descriptions were brutal but the sounds were delicate. As she spoke of the delicious wetness of the uncle's kiss, of her nervous excitement, the actors on the stage began to undress. The blond boy slowly unbuttoned the older man's trousers and took out Pano's fleshy purple cock. The audience breathed as one. The woman described how it felt to first have a penis in her mouth and the young boy took Pano's cock and began to suck.

—Fuck him, yelled a voice.

Maria stopped, scowled, inspected the audience. She proceeded with her tale. I could feel my own erection stirring in my pants. The boy had his back to the audience and continued to fellate Pano. Maria's voice was now breathless and she was almost singing the words.

—My uncle's monstrous cock astonished me, and I was crying as I tried to fit it into my mouth. His fingers were exploring my virgin arsehole and I was shaking from fear, fear that his terrible cock would be inside me, shivering with the anticipation of it.

On stage Pano raised the boy to his feet, then slowly unbuttoned the boy's trousers, which fell to his ankles.

—I wanted him to fuck me, sighed the woman on the stage. I wanted to feel his cock deep inside of me.

The pornographic words fell out across the audience, and slowly the men began to touch hands and feet, began caressing the half-naked waiters standing around them. I watched money—euros, sterling, dollars—slip from palm to pocket, slipped in between the suspenders and bare flesh. In the back, in the half darkness, some of the men had unzipped, were undoing their trouser buttons, and had started to masturbate.

—He whispered to me, Remember I love you, nephew, and then he pushed his thick big cock up my arse. Maria trills, a melodramatic operatic shriek. Oh, it did hurt.

The boy on stage had been shaved, and his pale pink pursed arsehole appeared prepubescent. Pano was still clothed; only his cock was naked, only his cock was exposed. He lay the boy on the podium, turned him onto his back, lifted the boy's thin smooth legs over his own tuxedoed shoulders, and he entered him. In the middle of the room, a shower of semen arced, reflecting silver as it was touched by the candlelight.

—But as his thrusts continued into me, the pain became indistinguishable from the greatest pleasure I had ever known. Fuck me, Uncle, fuck me!

From where I stood, I could see the boy's face. His eyes were screwed shut, and every time Pano bucked into his frail body I could hear tight, pained grunts. His pain excited me. The boy's thin body shuddered and as I looked down at him it seemed that his skin had fallen away and his very bones were visible; and when I searched his face it had darkened, his hair was now black, not fair, and the gaunt face that leered up at me was looking straight into my eyes and his eyes were shining, they were laughing, and I knew those eyes, had always known those eyes.

Fuck me, screamed Maria, and the boy was laughing and Pano was slamming into him and I turned away but not before my own cock twitched against my jeans and I felt a warm ooze jerk from inside.

I rested my face on the cool wall. Maria continued to sing her song but I was no longer listening. I did not know where my shame was coming from. I had seen sex acts before, and hadn't I even paid for sex with an Athenian whore only a few weeks ago, who, if I was honest with myself, would not have been much older than the boy Pano was fucking on the podium? But whatever its source, the contempt I felt for myself was rich, righteous and mortifying. If I could not be sure if I was ashamed of being a man, or of being a man who was a fag, or of both, or of being a white man in an Eastern city, or of all of it, I knew enough to know that I was ashamed of being human. *You are in Hell*. This time I whispered the words to myself.

o O o

Mathilde was still sitting in the room. I sat on the dresser and offered her a cigarette again. She glanced quickly at the door and took it from my hands. She smoked nervously, quickly, and after the third puff she gave it back. We sat and waited in silence.

When Maria returned she did not look at me. She said something quickly to Mathilde, who followed her immediately behind the curtain. After a few moments Pano burst into the room. Ignoring me, he began to strip. He threw the bow tie and his clothes and shoes in a pile on the floor. Standing naked, he wiped his cock, then shouted for his wife, who emerged from behind the curtain with a bundle of clothes. On the pale pink of his upper left arm, I saw the Star of David, the coarse yellow lines blurred with age to a mustard colour. I almost reached out to touch it. Syd burst laughing into the room. He sat beside me and winked at Pano.

—They love you.

—Have you my money? I noticed that Pano had turned away and hastily put on a shirt to cover the tattoo.

Syd took a roll of bills from his pocket and handed them to Pano. Mathilde came up next to her husband, grabbed the roll of bills and placed them inside her bra. She said something to Pano.

But Syd shook his head.

—No, you can't leave yet, someone has paid for you tonight.

—I can't tonight, answered Pano, smiling at his wife.

—Suit yourself. It's three hundred American.

Pano smiled ruefully at his wife. He spoke to her in Russian and she, glancing first at Syd, slowly nodded.

—Who is it?

—Guess. Syd looked over at me. Your friend Stephen is a fool with his money.

Maria came from behind the curtain, wearing the dress

she had worn back at the party. Syd held out another bundle of notes. Wordlessly taking it from him, she sat before the mirror and counted the money with a cigarette in her hand. Pano pulled on a pair of jeans.

—It's all there.

She ignored Syd. He turned to Pano.

—Come upstairs. The schmuck's waiting. He turned to me.

—And you?

—I'm going to go home.

—Steve's going to be a while. He's paid enough for it. He's going to take his sweet time.

—I want to go home.

—No you don't, said Syd. I have a present for you.

—What kind of present?

Syd called down the corridor. As Pano pulled the foolish fake moustache from his upper lip, a young boy came into the room. He was dark, small and thin, and he had large shining green eyes. He was dangerously young. There was a fine down beginning to sprout on his upper lip.

—Sedat, said Syd, and the young boy looked up. Syd pointed at me. The boy came and took my hand. The face that looked up to mine was resigned, emotionless. I shook my head, and Sedat, now confused, dropped my hand. In the mirror I could see Pano staring at me. I knew that what I was doing was not an act of a moralist. I was only trying to impress this strict Russian, to convince him I shared nothing with the men in the club, nothing with Syd, nothing with Sal Mineo. The boy was now sheepishly looking at Syd. He had only wanted to please, and he was fearful that he had failed to do so.

Syd shrugged his shoulders and signalled for the boy to go over to him. Sedat smiled and went over. Syd fondled the back of the boy's neck and Sedat closed his eyes and smiled. Syd kissed his brow. He then put his open mouth over the boy's, watching me; daring me to look away. I did not take my eyes from them. Syd's hand moved down the boy's vest, the other hand cupped his crotch. The boy sank into the colossal girth of the slobbering man.

I wanted to kill the filthy fat fuck, the urge to do so felt as if it were the very liquid of my bloodstream, that it was the source of Heaven and Hell and Earth itself; the urge was my very soul. But I knew that however primal the urge to kill and to rip the flesh and skin off the Jew, it was nothing compared to my envy of him. I wished it could be me, that it was I who would be taking this little boy, that it was I who would be turning him over as I had seen Pano do to the Czech boy on stage. I'd turn him over and I'd be just cock, just a cock ripping into the guts of the young boy. I would know—it would not be just a fantasy, not a guilty dream but reality—the anguish and the terror, and yes, the sweetness of fucking a child, of tearing into him, of making him bleed.

I became the urge that stopped me moving closer to Syd and Sedat. To move any closer was not only to give in, to fuck. To move closer was to destroy, to kill, to be consumed. To move closer was to become one with them both.

—Go, Pano, said Maria in English. Be quick.

I opened my eyes. Syd had his right hand extended out to me; his other was still caressing Sedat's throat. I shook his fleshy palm, shook it silently. I turned away from his gaze, refused it. It was as if he had seen into me, to the source of me. A thin trickle of cold semen slid down my thigh. Syd took the boy by the hand and left.

Pano sniffed, rose and looked at himself in the mirror. He kissed Mathilde; she clung to his neck, then let him go. I got up to shake his hand but he had already turned and opened the door.

He spoke rapid Russian to his mother and then turned to me.

—That filthy Arab boy, he is a virgin, he's just arrived. His brother works here as well. You are cruel to not have him. Now it will be one of the old faggots who will break him. Pano slammed the door.

Maria smiled across at me.

—Forgive my son, he is a very old-fashioned Russian man. To be accurate and even though he would never admit to such a thing, he is a very old-fashioned Soviet man. He detests the homosexuals.

—I can see why.

—Really? It simply strikes me as ignorance.

She began scrubbing the make-up off her face.

—Does Syd own this club?

—Yes.

—Is he very rich?

—Very.

—Pano must hate the Jews as well.

She turned around then and slapped my face. It stung. Mathilde looked up, shocked, but on catching my eye she immediately looked down again at the floor.

—My son is no fascist. At least the Jews and the homosexuals give him work.

I stood up.

—I should leave.

—It is possible you escort us home?

—Gladly. I was humbled by her reprieve.

Maria turned and spoke some instructions to Mathilde, who grabbed a bag and quickly wiped the dresser clean. We waited for her. The corridor looped to the right and there was a small rusting metal door that opened up to an alley. We bent, crossed under, and were in the night breeze. I looked up the side of the black stone at the faint lights glowing through thick curtains on the second and third floors.

—What is upstairs?

—The bordello. Maria gripped one of my arms, and Mathilde, after hesitating, took another. The younger woman suddenly surprised me by kissing me and mumbling something rapid in Russian.

—She's blessing you. She is mad for God, that one. It disturbs me. Her generation have disowned politics for religion. Maybe I am just old but this seems very ridiculous to me.

Mathilde hugged my arm tight as we stepped over a sleeping body in the alley and began to walk up a narrow street snaking away from the river.

—Do you believe in God?

—I don't know.

Maria mused on my answer.

—Do you believe in anything?

I was silent. She punched me lightly on my arm.

—Well? Answer me.

—In Australia I believe in lots of things. Here, in Europe, you all make me feel a little stupid. Do you understand? I don't know if I believe anything in Europe.

—Australia seems a perfect place in which to finish one's life. I imagine it is a very quiet place, a very safe place.

I laughed. A woman in a tight black bra and short denim skirt glanced at the three of us, then called back to a companion, another whore hiding in the shadows. They called after us for cigarettes.

—Why do you laugh?

—I don't see why that is anything to be ashamed of.

It was her turn to laugh.

—And that is what surprises us Europeans about you Australians. That you would think that is something to be embarrassed by.

—Most Europeans know nothing of Australia.

—That's true. We do not care.

—And you, do you believe in God?

Maria shrugged.

—No. I was never religious. Neither were my parents.

They were very good Bolsheviks. Even though they lived every moment of their life in fear, they were proud Party members.

I couldn't pretend to understand the depth of malice in her voice. So instead, I squeezed her hand. When she spoke again, her tone had softened.

—My grandmother was a Jew. She was very superstitious.

—That makes you and Pano both Jews, doesn't it?

The only sound in the city was the tap of heels on the cobbled street.

—Syd does not know. He would not employ us if he knew. He is obsessed with taking revenge on history. But being Jewish was never of importance to me. I did not even circumcise my son. You noticed his tattoo? He did this to spite me. Of that I'm sure.

—Your name is not very Jewish.

—Was not Christ's mother a Jew?

I blushed. And she laughed.

—I am not named after your Virgin. I would like to believe I am a descendant of another Maria, or to give her the true name, Miriam. She was a Jew as well, living in Jerusalem when the Temple fell. There was a great hunger and a great death when the Romans took the city. The people feared both the powerful Romans and the fanatical Jewish rebellion. Rather than letting her children suffer she killed them and ate from their flesh. When the rebels came upon her she offered them the meat. Maria paused, and then spoke in a language that I knew was not Russian.

—Was that Hebrew?

—Isaac, I am so disappointed in you. That was your language, that was spoken in the tongue of the ancient Greeks.

—That is not my language.

She translated for me.

—Eat, for I have already eaten. Can it be you are afraid? Are you weaker than a woman, weaker than even a mother?

She then touched my face. We had stopped before a tall apartment block, its blue paint chipped, its windows cracked and dirty.

—Next time you pray to your Maria, give a thought to my Miriam.

—Leave, I said quietly. The three of you should leave Prague.

—My daughter-in-law is pregnant, Isaac, who will protect her? Where should we go? Would you take us to Australia?

And for one moment, a grace of a moment, I thought I saw hope in her eyes. Then there was only a mocking tenderness.

—A pleasure to meet you, Isaac.

—Can't you go to Israel? The words came out in a rush and for a moment I thought she had not understood me. She touched my cheek again.

—It is possible. Maybe I go when my wanderings are finished. Maybe I go when God forgives me. When God forgives me, maybe the Russians in Israel will forgive me as well. She kissed me on the lips.

—Goodbye, Isaac.

I watched the two women walk, hand in hand, into the shadows of the night.

I walked the dark city, past whores and beggars, drunkards and dopers, revellers and madmen shouting out the varied names of Paradise and of Hell. I crossed streets and alleys and boulevards and bridges and I kept walking, exhausted, all the while repeating to myself, I once had a teacher, I once had a teacher, and he taught me there was a city called Prague and that once hope existed in this city, and I kept walking and walking but dawn came and I had found no hope.

He was waiting for me. He began beating me with his fists as soon as he saw me. His photographs of Pano were scattered all over the floor. Someone or something had scratched the prints; serrated tears ripped through Pano's face and body and neck. In the near-dawn light it seemed that the portraits were bleeding from their wounds. I held Sal Mineo's fists and whispered to him that I had not done this, I had not done this, and eventually he stopped hitting me and began to cry and I took him and lay in bed with him, stroking his shoulders, kissing his neck. I held him tight till sleep took hold of him instead.

In the morning I packed my things and Sal Mineo took me for coffee in the square. There were tourists with backpacks like mine and there were elegently suited young people sipping espressos in the sunshine. I looked across to the intricate figures on the cathedral dome and I said to Sal Mineo, You live in a beautiful city. While we were drinking our coffee, the old woman who was cleaning the cafe floor tripped over her broom and upended a bucket. The dirty water spilled across the cafe's smooth porcelain floor. The goateed waiter rushed over to her, screaming. He was pulling her arm, and the young people around us were laughing and pointing. I asked Sal Mineo what the waiter had said and he answered, That they will get rid of her, that she's worthless, that she's no good. The old woman, now crying, was wiping her hands on her stained blue uniform. She refused to look any of us in the eye as the waiter dragged her out back. I stood up.

—I have to go.

Sal Mineo kissed my cheek. Once, twice. A gypsy child asked me for money and I gave him the last *krona* notes I had left. The train arrived.

—You shouldn't do that, said Sal Mineo, you shouldn't encourage them. He then slipped a thick joint into my shirt pocket. Memento from Praga, he grinned. He became serious. Smoke it before the German border. It didn't use to matter, but, you know, these days, security. Of course, I answered, security.

And with that, without once glancing back, my friend turned and walked away from me.

THE SPARROW'S SONG,
THE SERPENT'S COURSE

STELLIOS LEPTOULIS HAD his blue cap rolled tight into a ball and he was crushing it with a tense grip. He was oblivious to what he was doing: what concerned him was that he had been ordered to wait in the town hall's tiny cold vestibule till the Colonel was free; and Stellios was fearful that he would be spied by someone strolling past the building from the street. He kept his head bowed low into his chest, crushed his cap even tighter, and tapped his left foot with growing impatience. He could hear voices in one of the rooms off the hall, he could hear sounds from the markets outside in the main square, and he could hear the soft lilt of music from a wireless coming from deep within the town hall's bowels. A heavy drop of sweat fell from his brow onto the cracked tile floor.

He wiped his brow with his cap and swore softly to himself. What the devil is keeping him? The Colonel usually saw him straight away; Stellios would answer any questions the man had for him, and the interview would be terminated quickly. Ten minutes at the most. Stellios would then leave through the back of the town hall and make his way back to the centre of town in order to finish his bartering at the markets. He was distraught that he was being made to wait today. An old woman, her black shawl wrapped tight across her skull, peered through the heavy wood doors and Stellios abruptly turned his head away. The young soldier standing guard called out to her.

—What do you want, Auntie?

—Nothing, grumbled the old crone, and quickened her

pace, almost tripping herself over in her fear and haste to get away. The soldier started to laugh, then looking back at Stellios, his young face turned sour and contemptuous.

What the devil is keeping him, muttered Stellios. He turned his eyes towards the clock on the vestibule wall. An hour and a half, the Colonel had kept him waiting close to an hour and a half. This was ridiculous: how was he to be back home before nightfall? Ignoring the suspicious eyes of the young soldier, he got to his feet, made his way down the short corridor and knocked three times on the door to the Colonel's room. He heard a hurried scraping of a chair across the tiles, a giggle, and then heard the Colonel's low voice call out in anger, What the fuck is it?

Stellios Leptoulis opened the door. Even as his hands were turning the cold brass handle he was beginning his obsequious complaint.

—I'm so sorry, Colonel, but I just cannot wait any longer. He stopped, his mouth fell open and a hushed blasphemy vaulted from his mouth.

The Colonel was tightening his belt. But this was not what made Stellios' eyes bulge and his mouth go dry. Sitting across from the Colonel, a mocking smile on her lips, was Lucia Panagis. Her mourning scarf had fallen lazily across her shoulders and her long flowing hair was scandalously exposed; the once raven black waves were now as white as the sparse locks of a dying old man. But what was most shocking was that her thick wool skirt and her cream hessian pantaloons were lying untidily around her feet. Lucia, with a small laugh, rose, and facing Stellios, she hoisted her skirts back to her waist; but not before he caught sight of her thick white bush. He dropped his eyes.

—What the fuck do you want? repeated the Colonel, his tone now calm and taunting. Without a word Stellios shut the door and rushed back to his seat in the foyer.

It was true what the village gossips said: Michaelis Panagis' wife was mad. He cursed his brother, for if it wasn't for Antonis, Stellios would not have come to town. Instead of walking into an abomination he would be now tending his flock, and preparing his fallow fields near the Cold Water creek. But Antonis had convinced him to make the journey, urged him to make an appointment with the Colonel one last time. Antonis' son Giorgos had come of age and Antonis was determined that if his boy had to do time in the army, he should serve as far away as possible from the mountains and borders. The war was officially declared won by the government but the bandits and guerrillas still roamed the winter mountain peaks, increasingly desperate now that they were scattered and hunted. Any uniformed soldier they came across, they finished off immediately. Stellios honestly wished the guerrillas no harm. He was quite happy to see them flee to Albania and to the Slavs' lands and leave Greece far behind: he was not vindictive but a fair man, and was grateful that the bandits had led the resistance to the German occupation. But he had lost patience with them over the harsh years of the civil war. They had pilfered his flock and this last winter they had demanded most of his stored provisions. With his children hungry and sick, he had even remonstrated with the two men who had come to take the cheese, the corn and the wine from his cellar. They had ignored him and ignored the cries and screams of his youngest daughters. Stellios had once been in sympathy with their cause. Now he damned them and all politics, all governments and all nations. God, just grant us a little peace.

His brother was far less forgiving. The Germans had plundered the whole village and had stolen from across the valley, but once they had left, Antonis' fields had flourished. It was as if the Devil had protected him. That first year after the Germans had fled, the village's harvest had been disastrous. Other men had seen their crops fail, their seedlings puny or mouldy or poisoned. Antonis had begun to rent out his own fertile fields, charging a small interest. Of course, there was grumbling and insults but it was acknowledged that the eldest Leptoulis had always been a crafty schemer. He gets it from his great-uncle Mitsos Bertes, it was said, Mitsos Bertes being a young man who had managed to gain a favoured position in the court of the last sultan. Mitsos Bertes had ended up stabbed ruthlessly to death by a Greek patriot on the streets of Constantinopoli and there were many men in the village who were keen to see his great-nephew suffer a similar fate. There were few tears when the guerrillas came into town and announced that Antonis Leptoulis had been convicted in absentia by a people's court which had found him guilty of capitalist usury. His rich crops were all plundered, his fields denuded and most of his stock of goats and chickens stolen. For good measure they had given the man a whipping that left him bruised, humiliated and blind in one eye. Though people had thought it quite merciful of the guerrillas not to have executed him, Antonis did not quite see it this way. He swore to avenge himself on the bandits and forced his brothers to do the same. However, he was loath to lose his oldest son to that struggle.

Stellios looked up as he heard the heavy tread of the Colonel's boots across the tiles. The Colonel was a tall man, and though the years of war had trimmed his solid frame, he was still imposing. He had a thick moustache that he wore in the Cretan style, and which reminded Stellios of Stalin. Not that it would do to tell this to the Colonel—better to not even try to make of joke of that.

—Come, barked the Colonel, and Stellios followed the man into his private office. There was no trace of the mad whore. The room was cold and sparsely furnished with a long desk and two small wooden chairs. A photograph of the King and a silver crucifix were the only adornments on the walls. The walls themselves were cracked and peeling from the shelling during the war.

—Sit, ordered the Colonel, and Stellios perched on the edge of the wooden chair, his grip still tight on his cap.

—What news have you for me?

He's not even looking at me, thought Stellios. The Colonel lit a cigarette without offering one to the other man.

—Excuse me, Colonel, but I have a favour to ask of you.

—And what news have you for me?

Stellios stirred uncomfortably in his seat.

—Colonel, nothing to report. All the bandits have fled our village.

—And their supporters?

Stellios said nothing. Who can tell anymore, he wanted to reply, but he knew that would be a damaging retort.

The Colonel turned from the window and looked at him. His eyes were large, dark and smiling. Stellios distrusted them.

—How about Paparaklis?

Stellios frowned. Sotiris Paparaklis had died the last winter, an icy landslide had buried him.

—Colonel, Sotiris Paparaklis is dead.

—But not Vasilis Paparaklis.

Despite his fear, Stellios could not help laughing.

—But little Vasilaki is not yet twelve, Colonel.

The Colonel leaned into the desk and blew a thin stream of smoke through his thick pale lips.

—I have it on good authority that your little Vasilaki, that little bastard, has been carrying messages to the guerrilla captains. I have it on good authority that your little Vasili Paparaklis is a communist.

Stellios kept his mouth shut. He thought of Sotiris' widow and her three young children, her oldest son fighting desperately up in the mountains. I will not say a word, Stellios resolved to himself.

—What do you have to say to that, Kire Leptoulis?

—I know nothing of this.

—Then what the fuck are we paying you for? The Colonel butted out his cigarette on a tile and spat after it.

Stellios blurted out his prepared speech.

—Colonel, my nephew Giorgos is to be drafted and his father fears for his safety as the bandits are already suspicious of his allegiances. Please, Colonel, you who have been so good to our family, could you use your influence to ensure that he serves somewhere far from us? Stellios hesitated. The other man was again lost to the sights outside the window. A faint note of panic, a desperate shrill, now entered Stellios' voice.

—Please, Colonel, can I ask of you this one last small favour? My brother was slaughtered doing his duty on those damned devil mountains around Karpenissi. When we found his body he had been beaten so savagely by those madmen that I could not recognise his face. We identified him by the Cross he was wearing.

The Colonel's eyes were still smiling as he turned and faced Stellios.

—My brother did not fear his duty.

The two men stared at one another. Stellios dropped his gaze.

—What news have you for me?

Stellios now sat upright on his chair. Forgive me, God, he whispered to himself, and quickly patted his foot on the cold tiles. I step on you, Satan, he mouthed.

—In the coffee-shop, Colonel, I overheard Costas Meniotis condemn the banning of the Party. Stellios spoke firmly and coldly. The Communist Party, he added quickly.

Stalin's moustache twitched furiously.

—I know which fucking party he meant. The Colonel lit another cigarette. Stellios did not dare ask for one.

—I'm not interested in gossip, Mr Leptoulis.

Stellios looked up at the silver crucifix on the wall.

—Vasilis Paparaklis, they say, is often seen wandering out

of the village at nights. Since he was a young boy he has not feared the night. I don't know where he goes. But he returns before dawn. He has an aunt in the village of Gravitas. I think he stays there. If your men were to keep a watch on her house you will be able to follow him.

The Colonel nodded and rose.

—I'll see what I can do about your nephew.

Stellios shook the Colonel's hand and walked out of the office and out through the back of the town hall. A latrine stood in the far corner of the yard. Stellios squatted over the hole and a long hard turd emerged from his body. He wiped his hands across his buttocks, then on some tall wild grass and hitched his trousers. He turned and spat into the hole and for one moment stood in silence, watching a swarm of flies dance merrily over the dirt and the shit. You are running very late, he reminded himself, and he walked away.

He quickly finished his chores at the markets, and placing the pepper, the coffee and the salted meat into a thick hessian cloth, he tied his purchases with a tough weathered rope, and placed the bundle under his arm. The sun was high in the sky as he began his journey and he knew that it would be dark before he reached the village. He made his way out of town.

As he was travelling along the thin dusty road, he heard his name being called. He turned around to see Lucia Panagis following him. Damn that woman, he cursed to himself, but he slowed his pace and allowed her to catch up to him. Her young daughter, Reveka, marched alongside her.

The little girl was going to be a great beauty, like her mother. Her round face was pale from the winter dark, and her hair was long and black. Stellios had been one of the boys who had fantasised about making Lucia his wife, and in his youth the Devil had often sent temptation at night in Lucia's guise. Now, looking down at the little girl's stern shy face, he felt the familiar stirring in his crotch. He knelt and kissed Reveka.

—What's wrong, Reveka *mou*, aren't you going to give your Uncle Stellios a kiss? Reveka tried to hide behind her mother's legs. Lucia laughed, then quickly slapped her daughter.

—Go on, you wild animal, kiss Mr Leptoulis.

Reveka gave Stellios a hurried kiss. He smelt oil and rosewater in her hair, and he closed his eyes.

—And did you have a good interview with the Colonel, Stellio?

He rose to his feet, placed his bundle back under his arm, and continued his journey. Lucia fell in step behind him.

—How is Michaelis? he asked her.

Lucia was silent. Stellios smiled to himself and kept walking. He could hear Reveka's rushed steps, trying to keep up with the steady gait of the adults. He turned and smiled at the girl.

—Would you like to ride on my shoulders, Reveka?

The little girl looked up at him suspiciously, then nodded slowly.

—She's heavy, cautioned Lucia, but ignoring her, Stellios lifted Reveka to his shoulders, waited for her to relax with her long warm legs falling across his chest, and the three of them continued their way up the mountain.

From time to time, Stellios would glance back at Lucia. She was still a beautiful woman. Michaelis Panagis was lucky to have this to return to every night. Then he thought of little Christaki, the poor departed one, and his face saddened. Stellios bore Lucia no ill: far from it. He only felt a deep sadness for what had befallen the couple. He had heard Lucia's screams of pain the night their son had died. The howling had lasted all through the night, and it was as if the very sky itself was screaming with her. Her shrieks had seemed to echo throughout the valley for days, for weeks afterwards. Lucia had been driven demented by Christos' death and had even accused her own mother-in-law of killing the child. Stellios believed that Maritha had indeed been a witch. Even though his own mother had always called for her assistance when one of the children had fallen ill, she had also warned them against the *Albanesa*. But he refused to believe that Maritha was capable of evil towards her own grandchildren. No, Lucia had done great damage to her soul by condemning Maritha. Evil had come to their village and it was the old woman Panagis who had ensured that evil had also been banished.

Stellios had been the one who had dug up the body. The boy's corpse had not decayed at all: the skin was grey and clung like a shroud over the boy's skinny frame. The mouth was contorted in a wide imbecile grin, and even the eyes had remained whole: in those empty glass eyes, Stellios had seen the summons of his own death. He had screamed, and would have fled if old Papa Nicholas had not grabbed on tight to his tunic. The priest had washed Stellios' hands in holy water, blessed him, had the man kiss the Holy Book, and together they had prepared the pyre. There was no smell to the boy, and Stellios noticed the short stubby penis.

—Was he a Mohammedan, Father?

The priest had not answered. It had been then that Stellios had understood. The boy had been a betrayer of Christ. He spat on the ground and threw the corpse roughly on the pyre of tindersticks and coal. He gave a quick sharp kick at the inert body.

—What are you doing? screamed the priest.

—Forgive me, Father, said Stellios, but it is a rare chance a man has to kick at Satan himself. I'll get to Heaven.

The priest poured oil over flesh, over wood and coal. He had told the gravedigger that it had been Maritha Panagis who had urged him to unearth the body. Stellios had not been surprised that the old woman and her grandson had died. It was certainly no accident. It was the damn Judas' final satanic revenge. Lucia had no right to condemn her mother-in-law. Maritha Panagis had saved their village.

Night fell quickly as they began their steep ascent. Lucia had ordered her daughter off Stellios' shoulders, and they now walked hand-in-hand behind the man. Reveka kept close to her mother, her bright black eyes darting in fright at the forest's evening music. Is that a wolf? she cried. No, laughed Stellios, that's the wind running down the mountain. Is that a demon, Uncle Stellio? No, shushed the man, that's the moon yawning because he's just awoken. But Stellios too believed the night belonged to the wolves and the demons and he prayed as they climbed. He heard Lucia chuckle.

—I thought you a brave man, Stellio, a gravedigger. Why the hell are you praying?

—All we have in life is God's protection, Lucia Panagis.

—You are a fool, Stellio Leptoulis. This is the Devil's mountain. God doesn't live here.

It was the little girl who first heard the sobbing. She stopped and tugged fiercely at her mother's skirts.

—Why have you stopped, you stupid beast?

—Listen, whispered Reveka, someone is crying.

The adults listened to the night and they too heard the fits of grief.

—She's right, nodded Stellios, I hear it too. He turned to the woman and her daughter. You two stay here, I'll go and have a look. Crossing himself, he followed the sound of the sobbing.

Stellios came to the edge of a clearing and in the benign light of the half-moon he saw a young boy kneeling beside three misshapen forms. It was the boy who was crying. He looked up at Stellios' approach and pulled a knife from his belt.

—Vasilaki, don't be scared, it's only me. It's Stellios Leptoulis. I'm returning from town.

Vasilis Paparaklis hesitated, then he placed the knife back in its sheath and angrily wiped tears from his eyes. Stellios approached and looked down at the three figures lying still on the ground.

He guessed that they had been bandits. The two dead men had long black beards, and the dead woman had worn the stiff grey hides of the guerrilla army. The skin on the faces of the corpses had been burnt away, as had much of their dress. Red scars and boils were visible on the exposed flesh. Around them, visible even in the half-moon light, the earth itself seemed burnt and scarred, as if the sky had rained fire. The smell was putrid: death, rotting, and something unrecognisable. Something new, not of nature, something chemical, like the residue that clung to the one photograph Stellios possessed, of his mother and his father, God have mercy on their souls. He turned away from the abhorrent sight.

—They've killed my brother. The boy pointed at one of the corpses. This is his dagger.

Vasilis broke down again, and in his humiliation he turned away from the man. Stellios looked back at the forest path, and seeing that Lucia had not yet followed, he quickly made up his mind what he was to do. He knelt before Vasilis and violently shook his shoulders.

—Hush, Vasilaki, you will have plenty of time for grief later. Your life is in danger as well. They know you have been helping your brother.

The boy stopped crying and an angry suspicion filled his face.

—What do you know?

—I was in the town hall, Vasilaki, I had some business there in town. I overheard Lucia Panagis talking to one of the Colonels. She betrayed you to him.

—Are you certain?

The man nodded.

—Go, Vasilaki, go and tell them about your brother. But then leave immediately for they will be coming for you. Run, don't hesitate.

The boy did not move. He looked down at the three bodies.

—Run, insisted Stellios, save yourself. I swear to you on my children's lives that they know you are involved. Your mother has already lost one son, don't let her lose another.

The boy rose and began to run. Stellios heard his rapid footsteps taking the forest path. The rank smell of the corpses reached his nose again and he had to turn away. He heard a tread and saw Lucia and Reveka walking out into the clearing.

—Don't let the girl come close, he warned, and ran and took Reveka in his arms. They both watched as Lucia walked up to the bodies and surveyed the ground around them. She turned, and in the moonlight, Stellios was shocked to see a triumphant smile on her face.

—What killed them, do you think?

Stellios did not move. He shrugged his shoulders.

—They say the Americans have a bomb that rains fire from the sky.

Lucia laughed loudly at this and clapped her hands. And then, slipping off her pantaloons beneath her dark skirts, she crouched beside the bodies and began to piss. The thick gold stream sent clouds of white steam up into the starry sky. Stellios tried to shield the young girl's impassive eyes from the horror of her mother's madness. She is a wild animal, thought Stellios, the Devil is certainly in her. Lucia pulled up her pantaloons, adjusted her skirts, and came over to Stellios and Reveka.

—Give me my daughter.

Taking Reveka's hand, she started to walk back to the path. She stopped and turned to Stellios.

—Who was it that was sobbing?

—Their souls, whispered the man, his voice harsh and trembling. We must have heard their souls.

Stellios Leptoulis' favourite spot on the mountain was a wide cleft step perched on the edge of a cliff overlooking the valley below and the setting sun above. The step was wide enough for a small natural garden to have formed, and Stellios tended it by removing any overgrowth of nettles, pruning back the grassy knoll on which he sat and looked over his world. It was between the twin lofts of the neighbouring mountain that the sun set. It had been a terrible winter, thought the man, the worst he could remember, and he feared that his strength was beginning to fail him. He had grown very thin over the winter, his hair had started to whiten, and he was filled with guilt and anxiety for his soul over the acts that war and hunger had forced him to. But even with his failing strength, he had managed to protect his family, and now that the winter was passing and the wars were over, he took his seat on the knoll and thanked God that his family had survived. Stellios sat on the edge of the cliff, feeling the last warm rays of the setting sun, glad to be up above the world, away from the inanities of man. That very morning he had heard the first thrilling song of the sparrow, and in the middle of the day, with the hot white sun above him as he had been digging in his orchard, he heard a rustle in the corn grass. Bending on one knee and flicking back the cornstalks, he saw a serpent's course outlined in the soil. Spring, Easter was coming.

Looking down at the valley, he heard the church bells ring. Glancing across, he could make out a bent figure kneeling at a graveside but he could not tell who it was or whose death they were still mourning. I'm too old to dig many more graves, Stellios thought to himself, and he smiled, thinking of his oldest son, Gerasimos. It's your turn, son, he murmured, your turn to become a man. He looked back at the valley and wished he could stay on his secure warm ledge forever. The trees, the wind, the sun, the sparrow and the serpent, all these belonged to God. It was the world of man that belonged to the Devil. But as the sun began to drop beneath the twin lofts, Stellios rose to his feet and began his walk back to his home and his village.

Michaelis Panagis also rose as he felt the sun's warmth fading. He had been kneeling before his family's tomb. His face was cold and still. He allowed himself three prayers. First, he prayed for his son, Christos; then he crossed his heart three times to honour his mother's soul; and three times he honoured his father. He then hesitated. Was it true, what the villagers had said, was it true that she had lain with the Devil? As he rose to his feet, his fingers searched his jacket pocket and he found some crushed camomile flowers there. May God forgive him, but whoever had murdered Lucia had done him a great favour. He was finally released from her enchantment. It must have been mercifully quick. When he had found her by the goat-shed she had been lying on the dirt floor as if asleep. There was a bullet wound at the back of her head. There were some in the village who gossiped that it was he himself who had murdered his wife. He hadn't, but again asking understanding from God, he sprinkled the crushed camomile on Lucia's grave and was grateful.

COLIN HAD BEEN arrested twice in his life. The first time was when he was eleven and he was caught for shoplifting a small transistor radio from a store in High Street, Northcote. The second time was when he was fifteen. Along with two other boys he had taken the train into the city, from there a tram to the beach, and after scabbing enough money from passers-by to pay for two cheap bottles of bourbon, they had ended up drunk, and scaling the high wall of the East St Kilda cemetery. Once inside, they attacked and desecrated a row of Jewish graves. The alcohol fuelled both their recklessness and their hatred. They had not noticed the surveillance camera in an alcove in the high brick wall. The cops arrived and interrupted their rampage. Colin spent that night in the Caulfield lock-up.

—What did it feel like?

—What do you mean?

—How did it feel destroying those headstones?

—It was fun.

—You weren't scared?

—No, I wasn't scared. I was high. I thought I was doing God's bidding. I thought God was on our side.

—So what did it feel like?

Colin had turned away from me. I kissed his freckled shoulderblade.

—It felt like I was fucking flying.

—What exactly did you do?

—I didn't smash any headstones. The others did that.

251

—What did you do?

—I pissed on one of the headstones. He turned around and faced me now.

—There was no English on it. It was all Hebrew script and I remember it shat me off that I couldn't read it. I let my piss flow all over the grooves of the script. I couldn't stop laughing. The others wanted me to shut up but I couldn't stop.

I turned away from Colin and looked up at the ceiling, examined the fine cobwebs suspended from the lightshade. I wanted to look anywhere but in his steel-cold eyes.

—You must have really hated the Jews.

Colin said nothing.

—Maybe you still do?

I felt him stiffen.

—What's with the fucking interrogation?

—Do you?

He got up from the bed and looked around for his overalls. The streetlight fell on him and painted his pale skin a golden hue. He found a cigarette and lit one. I reached out for one as well.

—It's as if I hated the very word. Jew. I hated the very sound of the word, does that make sense?

—No. I could tell he was uncomfortable with the conversation but I also knew I needed it to happen. The swastika tattoo was invisible in the dark of the bedroom but it was as concrete an obstacle between us as a mourned past lover.

—It wasn't as if I knew any Jews, Isaac. It wasn't as if they were the only ones I hated. I was full of hate. I hated everyone.

—And what did you hate?

—If I saw a father playing with his son, I hated them both. If I saw some migrant woman tending her beautiful vegetable garden in the sun, I hated her. I hated the actors on the movie screen, I hated the politicians on the news. I especially hated anyone who spoke of justice and right. I hated those cunts who used to come around pretending to care about Mum and me. I hated social workers. I hated social workers and teachers much more than I hated the Jews.

—So it was indiscriminate? My voice must have sounded hopeful because he looked hard at me. He was guarded, suspicious. But I continued to talk, finding hope in what he had just said. I wanted his hostility and hatred to have been random, purposeless; or at most the inevitable consequence of an adolescent raging against the hypocrisies and inequalities of the adult world. You didn't really hate the Jews, I continued, my words tumbling out, hopeful, expectant. You just hated everyone.

He had turned his face away again.

—I did hate them. I hated them completely, passionately. It was a joy to experience such a hatred. Such a pure, directed hatred. I think it stopped me going mad. I hated everyone and everything but I could focus it all on one thing. That one word, Jew. That's what made me feel alive, when I was pissing on that old Hebrew grave. I hated everyone and everything but they were at the centre of my hate.

—Do you still hate them?

—The cops congratulated me. As they were taking my shoes and socks, before throwing me in the lock-up, one of them knelt and whispered in my ear, Good on ya, son.

—Answer my question.

Colin pointed to his tattoo.

—I am ashamed of this, Zach. I'm forever ashamed of this.

—Do you still hate them? I had raised my voice. I could barely conceal my contempt. He took my hand but I tore it away from his.

—I don't have any of those old hates any more, Isaac. I promise you that. I have my envies. I can't fucking change that.

—What are you saying now? That you envy the Jews?

There was a pause before he answered. When he spoke, there was wonder, surprise in his voice.

—No, no, I don't. I still envy the rich. I envy you wogs because you can be passionate and touch each other without cringing. But I don't envy the Jews. I've exiled myself from the Jews.

—What the hell does that mean?

That moment I did hate him.

—You know how you can see a black man on the street or an Aboriginal woman or an old Vietnamese geezer and the first thing that you are aware of is their difference from you? You understand that?

His tone had become cold and distant, but there was an urgency to it. I reluctantly nodded.

—And then you know how you can talk to the stranger, get pissed with them, ask about the weather, the football, talk about a film, and the difference just disappears? It's no longer about skin colour or language, it's just you and the other person, does that make sense?

—Yes.

—Well, that can never happen between me and a Jew. He tapped his arm. This tattoo, it's not ever going to go away.

I leapt out of the bed then. In the toilet I punched the wall. It was him I was wanting to hurt. You fucking romanticise your past, I wanted to say to him, you fucking use everyone as a scapegoat for the idealisation of your own poverty and pain. You're still proud of that ugly cheap tatt, you're such a working-class hero that you can't tolerate the reality of a suffering more real, more painful, more fucking noble than yours. Fucking gutless white trash scum.

I returned to our bedroom determined to leave him. I loathed him.

He had put the light on, was sitting on the edge of the bed, and he was wearing boxer shorts and a ripped white t-shirt.

He looked up at me with an acute sadness. I would have done anything to make him smile, to give him peace again. I held him tight.

—It doesn't matter, Col. It's all in the fucking past, it doesn't matter. I kissed him, held him as he cried, wiped the tears away. But, of course, it did matter. For something was exchanged between us that night. If with me Colin had found someone prepared to accept his shame, I now shared something of his exile. As I was holding him, loving him, my own dark arm brushed against his pale flesh, and against his tattoo. The ink was on my skin too.

I was sick. A fierce nausea consumed me as soon as the train began the exit through the western suburbs of Prague, but I assumed that it was nothing more than the just consequence of my indulgent time with Sal Mineo. I was fortunate that my train carriage was not full and there was space for me to stretch my legs. But as the train hurtled towards Germany the nausea worsened. I was nearly paralysed by an impossible hunger: I say impossible because nothing could satisfy it. I ordered a greasy tub of chips from the slack-jawed attendant in the catering car but at the first taste of the food I began to retch. I apologised to the scandalised passengers in the carriage, and their multilingual murmurs of disdain followed me as I made my uneven way to the toilet. I emptied the chips, and what little solids were in my stomach, into the soiled bowl.

I took in nothing of the scenery that whizzed past. My only reality was the burning pain that attacked my stomach and my bowels. But if I was insensible to sight and to sound, I was acutely aware of smell in a way I never had been before. The seat stank of acrid human sweat, and of the faint chemical dew that was sprayed across it to disguise the stench. Of my fellow passengers I was aware only of their perfumes and their odours. The stink of my own vomit and the reek of the shit-stained toilet permeated the carriage. I was aware of the musty reek of the marijuana in the joint in my pocket; I couldn't believe the glum Czech guard who had inspected my passport could not smell it, did not immediately haul me away. But he only glanced at my documentation, flicked it back at me and left me alone. I closed my eyes and laid my cheek against the cool train windows. I think I must have prayed for death.

It was then that I sensed her. She had taken the seat on the other side of the aisle from me. Her stink was powerful and I knew at once that she was bleeding. The smell itself seemed to have a coarse corporeal solidity to it; the only word to describe it would be velvet. I could smell the velvet in her cunt. I opened my eyes and looked across. She was a short, dark woman, with two large gold hoops dangling from her ears and wearing a strapless black dress; her slim naked shoulders were richly tanned. She was young, a student. I lifted myself out of my slouch and smiled over at her. She had lit a cigarette and was absentmindedly looking over in my direction. Cautiously, she returned my smile.

The pain in my stomach, the call of my intolerable hunger, had not vanished, but it was as if by inhaling her aroma I was able to steady myself, to right the shudders and quakes of my racked body. My mind was racing. My desire for her was such that I contemplated the most sickening of fantasies. Taking her, assaulting her, devouring her. Instead, I coolly planned a seduction.

I leaned over and introduced myself, and began to ask a series of innocuous questions. She responded, initially diffident, but I was charming, and soon I was sitting across from her. She was a graphic design student from Sao Paolo and she was on her way to Berlin to meet up with friends. She had, she told me, fallen in love with Prague. In her excitement she fumbled and skittered over the English language but I continued to smile and encouraged her reminiscences. No, no, your English is excellent. She listed the various sites and attractions of the city and I too pretended to be enthusiastic about the cathedral in the Old City, about visiting Kafka's sister's house. I too gushed about the beauty of the city's architecture. The culture, it is magnificent, she rhapsodised, and I echoed, yes, yes, it is magnificent. I told her that I was a photography student and I eliminated ten years from my age and hoped that she would be kind enough to not openly doubt me. All the time, the vinegary perfume of her cunt filled my nostrils, touched all of my senses; the aroma expanded and filled my head and my lungs. The conversation took a turn towards music and from there I quickly steered it towards a discussion about drugs. Did she smoke? Yes, occasionally. I patted my shirt pocket. Would she like to share a joint with me? She hesitated and scanned the passengers in the carriage. I indicated the toilet car. She slowly nodded.

It took all my will to control the fierce violence in my stomach. The marijuana seemed to have no effect on me at all, but it must have been potent, for after a few puffs a smoky glaze clouded her eyes. In the small space, I was looking directly into her eyes, her body was touching mine, and I was aware of both her youth and her shyness. I leaned over and kissed her neck. She neither responded nor moved away from me. She remained looking into my eyes. I kissed her neck again and this time I touched her thigh. She shivered, then kissed me on the mouth.

It was agony not to push her against the wall, rip off her dress and devour her. But I controlled myself, kissing her softly, and all the time my fingers were stroking her thighs, feeling underneath the cotton of her panties where her sanitary pad was. I brushed the rough coils of her pubes and she lightly slapped my hand away. I sensed her embarrassment, but even more I sensed the sweet, rich blood that was flowing out of her. It's okay, I whispered, and then kissed her again, I don't mind. My hand moved back up her leg and this time I lowered her panties, rubbed the raised tender curve of her mound and slipped my fingers inside: I was immersed in the slush of her moist meat. I dropped to my knees.

Her body stiffened but I forced her legs apart and pushed my face into her groin. The smell was overpowering. It was as if her cunt was a cellar filled with a heady store of wines and spirits, all emitting wafts of gaseous bouquets that recalled all the possible eruptions of the body. She smelt of farting and diarrhoea, shitting and pissing, burping, bile and vomit. I forced my tongue into this churning compost. Her blood was calling me. My tongue furiously worked the craters of her cunt and I felt the blood, coarse and thick, trickle onto my lips and into my mouth and onto my tongue and down my gut and I forced my lips over her clit and sucked on it till I felt I was drawing her into my very body and the blood kept flowing onto my lips and into my mouth and my guts and I rubbed my face across the hair and skin and meat of her and as I licked at her cunt and arse I opened my mouth wide and bit into her thigh and I did not hear her squeal for all I was aware of was the clean neat puncture and the blood that began to flow from it which fell onto my tongue and into my mouth and my gut, and her blood pumped through me and calmed the agonies in my belly and head and I knew I was alive; and laughing, drawing away from her I was aware that above me a body was heaving and I pushed my face back into her, all my fingers, my tongue, my chin, inside her: a bitter cool spray washed across my face. Her body convulsed, shuddered, trembled once more, and then fell to stillness. She had come.

I look up at her and smile. I feel the wet uncomfortable spread of my own semen fill the pouch of my underwear. She crouches down and wipes my face. I am still laughing loudly and she spreads the fingers of one hand across my mouth to stop me. I wash my face, and kiss her on the mouth as I wipe my cock with toilet paper and piss into the foul bowl. I leave her in the toilet and walk through into the carriage. The whole world is ablaze with golden light. Through the windows I can see details that are miles and miles into the horizon: squat village houses, a flimsy scare-crow in a field of corn. The light that pours into the carriage is warm and it feeds me. I breathe it in, smile at my fellow passengers, then drop into my seat and am promptly fast asleep. I am awoken by the German guard demanding my passport. I look across the aisle but the Brazilian woman has gone.

In Berlin, where I have to change trains, it is raining. I am ravenous and I walk through the station underpass and into the first fast food place I see. Under the comforting yellow, red and orange banners of McDonald's I order three quarterpounders, two large fries and a German version of the ubiquitous sloppy dessert. I wolf it all down with a giant Coke. I burp and I am happy. It is night in Germany and I have five hours' wait for the train to Paris.

I can recall every moment of the last few days. I can map the contours and recall the textures and minute details of every face: the doomed old couple in Venice; the smiling waitress at the Café Beirut; the sailor who fucked me contemptuously in the sleazy hotel in Brindisi; Pano and Milos, Maria and Syd; the woman on the train. If it had been demanded of me, I could have scripted every word and nuance of the conversations between Sal Mineo and myself. I am all too aware that the events that have occurred on this journey through Europe are objectively perplexing and disturbing. But I do not feel distressed. Instead I am experiencing a remarkable clarity. Without a tremor of guilt or betrayal, I am clear about Sal Mineo's dissipation. He is whoring his art. I understand that the sexual encounter with the woman on the train had nothing to do with lust, and everything to do with nourishing myself on her blood and her spirit. None of this shames me. Of course, I can give it no clear sense or meaning. This journey seems to be taking me further away from myself, from all my certainties, from even a sense of my own origins.

I let out another large burp and stare around at the sterile space of the restaurant. A dishevelled old woman, a bundle of her belongings held tight underneath one arm, is sipping slowly on a coffee. When I catch her eye, she quickly looks down. Some atrocious pop song, sung in a little girl's voice, is playing on the radio, and a group of dark-haired, dark-skinned boys with blonde-haired, pale-skinned girlfriends are crammed across a tier of seats. They wear a global street style, all brand names and sportswear. There's a grin on my face. I have clarity and I am in control. I feel contempt. The shitty pop song, the frightened old homeless woman, the faux-Yank niggers with their slutty white-trash girfriends: all of them shit, refuse. Nothing.

I deposit my backpack in the railway station lockers, but take my camera. I am not interested in the faces and bodies that I pass as I walk the grim city. Berlin seems devoid of colour. The only splashes of brilliance that pierce the night are those emanating from the plasma television screens that dominate the shop façades. Otherwise, the streets are bleak and dark. But I have no fear of the night and its shadows. Beggars, cops, drunks, teenagers, sullen men, defiant women, gay men in leather, financiers in suits, blacks, whites, Arabs, Turks, Asians, they all pass by me, smoking, laughing, drinking, scowling, grimacing, throwing me looks of hate or diffidence, or curiosity when they spy the camera in my hands. There are the sounds of the city: cars, bars, music, shouting, laughter, fighting. And there are the smells. The whole city stinks, a putrid sewer of filth and waste. The smells are chemical, of the city. There is nothing organic in any of it. I walk and I wander, a huge smile on my face, aware as I have never been before of my separation from the mass of bodies that throng this metropolis. The whole human species exudes a foul, bitter stench.

It does not cross my mind to take a photograph of any human. Instead I photograph the bricks and steel and mortar and vinyl and plastic and wood and silicon. My flash illuminates a bare automatic teller machine wedged tight between two shopfronts. I capture buildings and streetlights and billboards. I rid Berlin of its people and capture instead the evidence of their passage. I am fascinated by the banal modernity of the city. It is as if history refuses to be trapped in this sterile landscape, as if history never happened. The flashlight falls on the last negligible vestige of the old Wall, and as the light quickly fades, there is a whirr from my camera; my film is exhausted. I buy a kebab at a kiosk and wolf it down. A radio shrieks a Lebanese lament. I lick the juice from my fingers.

I make my way back to the station and I buy a coffee, an English-language copy of *Rolling Stone*, another pack of cigarettes, and I book into an hour session at an all-night internet cafe. I experience no loneliness, no fear. I am not even a tourist in this city, for to consider myself a tourist I would require a home to have begun my journey from. I am above all that. In this heightened state of omnipotence, I don't even miss Colin. I am alone in this world.

But Colin has emailed and I smile to myself on reading his short, restrained message. The cats are well. There is spinach in the garden and the lemon tree is finally producing abundant fruit. I miss you, I love you, he finishes. Colin has an antipathy to the computer. I am touched by his effort. There is an email from Sophie, and she writes about our mother and about my nephew and niece. There's also a message from Clem, who works with me at the video store, and who invites Colin and me to a party the weekend I am to return to Melbourne. I have to scroll through one hundred and seventy-eight pieces of junk to find these three stray missives from family and a friend. There are two hundred and four messages remaining unread when I look up at the cafe clock and realise I have only ten minutes left on my time. I load page after page of electronic text and scan rapidly through the email addresses. Porn, penile extensions, miracle pills, cheap drugs, insurance advice, gambling opportunities. The list confirms the puerility of the human race. I don't mind, I don't mind it at all. I am experiencing pure joy. The machine is slow in loading new pages and I am tempted to log off and ignore any possible messages from friends. Or the promise of someone, some agency, wanting to look at my photographs. That is what I am really searching for.

In acknowledging this desire, the sense of completeness and power that has buoyed me in this city begins to desert me. Not that I am aware of it immediately. As if descending from a drug rush into a pleasant plateau of stillness, I become slowly aware of my physicality, my body in this space. The computer screen is dusty, the chair I am sitting on too hard, the fluorescent lights in the cafe too harsh. I watch the electronic words tumble across the screen as I keep my finger firmly pressed on the computer mouse. An address captures my attention. The postfix is *fr*: I know no one in France. I look across at the subject attachment, and then I take a deep breath. *Are you the son of Vassili Raftis?*

Vassili. Bill. Billy boy. Lucky. The various names my father was known by. It was never Basil. That prim English rendering of my father's name never suited him. Of all his names and nicknames, it was Lucky that stuck and the nickname most suited to the continent he was to make his new home. It was a name my father carried well. He was cheerful, he was easygoing, and despite my mother's half-hearted sporadic attempts to make him responsible, he was always looking for a good time. Lucky, a bastardised abbreviation of the Greek Vassilaki, which means Little Bill, may have an echo in the tender English appellation of Sweet William. He's sweet, your old man, it was said to me of my father. Not cute, not effeminate. Sweet as in alright. As in a good man. My dad was Lucky.

He wasn't Lucky in France. In France he was Guillaume. On the mantelpiece above our gas heater, I have placed an old photograph of my father taken when he was nineteen, and a student in Paris. It is a small black and white photograph. My father is one of a trio of young men, squinting in the sunlight, their arms across each other's shoulders, on one of the bridges that cross the Seine. The three men all have well-groomed, slicked hair, all are wearing identical white shirts and black trousers; they are handsome and smiling. The other men are wearing thin dark ties but my father's shirt is unbuttoned at the neck and a packet of cigarettes is visible in his shirt pocket. My father rarely talked about his two years as a student in France. I know he studied philosophy and politics, and that he still read French literature right up to his death, never wanting to abandon the language. When we were children, Sophie and I would be embarrassed by his eagerness to speak it. We would be on a tram and he would hear French spoken and immediately interrupt and introduce himself to the speaker. Our embarrassment was also laced with a certain resentment that he never introduced the language he loved to his own family. It was a point of separation between himself and his children, and between himself and his wife. French marked another life, another continent, and I believe, another class. You sound like a bloody Kraut, he would answer my stilted attempts to speak high-school French. When he spoke the language I could hear the beautiful measure of it. I was ashamed by my nasal pronunciation. My French is pitiful, but Dad could not help but instil a love for the country in his children, and when I first arrived in Paris as a young man, I unconsciously dressed as my father did in the photograph I had of him. All austere black and white.

Sitting at the terminal, I am now remembering my father without sadness. I am remembering his unshaven face, the short sharp black bristles that as a child I loved running my fingers across. His clear bright eyes that would seem to implode and be masked by a cloud of film every time he took the heroin into his blood. My hands have dropped to my sides, off the mouse, off the keyboard. I do wish the bastard had not died, that he had had the opportunity to meet Colin. I do wish the fucking prick had lived.

—Why did your father come to Australia? Why didn't he just go back to France?

—My *Papou*, my grandfather, insisted he migrate here. He didn't want him to go back to France because he blamed France for my father's politics. Anyway, from what I can understand France was caught up in the Algerian mess they made for themselves and were reluctant to take on any Greek commies. I think *Papou* thought that if Dad was to remain in Europe he'd just be caught up in politics again. He thought Australia would be safer.

—Did he have to leave?

—*Papou* thought so. Dad was already blacklisted, thrown out of university. His family was terrified the next step would be to put him in prison.

Colin finished his coffee. His fingernails were black from the earth and he pulled up his torn pair of trackpants in which he always gardens. His faded indoor-cricket t-shirt was also full of holes. He walked off the porch and began weeding.

—He should have returned to Paris.

His back was to me. I know. Guillaume. Not Lucky.

o O o

I open the email. The message is short and the grammar is awkward. He is an old friend of my father and he realises I probably will not remember him. He wishes me to contact him when I reach Paris and he has forwarded a mobile phone number. He signs off, simply, Gerry. No surname, no address, no further details.

I don't remember Gerry. I certainly don't remember any French mate of my father. I write the phone number down on the back of my return plane ticket, and I am about to reply to the email when I receive a message that my time is up. In an hour I will be on the train to Paris.

Berlin. It is my second time through this city and once more all I have seen of it is the railway station and the cold bleak office buildings of its commercial heart. My euphoria has waned and I am tired.

Fuck the Germans, my father had roared, fuck those treacherous Poles and those swindler Czechs. Fuck them all. If the fall of the Berlin Wall had seemed to inaugurate a moment of universal happiness, it was not so in my father's house. They've got what they've always wanted, those dirty Poles: fascism. Same with all of them—fucking dirty Eastern European scum. He spat at the television screen. May your children die in poverty, he roared at the jubilant Hungarians, may you sell your whore bodies to the Americans, he cursed the East Germans leaping through the shattered concrete of the wall. He took their jubilation about capitalism as a personal betrayal, and every slab torn from the wall he saw as an attack on his very own home, his very own property. My father did not believe in a soul, but his spirit hangs over me as I impatiently await the train to Paris. The German faces I brush past in the underground corridors of the railway station seem mute and distant. I can't relax in Berlin; my father's soul won't let me.

The train comes, I board it, take a seat next to a sleeping man, his backpack his pillow, and squeeze past the knobby knees of a young woman. She smiles at me and I drop into my seat as the train begins its slow chugging journey out of the metropolis. I know I will never return to this city.

—Where you are?

There is still a faint trace of Australia in his voice.

—At the Gare du Nord.

—You know how to make the Metro?

—Yes.

He barks out a destination and I ask him to repeat it.

—I will be there.

—How will I recognise you?

—Do not worry. I will know you. I will see Lucky in you.

The sharp Slavic cheekbones. I share those. I have his thick black hair. I look like my father.

In the end, I did recognise him. We met outside the final suburban Metro stop on the eastern line. Whereas I had descended into the underground from a clean pristine Paris, I ascended into a bare concrete vault, littered with rubbish and cigarette butts. There was garish graffiti on every spare surface, and a homeless woman was peeing on the concrete. I walked past her and she screamed out for money. I ignored her. Outside the station was a huge concrete car park and a long stretch of motorway; beyond that, empty, barren fields. Behind the fields, blocks of grey high-rise apartments stretched for miles across the blighted plain. The sky was dark with threatening clouds.

I heard my name called. He was now an old man, much thicker around the middle, but he was still tall, imposing and bear-like. His hair was chalk-white, but still thick on his head. I was very young when I had last seen him; he had been one of those figures on the periphery of my childhood for a few summers, and then he was gone. I did not know if I had ever registered his going. I know that he and my father had been very good friends because I could only recall my father's happiness at being with him. The memory came back of slipping out of bed one night to see the two of them engaged in a loud boisterous argument, one moment shouting, one momnt with their arms wrapped around each other. But there was little else I could remember of him; he must have slipped out of our lives at a time when I was still too young to realise that there could be anyone of more importance to my parents than their own children. My most vivid memory of him was as one of a group of stocky men, seated in their singlets, in high summer. They were in Tassios' garage, drinking beer. On that occasion it was not clocks they were dismantling but ugly, ostentatious sofas and footstools. They were slicing open their cushioned backs. My sister had climbed up on the milk crate alongside me and we were looking through the dirty louvres into the garage. My father then laughed and held up bags of powder that he had pulled out of the furniture. My sister whispered, too loudly, and the men had looked up. Tassios chased after us, shouting and kicking at our bums. The man who was now holding out his hand to me in Paris had said nothing on seeing our young, curious faces. He had continued doing his work. I don't ever remember him having a name. He was always the Hebrew, that was how the Greeks always referred to him. That's what Dad had called him. The definite article was important. Back then I thought he was the only Hebrew in the entire world.

He took my backpack and waved off my attempts to assist him. We walked to a small Mercedes truck, battered, rust visible on its underside. A colourful mural of fruit and vegetables was painted across one side of the truck.

—Get in, he ordered. The van smelt and I fought off an urge to sneeze. As soon as he started the ignition, George Jones came in midway through a song about heartaches and hangovers in his baritone voice. The volume was loud and it was only when the song finished that the old man lowered the sound and spoke.

—Do you remember me?

Again, a faint echo of Australia.

—Yes, but I don't remember your name.

—Gerry. Then he smiled across at me. Or the Hebrew. He used the Greek word.

I laughed at this.

—Yeah, I remember that.

—How did Lucky die?

I only hesitated a moment. I knew instinctively with this man that I did not have to pretend. I mimed pumping a syringe into my arm. He nodded slowly.

—I always say to Lucky that he is a fool for taking that shit. He spoke slowly, as if it had been a long time since he spoke the language. The words were full of French inflections: the long final diphthong when he said my father's name; the stretching of the obscenity into two syllables, *shee-it*.

—And your mother?

—She's clean. She's been clean since his death.

—Pardon? I'd confused him.

—She doesn't use heroin anymore.

Gerry let out a long sad whistle.

—Your father very wrong for doing that to your mother.

I had nothing to say.

He exited the motorway and almost immediately he pulled up in front of a square squat block of flats. The building was isolated amid the criss-cross grid of motorways. In the distance, rows of tower blocks seemed to fall into the horizon. I grabbed my backpack and followed Gerry up a flight of stairs. He pulled out a bunch of keys and inserted one into a flimsy white door, then he ushered me into the flat.

It was sparsely furnished: a small television, a white electric kettle, a camp stove with two rings, a black vinyl couch, and, incongruously, a junk photographic print of a Bondi Beach sunset on the wall. A door led into a further room with a single mattress on the floor. Gerry indicated the bedding he had ready for me. A small alcove contained the shower and the toilet.

—You can stay, he said. The new tenant is not moving till next week. It is yours till then.

—I'm not intending to stay more than a night or two.

—As you wish. Do you want a coffee?

He went to make the coffee and I took a seat on the couch. The bottom springs had collapsed and I sank into the vinyl. This was not a Paris I knew at all. Outside the window I could see a supermarket in the distance, and there was the constant drone of the motorway traffic. It was a flat-blasted concrete shithole as far as the eye could see, and apart from the French type on the banners for Pepsi and Nike flying across the shopping mall exterior, I could have been in any outer suburban allotment in Melbourne.

Gerry handed me a cup of instant coffee. He had not made one for himself.

—How did you get my email address? The question blurted out sounding much more aggressive than I had intended.

—It was very good luck, Isaac. I ring your mother and she tells me that you are in Europe. I wished to ask of her a favour.

—I didn't know you were in contact with Mum. I was fiddling with my cigarette packet and he asked for one. I lit it for him and he inhaled deeply.

—How is Reveka?

He pronounced my mother's name in the Greek manner.

—She's okay. She's retired so she's a bit bored. But she's good. I'm glad she's finished work. She was getting exhausted.

—Factory work?

—Mostly. In the end she was working as a cleaner. She said that was easier on her.

—Is she still beautiful?

I laughed.

—She's old.

—Of course, he snorted. We are all old. He continued to smoke, sucking on the cigarette. The silence grew awkward between us and I was suddenly nervous. The man was anxious. His sweat was pungent and masculine, and he also smelt of the earth, of soil and dirt. I was reminded of my lover's smell. Gerry's hands were large, knotted and scabbed, and he was wearing a simple cheap cotton shirt and worn white-streaked denim jeans. He noticed me looking at his hands and he stretched them out.

—A worker's hands, eh, Isaac?

I nodded.

—Like your father?

—On and off.

—Yes, and the old man smiled. Lucky never liked too much hard work. I tease him much about that. He always talked of the working class but Lucky was no worker.

I launched into a defence of my father.

—He looked after us. He worked in factories all his life. He was a bloody worker.

—No, disagreed the old man firmly, he was not a worker. He think too much, he argue too much. He always tell the manager to fuck off. Lucky always in trouble with the bosses.

—Did you and my father work together? I lit a cigarette. Gerry didn't answer me. I was remembering the pouches of powder they once pulled from inside the cushion stuffing of a gaudy faux-baroque sofa. I was also reminded of my first love, of Paul Ricco, another man who smelt of the earth, of soil and dirt. I was aware that Gerry was examining me, that he was making up his mind about me. I wanted to impress this strong, severe man. When he finally spoke it was not to answer my question.

—I rang your mother to ask for help. When she tells me that you are in Europe I think I am fortunate, that maybe Lucky's son will be the one who will help me. He was careful with his words, speaking slowly, ensuring that he pronounced the English accurately.

—How long had it been since you'd spoken to Mum?

—I leave Australia in nineteen seventy-two.

—Jesus. That long?

—Yes. A very long time.

—And what's the favour you want to ask of me?

Again he fell silent. The cigarette had burnt out in his hands and he flicked it into my now-empty coffee cup. When he spoke again he did so in a rush of words, a long complicated sentence that he forced out as if he'd rehearsed a speech, as if it was crucial he got the order of the words right.

—I wish to bring a young woman to Australia. I will fix her passport, I will arrange all her papers—you have nothing to worry about, I promise, it will all be on my expense and all I ask is that you look after her, to find her place to live, help find her job. She is good woman, she is brave woman, Australia will be good to her. He stopped. His next words were bitter. Europe is no place for her, Europe not good for her.

—Is she a relative?

—No. I have only my wife, Anika. I have no other family. The Hebrew. The only one in the entire world.

—Who is she, then?

—She is a refugee, like your father. She is very like your father. She too had to escape her home.

—Where's she from?

—From the wars.

—But *where* exactly is she from?

His smile was bitter.

—That does not matter. The important matter is if you will help her.

I looked at the old man's face. I could not summarise his features. His skin was a Mediterranean olive but he was no Mediterranean. He was no Slav. He was no Turk. He was certainly not an Eastern European. Where was he from, I wondered.

—Is she a Jew?

There was a flash of anger on his face, then it was gone.

—No. If she were a Jew she could go to Israel. Or she could stay here. I would not need your assistance. Unfortunately, she is not a Jew.

—I'm not sure what you want of me.

—To help her, to help her come to Australia. That is all. And that you tell no one her secrets.

—Why can't she stay in France?

—It is difficult here. France, Europe, they ask too many questions of her. She is living in hiding now. She will be free in Australia.

Nineteen seventy-two, it was such a long time ago. He was sweating heavily and I noticed his left hand was trembling.

—It's also difficult in Australia now, I reply. Things have changed. It's harder for people to get visas. I don't think I can help you.

—I tell you. I arrange passport, I will prepare the papers.

—If she doesn't have official papers, there's nothing I can do. If they find her they'll send her back, or put her into detention. Do you undertand? It's like a prison. I searched for the words. No, it's like a concentration camp.

He looked at me blankly. I didn't know how to tell him that the country he had dreamt of no longer existed.

—They're just as suspicious as here, I spluttered, it's just as fucked as here, maybe more so.

—I have passport, I will prepare her papers.

He was not listening to me. I was both frightened and

shamed by his request. I had a multitude of reasons why what he was asking of me was impossible. I could tell him that he had forgotten the xenophobia and suspicion of strangers that had long been part of the Australian character. I wanted to rationally explain the difficulties now involved in attaining an Australian visa, an Australian identity. I wanted to tell him about the detention centres for asylum seekers, I wanted to tell him that this woman's life would be no better in Australia than it would be here. Not better, not more safe. Nowhere was safe anymore. I had a multitude of good, rational reasons but I felt shame because I knew the real reason why I would not take this risk. I was scared. I was terrified to take such a risk. I was chickenshit scared. I didn't want to risk my own security for a stranger. I shook my head. No, I will not do it.

—Five thousand euros, he announced coldly, I will give you five thousand euros if you assist me.

The room had gone quiet, the world had gone quiet.

—Five thousand euros, he repeated. They are yours. I can give them to you now.

I could smell his anxiety. I could sense the cost for him in doing this, in asking this of me, the cost of his pleading.

There was a tremor in my stomach. It was only for a second, but I instantly recognised it. It was hunger, it was stirring. The tremor went, but it had not vanished. It was coiled, a sleeping serpent in my belly. It was waiting.

I shook my head again. I did not need the money. The money would help, but I didn't need it. Colin and I both, Colin and I together, we did not need the money. This was freedom. The money was not a temptation. The old man glimpsed the relief on my face. He did not attempt to cajole me further. He rose from the sofa.

—You are free to be here for a week if you wish. I will take no money.

—I only need a place for a night, two nights at most. I

began to stammer out an apology, but he wouldn't allow me to finish.

—Come, he interrupted, I will introduce her to you.

She had the apartment next door. Gerry did not bother to knock, and we startled the woman as we entered. She was wearing a pale blue scarf over her head and her round ashen eyes flitted angrily from me to the old man. Then, bored, she turned back to the television. The layout of the apartment was identical to the other one. Her small kitchen alcove was full of jars. Chickpeas and lentils; the room smelt of spices, cardamom and garlic, cinnamon and rosewater. There were no photographs or pictures on the walls. The woman picked up a remote control, turned off the television and indicated for us to sit on the jumble of pillows forming a half-circle around a low rectangular coffee table. She turned to me.

—Do you speak any French?

—None.

—Fine, she said, then we shall speak English.

I was surprised by the American twang to her accent. She offered us a coffee but Gerry refused and turned to me.

—You will come to my house for dinner tonight. The statement brooked no refusal and I found myself nodding in agreement.

—I will give you directions.

—I will take him, the woman answered for me.

He said something sharply to her in French and she replied even more sharply. He turned once more to me.

—You will meet me at my work. You still have my telephone number?

—Yes.

—Good. And he was gone.

The woman visibly relaxed once the old man had left.

—I will make us a coffee. Do you take it in the Lebanese style?

I still felt shame from my refusal of Gerry's plea. I didn't dare tell her I preferred Turkish coffee. I smiled and said, Yes, that would be lovely.

—Good. My name is Sula.

—Isaac.

On hearing my name she hesitated and looked towards the door, as if searching for the old man.

—You too are Jewish?

—No. I hesitated. Greek Orthodox, I guess, but I'm not religious.

—And you are the one who will offer me safe passage to Australia?

Her grin was sly.

—I don't think I can, I said slowly.

—No, she replied, I did not think you could.

The coffee was far too syrupy and sweet and we sat across from one another on plump red pillows while she fired off a dozen questions about my work, my family, my house, my relationship. When I told her about Colin she did not flinch. If anything, it softened her attitude towards me. She took one of my cigarettes and asked if I would like to see Paris with her.

—I'd love to.

—I will prepare myself.

She returned from the bathroom with make-up on her face. The thick scarlet lipstick and the blush of lavender eye shadow had the effect of making her appear older. She had coated her eyelashes with a thick black gel and her round eyes seemed darker and almost too large for her soft fine face.

—It is easier if I leave the apartment looking like this. I am less conspicuous.

—You don't mind?

—Of course I mind, but it is easier.

She swung around.

—What did the Jew say about my situation?

—That you are a refugee.

—And?

—That's it.

—He did not tell you that I am asked for by the authorities?

—No.

—That he should have told you. She walked past me and back into the bedroom. Please excuse me, she said, I desire to change my clothes.

When she emerged from the bedroom, she was wearing a thin wool white sweater and a black thick skirt that fell below her knees.

—Do I look European? She pulled her silk scarf off her head and wrapped it around her neck. Her thick, dark shoulder-length hair shone black and cobalt in the light.

I looked down at my old jeans, stained with sweat and come, and my navy hooded top with streaks of tobacco ash covering the front.

—I should change.

—You look fine.

—I'm afraid I stink.

—Of course, you have had a long journey. Would you prefer to sleep? I can awake you in the evening.

—No, I answered. I wanted to see the city through her eyes. I can sleep when I get back to Australia.

—Good. She slung a white compact handbag over her shoulder. Then we shall go.

The afternoon I spent with Sula would forever alter the adolescent romantic notions I once had about the city of Paris. When I had first travelled in Europe I'd bunked down in a hostel near St Germain des Pres and though I walked miles across the mythical city, and though I travelled widely through the belly of its Metro, I realised now that I'd seen only a fragment of Paris. Of course, when we travel, when we are tourists, we only see that part of a city which has given itself over to the trade of travel. I knew it back then, that the gloriously pretty city of classical architecture and narrow sloping streets was not the whole story. But I believed it to be a significant part of the story. I was enchanted by the beauty of the French capital. Why couldn't our cities be more like Paris? I moaned when I got home. I detested the wide empty streets and grid-like patterns of Australia's modern metropolises. I couldn't bear the vast tentacle reach of suburbia. But the confident young woman who led me through her Paris that afternoon did not take me anywhere near that safe, contained, delightful city. She showed me a harsh place, a tough, crumbling, decaying, stinking, dirty city. The city beyond the Metro.

We waited at a filthy bus shelter that reeked of vomit and piss. Don't sit, she barked at me as I was about to plonk myself on the seat; I looked down and saw a seeping mash of shit splashed across the bench and dripping through the slats to the concrete beneath. I had to fight back the impulse to retch. When the bus arrived, mine was the only white face among the passengers except for a pale teenage girl, her right ear spiked with an array of hoops and rings, whose head was slumped on the shoulder of her bored African boyfriend. Most of the other passengers were also African, the women in colourfully patterned burkas and shawls, the men in thriftshop sport jackets and polyester trackpants. The passengers who were not African were either Asian or Arab. I had my camera around my neck and I held it close to my chest with one hand while the other hand jabbed my wallet deeper into my jeans pocket. Sula paid my fare and the young Vietnamese driver impatiently handed her two tickets. The bus jolted, lurched and picked up speed until it abruptly stopped for an old French couple. The frail old woman required a walking stick and her husband solicitously assisted her to a seat near the front. With extreme care, with diligent purpose, the old man and the old woman made sure that their eyes were not once in contact with anyone else's on the bus.

When the white French couple had boarded, I automatically felt lighter. I could suddenly merge into one with the rest of the passengers on the bus. The old couple looked at their feet and said nothing to each other. With my tanned skin and dark features I too blended into this mob of faces which was and which was not Europe. Only the camera that hung around my neck gave me away. I fingered the lens. I raised the camera and brought the old couple into focus. In the foreground there was the bright sunshine-yellow burka of an African woman and I could sense her back stiffen at my action. The old couple looked away from me; the old man scowled. A young Arab man, sunglasses on, an unlit cigarette in his mouth, was sitting across from me, but he smiled at my camera. I took his portrait. Sula ignored me. I noticed a torn sticker on the window of the bus. There was the outline of the map of France and within the borders of the map there was a jumble of symbols: the Islamic Crescent, the Star of David, and a caricature of a veiled woman. I could not make out the French. What does that say? I asked Sula.

She sniffed dismissively.

—That is a fascist sticker. It is anti-Semitic.

I pointed to the half-moon crescent.

—And anti-Arab.

—What did I say? There was fury in her voice. Aren't I a Semite as well?

Why anti-Semitism? Colin once mused. Why is that one form of racism the only one given a name? And why that divisive name? Do you think, he continued, that it was all planned, the playing off of the Zionists against the Arabs, the bungled administration and handover of Palestine, all deliberately organised by the European Christian powers to split the Jew and the Arab?

I laughed out loud over my coffee.

—You're exactly like my old man. That's what unites the fascists and the bolshies. A love of conspiracy theories.

—And you're a classic fucking democrat. You don't want to believe that those with wealth and power would deliberately organise and conspire together. And you're the one who went to fucking university.

The Crescent, the Star of David, a veiled woman. I fumbled in my pocket and found my pen. I leaned across Sula and I daubed a crucifix into the French borders. I smiled as I was doing this.

—See, I said gleefully. Now everyone can relax. Now it is truly France, as it has been for centuries.

Sula looked at the graffiti I'd added to the sticker. She said nothing, she stared ahead.

We got off the bus at a square that reminded me more of the Paris I'd encountered on my previous travels. Sula pointed out the beginning of the Metro line; we were in a small valley between two hills: the shopfronts were a jumble of modern steel and concrete, and eighteenth- and nineteenth-century terraces. Many of the shop windows had Arabic as well as Latin lettering advertising their wares, and the square was full of young people: white, brown, black, Arab, African, European and Asian. We took a seat at an outdoor cafe and I watched the youth casually flirt with one another. Destiny's Child was singing 'Independent Woman' in one corner and from across the square Youssou N'dour was challenging with 'Allah'. A huge banner flew from the entrance to the Metro: a thick-necked man with a basketball in his arms was holding up a soft drink. The enticement to drink was in English, not French.

—He looks like a monkey, doesn't he? Sula had lit a

cigarette and was pointing at the poster. I was shocked by her casual racism. The man's dome was shiny and mahogany, his teeth a preposterous white.

—I think he's handsome.

—The Americans have been successful at getting their minorities, their Jews, their Blacks, to become their propagandists, she said suddenly.

The gospel-inspired chanting of Destiny's Child was proclaiming their independence.

—Also the homosexuals. Don't forget us. We love to shop. We're the frontline of capitalism.

She smiled at this. A waiter arrived and she quickly fired off an order.

The sun had come out through the clouds and in the afternoon light I was again struck by her youth. I blurted out a question.

—Is Gerry your lover?

She was confused for a moment, then she laughed so deeply that she ended up spluttering and coughing. Her joy made me laugh. When her convulsions finally stopped, she took a drink of water and wiped the tears from her eyes.

—Gerard is a very kind man, but no, we are not lovers.

—How did you meet?

She hesitated. Her gaze was similar to the one the old man had given me when we were sitting in the apartment. She was taking stock of me, making up her mind. Her next question surprised me.

—In what do you believe?

The question made me flounder. I had no ready answer. I had no God, nor faith in any doctrine. I was not proud of this; I didn't believe that it indicated any intellectual authority or wisdom. If anything, it betrayed a lack of knowledge, a pampered naivety. This woman, so many years younger than me, had made decisions and come to conclusions of which I was yet incapable. I'm still working it out,

I finally answered. Col, I added, I guess I believe in Colin.

—Gerard, she said suddenly, is paid money to bring people into France. Do you understand?

I was shocked.

—A people smuggler?

Her face hardened.

—Yes, she echoed hollowly, a people smuggler.

I touched her hand and she pulled it away from mine.

—I apologise. I didn't mean to insult him.

—He is a good man, the Jew. He saved my son and me.

—Where is your son now?

A weariness crossed her face.

—I have had to orphan my son. She changed the topic immediately. As I said, Gerard was very kind. He offered me the apartment, he ensures I have money for food. We are not lovers. He has asked for nothing in return. She laughed again. It is ridiculous, I cannot imagine he and I together. He is a peasant, that man. You must see that.

—And what about you?

—I was a spoilt pampered child, I was a foolish little girl. And now I am a fugitive in Europe.

It was at that moment that I made a decision that I knew I would only, could only regret. I had no right to make such a decision. Not on my own. Not without discussing it with Colin first. I didn't have the strength or courage for such a decision but I made it anyway.

—Sula, come to Australia. I'll take care of it.

Her laugh was almost hysterical. She leaned back in her chair, her hands across her belly, and her chuckles rang through the square. People turned to look at us. She took my hand.

—Isaac, no, no, she finally chortled, I have no wish to come to Australia. It is a fantasy of Gerard's. It is he that wishes to return. As I said, he is a peasant. When he talks of your country he talks of land and gardens, of space and wild forest.

Her grip on my hand tightened. I have met very few Australians, Isaac, but I have always been struck by their innocence. They remind me of a character from Henry James, they have an innocence that the Americans have now lost. It's very seductive but I think that if I was to live in Australia I would learn to hate that innocence. I think it would drive me mad. No, thank you, but I will remain in Europe.

I was relieved, I was fucking relieved. She let go of my hand, and from that moment our conversation lightened. She paid for our coffee and again refused any money. We did not touch on the subject of her life: we did not talk about her child, her exile, her crime. Instead, we wandered through the maze of shops, and we tasted baklava and she told me a little about contemporary French politics. As the afternoon light faded she walked me to the Metro and gave me simple directions to Gerry's shop: ascend the escalators, turn left and then turn left again into the first alley. I would recognise his truck.

—He always parks his van outside the factory, she told me. She kissed me on both my cheeks.

—Let me give you my address, I said, I will give you my email.

She shook her head. No, it is not safe.

I walked through the Metro station. A stiff elderly Indian man, dressed in a blue uniform, a gun in a holster at his side, waved me through the metal security detectors. I was entering the proper Paris.

It was not a factory, but a warehouse, and the old Mercedes truck was indeed parked outside. I knocked on a stained aluminium door but no one answered. I tried the knob and it opened. The cavernous space was packed with crates of vegetable and farm produce piled up to the rafters. Men were busy stacking the crates, or sifting through them, or smoking cigarettes and talking to each other. They ignored me until I walked up to a stout Arab youth and in appalling French asked for Gerard. He indicated an office at the far end of the warehouse. A forklift made a loud din, as did the radio which was playing a wailing song by Fairuz. Gerry was at his desk. I knocked at the window and his face beamed up at me. Come in, he indicated.

His desk was a plain laminex top on four wobbly limbs. The computer on it was old and dusty, and the tabletop was littered with paper and accounts. The flimsy alabaster walls were covered with calendars and pornographic pin-ups of large-breasted women. There were two posters pinned to the back wall. One was an Air Israel poster of Jerusalem. The Dome of the Rock glistened gold. The other poster was of the island of Santorini. The white sun-blasted houses of the island looked over an impossibly sapphire Mediterranean sea. A group of upturned green plastic chairs sat under the posters, and Gerry rose, took one and offered it to me.

—What did you think of Sula?

—I like her a lot.

—But you will not help her?

His tone was teasing and I was not offended.

—She doesn't want my help.

I had placed my camera on his desk and he picked it up and shoved it at me.

—You will take my picture. You will take my picture to show your mother. You will show her Gerry in Paris, show her all I have.

As soon as the camera was in my hands I felt a tremor in my stomach. This time I could not make it disappear; it rose and fell and created a wave of tickles in my belly. I was about to take a photograph but Gerry stopped me. A close-up, he ordered, pointing back at the pornography on the wall. None of the bad pictures, I do not want Reveka to see any of the dirty pictures.

His tough, hard face filled the frame. I took my shot.

He pulled me out of my chair, kicked open the office door and spread his arms to the warehouse.

—Take pictures. Take plenty of pictures. Show your mother my life in this world.

I knew that the first few photographs I'd taken would be terrible. I was clicking the shutter automatically, not thinking about the frame, not thinking about the light. But after the first few shots I began to take pleasure in what I was doing. I asked Gerry to open wide the roller-door at the end of the warehouse and the dying afternoon light flooded the space. He introduced me to the men who worked for him and they all seemed to be called Mohammed or Ibrahim or Hussein. At first they eyed the camera nervously, suspiciously, but when Gerry explained to them that I was an old friend's son from Australia, they relaxed and soon they were laughing and mucking about for the camera. The rich fetid stench of the vegetables filled my nostrils, seeped right into my blood and lungs, and again I was conscious of my stomach twitching. But the act of adjusting the camera lens, the act of focusing on an image, seemed to alleviate my anxiety. I took shots of the men in groups of twos and threes, with wide grins and their arms around each other. I posed a trio of young men, instinctively asking them to arrange themselves in the pose of the old French photograph of my father. But before too long, the men were themselves dictating the kind of photographs they wanted me to take. A skinny African youth lay in a crate of shiny purple aubergines, his white teeth shining like pearls amid the dark tones. Another man, a burly Egyptian youth—another Mohammed, another Hussein—hung precariously from the forklift. All the time the men asked me questions about home. Their English was largely negligible, but adequate for the answers they so obviously wished to hear. Yes, our houses are large and many of them have gardens. Yes,

Australia is very big. Yes, there is much money in Australia. And all the time, Gerry supplied a proud running commentary, slipping from French into English and into Arabic. You are unlucky bastards, he jeered, to come to Europe and not to Australia. Australia is good. Australia is the best country but Australia doesn't want you. He mimed the slitting of his own throat. No niggers, no Arab monkeys for Australia.

One moment I was the centre of the action, the next the men suddenly drifted away. While I had been taking my photographs, the radio was playing agreeable Oriental rhythms. But a new voice rose across the warehouse, the call to prayer from the radio. A mullah chanted from the Qu'ran and a section of the men silently returned to their work. But a few of them walked to the back of the warehouse and entered the toilets. They emerged shoeless and unrolled mats, knelt and faced Mecca. They began their prayers. Gerry touched my shoulder and pointed to the men working.

—You can tell the communists, he whispered. They're the ones not praying. Come, he continued. Come to my house; come meet Anika.

The drive seemed to skirt the edges of the city. Paris, with its mythical spires and labyrinthine streets, was always in the distance. Untouchable, unapproachable. We were driving northwards and very quickly the endless rows of apartment blocks fell away from view, and we were driving through miles of endless suburban estates. Country music was on the stereo and my stomach was performing its somersaults; the smell of the decaying fruit and vegetables sickened me. I forced myself to listen to the music, to try to make out the words, Loretta Lynn singing that she was a coalminer's daughter, Merle Haggard declaring he would never love again. I battled with all my will to conquer the convulsions of my body. I was sweating, I could taste my foul, anxious perspiration. Gerry turned into a cul-de-sac, a circle of red-brick terraces, small patches of manicured lawn. He pressed the button of a remote control and a roller-door began its whirring. We drove into a garage.

—My house, he announced. Johnny Cash died in mid-song, eighteen minutes to go.

Gerry touched my arm as I was about to jump from the truck.

—My wife is very different from me.

If the old man was at ease and cheerful in his warehouse, he seemed uncomfortable in the compact bourgeois elegance of his modern home. Anika, his wife, was dozing on a settee when we arrived. Gerry shook her awake. She saw me standing behind him and drew back in alarm. Before she could speak, Gerry placed a finger on her lips.

—This is Isaac, he introduced me. He is Lucky and Reveka's son. He is visiting us, all the way from Australia.

Anika was indeed different from Gerry. She was strikingly thin, with a long neck, and her short grey hair was cut into a bob that suited both her face and her age. She was wearing a simple black dress with a burgundy scarf wrapped across her shoulders. I could tell that she had been very beautiful in her youth; despite the deep wrinkles gathered at the edge of her mouth and spreading out from beneath the slight slanting curves of her eyes, she was still a formidably attractive woman. The old man at once seemed coarser, almost brutal, next to her. Her alarm had disappeared and her manner was now reserved and formal. She offered me her hand and then kissed me on both cheeks.

—You will shower.

It was an order for her husband and she spoke in English. While the old man washed, she showed me through the house. It was simply furnished but every item spoke of her good taste. I was immediately drawn to a handsome polished cedar bureau in the lounge room. Elegantly framed photographs sat on top of it. They were all from the past, all black and white except for one colour portrait of a younger Anika sitting confidently on the arm of a sofa. She was smiling at the camera and behind her the white lace curtains revealed the rooftops of Paris. The copper-orange tiles shone brightly in the summer light. Her classical beauty was intimidating, as if it belonged to a different firmament from the one that shrouded the contemporary world. I must have paused in front of the portrait for a long time because she suddenly laughed.

—I was very young then. That was the apartment I lived in when I first arrived in Paris.

I examined the other photographs. There was not one of her and Gerry together, nothing of their courtship, their marriage, nothing of their time in Australia. A long rectangular frame across the middle of the bureau contained three square sepia photographs of a family dressed in their winter finery: the matron in a tilted black-plumed hat, a fur coat buttoned to her neck; the patriarch fat and beaming, his suit well-cut, his moustache thin and waxed; the two daughters, one of whom I immediately recognised as Anika, dressed in identical fur stoles and dark berets. They were both laughing.

—This is my family, in Amsterdam, before the war.

—Is your family still in Holland?

—They were all killed in the war, she answered coldly as she moved me on. I was the only one to survive.

The kitchen smelt of spices and roasting meats. From the window, in the evening light, I looked out into the small patch of garden. The interiors did not feel like the old man's house but it was clearly his garden. Thick, long zucchinis grew amidst ropy vines. I could make out three tomato plants and a small row of pots along the back wall with herbs growing in them. It was a tiny space, not more than a couple of metres long and a metre wide and now I could understand the old man's nostalgia for his Australian home. Sula was right. This was a peasant's garden and it was calling for more space, more soil, more earth.

Anika had opened the oven door and I caught a whiff of burning meat. My stomach turned and I steadied myself on a bench. I was dreading the thought of dinner.

When Gerry returned from his shower, he had replaced his old work shirt with a frayed denim shirt, and wore a pair of old tracksuit pants.

Anika said something sharply to him in French.

—This is my house, he replied in English, and I will wear what I want.

He turned to me.

—What would you have to drink? Wine? Vodka?

—Have you got whisky?

—Just like Lucky, he laughed. Anikaki, does he not remind you of Lucky?

—I barely remember Vassili. There was a chilly anger in her voice, and realising it, the face she turned to me had softened and she smiled warmly for the first time.

—It was all a long time ago, darling, since I last saw your parents. She took a long look at me.

—Yes, I see Vassili in him, but I also see Rebecca. Yes, he is Rebecca's child.

My nausea escalated as Anika brought the meal to the table. She apologised for not being prepared for my arrival but there was no need. The meat she had been roasting was a succulent cut of beef, and she had reheated a tray of grilled aubergines and peppers. I forced down what I could, making my tongue work its way around each morsel, clamping my teeth into the food, driving it down my gullet, down to my protesting belly. Gerry, I noticed, ate nothing. He sipped at his whisky and watched me eat; I thought I saw a playful, teasing grin on his face. Anika only picked at her food. She explained that she had friends arriving for lunch the next day and it was for this reason she had cooked a roast.

—How about your husband, the old man interrupted her, didn't you cook it for me?

Anika ignored him and instead asked me questions about my life in Australia. She was obviously saddened to hear of my father's death.

—I admired your father, he was an intelligent and learned man.

—Unlike your boor of a husband, no?

Gerry slapped my shoulder to show he was joking, then continued.

—I always believed Lucky and Anika should have left together for Europe. They belonged here. I would have been happy to stay in Australia with your mother.

—You are talking nonsense, his wife retorted. Lucky adored Rebecca. She was not like the other migrants. She was raised in the city.

Anika turned to me.

—She is a very smart woman, your mother. Of course, she was not educated like your father was, but she could laugh at him. She has great strength. And she was truly beautiful.

The talk of their shared past with my parents had momentarily stilled the burning inside me. I wanted to hear more.

—How did you all meet?

—My husband shared a house with your father before we were married, before any of us were married. They were comrades together. There was a biting resentful tone to her answer but she smiled as she continued her recollections.

—The men would take Rebecca and me to communist dances. They were truly insipid affairs.

—We make fun together, Gerry objected.

—The precious moments of dancing and singing were not worth the boredom of those harangues we had to listen to.

—No, of course not, you always prefer the rubbish and lies of the rabbis.

—I never forced you to Temple.

—You did not? Your memory is mistaken, my sweet Anika.

There was ice in the room. The torments in my belly had returned. I was sweating. In order to fill the suffocating silence I stammered out a question.

—Are you religious, Gerry?

He did not look at me as he answered. His fierce gaze was firmly set on his wife.

—I was born a Jew. It means nothing. It means shit. There is no God.

I could see that Anika's hands were shaking. It was as though I were no longer at the table, that they had forgotten I was ever there.

She spoke in French and he let out a wild, derisive laugh.

—See, Isaac, she is very religious, she is very righteous. She condemns me to Hell.

—That is not what I said. I said that you are in Hell.

I stared back down at my plate and attempted to force a limp garlic- and tomato-coated slice of eggplant down my throat. It felt like elastic. I realised that this man and this woman detested one another.

—What do you do for work, Isaac?

Her voice was again pleasant.

—I am a photographer.

She nodded but she was clearly uninterested.

—And you, I replied, desperate that the table would not once more descend to bleak silence. Do you work with Gerry?

She seemed shocked. Her eyes widened, she flashed an

angry gaze at her husband, and then quickly she composed herself. She chewed, swallowed and then smiled.

—Did my husband take you to our business?

—Yes, this afternoon.

—I have not been there for a long time. Not since the fire.

This surprised me. Gerry had not mentioned it, and I had not seen any evidence of fire in the old structure, or spied any trace of renovations or remodelling.

—It was years ago, she continued, a tragedy. Many men died in the flames. My husband takes care of the business on his own now. I want nothing to do with it.

—It has made you rich.

She glared at Gerry.

—It has made me comfortable. It was not worth the lives that were lost. Her voice was sad.

Gerry reached across the table and tapped my hand.

—May I have cigarette?

—Let the boy finish eating.

—No, I exclaimed eagerly, glad for the opportunity to interrupt the torture of the meal, I'll have one as well.

—Come outside, commanded the old man. We'll smoke in my garden.

—Look at this one, Gerry said proudly, tapping a long, stout zucchini. Look how big I grow them. Did Lucky grow zucchinis this big?

—It was Mum who loved to garden. Lucky didn't garden at all.

—Yes, Lucky was a man of the city. Like my wife.

It was a mild night but I was sweating profusely. I needed another drink to settle the tremors, to steady myself. The old man was oblivious to my fever.

—If I had met Anika here in Europe, we never marry, we never even talk. You know the San Remo Ballroom, in Carlton?

—Yes. The talk of home, the naming of a familiar suburb lurched me into a strong wave of homesickness. I wanted to walk down Nicholson Street, to buy a roll from the Italian deli, to hunt for old music in the second-hand music shop. I wanted to be with Colin.

—It was a big dance, he continued, the Greeks, the Italians, the Jews, we always had big dances in the ballroom. I saw her dance. I fell in love. Like that.

He let out a low moan, cursing in a language I didn't know. It wasn't French or European, it wasn't Yiddish. It didn't sound European.

—She bewitched me with her dancing. She had no one. She needed a strong man. She wanted me then. But if I had met her in Amsterdam, she would not look at me. She would not even spit at me. She would be ashamed to be seen with me.

Such hatred, I could hear such hatred in his voice, and so much passion.

—In Australia, all she speak of is Europe. Europe destroy her family but she never stop talking about it. I'm European, I'm European, she say all the time, I no belong here.

—But you're European too. Didn't you feel that way? My mother does, I wanted to add, my father did all his life. It was the migrant's song.

He laughed at my question.

—Me, I'm a Turk. He waved towards the house. That is what she call me.

—Where are you from? I was searching his broad face, looking for clues, but I couldn't decipher the mystery of his skin and features. He certainly wasn't Turkish; he wasn't European; but he wasn't from the East either.

He pronounced a long complicated word.

—What's that?

—It is a Bulgarian word. It means the place where the wolves fuck.

—So you're Bulgarian?

—Who knows? This time his laugh was bitter. Where I come from doesn't exist now. He snapped his fingers. Poof, it has disappeared. The wolves no fuck anymore.

He tossed the cigarette butt into his garden.

—It has been erased. God has erased its name.

The table was cleared and coffee was brewing in the kitchen. Anika was on the phone and hastily put it down when we returned.

—Who were you phoning? Gerry's tone was suspicious.

—I was speaking to Helene. I have cancelled tomorrow's lunch. I am not feeling well.

She made us coffee and as I drank it the acrid liquid raced through my body. My eyes were weeping and I had to wipe them with a handkerchief. We were back at the dining table and the smell of the food was still overpowering and obscene to me, though the old man and woman seemed oblivious to my agonies.

I wanted to hear more about my parents' lives before I was born.

—How did you and my father meet?

—We are workers together at a factory in Abbotsford. We become friends.

—Did you work together for long?

—Not there. Gerry laughed out loud. Your father never work at one place for too long. But we become very good friends. Then, as my wife say, we move into a house together. In Park Street, Fitzroy. We have many parties there.

Here I was, in Paris, and the familiar street names of my childhood were being spoken. Anika remained silent. She seemed nervous. I felt like an intruder in her home. I knew she didn't want me there.

—Your father taught me to read.

Anika glanced up at this statement. It was as if everything her husband said was aimed at provoking her.

—You must understand, he continued, I was illiterate. A dumb animal.

He grinned at his wife across the table.

—I am just a dumb, ignorant peasant Jew. Once upon a time, there were so many of us.

—How did he teach you to read?

Gerry turned back to me.

—He teach me as if I am a child. He teach me letters and words. Like a proud schoolchild, the old man carefully, slowly, recited the English alphabet.

I laughed out loud.

—Excellent.

Anika laughed as well, but her laughter was bitter and poisonous.

—He still cannot read.

—I have no need. I use my hands.

Gerry spread out his hands on the table. They were enormous, with long calloused fingers. He pointed them at his wife.

—Anika hates my hands. They are a real Jew's hands. Hands of the earth, hands made for the land. These are not European hands. These are not a poofter rabbi's hands. These are hands for work and suffering.

I was finding it hard to breathe. It was as if the hatred in the room was pouring into me, merging with the toxic bile in my stomach and threatening to rip through me, to crush me.

—They are murderer's hands.

—Yes, he agreed, nodding in agreement at his wife's words. But his smile was arrogant. They are murderer's hands. They know pain and suffering.

—As do I. Her voice was powerful. Her answer was imperious, her tone commanding. Do not dare say I do not know suffering.

I thought of the photographs on the cedar bureau. The

laugh of a young girl that had been forever stilled, forever banished.

And Colin was there beside me. I could sense him. He too smelt of the earth. He was there, shirtless, the blue tattoo on his skin gleaming fresh and sharp.

I staggered to my feet. Dizzy, I grabbed the back of my chair.

—Where is the bathroom, please?

My voice cracked. Hands led me to a corridor, I stumbled into a small room and fell to my knees next to the toilet. I raised the lid and vomited a spray of such volume that the basin was covered in streaks of black and red and purple slime. I retched again and again, into the basin, onto the floor. A light was switched on and Anika was beside me, stroking my brow. I was enveloped in her arms. I closed my eyes. For a moment there was peace.

In the darkness, she spoke to me. You are hungry, she said. You must eat. You must feed. Do you know who I am? she asked. I am exiled, as you are, from Paradise. You are mine, she whispered, but there was no French lilt to her accent – instead the voice was childish, a boy's speech, he talked to me in my mother's tongue and the arms holding me then were thin and icy-cold. I felt a kiss on my neck, a hand plunging down into my crotch, it was freezing and with a start the blackness disappeared.

I was lying on the floor, my head on Anika's lap. She was stroking my hair, gently, soothing me. I was spasming.

—You fainted. She said it simply, calmly.

—I'm sorry.

—Do not apologise. It is a warm night, the food was very rich and you have been travelling. You are tired. Do not trouble yourself with the madness between my husband and myself. We are cursed to be together.

Yes, I am cursed as well. I lifted my head off her lap and slowly rose to my feet. She was still sitting on the floor, not looking at me. Slumped against the cold white tiles she looked old, frail and wasted. She looked exhausted. I wiped the saliva from my lips and, offering her my hand, I lifted her to her feet.

As she switched off the light, we heard the doorbell ring.

A policeman was at the door, speaking to Gerry. Anika offered me a whisky and I drank it gladly. The smooth, biting liquid stilled my stomach. When Gerry returned he resumed his seat and poured a large splash of whisky into his glass. He was looking hard at his wife. Anika had a small, discreet smile on her face.

Without looking at me, he tapped the ashtray, indicating he wanted another cigarette.

At this, Anika broke her silence and spoke in French. I understood, from the fierceness of her smile, by the cool jubilation in her tone, that she had uttered an obscenity.

The old man lit his cigarette, and he too finally spoke.

—I intend to live a long time. With you, a long time with you. I will never leave you.

His next words shocked me.

—Sula has been arrested.

—Why?

—She is an illegal.

I realised that though he spoke the words to me, his eyes had not left his wife's face. I was merely a witness. Anika's next words indicated that she too demanded this role from me.

—Those apartments belong to me, they are in my name. How dare you risk everything I have created?

—Yes. Gerry seemed serene, at peace. He was still taking slow sips from his whisky.

—I apologise for placing you at risk, Anikaki. Send them

all back, send them all to Hell. What the fuck do I care?

—Do the police wish anything else from us?

The look the man gave his wife was pure sorrow.

—No, we've done all we can to help them.

We sat in silence at the table. All I could think of was my burning bowels, the howling inside my body. I inhaled the aroma of the whisky in order to stay the rising bile.

—Would you like another?

I nodded and Gerry rose and filled my glass. He then approached his wife and stood over her. He touched her hair, lifted her chin.

—Tell me, he whispered, that it was not you who betrayed her.

Anika just smiled.

He broke her nose. There was a crunch, she gasped, cried out, and the blood splattered across the table. I could almost taste it, sinewy, thick, nourishing. I looked on as his fist hammered into her flesh, as the proud visage was transformed into an obscene pulp but all I was aware of was the blood. Finally, exhausted, the old man fell to his knees, his body convulsing, his moans bestial. The woman was splayed back in the chair, her body inert, blood slicking her face and neck.

I get up from my chair and move towards the stench. I take the limp body into my arms and hug her, pressing my mouth to her face. I lick her nose, her lips, her mouth, her neck, drinking in the vital carnal liquid; it is as if I can still trace the beat of her heart in the thick drops that course down my throat and into me. I lick her face clean. I falter. My hunger urges me to further depravity. I want more of her: she is such a slight figure in my arms, this old body, this frail spent body. I could snap her in two, I could devour all of her. But I drop the body back onto the chair and her eyes flicker.

The old man pulls me off her.

—Enough.

I watch him clean her; as he is ministering to her his voice is pained and apologetic. He speaks to her in a tongue that I do not understand; she makes no reply to him. She watches him warily as he cleans her face, washes her hair, puts her to bed. My hunger satisfied, I am filled with an impatience to leave the house and to be in the night. The whole world seems aflame with an electric light that warms me. The world is tame and not frightening. I belong completely to it. I want the old man to finish with his wife and to drive me into the city. I have no intention of spending the night in the cramped small apartment he has put me in.

—Are you finished? I blurt out. I have to get going.

He doesn't answer me but he kisses his wife goodbye, shuts the bedroom light, and I follow him to the garage. As soon as the truck reverses out into the clear night I am intoxicated by the smells and tastes of the earth. And of the city. I can smell chemicals and electricity, the stink of a million bodies. For the first time in my life I understand what it is to know that I am indeed the centre of the world. None of these bodies matter. The old man driving does not matter. Nothing matters except myself. Clarity.

—Can you drive me into the city?

—Your things?

—We'll pick them up, I confidently give my order. Was it only minutes ago that I was awed by this man, thought him strong? I look across at him. He's aged, he's near death. There is nothing to fear. We have entered a motorway and we are carving through a dark, grey tunnel illuminated by the glare of yellow streetlights.

—She does not understand what she did.

—Who?

—Anika. She was scared.

This makes me laugh and he flinches. I am sure that his

wife understood exactly what she was doing when she informed the police that a fugitive was living in one of their apartments. I did not believe it was fear that led her to such a decision. Or even something as commonplace as jealousy. It was revenge.

—My wife trusts no one and because of that she fears everyone. She was a girl when everything was taken from her. This destroyed something important in her soul. This was what was done to all of us.

I let him talk. He is convincing himself. He tells me the story of Anika's family, the grim tragedy of annihilation. But I cannot be moved by these lamentations. There is poetry after Auschwitz: I can taste a juicy drop of Anika's blood on the bottom of my upper lip. I lick it, feel it trickle down my throat and I breathe out deeply, flooding my nostrils and lungs with blood. There is poetry and life and adventure and pleasure and movement; always movement, it doesn't stop. Life doesn't stop, suffering does not end. Anika's suffering, Gerry's suffering, Sula's suffering which is about to begin again. I am in no mood for stories. Those stories have been told and will be told again. There is nothing to apologise for, nothing to regret, no sins or evil to make recompense for. I have nothing to be sorry for. At this wonderful moment I am alert to the glory of life, of rich satisfying bloody life. I cannot be saddened, I cannot be humbled. Every cell of my body is singing sweet electric life. I will never apologise again for life. It is worth killing for this life, it is worth any horror to be in this life. I taste the blood and I have clarity. Any brutality is worth this life. Be brutal, be cruel, be alive. It is as if the old man has read my thoughts.

—You know nothing of suffering. Only God knows what she has suffered.

Who, I want to ask? His wife? Sula? I am in no mood to be affected by his scolding. I am in no mood for God. I look out into the night and there are shapes and forms fleeing across the barren landscape. God created this suffering, I want to say to him. If there is a God. I let out a deep breath and my body is light. I am one with the vehicle I am in, flying through the air and through space. I am free of this ancient, spent God.

—Are you truly a murderer?

—I killed a man who was sheltering me. I was a youth. He was sheltering me and I killed him. I did not trust him to not betray me. I was a Jew and a partisan.

—There must be some reason you killed him. What made you think he would betray you?

Gerry's eyes are focused on the road.

—Why? I am insistent. I have to know. I am aware of the great blasphemies I have just uttered to myself. I am on a precipice and I see this. I am not scared. I am not in despair. I am challenging God, I am gambling with eternity.

—Why?

—Your father knows. I told your father.

—My father is dead. Tell me.

Gerry slides the truck off the road and it screeches to a halt. The noxious reek of the burnt rubber surrounds us. There is a young policeman standing guard at Sula's door, and he leans over the bannister to look at us. Gerry switches off the lights.

—He find me with his wife. He find me with my Jew cock in his wife's cunt. He screams that I am a filthy Hebrew and I have betrayed him. He says he will kill me. I kill him first. He gestures with his finger across his throat. I slit him like an animal and I cut his whore wife. I kill them both. Only Lucky and you know this.

I am laughing ferociously. I am crying tears of joy. I have won my bet. The old man starts laughing as well.

—You are like Lucky. The old bastard laugh too. He laugh and laugh when I tell him.

—You have nothing to be sorry for.

The old man eyes me suspiciously. I haven't stopped laughing.

—There are no apologies to be made, do you understand? I feel like singing, dancing, drinking, whoring, laughing forever. We have nothing to be sorry about.

I slip my camera into my backpack and Gerry drives me into Paris. Very soon the hideous suburban landscape is replaced by the bloated opulence of the inner city. I care nothing for the prim and pretty façades and ornaments of architecture; what excites me is the darkness and the shadows. Sweat, drugs, excrement and the caustic traces of the city.

Gerry drops me off at the Gare du Nord.

—When you return to Australia, you will go to your father's grave and you will whisper a farewell from the Hebrew. You will do that. It is an order. We never farewelled one another.

—Yes, I agree. Of course I can do that. My father will not hear but I will do that. What's your real name? I suddenly ask. It can't be fucking Gerry.

At this, it is his turn to let out a wild cryptic laugh.

—It does not exist anymore. It has disappeared with the land in which the wolves fuck. Let my name be erased.

With that last instruction, he starts the ignition, the truck rumbles and he turns on the car stereo. Waylon Jennings is singing 'The Bottle Let Me Down', and the Hebrew vanishes into the night.

I take my photographs of Paris. I take a photograph of a boarded-up old butcher shop, of two African drag queens outside a bar, of a girl selling illegal cds to customers at an open-air cafe. The intense euphoria I experienced in the old Hebrew's truck is waning but I am still happy and fearless as I trudge the streets. I take a photograph of two Arab men smoking cigarettes in a Halal pizza shop. There is no God but

Allah and his Prophet is Mohammed. I shoot the luminous spires of Notre Dame. Jesus Christ was the Son of God crucified and Resurrected on the third day in order to redeem us from sin. I capture the Hebrew lettering on the windows of a bakery in an alley off the Bastille. There is one God and the Jews are his Chosen People. The savage mythologies of ignorant, obsolete tribes. I am not tired, I am still elated. I am of this world, only in and of this world. Revelation. Every photograph I take is an act of defiance against God.

I will sleep on the train to Amsterdam and I will awaken refreshed and enter the city and take a room in a small hotel in the red-light district. I will wander the streets and cross the bridges over its canals and all the while I will glory in my omnipotence. The fire in my blood is still roaring and it is as if I can view this city and its inhabitants with a clear-sightedness that I did not have as a younger man. I will no longer be saddened by the rote masturbations of the whores parading their grotesque bodies in the clear glass windows of the brothels. I will look on at a young African woman, her cunt shaved, cupping her mammoth breasts in her hands, and it will make me laugh. She will be there for my pleasure. I will walk among schizophrenic homeless men and women and their snarls for money will appal me and I will understand the urge to wipe this wretched scum from the earth. I will enter a porn cinema and have sex with three men, a German, an Italian and a Korean: I wish to have my fill of bodies, to consume and devour. I will be the first to come and as I spray my scent on the face of the pale-skinned German, he will reach out for my hand and I will slap it away. I will zip my jeans, I will slap his hand away, I will extinguish them all from memory. I will then call Colin and tell him that I will be home within a week. I will feel no guilt, I will experience no shame. He will tell me he loves me.

I will pass by the house of Anne Frank and will not have the patience to wait in line to visit the apartment in which a young woman once sought refuge. I will smoke handfuls of dope and I will pay for sex with a young man who looks younger than the age he is advertised and who will tell me in faltering English that he is from a land that was not yet born when I last visited this city. He has a tattoo of the Nazi Iron Cross on his belly and he has a tattoo of the warm proud face of Stalin on his back. As I fuck him, I make myself hard by wondering how long it would take me to squeeze the life out of him, to tighten my grip around his puny adolescent neck. Before entering the brothel, I will have given my rolls of film over to a young woman at a photo-shop who will return them to me with contemptuous silence. I will laugh in her face. But when I will take them back to my tiny room and lay the photographs on the bed, I will stare hard at the damaged, bent, misshapen bodies that return my gaze. The young men in Gerry's warehouse are not laughing and joking. Their faces are contorted into death masks of sullen despair, of unbearable anguish and of never-ending grief. Their bodies are charred, blackened as if from fire and plague. Some of them have their faces turned from the camera, their bodies are limp, entwined, slumped. They are carcasses, they are meat. The warehouse is an abattoir. Those morose faces turned towards the lens are countenances pleading for a great silence: they are doomed. And the old Hebrew's face is not proud, it is not welcoming my mother's gaze into his European world. There is no expression on his face, it can't be read. He is Charos. For a long time I will hold up a photograph of Sula's face. It will not convey the smile she beamed at me in the suburban Parisian square but instead her eyes reproach me with despair and terror. I will feel a pain in my gut then, I will feel shame. I will hear the old Hebrew's laughter then and I will take my camera back out into the Dutch streets and I will continue to shoot photograph after photograph because it is all I know to do. I will walk among strangers and take my photographs, feeling no connection with anyone: whores and junkies and pickpockets and thieves; bored jewelled women and elegantly suited men; white faces black faces brown faces yellow faces orange faces pink faces. I will speak to none of them. I am not ill, I still have clarity. Every photograph is an apology, every photograph I take is an act of contrition before a mocking malignant God. With every shot His laughter rings out. I am nothing in this world.

IN THE GARDEN OF CLOUDS

IT WAS A cold place. Reveka shivered as she crawled under the long wooden beam and squeezed herself through the broken slats that lay across the cellar. She landed on her hands, and the squish of the damp mud floor made her shudder. But she did not hesitate. She fell into the mud, scrambled to her feet, and with her head bowed under the cellar's low roof, she listened carefully for noise from the world up above. She could hear shouting but from such a muffled distance that it could have been the wireless from the house next door. Gradually her breathing slowed and she crouched, looking around her at the dark walls. The only light came from the sun that poured in from the damaged slats, the beams of light forming thin gold stripes on her shoes and legs.

—It's all right, Angelo, she whispered. I think we're safe.

No, they're still there.

—I can't hear them.

They're still there, he insisted.

Reveka sighed and sat down in the dirt. She knew that she would be in trouble from Old Woman Kalantzis. But her only concern was to make sure that Roger and his friends did not find her. If that meant that her skirt and stockings would be soiled, then so be it. She could feel Angelo's presence next to her, feel his cold skin touching hers. There was a scampering from up above, and she froze. She looked up through the slats and saw Roger's cruel pale face smiling down at her. He pursed his mouth and then expelled a large brown gob that landed at her feet.

—I've found 'er.

Two other boys' faces peered down into the cellar. They blocked out the sunlight and Reveka shivered alone in the darkness. Angelo's icy fingers clasped her own. Roger had already begun to remove the slats and his hand was groping towards her. She felt rather than saw Angelo dart towards the lean thin arm.

Roger squealed, a high-pitched embarrassingly girlish screech.

—The dirty wog, she bit me.

The boys began to tear up the slats. Reveka shifted back in the darkness until she was pressing against the cold stone wall. One by one the boys dropped into the cellar. Reveka was suddenly aware of their smell. They smelt of dust and earth and boy. Angelo was still holding her hand. *Let me*, he pleaded.

—*Ochi*, she insisted. No.

—What did you say, wog?

—Nothing. She looked up at Roger. He was kneeling in front of her, a blue singlet hanging loosely across his scrawny shoulders. His mouth was too big for his face; he was all teeth and gum.

Let me. Let me. Angelo's voice in her ear was a chant.

I mustn't speak out, thought the little girl, I mustn't let them know that Angelo is here. The boys began to pull at her. Roger held her while the other two forced her out into the sunshine. Reveka glanced quickly across the small yard, over the tomato plants to Mrs Bruno's kitchen window but inside the room was dark and silent. Should she shout? She decided against it. The boys would only do worse things to her. Already Roger's fingers were pinching into the flesh of her hips. She bit on her tongue. She would not cry.

In the alley, the oldest boy, his face streaked with dirt and mud and snot, slammed her against a corrugated iron fence.

Roger pushed his face against hers. He was nursing his arm where Angelo had bit him.

—Why'd you bite me?

—I didn't bite at you.

—*I didn't bite at you*, Roger jeered at her accent. The other boys giggled.

—Why'd ya dob? he continued.

—I didn't dob.

—Yes you did, Rebecca, you dirty liar. Sandra said you dobbed to Mrs Cowan. That's how she found out we hid the paintbrushes.

—Sandra, she lie.

—You're a bloody bastard wog liar.

—You have paint. Your fingers have paint. That's how Mrs Cowan know. Her voice was now urgent, her words rapid. She saw the oldest boy form a fist with his left hand, she could feel Angelo's breaths quickening next to her.

—What are you talking about, wog? She did not know this boy at all. Unlike Roger and the oldest boy, he was not from her school. His black hair was as thick and as dark as a Greek's. But his smooth pale skin was of a whiteness that made her recall snow. And it had been two winters since she had last seen snow. In this new place there was no snow.

—What are you talking about, wog?

She looked up at the white boy's eyes. They were ugly with spite and distaste.

Reveka attempted to explain. She wanted to make them understand that Mrs Cowan had noticed the traces of blue and red paint on the boys' fingers. This was how the teacher guessed they had taken the paintbrushes. She tried to explain how Sandra's older sister, Maude, was jealous of Greek girls because Maude's boyfriend had become lovesick for young Anna Kiriakidis who lived in Charles Street and that Sandra too now detested the Greek girls and would do anything to get them in trouble. But in her fear and confusion, as she slipped Greek words into her English, as she truncated sentences and got the tenses of her verbs all wrong, the words came out making little sense. Angelo was no longer by her side. She wanted to turn her head, to see where he had got to, but she did not dare take her eyes off Roger. Roger had hurt her before. Roger enjoyed hurting children. Roger was what her father called the worst kind of Australian. She continued defending herself.

—Shut up, wog. Reveka abruptly stopped her defence. The boy had slapped her hard on the shoulder. We know you dobbed on us.

The very worst kind of Australian, Reveka mou, *is ignorant and violent.*

Roger pursed his mouth again, cleared his throat and spat into her face.

—That's for being a dobber. Together, the other two boys also spat on her.

And what I don't understand, my little angel, what I don't understand about these people is how proud they are of their ignorance.

She did not dare wipe at the thick froth sliding down her cheek and face.

Roger spat on her again.

—And that's for being refo scum.

The oldest boy's spit landed right in the middle of her closed left eye. When she opened it again she felt the thick sticky liquid soak into her eye. Roger laughed and spat one last time.

—And that's for being a greasy, ugly wog.

Criminals and prostitutes, Reveka, my poor daughter. I've brought you to a nation of criminals and prostitutes.

Reveka waited till she heard the boys' laughter fade as they ran through the alley. Only then, only then when she was sure that they had gone, did she bring the hem of her tunic to her face and wipe away the phlegm. Only then, alone, under the blazing foreign sky did she allow herself to cry.

We should have hurt them.

She did not answer. A huge lorry was attempting to reverse into a factory gate and Reveka stood and watched its progress. The truck wheezed and shuddered; it seemed likely that the massive square cabin would nudge the red bricks off the arch. Reveka held her breath. The truck slipped through the gate. Reveka expelled a large sigh.

We should have hurt them.

—No. It's wrong.

She could see he was hurt. They walked in silence down Church Street. A corner hotel was full of men who had just finished their shifts. She could barely glimpse their shadows in the dark dusty windows. Very soon they would be vomiting and urinating against the cool green broken tiles. She walked quickly past them and turned up the next street. The asphalt streets shimmered like liquid in the stifling summer heat. Reveka opened the gate to her house.

Old Woman Kalantzis was already home. She was sitting in the kitchen, drinking a coffee, her pale blue uniform unbuttoned and revealing a glimpse of white brassiere and brown skin. She was fanning herself with a stalk of silver beet.

—Shut the Devil's door, she roared.

Reveka watched Angelo creep up to Old Woman Kalantzis. He was crouched before her, his burning black eyes staring at the suggestion of breast. Reveka turned away and headed to the room which she shared with her father. There were things about Angelo she did not understand. She knew, for he had told her, how much he despised Old Woman Kalantzis. It was he that had minted that nickname for her even though she was far from old. She lay on the bed, her eyes following a supple line of cobweb stretching from the ceiling lamp to the curtain cornice. She shifted her head and looked out of the window. She knew that Angelo would be creeping up close to Old Woman Kalantzis, sniffing at her, sniffing at her woman's thing, maybe even daring to touch her there. She closed her eyes. She knew that Old Woman Kalantzis would shudder, that she would suddenly feel a chill, suddenly feel fear, and that she would bring her legs together, button the top of her uniform and make the sign of the Cross.

She opened her eyes. Angelo was lying next to her. He was breathing heavily. She grabbed his hand. It was cold and hard and rough; it was more like touching a piece of bark that had fallen from a tree than touching flesh. Let's go and play, she whispered to him.

Her father had a plot allotted to him in the far corner of the garden, behind the shed. Mr Kalantzis kept some tools and old boxes in the shed, but many of the roof shingles were damaged and rain always got in. The floor of the shed was muddy and slippery and the whole structure smelt of mouse-shit and damp. Her father's plot was tiny, barely enough for a few rows of tomatoes and a corner filled with zucchini flowers. But he had also planted blue and red flowers in beds he had made from old bricks and broken bluestone. The flowers were beginning to droop in the summer sun but their perfume masked the rank stink of the tumbling down shed. Two sheets of corrugated tin tied together with a thick piece of rope formed a gate to the alley outside. Reveka and Angelo loved swinging on the doors but they made an abominable sound and Old Woman Kalantzis would scream at them whenever she heard the rumbles and the squeals.

—What are you doing, you animal!

Reveka would quickly jump off the gate.

—You're worse than a boy, she would be scolded. Later, at dinner, the old bitch would complain to her father.

—Michaeli, you've got to look after your daughter more.

It's school that's causing this. She's becoming like a boy. There's no reason for a girl to be at school.

Reveka agreed. She wished there were no school either.

—It's the law, here, Mr Kalantzis interrupted his wife, and Michaeli nodded. And here, you have to obey the law. It's not like home.

—What kind of place is this? And with a grunt of disgust, Old Woman Kalantzis again attacked her food.

Reveka lay in the garden bed and looked up at the vast blue sky. The stalks of the withering tomato plants towered over her and Angelo.

What can you see?

The lazy sky was nearly empty except for a smooth wisp of blinding white cloud.

—There's a man sleeping on that cloud. Can you see him? *Tell me what he looks like.*

—He has a funny red hat and is wearing long black trousers and he has no shoes on. But that's because it is so soft when you live on the clouds that you don't need shoes. Can you see him?

I can see him.

They preferred it when the sky was low and dark and filled with mountains of cloud. Then, then, the world above them would be filled with palaces and turrets, hills and valleys. Some of the worlds in the clouds were barren like deserts. Sometimes there were huge grand cities with factories spewing forth thick black smoke. Sometimes the people in the clouds looked human. Sometimes they had the heads of lions and the bodies of goats. Reveka stretched her head all the way back, searching for more cloud, but all she could see were the thick stalks and flat green leaves of the broad beans. And the endless blue.

She began to search the clouds on the ship. The first days were terrifying. The women and the men were separated into different sleeping quarters and Reveka could not stop crying at the thought of not seeing her father. Old Woman Kalantzis spent the early days of the journey refusing to allow either Reveka or her own daughter Eleni up on deck. You have to keep out of sight of the sailors, she warned. Those days had seemed endless. The journey itself was smooth, for the waters were calm, but the heat inside the vast dormitory was suffocating, and the other girls and women rarely talked to the dark lonely child. It's because your mother was a witch, Eleni informed her casually, without malice, when Reveka asked her why she wasn't allowed to play in the circle with the other girls.

The world without day or night was interminable. They were fed every morning and every evening in a cavernous space in which benches and chairs had been nailed to the floors. Above them rumbled the ship's engines. The crew who served them were surly young men who would whisper to each other and then laugh loudly. Their laughter was full of sneers. They seemed uninterested in the children and the mothers and grandmothers. Their whispers and leers were all directed to the young women, like Eleni, who kept their eyes firmly lowered. The crew's quarters were above them and sometimes above the roar of the engines she could catch traces of masculine voices and shouts.

By the third day, the dormitories had begun to smell. The toilets were always overflowing and the combined stench of vomit, discarded diapers and the acrid odour of women bleeding was unbearable. Reveka longed to stretch her legs, to yell and to shout. She wanted to see sun.

On the morning of the fourth day she was awoken by a shout from the old woman who slept beside her. They're calling you. A red-faced young man, his cheeks unshaven and darkening, his white uniform soiled by grease and smoke, was standing in the doorway of the dormitory. The women were laughing at him and making sly jokes that Reveka did not quite understand. They were making fun of his age and his youthful good looks. *Look at our brave young sailor, he's dared to enter the lions' den.* Gushes of laughter. *Careful that we don't eat you up and leave nothing for the birds.* Squeals, yelps, hilarity. *What do you reckon, Spiridoula, if we left you two alone together how long before you gobbled him all up?* Spiridoula, who was nearly sixty, had one dead eye and was missing all her teeth, leered at the blushing young man. His face had become almost purple. Reveka came up to him and tugged at his sleeve. *I'm Reveka.* He took her to the light.

Her father was standing at the ship's rail, smoking a cigarette and staring out to a sea that was deep and black-blue, an immense dark reflection of the heavens above. Even the ship's stack, which when she had first boarded had seemed immense, towering over the other boats and ships and buildings in the harbour of Piraeus, was now dwarfed by the vastness of the two elements. Her father had turned and smiled. The sun hurt her eyes and she blinked back tears.

—What's wrong, my Reveka?

—The sun is hurting my eyes.

—Would you prefer to be below deck?

She shook her head violently. I want to be up here, but Mrs Kalantzis won't let me.

—She doesn't mean to be cruel. She's scared that you will get into trouble.

Her father took her hand. The dark grey and silver waves rolled till the horizon; she thought she might see a sea serpent. Her father carried her down some greasy metal steps and they entered a lower deck where massive steel blue and white containers formed an enormous train in the heart of the ship. The men had formed small groups against the side of the containers, sitting on their haunches playing cards, smoking cigarettes, sleeping with their heads on each other's shoulders. Here she could smell the musty harsh tang of men. The smell of grease and work and the salty sea. Her father pointed to a small clearing on the deck. He sat against the great hulk of one of the containers and began to roll himself another cigarette.

—It won't be long, my little one. Be patient.

—When will we see kangaroos? Will there be any in the village in Australia?

He laughed out loud.

—And what the devil will we do with a kangaroo? I don't think we can milk them. We can't even eat them.

—I can ride it.

He laughed again.

—There will be kangaroos everywhere, my little Reveka. Every village in Australia is full of kangaroos. You'll see. Let's just pray to God that we arrive safely.

—Abruptly, he stopped smiling and pulled her towards him. She felt his hands trace the hem of her skirt.

—They're safe, she whispered to him.

He patted her shoulder and she suddenly smelt the sharp whiff of alcohol on him.

—You're a very good girl. He cupped his cigarette from the wind and lit it. Stay up here on deck, you can play here. But don't leave my sight. I'll come and grab you every morning. Would you like that?

The grin on her face, her father would always remember, was as wide as the sea.

She had first created the game with the clouds to keep Angelo out of mischief. Bored at being trapped below with her, he had begun to play tricks on the women, pinching them, moving their things, pulling at their hair. She made him promise that as long as she allowed him outside on the open deck with her, he would stop. When she was younger, she too had been victim to Angelo's deceits and games. Then, when her mother was still alive, he had barely any time for her. It was her mother that he adored, whose knees he had clung to, whose breasts and thighs he had touched and stroked. Whenever her mother had attempted to take hold of Reveka, cuddle her own daughter, the spiteful boy would pull harshly at his rival's hair, spit at her, scratch at her. But at other times he would come and sit beside her and play games just like any other child. They would chase each other or play hide and seek, they would run around and around the courtyard or climb down into the cellar and climb the wine vats.

—His name is Angel, her mother had told her, he's an angel sent by God to protect us.

But when her father came into the house, Angel would become vicious. It was then he would fly at her, scratching, biting and slapping.

On the night her mother died, the boy had come into her bed and kissed her wet cheeks.

Can I sleep with you?

They had remained friends ever since.

She had invented the game with the clouds to keep Angelo out of mischief but very soon she too lived for the game. Huddled between the crevices of two containers, they would look up at the jutting chasm of sky, stare into the clouds and she would tell him what she saw there. And as the ship sailed on, as the sun got hotter and the air became thick with moisture, the worlds in the clouds would change as well. The broad smooth African clouds housed a world of ancient black kings and queens, who rode on lions and tigers and who lived in palaces made of bronze and gold. As they sailed east, the clouds became tinged with blue and silver and became the lands of the cannibals, wiry golden-haired boys and girls who lived on solitary wisps of clouds.

Sometimes her father would peek from behind one of the container walls and laugh at her.

—Who are you talking to, Reveka?

—The Angels.

—Good, he would whisper, and leave her in peace.

By the time they had left India, where dark brown boys had beckoned and smiled up at the passengers on the decks, imploring them in their shrill voices as they held up rich textured fabrics, the women below had started to go mad. Increasingly they ventured out on deck. More and more, they fought and gossiped. More of them became ill. The sailors gave them lemons to suck on to keep the fever and evil at bay. It was during this time, when the air below deck was filled with spite and venom, that Stella found her gold chain had gone missing.

Stella had large breasts, and though barely fourteen, every day one or another of the sailors would comment favourably on her long raven hair and smooth milky skin. As the men far outnumbered the women, and as Stella and her mother were travelling alone to meet the father that Stella had not seen for eleven years, her mother had staunchly refused to allow her daughter to venture onto the open deck.

—They'll eat you alive, her mother warned.

She's ready for it.

—Ready for what?

Angelo cackled.

Her cunt is always juicy.

Reveka put her hands to her ears.

Stella's gold chain had gone missing. It had been a present from her godfather at her birth and she kept it in the sleeve of a cardigan she had rolled up tight underneath her pillow. The morning she discovered it was gone, Stella had let out such a ferocious scream that everyone had awoken. The young woman, in her thin nightdress, her thick black hair tumbling over her shoulders, rushed from bed to bed. She pulled at blankets and sheets, overturned baskets and suitcases. The dormitory was in an uproar.

Stella found the small gold necklace lying underneath Reveka's warm pillow. She slapped hard at the girl.

—You witch! You thief!

—I didn't take it.

Reveka was horrified.

Mrs Kalantzis came to her and began to shake Reveka's shoulders.

—Don't lie. What's it doing here?

The little girl looked up at the woman's angry face and then hung her head. Mrs Kalantzis slapped her. Then Stella slapped her again. When her father arrived at the dormitory to take her up to the world outside, he was told of her indiscretion.

—Reveka is not a thief.

—She is, Michaelis, intoned Mrs Kalantzis grimly, she deserves to be punished.

Reveka looked up hopefully at her father. His face was heavy and sad.

—She has her mother in her, she heard a woman whisper. Beside her, she could feel Angelo bristle. She placed a warning hand on his arm. Without a word her father turned and walked away.

I want to visit the clouds.

—We can't.

I want to visit the clouds.

Reveka rolled on her side. It had been days and she had not seen sky. The women and girls refused to speak to her and she was even forbidden to visit the dining room. Instead, Mrs Kalantzis brought her back a few pieces of bread, some rice, a slice of apple. These were also given to her without a word.

I want to visit the clouds.

—Shut up, she hissed at him. If you hadn't taken the necklace we could.

I didn't take it.

She did not believe him.

I didn't, he insisted. *Stella put it under your pillow. That bitch has gone mad with lust. She's crazy. All she can think about is that sailor Manolis. And he never looks at her. But he's always got a compliment for you when he sees you. Stella's gone mad with jealousy. Can't you smell it on her?*

Reveka propped herself up on her pillow. She could hear the snores, the wheezes of the women. The cabin stank. Reveka strained her eyes in the darkness. She could just make out Stella lying next to her mother. The young woman was lying on her back, the sheets at her feet, her hand clasped firmly between her pale thin thighs.

She's thinking of fucking him. That's all she can think of, Manolis' cock.

Reveka was filled with hot brutal spite.

—Are you sure she hid her chain under our pillow?

I saw her.

Reveka wanted to scream.

What did you say?

—I wish she was dead, whispered the little girl.

The clouds did not come. The sky remained empty and blue. Reveka heard voices from the front of the house. Eleni must have come back from work. But she did not move from her bed in the garden. If Eleni had just finished work, then her father would still be at the pub, he would be drinking his beer fast, the warm brown liquid spilling over his chin and throat, drinking until the barman jostled them out at six o'clock. She heard the young woman's quiet soft step coming down the lawn.

—Reveka, are you there?

The girl and Angelo held their breaths.

—Come on, Reveka, come and help us cook?

Eleni's flat black shoe came into view. She pulled Reveka up from between the long green stalks. Eleni slapped the dirt away from Reveka's skirt.

—You're such a dirty gypsy.

She marched the girl into the kitchen.

They had baked potatoes in the burnt stone oven, potatoes cooked golden, with chives and oregano. But when her father came home he was too drunk to eat. Instead, he sat on one of the kitchen chairs with his legs outstretched and patted his right thigh. Reveka jumped on his lap.

—Oof, he joked, you are getting so big.

Old Woman Kalantzis shook her head and whispered something to her husband. Michaelis looked up.

—What's the old bitch saying now, Stellio?

Reveka could smell the lager on her father's breath. He still had on his streaked overalls and she could smell the grease on him.

—He's drunk, replied Stellios to his wife, and kept munching on his potatoes. Old Woman Kalantzis groaned and slammed her knife on the laminex table. Eleni was looking down at her empty plate.

—Your rent is due.

Michaelis laughed.

—All you ever fucking talk about is my rent.

—Don't talk to my wife that way. Michaelis glanced over at the other man, then bit his lip. He pushed Reveka off him, reached into his overall pockets, and brought out a sheaf of notes and a few copper coins. He put a bill and some coins on the table.

—There's our rent.

Old Woman Kalantzis swept her hand across the table and grabbed the money.

Reveka followed her father to bed. He was cursing and swearing, bringing down disease and rage on the family in the kitchen. Reveka watched him as he crossed and recrossed the room. He was cursing Australia. She knew that if he did not sleep soon, he could be up all night, lamenting his life, his fate. He always talked about America then, always cursed himself for leaving America and returning to Greece. But then he would spy his daughter and gather her up in his arms, kiss her face. *Then I wouldn't have you, Reveka* mou, *he would cry out, what would life mean without you?* She hated to see him so unhappy. She would often cry with him. There was nothing she could do. But blessedly, tonight, in mid-curse, he fell on the bed and immediately he began to snore. Reveka untied the laces of his boots. She pulled them off his feet and placed them neatly at the foot of the bed, stuffed his socks into the boots, and then began to unbutton the overalls. She struggled to get the clothes off her father. Michaelis grumbled, turned over, and began to snore again. With a grunt she pulled the overalls off. Her father lay on the top of the bed, his white singlet and white shorts luminous in the dark. She could see Angelo snuggling up close to the man, his cold thin hands roaming the man's chest, his blue-tinged lips kissing the man's neck.

—Leave him alone.

Angelo ignored her. His hands were now creeping under her father's shorts. She slapped them away. The boy's eyes flashed violence and then a sly insolent grin replaced his fury.

Don't you have to piss?

She blushed, for indeed her bladder felt full and painful. She opened the door and crept down the hallway. The family were now in the living room, and the kitchen was dark. She did not turn on the light. She felt her way into the dark night, past the garden and the shed and she emptied her bladder into the dark gaping drain. On her way back to the bedroom she could hear Old Woman Kalantzis arguing with her husband.

—He's a drunk.

—Leave him alone.

—He's never on time with the rent.

—He's had much misfortune. You know that.

—And she's a devil, just like her mother.

Reveka bit her lip and entered the bedroom. Caressing moonlight streamed through the curtain. Angelo was lying next to her father, whose singlet was now crumpled above his hairy belly. His white shorts stretched across his thighs and his lean long thing lay sluggish and wet across his black thick crotch. She pulled his shorts back up and his singlet down over his belly. Her father did not stir.

She turned around.

Angelo's bright eyes gleamed in the dark.

—I hate you, she whispered.

She heard the boy chuckle and she had to bite her lip. She watched him glide over to the bureau with the broken legs in which they kept their clothes. His hand rummaged through the bottom drawer.

—Don't, she hissed.

I just want to see them.

—You can't. They're not yours.

They are.

—They're not.

His eyes flashed furiously in the light. He struck at the bureau. On the bed her father stirred, then began to snore again. Angelo was holding the small wooden box. It smelt of home, it smelt of the mountain.

Open it, he hissed.

—No.

I just want to look at them. Let me look at them.

She was tired. And he had protected her, had bitten Roger. She crept to where her father's trousers were scattered on the carpet and she began to search the pockets. When she unlocked the box and lifted the lid, the jewels threw flickering pins of light around the room.

Where are the others?

—We had to sell them. To come here.

You had no right. They're mine.

Angelo's hand reached towards the jewels and she

slammed the lid firmly, locked the box and clutched it to her chest.

You had no right.

—Shut up.

—My little Reveka, what is it?

The boy and the girl froze.

—Nothing, Papa, go back to sleep.

She pushed the box back into the drawer, lay next to her father and closed her eyes. She could almost see Angelo's sulky gaze, she could hear his furious sharp breaths. She bit her lip and closed her eyes tight.

Stella had become sick when Angelo had started going to her every night. Reveka would wake up in the dark and see Stella with her legs outstretched and the boy between her thighs. He would lift his thin face and grin mischievously back at her. Sometimes, in the darkness, it seemed to her that his smiling face was streaked with blood. Sometimes he would retch when he returned to bed.

Filthy Greek.

He wiped his lips.

Filthy Greek cunt. She tastes worse than that whore who gave birth to Jesus Christ.

—That's evil. She slapped at her own ears, not wanting to listen to his obscene words. He laughed at her, kissed her on the brow. His lips were cold. She shivered.

Stella became delirious. She swore to her mother that Manolis was coming to her every night, that she was heavy with his child, and the other women shook their heads and said it was a sin to have young women so close to men. They tried medicine and prayer, herbs and witchcraft, but nothing helped. The girl grew pale and thin. Stella was dying.

—I didn't mean it, whispered Reveka to Angelo, terrified of what she had done. Let her live.

She's already dead.

—Stop it.

I tell you I can't. It's done.

—Stop it.

She's just a whore. Why do you care?

Reveka began to pray. Angelo cowered at the edge of the mattress, his body jerking with fury. Reveka prayed louder.

And still Stella died.

o O o

It was soon to be holidays. Reveka was almost asleep; the smooth, soft voice of Mrs Cowan was reading the class a story. She felt something land on her back. She turned around. Roger was throwing spitballs at her.

—Stop it, she whispered.

Wog, he mouthed, dago, refo, grease-ball pig.

She turned and faced the blackboard. The wet paper projectiles kept landing on her shoulders and the top of her head.

It was the last recess before the holidays. Reveka hoped that she would never have to come to school again. She didn't see why she couldn't join Eleni in the factory, assist her in working the sewing machines. The factory was full of Greek girls, not like school. She sat underneath the wooden steps, sheltering from the sun, watching the girls play their games with rope and string. She could hear the yells of the boys at the other end of the playground.

—There she is.

Roger's blue eyes were looking down at her from above the wooden steps. She turned to run from her shelter but she felt the strong grip of another boy's hands. She could not even see who it was. She just wanted to run away from the leering Roger.

—Hey, relax, said the boy, I've got a present for you.

She squirmed and tried to bite the hands of the boy holding on to her. The girls had stopped their game. They were all looking in her direction.

Roger slapped her hard across the face.

—Wog, he sang.

—Wog, answered the other boy. The girls began to twitter and laugh. *Wog, wog* began the chant. Reveka fell quiet and the boy's grip on her body tightened. It was Andy McBride, she was sure of it. She could smell him. It seemed all her senses were sharp and clear and strong. She could smell Andy and Roger and the girls. She could smell her own fear. Had she pissed herself?

No. In his hands Roger was holding a small milk bottle. A neck of foam, the liquid thick and gold. She could smell it. She gagged.

—Not yet, laughed Roger. He brought the bottle to her nose. The stench of the urine made her gag again. The boy tried to open her mouth and she fought hard against him. He simply laughed. Another boy was now behind her, holding on to her legs. She bit Roger's finger, and he punched her hard in the stomach and as she fell to her knees in pain, her mouth open, he grabbed a handful of her hair, jerked her head back, and poured the contents of the bottle into her mouth, over her cheeks and chin and ears and eyes and hair. The liquid burnt her tongue and gums and throat. The girls were shouting with laughter. *Dirty wog, dirty wog, Rebecca is a dirty wog.* The boys let her fall. She fell to the ground and as the urine stung, as its stink filled her mouth and nose, she began to retch. Above her Roger was laughing. Her eyes burned and she found that she could not open them. The world was dark and she was spitting out bile. She heard her voice and it seemed to float above her. It was in Greek and the boys and the girls did not understand, and they kept laughing, but beside her she felt Angelo's freezing hands grip her shoulders.

What did you say?
I wish they were all dead.

That summer was full of mourning. Mothers nursed their feverish children throughout the night. The doctors prescribed medicine. But still the children died. The adults feared an epidemic. A rumour began that it was an exotic disease, a plague brought into the country by one of the filthy refos. The refos themselves kept silent, though in their own homes they agreed that there was truth to what the Australians were saying. Their own children were indeed safe. This was not an illnes to be cured by doctors and medicine. They prayed. They prayed, but they also placed garlic under their children's pillows, offered supplications to their saints, rained down curses on their demons, implored their One God while secretly doing penance with pagan spirits. At last, the children stopped dying. But not till thirteen small caskets had been lowered into the ground. Only then did Death stop his visitations.

Reveka remained inconsolable throughout all this time. Michaelis attempted to assuage her fear and guilt, first with gifts, then with kisses, then with pills. Nothing would do. Can't you see him, screamed the little girl, the Devil, can't you see him? He's right beside you. She was taken to the priest, who warned that she was possessed and who brought frankincense and the Bible into the house. The girl sickened and refused to sleep. Her eyes widened, her face thinned. I did this, she screamed at the priest, I'm guilty, it is all my fault. As February moved into March, as summer began to vanish and the girl remained sleepless and ill, Old Woman Kalantzis offered her advice.

—Michaelis, she said, take her to Dora. Dora will help.
—I don't need witches, he answered angrily.

—You do, replied Old Woman Kalantzis, her voice firm and kind, take her to Dora.

The old woman who opened the door wore black, her house smelt of cat's piss and her eyes were round and smiling. She took Reveka in her arms and attempted to soothe the little girl.

—Can't you see him? Reveka screamed. Can't you see that the Devil is always with me? He makes me do things. It's him, it's him.

Michaelis hung his head. The old woman could smell the lager on his breath. She smiled down at the little girl.

—Of course I can see him, she replied and she touched Angelo's shoulder; he turned to her and bit at her wrist.

The old woman just laughed and slapped him. She showed the flaming pink bruise to Reveka.

—See, he's not that powerful. We'll deal with him quickly.

She could see Angelo thrashing furiously at the old woman's back. His face was clouded with hate; black and fierce with hate. Reveka closed her eyes tight.

—I don't want to see him, she screamed. Make him go away, make him go away.

The old woman rested the girl on a couch covered with a thickly woven shawl, and took a small green bowl of poppies from the top of a creaking heavy wooden wardrobe. She turned to Michaelis.

—Go and have a cigarette in the night air. It is not necessary for you to be here.

He hesitated, but her tone had been as firm as it had been kindly. Stooping to kiss his shivering daughter, he left the room. The old woman offered cucumber and tomatoes to the little girl, who refused it all.

—Suit yourself. The boy lunged again, this time with a force that nearly knocked the old woman off her feet. She swung around and pummelled the empty air. Angelo was laughing.

The old woman ignored him. Sitting down, she grabbed a knife and began to slice at the wizened skins of the fruit. A small stream of sap and water fell onto a dish. She rose and took a large heavy wood crucifix off the wall. Come, she ordered Reveka, come to the fire. Reveka could hear that Angelo was calling her to stop. But the old woman's grasp was strong and she forced the little girl to kneel before the dancing kitchen fire. Angelo was now pounding his fists on the woman's legs but she just laughed and jabbed at him with the crucifix. This only maddened the boy further. He bit into the wood. Reveka tried to run from the old woman's grasp but her nails bit hard into Reveka's flesh. She could hear the woman chanting. She was singing out names. They were the names of saints, then the names of the Trinity, then the names of the prophets; and then there were names that were older even than these. Angelo was now shrieking in fury; he roared through the small wood house, drowning out the rumble of the cars and trams, the whistles of the kettle, Michaelis' pained sobs outside, and the angry hissing of the cats. The old woman placed the dish above the flames and pushed the little girl's face towards it. Breathe it in, she ordered, and the smell was putrid and the little girl resisted and held her breath but the woman's grasp was strong and the smoke stung at Reveka's eyes till finally she had to inhale and when she breathed again she could hear the boy's furious screams and she could still hear the old woman chanting, searching for the name. It seemed that all there was in the universe was this litany of names. The terrified boy's hands reached out to her. Again, Reveka attempted to rush from the old woman but then one name was chanted that filled the world with silence.

Elias. The world was in this name. Elias, the woman repeated, Elias.

The little girl collapsed to the floor.

—You can come back in, Michaeli. Her father rushed to

the stricken figure crumpled on the cracked linoleum.

—What have you done to her, you old bitch?

Dora lifted the dish off the flame, knelt before Reveka and leaned over to kiss the little girl's brow.

—She's fine, I'll get her some water.

The number 72 tram rumbled down Church Street. A factory whistle blew. Reveka slowly sat up and drank greedily from the water. Her eyes were languid and far away but for the first time in months a contented smile was on her face. She looked around the room. She could see her father, the old woman, the cats. But no one else. Should there have been someone else? She smelt again the sharp stench of the poppies' juice.

—Can I have some more?

The old woman nodded. Reveka inhaled, breathed in the glorious dreams of the fumes, and she fell asleep.

Dora and Michaelis sipped their coffee and sat in silence. The fire wheezed and sparkled in the kitchen hearth and the room was warm. Michaelis took a small box from his pocket and handed it to the old woman. Dora's eyes flashed wide at seeing the exquisite scarlet and silver stones inside. She slipped a charm over her wrist. The demon's bite had all but disappeared. But reluctantly she took it off and laid it back in its box.

—They are the Devil's, Michaeli, she whispered, do not keep them.

The man said nothing; he stroked the hair of his sleeping daughter. Reveka did not stir. Her arms tight around her father's strong neck, her body slumped across his knees, the little girl lay in grateful, contented, serene sleep.

THE NIETZSCHEAN
HºTEL PºRTER

IT WAS AN Enid Blyton morning when I finally cleared English customs. The ferry from Rotterdam landed in Harwich at seven in the morning and it wasn't till just before noon that the customs official handed me back my passport and waved me through. They'd checked my bags and asked me a hundred questions. *How long do you intend to stay? What do you have to declare? How much money do you have on you? What is your purpose for being in the United Kingdom? Do you have relatives who reside in the United Kingdom? From Cyprus? From Greece? Are you sure? Would you be prepared to sign a statement to this effect? Have you ever been convicted of a criminal drug offence in Australia? Have you ever been convicted of a criminal activity involving a minor? Have you ever been a member of an organisation designated as a terrorist organisation by the European Union?* I answered in the negative, I declared that I had the equivalent of two hundred and thirty pounds to last me the week in their country, and I showed them my plane ticket confirming that I would fly out of Heathrow the following Monday evening. The customs official was all blank eyes and clear pale skin. She was young and officious, with an insipid smile and a polite blank expression, even when asking if I was carrying a bomb or if I was a child rapist.

It was a contrast to the last time I entered the country. Then, the customs official could barely bring himself to look at me without making his contempt clear. I remembered him distinctly. He was short and reeked of tobacco, balding, bony and wiry, and his leathery skin reminded me of the faces

I had seen on countless late-night black and white English movies. An Ealing face, a kitchen-sink face. The young woman relentlessly interrogating me this time was a new face of England, a post-Thatcherite face. Youthful, officious, pretty and blank. No, I answered, I have nothing to declare. No, I have never knowingly consorted with terrorists. No, I answer, I have no intention of working illegally in the United Kingdom. She handed me back my passport and waved me through. I knew I was fortunate. Those with Oriental features, or with African faces, those with the broad flat faces of the Europeans not admitted to the Union; they were all made to wait, and were eventually taken through into private interrogation rooms. She accepted my answers at face value. She searched my bag but did not take away my passport, she didn't ask me to strip, she didn't demand to search my mouth, my hair, my arse. The Asians and the Africans and the Slavs were not afforded that luxury. Their papers, their bags, their arses, their cunts, every pore would be checked.

She smiled clinically and waved me through into England.

The world I entered was green and lush, and there were birds trilling in the trees as I walked across to the railway station. The elderly head-scarfed English woman at the kiosk called me love and promised to make my coffee strong. I bought *The Guardian*, a packet of Marlboro Lights and sat down in the sun. Pure happiness.

Colin, whose ancestors' Celtic blood had mingled for generations with the Anglos and the Saxons, told me that every moment he was in England he felt estranged and wary. I didn't feel that way at all. The first time I visited here I had been surprised to feel comfortable and at home. Not a sense of home as in belonging. Nothing of that. It was in Greece where those emotions and contradictions played out. I was simply who I was when I was in England. A stranger. Myself. There were no colonial ties. I was blessedly free of identity.

I was not a wog in England. It was Colin who was a wog in Europe.

—Where you from, love?

—Australia.

The old woman's face lit up, and then she looked puzzled.

—You don't look it.

I smiled and opened *The Guardian*. There was news of terror and security. The Europeans had become New World. They were puzzled by the senseless attempts of the world to place obstacles to their pursuit of happiness. For myself, under the caress of the fine English sun, I was just content to not be feeling the call of blood. I was not hungry.

There was a train leaving for Cambridge in an hour. I took out my tattered address book and searched for a number. I asked the old woman for a pay phone and bought a telephone card from her. The phone was answered on the second ring.

—Yes?

His voice had not changed. It was as gruff and as deep as it was when I first knew him.

—Sam, it's Isaac.

There was a moment of silence, and then his laugh sang down the line.

—You bugger. Where are ya?

—Harwich.

—You fucking wog, you don't pronounce the 'w'. It's *Haridge*.

—I'm in fucking Haridge then.

Immediately his manner changed. He became serious and reprimanding.

—Why didn't you phone before?

I didn't have an answer to that.

His manner changed once more and again he was laughing and sounded pleased to hear from me.

—Come on over.

—Can I stay a few nights?

—Of course.

I told him what time the train would be at the station at Cambridge and he promised to pick me up. When I put down the phone I could hear something poppy coming from the tinny radio over the kiosk counter. I found myself whistling along to it. A boy, not much older than fifteen, was standing alongside the old woman, smoking a cigarette. She took it from his mouth and had a drag. Though he had ebony skin, he had her eyes. Grandmother and grandson? Mother and son? There was nothing Enid Blyton about them.

The train wove through the orderly English greenery. An old man in a threadbare tweed suit shared the carriage with me but he immediately fell asleep to avoid conversation. I had the newspaper with me but I didn't read it. Instead, I thought back to the last few days in Europe. I found myself childishly wishing that the crossing of the channel had somehow delivered me from my curse, that the journey across the waters had shaken off my demons. I was convinced by now that it was indeed demons that had been following me incessantly on my journey across Europe. But I was too much a child of both my father and my mother. Her Orthodox superstitions were in my blood, and I pondered the worth of exorcism. And then I heard my father's rationalist scorn. I wondered if it was psychotropic drugs that I needed instead.

I was missing Colin greatly, his size, his affections, his love. More than God or medicine I felt the need for him. I found myself praying to him, my eyes closed, the rhythmic rumble of the train leading me into a mantra. I promised him that I would return, that from then on I would stay safe in his arms in the home he had created for us. I disavowed my ambition and my art. I would not seek fame or success, I would be humble, I would be ordinary. I was sick, sick to the soul, of wanting, desiring greatness, of never being satisifed. More,

I was always wanting more. I was always hungry for more. This was the nature of my illness. I would forsake the world for him. I opened my eyes. The old man was snoring. I unzipped my backpack and took out my camera. I pulled free the lens cover and took aim at the old man sitting across from me. There was a flash of light as I pressed down on the shutter.

By the time the train pulled into Cambridge station the clouds had rolled across east England, the sun had been banished and it was a grey, Orwellian afternoon. Sam was waiting for me under a large black umbrella. I was struck by how much he'd aged. When he taught me at high school he'd been the epitome of the hippie teacher: long unkempt hair, a shaggy moustache and baggy ugly earth-tone clothes. His hair, now cut close to his scalp, had gone completely white, as had his stubby thick moustache and close-cropped beard. I chuckled as I approached, on seeing that he was wearing neat cotton trousers and a freshly ironed shirt.

—Very smart, I teased.

He grabbed me in a huge hug and kissed me on both cheeks. Then he kissed me again. We pulled apart, and though we were both grinning happily, there was a brief moment of embarrassing silence. He stooped and picked up my backpack. He rolled his eyes at the drizzle of rain.

—Welcome to sunny England, Zach.

My teenage nickname. I wondered how I appeared to him. Though we had briefly caught up when I had first travelled to England, that had been in a London bar full of bodies and smoke and I was only a few years out of my adolescence. We'd still been caught within the clear pedagogical boundaries of student and mentor. Now I was thicker around the waist, older. I had, in name at least, a vocation and a pur-ported direction—one in which he had been instrumental. I was dreading the inevitable questions he would soon ask about my photography. Instead I pumped him for information about Cambridge. He was pleased to oblige; still, after all these years, the teacher. We walked across the railway bridge and he pointed towards the spires of the Colleges and the old town. We walked in the opposite direction, which, he explained, was where the 'townies' lived. Cambridge, he proceeded to tell me, was divided between academics and students, and then those who lived and worked in the town. He was obviously proud to be one of the latter.

—Are you teaching at all?

His face became stern. He shook his head.

—Can't, he said. But I've got some work in a place not far from here called St Ives. They've got a small museum. I work as a guide there, do some of their publication stuff. It's alright. He grinned. It still offers me an opportunity to pontificate.

His house was on a narrow street filled with identical compact two-storey cottages, each with doors that opened to the street. His was number eleven; the door was painted a glaring Mediterranean blue. Inside, the dank house smelt of cigarette, lavender and damp. Sam threw open the curtains to the living room. There was a small television and a lumpy red couch.

—How long you want to stay, mate?

—Only a few days, Sam. I'm leaving for Australia in six days. I'll stay a couple of nights here and then I'll be off to London.

—Suit yourself. But you'll have to bed down with me.

—That's fine.

—No bloody funny business.

—Can't promise that.

He laughed and tousled my hair.

—I share with a couple. Come. I'll show you the bedroom.

His room was upstairs and at the back of the house. There was a tiny bathroom with a bath but no shower.

—No darkroom?

—There's no fucking room, mate. Why?

—I want to develop some photos.

He looked pleased. Still a teacher.

—Hand them over, he said. I use a mate's place down the road.

I threw my backpack on the bed, ripped the roll of film out of the camera and gathered the rolls of film I had taken in Holland.

—Are you sure? I can take them to a lab.

—Not a problem, Zach. It'll give me something to do. You get some rest, have a kip. I'll wake you when I get back.

I could hear England in his accent.

It took me ages to fall asleep. The room was lined with books. On a drawer there sat a small television with a VCR underneath. After fifteen minutes of restlessness I got up, switched on the light and searched the room. On the bottom of one of the bookshelves there were rows of videos. *Blade Runner*, *The 400 Blows*, *Double Indemnity*. Then there were a pile lying flat with no cases. I selected one titled *Harem Gang Bang*, and slammed it into the VCR. A petite blonde in her forties was servicing a room of enormous beefy Turks, three of them ridiculously dressed as shieks, and three of them dressed in ill-fitting business suits that were far too small for their flopping bellies and broad shoulders. I got hard, turned down the volume and proceeded to wank. When I was finished I removed the tape, put it back on the pile, turned off the set, switched off the lights and threw myself under the covers. I fell asleep.

I dreamt that I was flying into oblivion. The world was dark, night, but there were no stars or light in the firmament. Endless flight. Then there appeared a light. I was moving towards it. As I approached it the light splintered and I was flying over a great city, a magnificent metropolis. I could not tell if it was ancient or modern. I was flying towards one of the great buildings in the city and it was both a temple and a skyscraper that seemed to dominate the horizon. It curved and slid across the centre of this world and I saw that this structure was in the form of a serpent. Its scales were bricks and its ribs were pylons of steel. I was flying towards the great serpent's head and I could see that its eyes were composed of myriad windows. Light shone from every window and in every window I could see myself. In one room I was sitting alone and bowed. In another room I was immersed in great wealth. I was being propelled with greater and greater speed towards the serpent's head. I began to panic. I was no longer soaring but I was being driven towards my death. I gazed into the serpent's eyes.

I awoke with a start. The room was completely dark and there was a shadow by my bed. I must have called out because Sam laid a hand on me and whispered, It's just me, mate.

He switched on the light. He threw a set of proofsheets across the bed.

—What the fuck are these, Isaac?

They were the cities of modern Europe. The modern streets of Europe: Alexanderplatz, Rue d'Alsace, Kalver-straat. The streets were modern and sleek but the bodies in these cityscapes seemed ancient and damaged and broken. In print after print, there appeared the same reptilian face. The dark, ghoulish boy, his face sometimes leering, sometimes grinning, always emaciated, always hungry, always reaching out grimly towards my gaze.

—What the fuck are these, Isaac? Sam's voice was shaking. He was furious. He was perplexed.

—I don't know, I answered.

I could hear noises and banging from downstairs.

—Zivan and Vera are home, he said.

Sam began to pick up the sheets. They're beautiful, he said finally, they are beautiful photographs.

—They're fucking ugly, I roared. Rip them up, rip them all up.

—Who are these people?

—I really don't know. Believe me. These were not the shots I took. I promise you.

I rummaged through the proofsheets. I found the shot of the old man in the train carriage. But in the photograph he was not asleep. His terrified eyes were wide and bloodshot and his toothless thin mouth was stretched in a moan to the camera. I pointed at the photograph.

—Sam, I took this shot this morning. On the train. The old guy was asleep. The fucker was asleep. I had begun to cry and I was shaking in the bed. Sam looked down at me but he did not make a move towards me. I wiped at my eyes and lowered my head. Our silence was only disturbed by the sounds downstairs. Sam walked to the door.

—Mate, I don't know what drugs you took in Amsterdam but I'm running you a bath. We're all cooking you up a meal. You need to eat. And then he smiled.

—Your photographs are shocking, mate, they are. But they're beautiful. They're not filthy, Isaac. They're far from that. Don't you dare apologise for them, Zach.

I reached for the prints again. Sam's parting words forced me to feel something I had not attempted in a long time. Courage. Fuck you, I muttered. I don't care if it's the Devil or if it's God. Fuck you.

I looked at the prints. Sam was wrong. Or rather, he was not being critical enough. They were not all beautiful or powerful. There were many in which the lighting was bland and dull, a few that suffered from a lack of contrast, too many in which the shapes of the figures were uninteresting or in which the landscapes I had chosen were prosaic, ordinary. I searched the proofsheets and then stumbled through Sam's drawers for a white pencil. I marked the shots I liked on the proofs and then tidied the bed, put on a dressing gown and went into the bathroom.

I washed myself thoroughly. The water was warm. I squeezed my nose and put my head under. I washed under my arms, my neck, my ears, my hair, my arse, my genitals, my feet, my hands, my legs. Fuck you, I whispered to the night air, fuck you, fuck you, fuck you. I took those shots, those images, they belong to me. They're my photographs. I could sense a trembling, a disturbance in the steam and humidity of the bath. I was not afraid. I hissed. I started laughing. Fuck you, fuck you, fuck you. I was not afraid. I would not be afraid.

It was a warm night and I dressed in a t-shirt and long shorts. At the bottom of the stairs, a young blonde woman with a long face and dull grey-green cardamom eyes greeted me. She held plates and cutlery in her hand.

—Welcome, she said in a thick accent, I am Vera. Come, you must be very hungry.

Vera had laid a white cloth across the small table in the lounge room and there were cushions spread around it. She set down the plates and the cutlery, then poured me a glass of wine.

—The men are cooking, she said, and led me to the kitchen. Sam was briskly stirring a hissing wok. The other man, who seemed a giant in the cramped tiny alcove, had his back to me.

—Isaac, this is Zivan.

The man who turned and smiled was at least six and a half feet tall. But more than his height, more than the undoubted beauty of his strong broad face, what struck me was the warmth of his wide smile. I could not help beaming back at him, immediately. He grabbed my hand, shook it firmly, and welcomed me. Then, turning back to his cooking, he ordered me to sit, to drink and to smoke.

—It will not be long. But you have time for a cigarette.

I immediately wanted to photograph him. I wanted to take shot after shot of his smile. Vera offered me a cigarette.

She too was striking, but it was an austere beauty, there was no softness to her face. Her fair hair was long and fell in subtle waves across her cheeks and her shoulders. Unlike her husband, her mouth did not fall naturally into the slant of a smile. There was sadness in her weary eyes, and a wariness across her thin mouth. She sucked on her cigarette, vehemently drawing in the fire and speedily expelling the smoke. She had finished her cigarette and had lit her second while I was still nearing the end of mine. Choose some music, she insisted.

Their cds were all piled across and under and by the side of the television. I could tell immediately that none of the occupants of the house were passionate about their music. There was a spread of titles. Classical and opera, rock and roll classics, a few Slavic titles, a few ethnic titles and the soundtrack to *Blade Runner*. Nothing to indicate a collector, no indication of a grand passion for a genre or a style of music. I chose the Rolling Stones' *Beggar's Banquet*.

She smiled at the first whiplash yelps of 'Sympathy for the Devil'. She swayed to the music, and then fell about laughing. Laughter made her pretty. Laughing, she looked girlish and young. Unsmiling, her face had no age.

—I love to dance to this, since I was a very young child. She indicated a small height with her hand. Is such a sexy song.

—It is.

She pointed to the wall opposite.

—See, Isaac, I have had you looking at me for months.

It was a junior effort, done when I was in Sam's class. A self-portrait. I was sixteen and sitting against the school fence on St George's Road. I look weaselly, a coarse coat of fluff across my top lip, as I squint in the sun. I had thought myself so ugly then but all I saw now was my youth, my impatience and my trepidation.

—It smells good, I said, nodding towards the kitchen and taking a seat next to her on a cushion.

—And you are still a photographer?

—Yes, I am.

—Yes?

—Yes, I am.

—I admire photography. She laid equal stress on each syllable.

—What do you admire about it?

—It is the most truthful of the arts.

I was about to launch into a well-refined counterargument. Then I remembered the prints upstairs. I realised that I agreed with her.

—And are you a student?

She shook her head savagely and drummed her fingers hard against the table. Where are the men? She shook her head again.

—I was a student in Yugoslavia. No more. Now I clean for students. I am a cleaner, at the Cambridge University.

—What's Cambridge like?

She snorted.

—Big. There is a lot of cleaning.

—It is a fabulous university.

Zivan had entered the room, balancing three plates in his hands. Vera threw up her hands in objection to her husband's comment. She gave a scornful whistle.

Zivan and Sam brought in the rest of the food. There was a steaming roast of lamb with baby onions and finely sliced potato. There was a Mediterranean salad of tahini and eggplant and long green beans stewed in a tomato sauce. The room quickly filled with the fragrant smells. I attacked the food immediately, spilling oily potatoes on my plate, biting into huge chunks of the sliced garlicky meat. My appetite had returned, it was normal. I was in England, I knew the language, I knew the rules. Maybe everything had returned to normal. Sam came in from the kitchen with a bowl of bread and sat beside me. He hugged me and raised his glass.

—To our Australian friend.

Zivan towered above us. He had his plate between his legs and Vera had one arm draped across his jutting bony knee. I stole glances at him throughout the meal. He caught me at it and smiled back. His messy hair, blends of yellow and cinnamon, fell across his forehead; he kept flicking it away from his eyes. His eyes were noon blue, as wide and open as his smile. His mouth, his eyes, were too big for the lean, wide face. They made him appear boyish. Sam had told me he had recently turned thirty. If I had not known that, I would have assumed the man across from me was in his early twenties.

Vera's face, her body, seemed all sharp planes. The clothes she was wearing, a loose linen blue tunic and a long, straight black skirt, deliberately hid her body. There was a puritan efficiency to her, evident in the way she chose to dress. And in her wary, cautious gaze. But as I watched her eat, attacking her food with the same compulsive appetite as she smoked her cigarettes, watching her attentive sharp eyes dart from her husband, to me, to Sam, to sounds outside the room, outside the house, I found that I was becoming captivated by her.

Each of us was making sounds of pleasure as we ate, as we chewed on our food and drank our wine. Happiness was coursing through me and with it an inevitable distant longing for home. Colin, food on the table, the radio or the stereo or the television in the background. Home.

As if reading my thought, Sam asked, How's Colin doing, Isaac?

—Same. Col's well.

—And your mum?

—She's good. A bit old, a bit of gout. She's alright. Immersed in the grandkids.

—And what's happening in the old country?

Three pairs of eyes were on me.

—Not much good.

I thought back to *The Guardian* I was reading at the train station at Harwich that morning.

—Same as here, really. It's all national security and fear about terrorism and refugees. The old country's fucked.

Vera, her mouth full, exploded.

—Terrorism, bloody terrorism. I am sick of hearing about terrorism.

—Do you have many refugees in Australia? asked Zivan.

—A few. We lock 'em up.

I looked down at my plate and picked at the beans. I didn't want to speak: talking about Australia in Europe still shamed me.

—That's not quite true, Sam interjected, we lock up asylum seekers, not refugees.

I was surprised at his pedantic distinction.

—Technically, yes. But most asylum seekers are still refugees.

—There has to be a process of ascertaining genuine refugee claims.

I was disconcerted by his measured counter-argument. I had expected him to share my outrage.

—And that includes locking them up, in the fucking desert, even children?

He shook his head. Vera put down her fork.

—You lock up children? In the desert?

I nodded.

—Has it always been like this?

—No, answered Sam for me, let's just call it ultimately another by-product of terrorism.

Vera groaned at this and broke off a chunk of bread.

—They justify everything, every evil, under the myth they are protecting us from terrorism.

—Quiet, Vera.

—You be quiet, Zivan. I will say what I like. The real terrorists are the Americans.

Sam put his plate down.

—Those people who died in New York, those people who died in the World Trade Center, they were not terrorists, they were murdered by the real terrorists. His voice was steel.

Vera scowled.

—Do you wish me to lie? I will not pretend a grief I do not feel. My grief was exhausted a long time before that. No, Sam, I was happy to see New York bombed. So they can understand, finally, what it is to suffer.

—You are alone in thinking like that. Sam's voice was shaking.

—That's not true.

Everyone's eyes turn to me.

—My mother felt that way. I was watching it with Colin, and you have to remember, it was late at night, and we were both transfixed to the screen. It seemed both real and surreal all at the same time. And then I called Mum because she's all alone and I thought she might be really frightened but when I called she sounded very calm and the first thing she said, the very first thing she said was, *epitelos*. I repeated the word. *Epitelos*.

—What does that mean?

It was Zivan who answered Sam.

—Finally. It means, at last.

—See, Vera's tone was quiet and firm, I am not alone.

Zivan piled salad onto his plate. He took a bite of cucumber, chewed it carefully, then sipped his wine.

—I cannot be happy when so many people are dead.

I turned to him.

—I don't think my mother was talking about the deaths. She was horrified by it all, of course she was. But she's a fucking Greek, don't forget, she believed that the Americans had it coming to them. Christ, I'm an Aussie and I felt some of that.

I turned to Sam.

—You must have felt a bit of that yourself.

—No, I certainly did not. I have friends in New York, Isaac. I've been to New York. I couldn't feel that. I love that city.

—And I loved my Sarajevo, look what happen to that.

—Vera, Sam was firm. That's a very different situation. And the Americans did not cause the civil war in your country.

—Bull-shit. Equal stress on each syllable.

—They did not.

—Their money, their greed, their interference. They caused it.

I was looking at Zivan. He had put down his fork and his eyes were darting from Sam to his wife. He was silent.

—We've had this argument, Vera. I am not having it again.

—Of course not, you want to believe that the civil war in Yugoslavia was caused by stupid Slavs who were barbarians and had to depend on the civilised West to assist them from the chaos we make. That is what you believe.

—I believe that Bosnians wanted independence.

Vera slapped her forehead loudly with her palm.

—I am bloody Bosnian. I born in Bosnia. I wanted no independence.

—That's because you're a Serb.

—No! She screamed out. I was born Yugoslavian. I am Yugoslavian. I die Yugoslavian.

—Zivan, I asked, what do you think?

He was still smiling; still boyish, but sad. He leaned over to his wife and kissed her.

—I am not like Vera. I am not a proud Yugoslavian. Yugoslavia is finished. But I was happy there, I was happy listening to the Rolling Stones and swimming with Vera in the Adriatic. That's what I remember.

His words created calm.

Vera scooped the last juices from her plate, finished her wine, refilled her glass and those of the men, and then lit a cigarette. She pointed it to Sam, and then she looked at me.

—Do you think your teacher has changed?

—Yes. I think he has.

—How have I changed, Isaac?

—You've gone grey.

He laughed. Anything else?

—You used to hate America. You were such a bolshie.

—Used to be. Now, I think that the Constitution and the Bill of Rights of the United States of America is the only creed worth defending in the world today. I really believe that, mate. I am a democrat. That's how I hope I die.

He shrugged.

—Don't get me wrong, I'm not defending American oil interest or denying that as an indulgent over-developed society it's fucked. But those are consequences of imperial power. I'm talking about fundamentals of politics, not economics.

—Economics *is* politics.

—No, Vera, I disagree.

—But, I interjected, isn't there a contradiction between espousing democracy and then trying to impose it on everyone?

—It's a contradiction I am willing to live with.

—Then you're a fundamentalist democrat. Zivan's smile was wide and glorious again.

Sam laughed ruefully.

—I think that Islamic fundamentalism is much more dangerous, ultimately, than democratic fundamentalism.

Vera had finished her wine and poured another.

—But this is nonsense. It is not one or the other, as if our only choice is between America and the mullahs. This is indeed nonsense.

—That's what the mullahs preach.

—So? She raised her hands in disbelief. And the bloody Pope preaches that you will be condemned to Hell if you are not a Christian. He says I am not allowed to have abortion. He says that Isaac is condemned to Hell for living as a homosexual. How is the Pope different from the mullahs?

—He doesn't want to control the politics of a nation.

—Fuck you. Equal stress on each syllable. He wished to have Poland and Croatia and he has them.

I had rarely seen Sam raise his voice. He did then.

—No, the Poles and the Croatians wanted independence. And with that, the choice to be Catholic.

—And the Arabs want the choice to be Muslim. Bloody religion. When I a teenager, none of my Muslim friends cared for religion. They prayed, they had their rituals and that was that. We studied together, we played together, we holidayed together. We argued and drank together. Now, now we are all religious.

She brought out a small gold crucifix from beneath her tunic. Even I. I too am now religious. She looked genuinely puzzled as she examined the Cross. She tucked it away. How this happen?

Zivan was looking at me.

—And you, Isaac, what do you think?

I was scratching circles on the greasy surface of my plate with my fork.

—You know, when I saw those planes hit the World Trade Center towers I was scared. Terrified. I deliberately did not look at Sam. But what shocked me about my response was the excitement I also felt. I thought it could be the end of the world and part of me wanted it to be the end. I thought it would be good if the whole world did go to fucking Hell, that it was the start of Armageddon. I thought that would be just. Maybe I still do.

Zivan was nodding slowly.

—Isaac, I think you are correct with your choice of that word, just. I believe it is notions of justice that are the problem.

—What do you mean?

Sam leaned over and whispered, loudly, pretending to be conspiratorial.

—Watch it, Zach, he's a Nietzschean. He has a doctorate in philosophy.

—That is true. My doctorate was on Nietzschean philosophy. But I would not call myself a Nietszchean. He was hopelessly a romantic. I am a refugee in England now. I must be a realist. But I believe that the Americans and the mullahs have much in common. A sense of morality, of justice, that originates from the desert. The desert is the original source of puritanism. You, Sam, you admit that Americans do not cope with imperial power very well. Why is that? Because they believe it is immoral. They have the great wealth and power of the supermen but in their minds they wish to believe themselves as commoners. That is indeed ridiculous. They are, if you listen to them, through their movies, through their television, through the words of their President, they still believe they are a part of the world's great poor and the great dispossessed. And they also believe, again like the mullahs preaching in the desert, that this dispossession also comes with being chosen by God for specific revelation. This is Christian and this is Islamic. But both these faiths are simply children of the greater faith that worships one God. Judaism. They still think they are the Jews of the desert. The Chosen

People. As do the Jews. They are not. They are not dispossessed, they are not slaves. If you will allow me to indulge in a Nietzschean pun, they are supermen who still think as slaves. That is why they are dangerous.

It was clear he had enjoyed the dance of his own monologue, the leaping of words and ideas. He filled his wineglass and stretched his long body against the couch.

—And Sam, before you correct me, he added, I am only speaking philosophically, not politically or economically. Politically and economically neither the Americans nor the Jews are slaves. Only morally, only ethically.

—Very cryptic, Sam returned.

—Not at all. Zivan lit a cigarette.

—Excuse me. I got to my feet. Can I use the telephone?

—Of course, Zach.

—I'm going to ring Colin.

That's fine. Go on, speak as long as you like.

Colin answered on the first ring.

—You're home.

—You beauty, I was just thinking about you.

—What were you thinking?

—How much I want to fuck you.

—How do you want to fuck me?

—Up the arse. On your back, your legs around my shoulders. I'd fuck you hard. I can't wait to fuck you hard.

—Six days.

—I can't fucking wait.

—Six days.

—I love you, Isaac. Where are you?

—At Sam's, in Cambridge.

—How is it?

—It's good. He lives with two Serbs, a cool couple called Zivan and Vera. We've been discussing politics and war and religion and philosophy. My head hurts.

—You poor ignorant Australian.

—You got it.

—Have they come to any conclusions?

—Religion's fucked.

—And capitalism?

—Fucked.

—Communism.

—Fucked.

—Australia?

—Very fucked.

—Europe?

—Doubly fucked.

—America?

—Arse-bleedingly fucked.

—I miss you.

Suddenly I was scared. Hearing his deep voice from the other side of the world. Who was it that was going back to him?

—Col, what would you say if I told you I'm giving up photography?

—I wouldn't let you.

I missed him like my heart was on fire.

—I love you. Six days.

—Ring me.

—Do you love me?

—Of course.

—Good. 'Cause I love you too.

I hung up the phone. I was normal. In Enid Blyton's England, everything is normal.

The conversation had gone elsewhere while I'd been out of the room. I leaned in the doorway and listened in. Vera rolled her eyes when Sam tried to convince her of the enormity of Stalin's crimes.

—I know that, Sam, she exploded in exasperation. Why do all of you in the West believe that you know more about communist history than we who lived it do? What do Stalin's crimes have to do with communism in Yugoslavia in the decade of the eighties?

—It's a legacy.

—Like the slave trade in the United States. Does that still affect your precious American democracy? At some point, Sam, you must allow for history to become history.

—Yes, that history still has effects and consequences for the United States today.

—But does it undermine the validity of your democracy?

Sam was silent. I bounded upstairs, into his room, put a new roll of film in my camera and brought it downstairs.

—Alright. Pretend I'm not here.

Vera waved me away.

—No. I look awful.

Zivan kissed her.

—You look wonderful, I countered, and clicked them in an embrace. I wrapped my arm around Sam, pointed the camera down at us, head to head, and blindly snapped.

—Colin sends you his love, I yelled, drunk now, waving the camera around. He'd love to be here, he loves arguing about politics and religion. He reckons he is a man out of time. I snapped Zivan's face. I'll tell him what you said about the three religions of the Goat-fucker.

—Goat-fucker?

—That's our name for Abraham.

Vera made the sign of the Cross. She laughed out loud.

—That is blasphemy, Zivan said, winking at me.

—Smile, I responded, I want to take a photo of you.

He was close-up in the frame. His enormous mouth, his unkempt hair. I could see wisps of dirty blond chest hair beneath the short yellow collar of his shirt. I wanted to kiss him. I took a photograph instead.

—So Cambridge is fabulous, I flirted with him, will you show it to me tomorrow?

I wanted to put my lips on his lips.

—I am not a student, Isaac. I work as a porter at a hotel in the city. It is a beautiful old bar. You will come and drink there tomorrow night.

—I promise.

Vera grabbed my camera. She pushed me against her husband. He put his long arm across my neck and pulled me into him, tight. Staggering, she snapped the photo. She handed me the camera and fell into the middle of us.

—You will meet me for lunch tomorrow, Isaac. I show you Cambridge. She pulled at Zivan's nose. It will be I who will show you Cambridge. It is not so fabulous.

Drunk, singing to 'Street Fighting Man' again, I helped Vera with the washing up. The kitchen was so small we bumped drunkenly against one another as we danced to the song. I kissed her on the cheek.

—Thank you for tonight, thank you for letting me stay.

—It is a pleasure to have you stay. It reminds me of being a young girl in Yugolsavia when my mother had parties and people would come and drink and talk all night long. England is not like tonight. She shook her head sadly. England is not at all like tonight.

She leaned close to me and whispered.

—I don't want my husband to hear. It make him angry. She put a finger to my lips. I hate the Jews, Isaac. The Jew Americans, what they did to my country. She kissed me on the lips, hard, wet. She was very drunk. I was glad to see those Jews jumping from those burning buildings. They deserve their towers to burn.

I was shocked at the venom in her voice.

The lights were out and Sam was in bed. I undressed and lay down awkwardly next to him. He started to cry. Soft slow sobs. I touched his shoulder.

—What is it, mate?

—I'm lonely, Zach. Having you here tonight makes me realise how lonely I am. It's been a very long time since someone's lain next to me in bed.

We made slow, fumbling love, the kind of love possible between a straight man and a gay man who have affection for one another. He had his eyes closed throughout and he came by masturbating. We kissed for ages.

Then we smoked a cigarette. And then another.

—Zivan loves to talk, doesn't he?

—The guy's a born teacher.

—You should be teaching too. Listening to you tonight, you still want to argue and debate. You should be teaching. You're a fucking great teacher.

—I can't.

—Do they know?

—I'm on the sex offender registry here.

—But how come? It happened in Australia.

—Don't matter. They know. I had to declare it.

—Has it got you in trouble?

—What do you mean?

—You know. I heard that local communities can treat people on the registrar pretty tough. You know, scapegoat them.

—Cambridge isn't that small. And I don't work with teenagers. He giggles. Anyway, there's a whole group of us here on the sex offender registry. We meet every Thursday night at one of the pubs.

—Really?

Sam burst out laughing.

—Nah, just having you on.

I laughed. I could feel myself stumbling towards sleep.

—Zach, do you ever see Lena?

Sexy pretty Croat Lena. With the long Hollywood legs, the smart mouth and the Debbie Harry dye-job hair. She was in my class at school. Everyone knew about Sam and Lena.

—She's in Queensland.

—She happy?

—Who knows?

We tried to fall asleep in each other's arms but it didn't feel right, didn't feel comfortable. We ended up on separate sides of the bed.

The next morning when I awoke my mouth tasted filthy and my head was pounding. I was alone in bed but Sam had left a note telling me he would see me in the afternoon. My face was drawn when I looked into the mirror, and large bags sat under my eyes. I had not shaved for a week and the thick bristle was black. I lifted a naked arm and wobbled my flesh. My weeks in Europe were telling. I missed the gymnasium. The sunlight beaming through the small bathroom window was warm but it was a tepid European sun. I wanted the harsh bright open light of home. It was my yearning for such a light that finally made the continent I live in my home.

The headache subsided with coffee, water and a swig of leftover wine but I was conscious of a gnawing in my stomach. It stirred, it was a living organism within me, and I knew, even as I begged it not to be so, that it was stirring, that it would seep through the lining of my stomach and enter my blood. It was an appetite. Over the sink, Vera—I couldn't imagine it being Zivan—had placed a square solid icon of the Orthodox Madonna. I found myself praying to it, but even in prayer I was ashamed, conscious of my blasphemies of the night before. In the middle of crossing myself I dropped my hand and turned away from the sink. I had no God to pray to.

Vera had left me instructions to meet her for lunch in a cafe in town. I wandered the narrow cobbled streets of old Cambridge. The dark streets curved and I found myself enjoying the smells and attractions of a medieval town. It was certainly one that had been made comfortable for tourists but it also felt functioning and real. I could not tell the students and academics from the townies. I could tell the tourists. Like me they craned their necks and looked up at high steeples and Gothic statues. I crossed the market square and walked down the basement stairs to the cafe where Vera was waiting. She was drinking a beer and wearing the universal pale blue coat of the service worker. A light yellow scarf was tied neatly around her hair.

We had a hot pie each, which I struggled to get through, another beer, and then she walked me across the narrow bridge over the Cam. The Colleges of the university were spread across fields of lush green. The tour she took me on was lackadaisical and irreverent.

—It is a very boring place, Isaac, she told me, these students are devoid of life. This town is like a village. It shuts at midnight.

But when I pressed her she admitted that she much preferred living in Cambridge to being in London, or Sheffield, which was where she had first been placed when she arrived in England.

—It was too big, too cold. I felt invisible. I felt as if I was nothing, I was an insignificant little insect when I was in London. It is good here. Zivan loves the libraries. He loves being close to the universities.

—Do you think he'll study again?

—He will always be a student.

I photographed her on a bridge over the Cam River and she took a photo of me perched precariously on one of the punts.

She checked her watch.

—I must go. I have a tea to serve at the College of Kings. She sniffed haughtily. They have visitors from South Africa and it is very formal. They make prayers in Latin and sing an old silly song. I'm sure the South Africans will be embarrassed.

—Who knows? It is Cambridge. They'll probably wet their pants at all that traditional shit.

—Wet their pants? They will urinate?

—Yes, I explain, we colonials get so excited by tradition we piss ourselves.

—Yes, of course, all that tradition. She rubbed her fingers together. Tradition makes them much money. She kissed me on the cheek, and with a cigarette in her right hand, she started a slow run across the green. I watched her disappear into the dour melancholy majesty of King's College.

I had my eyes closed to the mid-afternoon sun when Zivan found me. I heard a voice booming my name and I looked up to see his gleaming face looking down at me. He took the seat across from me and yelled out to the bored young waitress for a coffee. She was about to glare at him but his smile won her over and she smiled back. He took a cigarette from my shirt pocket.

—Did you meet with Vera?

—Yes. She gave me a tour.

—She is not very respectful, Vera. It is a wonderful university. I have been at the library all morning. I have had a swim. It is a good place to live. So many utilities, and as a townie you have some access.

—I don't think Vera likes the English much.

—They are okay. They are, as they themselves say, stiff. But you must know this already. You are Australian, after all. He took my hand and squeezed it. Don't judge her harshly, my Verushka. She wants to study. She is very jealous of these boys and girls who study in a place like this.

—I'm not judging her at all. I'd feel the same way. He slipped his hand off mine and I looked around at the chilly grandeur of the university town.

—I am jealous too, I continued. I understand her. They don't know how lucky they are, having the opportunity to study in a place like this.

He was silent and no longer smiling. I was uncomfortable in the silence and was glad when the waitress arrived with the coffee. He poured three sugars into the cup and stirred furiously.

—Zivan, can I ask you something?

—Let me take a photograph of you first. You look like a student yourself, sitting here, lazily sipping your coffee at Cambridge. Why not pretend to be a student for a day?

I smiled into the camera. I could smell him. I could smell that he had pissed and shat just before he sat down with me. His shirt smelt of dry sweat, his shoes of grass and oil, and an obstinate trace of dogshit. His messy hair was greasy. I could smell it. My stomach rumbled as he took the shot. My cock stirred.

—Last night, were you being anti-Semitic?

He handed over the camera.

—I don't believe so. Do you believe I was? He kept stirring his coffee, but his eyes were fixed firmly on mine. They were not angry. Just curious, patient.

I took ages to answer him. I was trying to comprehend Vera's fury at the close of the night.

—You believe that Judaism is at the root of the problems in the world today?

Zivan's laugh was a loud, merry outburst that startled the tables around us.

—You drank too much, Isaac. Or you do not listen well.

I was not offended by his remarks. If anything, I thought both observations to be true.

—Listen, he continued, in a very drunk manner I was making one point. That the moral categories of contemporary Islamicists and of contemporary democrats come from Judaism. Jewish ethics are very different from the morality of other people in antiquity. Isaac, he exclaimed joyfully, playfully slapping my cheek. It is nothing original. I was being vain, trying to impress. I was making a common banal point.

I insisted on challenging him.

—You argued that the Jews and the Americans no longer had a right to make use of that morality.

—I made the argument that they are not any longer dispossessed. And as for being chosen by God, I find that an unacceptable and irrational moral position.

—As do I. But you were saying that the Americans and the Jews had equivalent power in the world. That's certainly not true.

—They do not have equivalent power, but they are now bound to each other. The Jewish nation and the American nation are centres of power—economic, military, intellectual—in the world. That is what I mean.

—But that's where I disagree. Judaism is a religion, Israel is a nation. Jews aren't a country. They're a people.

—The Jews are a nation. Zivan, now impatient with me, began counting down on his fingers. The law of their God define them as nation. Israel is nation-state. Most Jews identify as a distinct cultural national body. And maybe most important of all, the Hebrew language binds the Jews as a nation.

—No, I disagree. An Australian Jew is an Australian. An American Jew is an American.

—And an Israeli.

—Okay, yes, they are a nation. My tone was defensive.

Zivan rolled a cigarette along his fingers. When he finally spoke again, his question took me by surprise.

—Are you religous?

Am I religious?

—No.

—But interested in theology?

I felt scrutinised. Zivan saw my hesitation.

—You were born Orthodox?

—Yes. But my father was an atheist.

—As was mine.

—And your mother?

—She became a non-believer. My mother's family was a mixture, some Catholic, some Orthodox, possible some Jewish. He laughed, a merry flicker of music. You are surprised?

I thought of Vera's insistent cruel words of the night before.

I blurted out my confusion to Zivan.

When I finished, I snatched another cigarette. Two women with freckled skins and short spiky hair took a seat next to us. Zivan was watching them.

—My Vera is impatient with Sam. They argue politics all the time. Her words to you last night were—how do I make you understand—she was frustrated. This explains her outburst.

—Does it? I was not smoking my cigarette. I was watching the packed tobacco burn. If I looked up at the square I believed I would see shadows move past me. My stomach was a clenched ball and my nostrils were full of Zivan. I could smell the perfume and bitter moisture on the skin of the two women across from us. Europe stank, it stank of ghosts and shadows.

—You did not listen well to Vera last night. She believed in a place called Yugoslavia, she believed in her home. Not blindly—not any more blindly than you believe in your home—but she loved it and misses it. Then Sam tried to convince her that it is a good thing, that it is just that it has disappeared. *Justice*.

He bit hard on the word and shook his head. Sam, of course, believes that his exile is identical to hers. Which it is not. He has a home to return to. It is possible to see my wife's anger as envy, *ressentiment*. Do you understand? Like your resentment of these pretty young students who have the opportunity to study at this fabulous university. Sometimes when I am too intoxicated by alcohol I can curse them too, blame them for all my problems, for all the problems in the world. His smile has gone. Do you understand?

—No. I still don't understand what Vera meant last night.

—The Jews at least have a homeland that can never be taken from them. It is God's to give. Can you understand how this may make someone like Vera feel? Envy, of course. Anger, certainly. Resentment, understandably. Her homeland has vanished.

Zivan pointed across the square, to the spires of the colleges and the cathedrals.

—Look, Isaac, there and there. The world created by the Greeks and the world created by the Jews. Alongside each other. Do they belong together? He was teasing me, his smile was across his every word. I was too dumb, too ignorant for his teasing. I looked at him blankly, embarrassed.

—That is Europe. He touched my chest. That is who you are. As for Vera and I, both the Greeks and the Jews considered us barbarians. And you still do.

He rose, pushed back his chair, and nodded at the two women. I have to get ready for work, my friend. Come and have a drink at the bar tonight. It is a lovely hotel.

As I walked with him, Zivan described the splendours of the building in which he worked, told me how much he admired the restrained British elegance of the architecture.

We stopped outside the hotel. It was restrained and elegant. It was very English. The hotel had originally been a four-storey bluestone Victorian mansion. An imperial dome crowned the structure, and the cornices and buttresses were all freshly painted in a calming mint colour. It was evening by the time we arrived and the streetlights flickered, sprang to life as the white-haired doorman swung open the door for us. The interior was dark and masculine, all wooden surfaces and deep blood colours: thick burgundy velvet curtains ran down the length of the windows to the floor. There were black leather armchairs in the reception area and the rug spread on the white sparse tiles was a plush swirl of scarlet and ochre coils. A young man with shining black hair smiled at us as we entered, and greeted Zivan warmly. A concierge sat beside a small desk, his eyes intent on a computer terminal. The only sign that this stern immutable building was now part of a chain of international hotels was the twisted black ensign engraved on the gleaming gold of the tags on the chests of the receptionist and the concierge.

—I must change.

—I'll come back tonight.

The pangs in my gut had been worsening throughout the afternoon. There were clouds billowing menacingly in the sky. This was a Patricia Highsmith England. Sam arrived at the house within minutes of my entry, with his arms full of shopping. He immediately went into the kitchen to cook for us.

I was unable to take more than a few bites of the steamed fish and rice salad he had prepared, and even so, I had to excuse myself and go to the toilet upstairs, where I retched for a good five minutes. Recognising that it would have cost a small fortune to prepare such a meal in England, I was mortified by my behaviour, but I was powerless to do anything about it. I looked into the bathroom mirror, at my gaunt, ashen face, and knew there was to be no deliverance.

Until Sam had got home, I'd sat in the dark lounge room, shivering and listening to the growling metamorphosis of my blood. I knew now that it was indeed my blood that was transforming me, making me ill. It was as if the very fluids coursing through my body were thickening, ballooning so that they could not be contained by the thin walls of my veins and arteries. It was as if my blood was resentful that I was refusing to feed it, and was deliberately spiting itself to force me to nourish it. It was not seeking mere food and water. In a terror, a vacant torment, I had allowed my nose to lead me through the house and up the narrow stairs into the bathroom where on all fours I crawled, seeking the odour that my senses had convinced me was in this very house. I was led to a small wastepaper basket where I clawed through tangles of hair, cotton and dental floss until I came upon two strips of bloodied bandage. I suckled on them as relentlessly and as intensely as a nursing baby would at its mother's breast. Throwing the bandages back in the wastepaper basket, sitting back against the cold bath tiles, I found a moment of peace and contentment. It did not last long but it allowed me to present a composed face to Sam when he arrived.

He had wanted to ask me endless questions about my photographs. I told him curtly that they were a response to Europe. But he wanted to know how I had achieved my effects. I pretended that the bodies were grafted from pornography and the vileness of the internet, and this explanation seemed to satisfy him. Of course, he exclaimed, they're montage. Yes, I answered, glad that he had remained ignorant of the intricacies of digital photography. You ignorant sad old fuck, I was screaming inside, it's film, it's real, this is not digital. I grinned at him. He must have assumed a thousand depravities about where I had found the models for my work. The only question he posed was of the dubious moral worth of using such traumatic real subjects. I answered that what I was doing was akin to what samplers did in utilising fragments of other people's work in their own creation; I also answered that, unfortunately, these very images were free and public on the convoluted garbage dump which was the internet. I was convincing myself as I spoke. The inert fear that had taken hold of me when I first glimpsed the photographs had now left me. Instead, I was delighted with them, aware of their disturbing evil, excited by their ability to move and confuse people. I was proud of them. This emotion swelled and met the ravenous call of my blood. I was famished.

Wishing to feel only this ecstatic swoon of pride, on the way back to the hotel I tried to lure a small ginger cat that was sunning itself in the last faint pools of sunlight. It was stretched across a slender windowsill and at first it eyed my tender crooning with just suspicion. But it raised its nose and moved to my outstretched hand. I was not at all clear about what it was that I was intending to do. I had a whiff of its vivid carnal smell. My intention was to grab its neck, break it, and to immediately bite into it and drink the dying blood. I don't believe that there was anything rational or conscious in this intention. It was an instinct. But as soon as the animal approached my hand and sniffed, it recoiled, raised its back and fur in brittle aversion and hissed at me. It disappeared, fleeing through my legs and out into the street.

I asked for directions to the bar.

I knew that Zivan was working and I did not wish to bother him. He had told me that he would find me in the bar. It was mercifully empty except for the ponytailed young woman who was waitressing and an older stiff-backed couple sitting in two lavish leather armchairs near the back wall. They were both smoking cigars, each immersed in reading; he a newspaper, and she a novel. Behind the cigar smoke I could smell something putrefying, something deathly upon him. She smelt empty of anything but weak animal flesh. No sweat, no sex, not even a trace of excrement; unlike the young woman at the bar, who smelt strong and alive. I asked for a whisky and I lit a cigarette. I held the glass of oily amber liquid close to my face, so that the alcoholic fumes would dull the smells of the world around me.

The first glass of whisky was lead pellets straight down to my gut. The taste was medicinal, not pleasurable, but the second went down better and by the third I could manage to ignore my hunger. Within fifteen minutes the bar had filled up and there was smoke and discordant conversation all around. Some football game must have just finished because a group of young men in bright soccer shirts had formed a half-circle of leather armchairs by the empty fireplace. They were yelling at each other, a mind-numbing drone. At a small table not far from the bar, a group of five effete gentlemen had ordered a bottle of wine and were hunched in close to each other, occasionally raising a disapproving eye towards the football crowd. From the snatches of conversation I could overhear, they were discussing an exhibition they had just been to.

The man with the loudest voice was in his late fifties, overweight, and with ridiculous coils of black hair jutting out like islands across the bald dome of his head. He was dressed completely in black, a thick poloneck top, and reeking limp woollen trousers. I could smell the residue of semen and piss and shit on those trousers; I would wager they had not been washed for months. The four men sitting around him were younger, all nervy and sallow, as if they were enemies of the sun. One of them had lank blond hair that hung lifelessly around his bony shoulders and as if to deliberately offend the footballers, was constantly fumbling with a pair of reading glasses that fell from a chain around his neck. Their conversation, that which I could make out, sickened me. It was pompous, overly educated, punctuated with *bons mots* and disparaging, catty remarks. They were discussing art but there was nothing about aesthetics or politics or ideas in their repartee. There was only gossip. Even though the youngest was barely into his twenties, there was something menopausal and jaded about these men. They smelt of mould, of something distasteful and decaying.

I turned and looked at the footballers. These men were burly and loud, with ruddy skin and shining eyes alive with bright Celtic hues. But their conversation, blaring through the intimate bar, was finally as noxious and inane as that of the dreary queens sitting near me at the bar. The footballers spoke of the game and of sportsmanship in cliches drudged from some asinine tabloid. Trading opinions and jibes, they moved from sport to television to alcohol, back to sport and endlessly repeated the cycle. *Arsenal. Man United. Big Brother. Who Wants to Be a Millionaire? Lager. Stout. Arsenal. Liverpool City. Big Brother. Lager Lager Lager.* I ordered another whisky and listened in between conversations. *Arsenal, Man United, Big Brother, he's drinking too much, he should drink more, terrible exhibition, top game, Lager, Lager, Wine, Wine, mundane, haven't I seen it all before, she's become boring, her art's always been boring, Arsenal, Man United, Lager, Wine, I've seen it all before, lager lager lager, wine wine wine.*

Will someone fucking kill the lot of them? The men of England, of Europe: working class, bourgeois, lumpen, aristocrat; all of them bloodless and effete. Someone just kill them all.

I felt his touch on my shoulder and turned around to see Zivan smiling broadly at me. His hair had been slicked back, he wore a crisp white shirt, a black tie and a black vest. The hotel's insignia floated across his chest. The old queen's eyes wandered the length of Zivan's body. I knew that Zivan was conscious of the attention but was studiously ignoring the group. The younger man followed the older man's eyes, spied Zivan, then deliberately sniffed, turning his back on us, and continued to play with his glasses.

Zivan looked even more handsome in his uniform; his height and fair beauty looked even more heroic in the conservative clothes he was wearing. The uniform could not contain him. He did not look like a worker. He took a cigarette from me and ignored the room, his eyes intent on my face. I assumed that Zivan's focus was always intense, always directed fiercely to whoever was in front of him. People must fall in love with him all the time.

He told me he was on a break and I offered to buy him a drink, but he shook his head.

—No, thank you. I am not allowed to have alcohol when I am working. But he beckoned to the woman at the bar and whispered to her to give me a discount. She nodded, and for the first time smiled at me. Zivan smelt of cologne, of some faint detergent, of bitter sensual sweat. People must fall in love with him every day.

—Are you ill?

He was searching my face.

—No. Why?

He shrugged.

—You are sweating. Your eyes are wide. Your lips dry.

—You sound like a doctor.

—Perhaps I am.

Was he teasing me? Before I could answer, a loud booming American accent filled the room and a bearded wolf of a man, with long black whiskers speckled with silver, and wearing a loose-fitting knitted jumper, was slapping the backs of the five queens. The man with the glasses around his neck screwed up his face in clear unabashed distaste but the American was unfazed.

—Well, what did you think of the exhibition?

The man in the black poloneck answered for the group.

—Fine. It was very fine. The tone was contemptuous, an exaggerated aristocratic sneer. The American called to the woman at the bar.

—A bourbon, honey. A double. He gestured towards the men. And another bottle of wine. His voice, though loud, was surprisingly high and feminine. One of the footballers glanced up, nudged a mate, and they giggled. Another footballer flapped his wrist and the whole team broke out into laughter. But it stopped immediately when a tall red-haired woman dressed simply in an olive-coloured strapless dress entered the bar.

Her hesitation, on seeing a room crowded with men, was brief. She moved purposefully to the bar and sat beside Zivan. All eyes were on her. She had a small, round face and her shoulders and back were pale and freckled. I understood immediately why the men in the bar had fallen silent. She was alive. Unlike them, she was life. The woman ordered a gin and tonic in an accent that was foreign to me. She looked straight ahead. The fragrance on her skin was sweet, the whiff of summer, but there was a darker pungent smell emanating from her. She was bleeding. My cock was immediately erect, my stomach churned and twisted, and I swivelled my stool towards the bar to hide my erection. I could see Zivan's mouth move, I knew that the American was arguing with the queens and I could sense the yells and laughter of the footballers. I could hear nothing but the sound of her blood, trickling, coursing, calling.

I turned to Zivan.

—I think I'm possessed.

He nodded, not at all thrown by my ridiculous statement.

—*I am*, I insist. Do you believe in possession, Zivan?

—What do you believe you are possessed by?

—I don't know.

—What can I do to help?

His eyes were concerned, warm. He was calm.

—Come, I answered; and taking my glass, I headed into the toilets.

One of the footballers was throwing up in a cubicle. I looked at my face in the mirror. In the strong fluorescent light of the toilets it appeared strangely white and I noticed I was thinner than I had been in years. I was immersed in my reflection and promptly forgot Zivan. I combed back my hair. It was damp from sweat and my hands were shaking. There was a loud fart from the cubicle. The toilets were drenched in the fetid stink of shit. Zivan screwed up his face but I breathed it in deeply, aware that there was the trace of blood and flesh in the diarrhoea. The footballer lurched towards the sink, washed his hands, gargled and spat out water into the basin.

I waited till the footballer banged the door shut behind him, then I raised my glass and smashed it against the porcelain basin. It broke cleanly into three pieces; I took the longest and sharpest and turned to Zivan. I took his right hand, brought it close, and drew the shard of glass across the top of his index finger. The blood formed a minute balloon and I brushed the thick warm flow across my lips.

The blood enters my mouth and at once my eyes are sharp and my senses concrete. I can hear the buzz of the innards of the hotel all around me. I can hear Zivan's nervous heartbeat. I can hear the individual muted voices of everyone in the bar. I am not greedy. I suck enough to feel my stomach loosen, feel it become calm, and I drop Zivan's hand. He runs cold water across his finger, then asks me calmly for a hand-kerchief. He tightens the cotton square around his finger. He grabs my hand and pulls me towards him. This will satisfy you for a matter of hours only, he whispers to me, you will soon need to feed again. His voice is that of a boy's, insistent and childish, he is speaking in my father's tongue. London is a large city, find your way there. His lips have not moved, Zivan's smile is constant and tender. What shall I do there? My own lips do not move. Feed, the voice orders me, feed till we are satisfied. In time, only with time, the need will be less.

How do you know this?

Zivan's smile vanishes. This time his lips move.

—Do you really believe that you have seen more than I have?

I have not heard this tone in Zivan's voice before. It is brutal and full of hate. Without his smile, his face is cruel. He detests me.

—No, Isaac, not at all. Zivan is smiling again. The glimpse

I had of him disappears, he is again the handsome hotel porter. I do not hate you. Why should I hate you? He brings his bandaged finger to my lips. My lips move towards the specks of red. He pushes me away.

—I have to return to work.

When he has left, I look again at my face in the mirror. I cannot believe how handsome I look at this moment. Colour has returned to my face. I am aware of the powerful muscles around my neck, aware of the glowing sheen of my skin. I touch my hands, my cheeks. I wet my face and go out to the bar.

Zivan has been called over by the man in the black clothes. He is nodding, and the man is touching Zivan's shoulder. The touch offends me. His desperate whining desire is clearly etched on the man's face; he stinks of it. It is a rancid dirty smell. He writes a note to Zivan, and Zivan, at first hesitating, finally accepts it. He turns and walks out of the bar. As soon as he has left the four young men break out in cackles of ugly laughter. I wish I could tear them all apart, extinguish their lives instantaneously, and throw their worthless carcasses out onto the street. For dogs, for waste. I know, I am sure of it, that this is what men descend to at the end of all empires, this whimpering effeminate posing. They disgust me. The ignorance and deliberate stupidity of the footballers also appals me but at least they contain within themselves a spark, a glimpse of past dignity. The enervated men sitting at this table are spent. They are at the end of time, awaiting their extinction. I am gloriously alive with an incredible sense of truth, of clarity. They are obscene, a final limp turd squeezed out by history. A fire, just and swift and magnificent, should rage through all of Europe.

The American is at the bar talking with the woman in the strapless dress. They are discussing a conference. I take a seat beside them and order another whisky. He refuses her offer of a drink and tells her he is driving back to London tonight. As soon as I hear his destination, I lean across.

—Excuse me, I say, smiling broadly, is it possible that you could give me a lift to London?

He is, of course, taken aback and eyes me suspiciously. I make up a quick and ready lie. I tell them that I have missed my last train and that I desperately need to be in London for the morning. I am polite, but firm, and eventually he nods.

—I have to head off soon, he warns.

—I'm ready. I offer to pay part of the petrol costs. At that he laughs, and shakes my hand. Out of the question. He asks me to meet him in the foyer in five minutes. I agree, finish my drink and head off to find Zivan. He is by the lifts, two suitcases in his hands. He is behind an expensively dressed young couple. The man is talking on his mobile phone and the woman is inspecting her long scarlet nails. Zivan sees me, and motions for me to wait. The bell rings, the couple enter the lift, and Zivan follows with their luggage. When he returns he is smiling and it is as if he has forgotten the madness of what occurred in the bathroom. But his amiable kindness shames me and I blurt out, quickly, Zivan, forgive me. He waves my objection aside. He has placed a small pink plaster on his finger.

I tell him that I am going to London but I promise to return the following evening. He shakes my hand. Behind us there is laughter and more of that damned cackling. The five queens are heading towards the exit. The older man turns and winks at Zivan. He mouths something to him, and slowly Zivan nods in agreement. The young man turns. There is envy and spite in his lean heron-like face. He turns and whispers loudly so we can all hear. *Pretty, but I'm sure she's dumb*. There is more laughter as the doorman swings them through. *I'm not in it for the conversation*. More laughter, and the doors swing shut. I wish them death. Through the glass doors I think I see a shadow cleave to them. They disappear into the English night. I wish them death, I whisper it, and Zivan can hear me. We both look out through the glass door, to where the shadow has descended around the men, attaching itself to them, caressing them. I have to go to work, Isaac. Zivan turns abruptly and leaves me in the empty foyer.

The American comes out of the lift and with him is a younger man. The American introduces himself to me as Robert James, but he wants me to call him Bob. Just Bob. His friend is called Nikolai. Nikolai is short, squat, with a flat handsome face and his body is clothed in an ill-fitting acrylic suit. The fabric stretches across his paunch. He blinks at me, shakes my hand furiously, and then stumbles past me into the foyer. He is staggering, pissed, but Bob James is unconcerned. The bill has been paid, he tells me, and I follow him through the doors.

The car is a wide metal-blue Saab and I move to get into the back seat.

—No, you take the front. Nikolai can have the back. A thin dark-skinned attendant opens the doors for us and Nikolai stumbles into the back seat. The car smells of pine and detergent. The interiors are clean and freshly polished. The American manoeuvres himself behind the steering wheel and his large frame is squashed up against the wheel. With a loud expletive, *fucking cunt*, he forces the seat back and Nikolai groans. The American apologises. We speed out of Cambridge.

Bob James explains that he is originally from Lexington and assumes I know where that is. From some of the details he drops, I assume that it somewhere in the mid-west of the United States of America. He works for AGFA, the photographic company, in marketing, in Chicago, and he tells me that Nikolai also works for the company, in Minsk. At this Nikolai leans over the back of the seat; I smell the chemical wash of the alcohol. He is searching his pockets and eventually finds his wallet. He hands me a card. I glance at it. In the dark

I can make out the AGFA logo and a Belarus address under-neath. He pats my shoulder. When you come to Menske, I look after you. My wife. Best cook. He slumps back on the seat and looks out into the darkness. Where we go?

—London.

—Fuck London, he spits out, shaking his head furiously. Fuck London, cold, cold London. No one talk to Nikolai in London.

He reels forward.

—Alcohol? There is pleading in his voice.

The American points to the glovebox. I open it and a bottle of Johnnie Walker falls into my hands. I hand it over to Nikolai, who clutches it to his chest.

Bob James starts bitching about the conference. I look out into the night. I am at complete ease, and I am satisfied. I am conscious that my appetite is momentarily asleep, but that it is coiled deep inside me and will possibly awaken at any moment. I am ready for it. I have my orders, I am prepared. I tell myself to relax, I take breaths. I am on my way to London.

The conference, apparently, was a failure. As part of their activities they had organised an exhibition of photographic art from the company's collection in one of the Colleges. As I had overheard, the exhibition had not been a success with the Cambridge critics. I almost ask which photographers were exhibited. I almost ask about the price the company pay for the artwork. I almost ask for a job. But Bob James smells of toner and offices and the noxious sting of air-conditioning ducts. He smells of commerce. I look out into the darkness instead. He isn't perturbed by my silence. He keeps on talking, his shrill voice bitching and moaning. The conference had been a failure; nothing had been accomplished. The Asians hadn't participated and he was sick of always carrying the Eastern Europeans. He speaks nostalgically of a decade earlier when he had first come to

Europe. It was the Wild West, he chuckles, money to be made everywhere. He had worked in Bucharest. The most compliant whores in the world, he tells me, but also the dirtiest. Prague. Over-priced and over-praised. Warsaw. The most stuck-up whores in the world. And Moscow. He had loved Moscow. He'd been treated with deference and respect. He had made a killing for AGFA in 1992. A killing. But all pissed up against the wall when they put the Russians in charge. Fucking Russians. Fucking lazy dogs.

In the back seat, Nikolai, who has drunk half of the contents of the bottle which he is nursing tight to his body, is issuing short rumbling snores. The passing headlights of cars flicker across his face. He is drooling.

—He's going to kill himself.

—What do you mean?

—Alcohol. It's going to kill him. There is a smugness to the pronouncement. The American reaches back and grabs the bottle, takes a swig. I look at Nikolai's bloated red face. Alcohol is poisoning his looks. But it has not destroyed him yet: there are still traces of charm and sweetness in that face. There is still life left in him, real and sensual. My cock stirs.

I don't have to go to London. I can make the American stop here on the motorway. I can turn over the sleeping senseless Nikolai, rip down his trousers, fuck him, bite him. Feed off him. I realise without emotion that there seems no trace of morality left in my appetites. I don't care. I feel grand. That's the word for it. I feel grand. *Ontopofthe-fuckingworld, man.* I feel alive. I turn away from Nikolai and look out into the black world ahead. I can sense the American watching me. There is a lewd smirk on his face, as if he knows all about my desires, as if he knows exactly what I need.

Bob James places a CD, the Wu Tang Clan, their first album, into the car stereo. To the chop-chop of the hip-hop beats, we enter London. The city just crept up on us. We were on the silent motorway, darkness all around, then a flitter of suburbia, and then we were in the city. Noise and light and cars and neon. I am ready for this city. I can smell the grime and the pollution, the stench of a million bodies. I can smell mould and rodents, rancid breath and foul, unwashed bodies. It is the putrid, accumulated odour of tense, neurotic bodies and it is the obscene effluence of the murky Thames. It is a charged, chemical stench and it hangs like a mutant nimbus over the sprawling city. I am ready for it.

Bob James and Nikolai are staying in a hotel in Earls Court. What the fuck is an Earl, queries Bob James, but he is laughing as he says it. Fucking Brits, fucking useless faggot Brits. The hotel is small and tucked unobtrusively between identical-looking Georgian terraces. A small gold laminated plaque is the only clue to its purpose. An attendant pushes open the swinging glass doors and comes out to greet us. Bob James throws the keys at him.

—Can you park it?

The African youth nods.

The American starts to pull Nikolai from the back seat. He stirs and starts searching for the whisky bottle. Still half-asleep, he pitches forward. Bob James slaps the Russian across the face.

—You fucking Russian cunt. Forget the fucking bottle.

Nikolai is rolling his head, his eyes closed, he is dribbling Russian words. I help Bob James get him out of the car and between us we walk him into the hotel.

A young woman in orange lipstick behind the reception desk glances at us nervously, but the American flashes a key-card and she immediately calls for a porter.

Struggling, the three of us carry the drunk man to the lifts, take him to a room on the second floor and drop him on the bed. Bob James hands a ten-pound note to the porter and asks him to retrieve the bags.

The American looks down at Nikolai, who is moaning softly to himself. He has pissed himself in the corridor and the left leg of his trousers is wet. The brutish reek of the urine is intoxicating. I can smell that he has also shat himself: there is the rich flavour of blood. The American tears the pants off the Russian, and discovers the trail of watery shit. He throws up his hands in disgust.

—That's the fucking Russian entrepreneurial class for you.

There is a knock at the door and the porter enters with the bags. Apart from a slight flinch on first encountering the stink, he shows no alarm at the sight before him. Bob James presses a twenty-pound note in his hand.

—Can you clean things up for me in here?

—Certainly, sir. His accent is flat, dull. He bows and leaves the room. Bob James turns to me.

—Are you going to stay?

I want to rip the Russian apart. Throw my face deep into the shit and piss, inhale him, pour my tongue into him and through him and rip my teeth into him, cover myself, sate myself in his stinking shit, his pulsing blood, his sweat and piss. The American is watching me, his arms crossed, his large bearish body standing in front of the lamp, blocking out the feeble light and casting the room in shadow. I shake my head. I must have thanked him, I must have left the room. I must have taken the lift to the ground floor and I must have walked through the lobby.

Shaking, hungry, awash in lust, I find myself on the cold streets of Earls Court sometime after midnight.

I can hear the sounds of traffic, I can hear shouts in the distance. I have no fear as I walk the deserted streets. London, with the English language everywhere, has always felt comfortable and safe. I draw sharply on the oily squalid air. It is thick with layers of sediment. Layers and layers of shit. History, manure, blood and bone under my feet. The dust of death, life, death, life, endless death and life, repeating repeating, this is what my body is propelling itself through, this is what life on this dirty soil means. I want to be home, in pure, vast Australia where the air is clean, young. I was not fooling myself. There was blood there, in the ground, in the soil, on the water, above the earth. I am not going to pretend that there is not callous history there. Everywhere the smell of the earth is ruthless but I want to be looking up into a vigorous, juvenile sky. The sky above me now is cramped and petty. I can't see the stars, I can't see the edges of any universe. The dome of London reflects back on itself. Europe is endless Europe. No promise of anything else.

I turn into Warwick Road. There are prostitutes outside the closed gates of the Earls Court tube station. I sniff. Rats and sewage, shit and piss and blood, it is all coursing beneath my feet. I approach the women. There are four of them, walking up and down their short strips of the main road. A boy jeers at them from a speeding car. I can see the blinking lights of an off-licence. I can hear the thump-thump of music.

I walk past each of the women. I am smelling them, testing their odour. I am not interested in their appearance. The first woman smells of heroin—was this what my father stank of?—and the abrasive caustic smell is unappealing. The second woman smells of decaying flesh. I know at once that she is dying. The third woman's odour is soft and appealing; she is young. But when I look at her she is startled by my expression and quickly walks off to join the others. I approach the fourth. In a hard cockney accent, almost comical in its television authenticity, she asks me if I have missed the last train. I can smell semen in her mouth, onion, KFC. The first woman yells out to her, Watch him, love. She looks at me, confused. I stand still and wait. She walks off to join the other women. They splinter and begin their pacing, except for the first woman, who keeps looking at me. I turn and keep walking. I hear her furiously tell me to fuck off.

I am approaching the intersection of Old Brompton Road when I first smell her. She has her back straight against the side wall of the off-licence, and is in the shadows, so I can't see her. But her odour is unique. I can smell woman on her: a cheap astringent perfume and something softer, sweeter, the fine dust of talcum powder. But she also smells like a child. I haven't ever been so intoxicated by a fragrance. It reminds me of being in the showers after gym, at school; a fresh pungent scent. I can also smell her fear. It excites me.

She emerges from the shadows. She is very young, with mocha skin and long shining black hair. Her lips are coloured a ludicrous scarlet that distorts her fine small face. You want fuck? She stammers over the coarse words. I nod and she points through into the alley. Twenty pounds. She blurts out the amount, nervously. She is terrified of me. I can sense that, I can sense her distrust and her terror. There is panic in the small oval eyes shining in the darkness. We need a room, I answer. I see her start at my accent. Forty pounds. Again she blurts out the words. I nod. She steps out into the street and I begin to follow her. She keeps turning to look at me, confused. I am craving for her and I am thrilled by the strange stirring of my desire. The mingling of scents has disoriented me and I am hungry purely for the touch of her, to have her. There is nothing of sex in my lust and I have never experienced this freedom from the constraints of the body. She is neither male nor female to me; she is hardly human. It is as if I am looking at the haunches of a dog or a cat walking ahead of me. She stops in front of a shoddy rooming house. She is shivering when she indicates to me to follow her up the stairs.

The corridor reeks of sex and excrement. The young man who hands her a key did not glance up from the magazine he was flicking through. There is no lift and we walk up three flights of the stairs. The door of the room is stained and pot-holed. She turns the key and we enter.

It is tiny. A bare mattress on the floor—emanating rats and semen and cunt—and a small dresser with a bowl of condoms. An uncapped syringe is lying beside the mattress and the girl flicks it with her foot to a corner of the room. She turns to me.

I think she knew that death was in the room with her. Her shivering had increased but she was frozen to the spot, looking at me with her frightened eyes. She had her arms clasped across her chest. I walked over to her and lifted her arms away from her body. She let out a small whimper and an Arabic prayer. She closed her eyes and waited, shaking, prepared. I lifted her slip. Her slim, undernourished body was dark and boyish. I gently stroked the small cups of her breasts. I could hear her. I could hear her heart speaking. It was asking me to kill her. There was a scar running down her left side, an ugly reddish streak. I touched it and for a moment—the only moment—she was defiant, and she pulled away from me. I grabbed her and pushed her onto the mattress. There was a breathing in the room, an excited desperate breathing. She could hear it as well. She was looking beyond my shoulder, in terror, somewhere into the vastness of Hell. I was the Devil. I knew what Evil felt like, was, could be, had to be: the extinguishing of consciousness. I placed my hand on her throat and began to choke her. She started to struggle, attempted to scream, but she was weak and I was stronger than I had ever thought possible. With a jerk of my fingers I could extinguish her life. I was ready. Her hand reached for my throat. She plucked uselessly at my shirt collar, then got a grip and pulled. The crucifix that Giulia had given me tore and fell across the girl's naked body. I looked at her, and now I could see her. She was a terrified small child and she was crying helplessly, desperately. She wanted to die but her body was willing her to live. I pulled away from her.

She did not move. Her eyes did not stray from my face.

I was crying myself now, endless apologies. I thrust into my pockets and found money. I threw the notes at her. A fiver. A twenty. Another. Another. All of my money for England. She was still, then looking at the money at her feet, she sprang up from the bed, gathered the notes, grabbed her clothes and fled. I could hear the tumble of her steps as she rushed down the stairs. There was a shout, an obscenity. I picked up my crucifix and looked at it. The craving had not subsided. I was not clean. But I had consciousness. I had to feed. No Christ, no God, could change that. I made the promise then. And as I made it, out loud, in that piss-stinking fuck-room, I made it not to God but to a man. To Colin. I would choose righteously. Not her, not someone like her. I would have to choose. I could not pretend it was only instinct. I had to feed and I had to choose. I was Satan and I was God.

The man from the reception desk was standing in the doorway. He held a long dagger. When he spoke, his accent was from the Caribbean.

—You gonna fuck off?

I slowly nodded.

—If I ever fucking see you again, I'll fucking slice you.

When I walked past him he spat at my feet.

There was no London as I retraced my steps. There were no revellers, no whores. There were no cars and no lights, no neon and no laughter. There was no asphalt, no sky, no brick, no night. There was nothing above and nothing beneath. There was no form in the void. There was only my breathing, the coursing of my blood. There was no one in the hotel foyer when I entered. There was no doorman, no porter, no receptionist, no concierge. There was no desk, no lift, no door. There was only a question, whispered to me, by the Thames, by the wind, by Europe itself. It was Andreas' question, Maria's question, Sula's question, Zivan's question. What do you believe?

I know how to answer it now. What I believe is that we will kill each other, that we will hurt each other. We will destroy our neighbours and we will exile them. We will sell our children as whores. We will murder and rape and punish one another. We will keep warring and we will keep hating and we will believe we are just and righteous and faithful. We will keep killing and selling one another and we will believe that we are just and fair and good. We will pursue pleasures and destroy one another in these pursuits. We will abandon our children. We will do all this in the name of God and in the name of our nature. We will create poverty and illness and we will create obscene wealth and the depravities that arise from it. We will think ourselves just and righteous, faithful and sane. We will hate and kill and piss and shit on one another. We will continue to do so. We will create Armageddon. In the name of God or in the name of justice or, simply, because we can. This is what I believe.

The American answers my knock. When he sees me, he laughs, a sly victorious cackle, and he opens the door and welcomes me. How had I not sensed it before? The putrid, spent stench of him. He is naked except for a white hotel towel tied around his belly.

—I thought you'd be back.

He sits in the armchair and the towel slips to the floor. His cock is wet and limp and red. He lights a cigarette and points to the bed.

—He's yours, you can have him.

The room has been cleaned and the bed made up again with fresh sheets. But there is the stench of vomit and shit, the caustic foulness of amyl nitrate. The Russian is lying naked on his stomach in the centre of the bed. His wide, fleshy arse. There is a trickle of blood there, it has dampened the fine tufts of black hair along his crack, and my resolve weakens as I smell it. I want to enter him. I walk over to the bed, my cock hard. I look down at him. His eyes are open and for a moment I fear he is dead. He is a man, I can see he is a man. His breathing is hoarse, there are silent tears falling, a constant stream. The side of his face lies in vomit. The empty brown glass amyl nitrate vial is clutched in his fist. The television screen flickers with images from CNN. A grim male newsreader with glasses. Flashes of desert, a handcuffed youth, scrawling letters.

—Don't worry, he's not dead.

I turn to the American. He is smoking the cigarette, stroking the thick grey fluff on his chest. His smile is cruel.

—Fuck him. It is an order, harsh, intoxicating.

I shake my head.

—Go on, you fucking cunt, that's why you've come back, isn't it? Fuck him.

I am startled by the venom but I am not afraid. I have nothing to fear.

He goads me in harsh, cold whispers, arousing himself with each threat. His hand has begun to stroke at his cock.

—This is what you want to do, I know. I knew it all along.

He has grabbed a tube of lubricant from the floor and is squirting it onto his limp cock.

—Go ahead, rape him. Go on—have you got the fucking guts? Kill the cunt.

I can smell the Russian. Blood and shit and sex. My cock is pressing against my jeans. Rape him. Kill him.

The American has risen and stands beside me. He looks down at the Russian. The Russian's eyes, unmoving, gaze somewhere beyond us. The American pulls the Russian's legs apart. There is a fart, then the smell. The Russian moans.

—Isaac, the American says slowly, deliberately; he is huge, he seems to fill the whole of the room. I order you to kill him. Get your revenge, Isaac. He's nothing, he's an animal. The American spits on the Russian. I command you. Destroy him, kill him, annihilate him. I command you. Slaughter him.

The Russian is moaning. I can do it. I can do anything to him. Meat, blood and flesh. I know then what man is. Meat. Flesh. Blood. He moans, low, desperate, ill. I sniff the air.

It is the American behind me. I can smell all of him. Lubricant, sweat, semen, muscle, blood, amyl nitrate, shit, piss, spit, soap, leather, cotton, denim, metal, plastic, steel, wood, alcohol, marijuana, coke, Pepsi, fries, wine, beer, plastic, steel, iron, leather, silk, satin, uranium, plutonium, petrol, chips, chocolate, gelatin, dollars, euros, pounds, Omo, Oreos, Oil of Ulan, porn, television, cinema, gold, silver, cash, stocks, bonds, insurance, tanks, guns, rifles, Versace, Gucci, Prada. Piss, sweat, blood, shit. God. The American stinks of Him. Piss, sweat, blood, shit. It stinks of Him.

Armageddon. How long must we sing this song, Lord? Sweet Armageddon, beloved genocide, Come to me.

I don't wish it to die straight away. I want to feel the liquid, thick and alive, course into me. I first bite into its upper lip. It does not scream, just a bare whimper as I tear the flesh off. Its eyes, horror swimming through them, catch mine but I have already ripped into its throat and it shakes, stammers and falls, slumping across the armchair. Its blood is on my face, on my lips, in my mouth, in my throat, pouring onto my body, the chair, the carpet, the walls. I feel its moment of death. Death makes a sound, a low rumble, a hoarse, desperate cleaving to life, then silence. Life is extinguished. The taste of the blood has changed, lost its potency, become stale. I wipe my face, lick at the blood. It has released its sphincter and bladder. Piss and shit run down its legs, drip onto the hotel carpet. There is laughter in the room, a boy's loud joyous exhilarated laughter.

There is a box in the corner; light dances and flickers across a screen. For a moment I stare, transfixed. Light dances from it, sounds come from within it, patterns forming patterns, sound echoing sound. Elated, I walk over to the bed. I am not yet satisfied. There is more to be had. The other creature on the bed is asleep, snoring. I lift its head, and for a moment the eyes flick open, there is rage there, but my teeth sink into its face and the eyes disappear forever. I pull away skin and muscle and bone and the blood gushes onto my face and neck and as it pours over me I can taste Creation but almost immediately I feel virile life being extinguished and this blood too is spent. I throw the carcass off the bed and lie down on the drenched silk sheets. As I fall into calm sleep, I hear the jumble of confused electric noise coming off the box in the far corner of the room; I am aware of the insistent humming of the bedside lamp above me; I can hear the dripping of the blood as it slides down the walls and falls in drops onto the carpet; the last sound I hear before blessed sleep is the violent, delighted laughter of the boy as he comes to lie next to me, wrapping his legs and arms around me.

THE BOOK OF LILITH

—EVERY CHRISTMAS THE Jews would steal a Christian toddler, put it in a barrel, still alive, run knives between the slats, and drain the child of its blood. Then they'd drink it. That's the first thing I ever got told about the Jews.

—I can't believe Rebecca told you that shit.

—I must have been about five when she told me. She made it sound like a fairytale . . .

— . . . some pretty fucked-up fairytale . . .

— . . . I know, I know. Dad told her off when he heard her talking about that sort of stuff. He told us it was uneducated peasant bullshit. He sat me down and gave me a history lesson. He explained where the Jews came from, told us that the Bible was their history, told us about the Holocaust. He even explained what the Ashkenazi and the Sephardim were. Being Dad, of course, he put his own Marxist spin on it. He always said that the tragedy of the Holocaust was that the Nazis destroyed the Jewish proletariat. And he told us that the Bible was all crap and not to believe in any religion.

—He was never religious?

—Maybe when he was a kid. But, nah, he hated religion. His religion was communism. And heroin.

—My Mum hated religion too. Typical Aussie, she taught me jack-shit. I had to go to school before I heard about Jesus. I believed in the Easter Bunny but I hadn't heard of Jesus.

—So how was she when you became a Christian?

—I was never a Christian.

—I thought you were . . .

385

— . . . I was fascinated by religion; I read the Bible because Steve made me. I'm glad he did. It made me fall in love with reading history. I know, that's not very Aussie of me. But I hardly knew any Christians. Just Steve and some of the kids at school. I knew the Catholics, the Orthodox, the Muslims. But they didn't give a fuck about religion except for some fasting at Ramadan or Easter. That was all religion was for them.

—I know exactly what you mean. It's all ritual, no theology. When I got older I yelled at Mum, said: Your bloody Jesus was a Jew, how could you tell me the things you did? *He was a Jew*.

—He wasn't.

—He *was*.

—Listen to me. He was born a Jew but he came to earth to announce a new Covenant, to replace the old Covenant between Moses and God.

—Now you do sound like a Christian.

—I just fucking hate that liberal bullshit that claims we're all brothers, that it's all the same religion . . .

— . . . it's the same bloody God . . .

—Listen, all I'm saying is that if you're a Jew, you claim to be a descendant of the twelve tribes of Israel. Your law is the law of Moses. You are the Chosen People. That's it. Your God doesn't give a fuck about anyone else. It's all there in the Torah. If you're Christian you believe in the resurrection of Christ, the Trinity and the new Covenant. If you're Muslim then Mohammed was God's last Prophet and you submit to the word of God as written in the Qu'ran. They are not the same thing. I can't stand New Age Christian preachers trying to humanise the Bible. I can't stand secular American Jews brandishing their copies of the Constitution as equivalent to Holy Writ and thinking they can be both Jewish and non-believers. Fucking bullshit. At least the Muslims are bloody honest.

You can't be democratic and monotheistic. Choose. It's one or the other.

—I disagree. That's too hard, much too hard. You can be ecumenical. You can have a rabbi, a priest, a mullah . . .

— . . . and they go into a bar . . .

— . . . You can have them get together, acknowledge differences but also accept similarities. Find common ground. Otherwise you are talking perpetual war. I can't agree with you.

—Listen, your mum didn't make that up about the Jews, not the blood libel. It's a fact. It's in the Gospels, I can't fucking remember exactly where, I think it's in Matthew. The Jews answered Pontius Pilate: let His blood be on us and our children. If you're a Christian, you have to accept that obscenity as fact. Your dad was wrong. Your mother wasn't speaking as an illiterate peasant but as a believer. That's the source of blood libel and I don't give a fuck how many bourgeois theologians attempt to explain it away by theorising about the politics of the early Church and the Roman state. What are you? What do you believe? Do you believe that the Jews killed Christ? Or do you believe that the Jews are God's Chosen People and his only people? Or do you submit to the word of God as revealed in the Qu'ran and unless you do you are doomed to Hell? This might offend your fucking democratic wishy-washy liberal pieties, but religion *is* war.

—Why are you so angry?

—Because people are cowards.

—Who came first? Abraham or Moses?

—Jesus Christ, I can't believe this. And you're the one who went to fucking university.

—They don't teach religion at university.

—They should.

—Why?

—It's history, it's politics.

—You sound like a bloody fundamentalist. Bullshit. God is dead. That's what you learn at university.

—Right, He's dead, is He? Go ask Khadijah and Bilal next door. Go ask your mum. Go ask the fucking Israelis and the Palestinians or the Hindus and the Pakistanis if God is dead.

—You haven't answered my question.

—Abraham was before Moses. He was after Noah. Isaac, your namesake, was his son whom God demanded he sacrifice. Abraham was prepared to do God's will. His other son was Ishmael, the bastard son he had with his slave, Hagar. The Jews come from the line of Isaac. The Arabs claim they are descended from Ishmael.

—Fucking perfect. Slavery and blood feuds. And that's religion? You can fucking keep it.

—That's history, mate, that's politics. Blood and servitude.

—So you're arguing that if you are going to believe in God, you have to believe fundamentally? You believe in Noah and the flood, Sodom and fucking Gomorrah? The Resurrection? That Mohammed received the word of God? That's your argument?

—Yes.

—And Adam and Eve?

—Yes. Adam and Eve and Cain and Abel. And Lilith.

—Who?

—Adam's first wife.

—What? That's not in the Bible.

—It's apocrypha. I like Lilith. She gave God the finger.

—Who the fuck was Lilith?

—First there was the Word. And the Word was Wisdom. Then there was God, Yahweh, and he created the heavens and earth and all that walks and lives and is on the earth. He created Adam after his own image and placed him in Eden. Then when Adam came of age he wanted a partner. So God passed all the female animals past him and Adam slept with them all but none of them satisfied him.

388

—You're making this up.

—I'm not. It's one version of her story, anyway. You want me to continue?

—Go.

—So God created Lilith from the earth, as he had done with Adam, and he created her in Wisdom's image. Sophia. You should know that word. It's Greek.

—Hang on. And is Sophia another god?

—Yes.

—But isn't there only one God?

—Moses told the Jews they could only worship the one God. But they had many gods before that.

—So Lilith and Adam get together?

—Yes. And they had children, which are now the demons that roam the earth. But Lilith wasn't satisfied with Adam and she left him. She wanted to be equal to him. She flew to the Red Sea and there gave birth to more demons.

—Fuck. What happened to her?

—She's still on earth. She departed Eden long before the Fall and, as she hasn't eaten off the Tree of Good and Evil, she's immortal. She will live to the end of time and God allows her to eat the blood of uncircumcised children. That's our first mother. Blood, you can't escape it. All religions know this.

—But they're fairytales.

—Or they're truth. It all depends on faith.

—But you must agree that they are of their place and time. You can have faith in God or Christ without having to accept all that superstitious shit from millennia ago.

—You can argue and disagree about the meaning of the words, but no, I don't believe you can pick and choose from religious moral codes as if faith is some kind of supermarket of beliefs. I'm with the fundamentalists. You make your choice. *You make your fucking choice*. You are either a believer or not. God makes his meaning and his character clear in the Torah, in the Bible and in the Qu'ran. He is not a God of love, he is a God of justice.

—So for me to believe in God, I have to believe that loving you, making love to you, being with you, is a sin and I am damned to Hell forever?

—Yes. You can ask God's forgiveness, but if you remain with me, you are damned.

—So do you believe in this God?

—I don't know. But I'll tell you this, my love, if there is the one God, I still choose you. I choose you above God. I've made that choice and I'll live with that choice. I choose Lilith and the demons, I choose Lucifer, who too knew love. I promise you, Isaac, if God is the righteous prick from the Bible, I choose Hell over Him. Fuck him. I choose to be with you. I choose Hell.

SHE HAD AWOKEN from her dream and was prepared for the telephone when it rang. In the cold of the August night, the room's temperature had dropped and she threw a blanket across her shoulders, and rocked back and forth in the winter silence awaiting the call. She had dreamt that she was a young woman again. The dream had been astonishing in its vividness. She was a young woman and she was approaching the graphite boulders that lay on the hill above her grandmother's house. She had not dreamt of home for decades. As a young girl she had loved to climb the boulders, for on the other side of them the ancient wind had carved shelves into the rocks which she would use as steps to skip down to where the mountain creek flowed south to the village. From the top of the rocks she could not only see her house and her village, but look back down the valley and see the village of Simshi, and, in the distance, Ta-Loukània. She could see the women working in the deep valley and she could see the monastery, perched so high on the mountain's summit that sometimes she believed it floated there beyond the clouds. She had climbed the same rocks again in this dream. She had been excited, anxious: would she see the silver-flecked waters of the creek rushing across the ashen rocks? But when she had reached the summit and peered down through the crevice of the boulders to the creek, on both its banks, on every rock jutting out from the rushing brook, there sat a coiled snake. Their scaly skins were the black of coal and they glistened in the aberrant sun. It was not a Balkan sun, this light in her dream. It was an Australian sun. She had been terrified, unable to move, for there was also a coiled snake at her feet. There were dozens of them. They were still and silent but it was as if every single one of them was alert, tense to her presence. Up on the hill, their backs to her, a man and a child were sitting. The boy was naked and his grey pale skin was the colour of death. The man's hair was as shiny and as black as the reptiles' cold skin. She knew at once that the young man was Vassili, her husband. She had called out his nickname. *Lucky*. But neither he nor the boy turned around. She could not go forward, could not go back. She was chained to the boulders. The boy had stood and pointed into the grotesque luminous sun. It was larger than the lowest full moon. She had shaken her head violently. No, she pleaded with them, she could not come to them. With his face still turned from her, her husband too had stood and pointed at the sun. She again refused, unable to defy the poisonous gaze of the serpents stretched before her. She had looked down again at the earth, at the snakepit, and then her heart had frozen. In the icy brook her son's naked body lay in the water, his eyes shut. She feared him dead. A giant snake sat on his chest, its head raised, looking straight into her. She had fallen to her knees. The boy was still pointing to the sun but now he had begun to turn his face towards her. She did not want to see his face, she did not dare look at his face. She feared him more than the snakes, the abnormal sun. She feared that boy more than the death of her own child.

She awoke, gasping for breath. She clutched a blanket tight around her frail body, bringing the soft wool to her chin. The hard electric light from the streetlamp outside the house brought the objects in the room to uncanny mysterious life. She glanced up at the icon of the Madonna above her bed and forced her hands out from under the blanket, forced herself to pray. She could not pray without a shameful sense of her ignominy and her sin. But she was aware that her dream had signified an ill omen and she knew she must pray. Further, she knew the boy in her dream, knew the face that would turn to her. Rebecca, believing firmly in the righteousness of justice and faith, knew that her sins were great. Her life, increasingly, had become a quest to make amends for these sins. Her small house was filled now with images of God, His Son and the Son's Mother. Her home was full of saints: Byzantine and stern, Catholic and soft. Her husband had mocked faith all his life and had often been furious when she tried to introduce religious icons into the house. He had allowed one small icon of the infant Jesus in the children's bedroom, and he had allowed her an icon of Agia Eleni in the kitchen. But he had forbidden anything else and insisted that there should be nothing of God in the rooms in which he dwelt. Nothing of God in the lounge room, in their bedroom. Instead, a painting of a severe Lenin admonished them from above the television, and her white bedroom walls—still smoky and burnished to ash from years of her husband's cigarette smoking—were bare except for their wedding photographs and a photograph Isaac had taken of Lucky just before his death. When her husband had died, she had filled the walls with God and the saints. She had left Lenin in his place, in memory of her husband.

—Please, Holy Mother, she prayed, take me, do what you will with me, please ensure that Isaac and Sophie are safe, that my grandchildren are safe.

The telephone rang in cruel blasts of sound. She threw the blankets to the floor and ran to the hall. Answering it, she recognised Colin's deep slow drawl at once. As always, his manner was direct and unemotional. Tonight she appreciated his strength. He told her the news quickly. He had received a call from England. Isaac was sick. No, he did not know exactly the cause of his illness, except that their friend in

England thought it was some kind of emotional collapse. Colin explained that he would organise a flight to London immediately. Did she want to come with him?

—Of course I will come. Then she started to howl. Colin, she screamed down the phone, I do not have a passport.

He had allowed her to cry, to lament, and then told her not to worry at all, that he would help her organise the passport, that she was not to concern herself with any such details. He would do everything.

The thought crossed her mind, even in her grief—and not for the first time—that if her daughter had married such a man she would have been a proud and vain mother-in-law. Oh, how she would have lorded it over the Greek peasant sows! Do you want me to come over, she heard him ask. Yes, yes, she cried into the phone. She could not bear to be alone.

She turned on the lights in the living room, fired up the gas heater. She rocked back and forth in front of the violet flames until she heard Colin's car pull up outside the house. She threw herself on him. That night they did not sleep. They drank coffee, worked out what they must do, spoke endlessly of Isaac. Near dawn, Colin had driven off and bought cigarettes. They both smoked their first cigarette in years. It was a drug, thought Rebecca, and like all drugs it brought relief. Allowed for patience. There would be interminable waiting ahead for them. Organising the flights, the flight itself, the vigil at the hospital, organising Isaac's return. She knew that she would be smoking through all that time.

Colin did indeed arrange everything. She had offered to pay but he had refused. I'm not going to take any money from a bloody pensioner. Sophie, too, had been marvellous. She had come down immediately from Canberra. The news from England was not good. Isaac was sick. The nature of his illness was never specified but every time Colin had got off the phone his face had been pale and stretched. She had been shocked when she received her passport in the mail. She was an old woman. She had only ever had two passports in her life. The first had been red, the now tatty and stained booklet she had as a little girl departing Greece. This blue Australian passport now confirmed her age, her feebleness. It was an old crone's face that stared out at her. Holy Mother, do not allow me to bury a son, do not let me bury a son.

Sophie drove them to the airport. Rebecca had become furious at the thoroughness and cold authority of the security staff. Since the birth of her first grandchild, knitting had become one of her keenest pleasures. She wished that she had discovered the hobby years ago. It kept her busy, kept her calm and at peace. While knitting, she could forget all that she had lost. Lucky, heroin, a country and a family. She had packed her knitting needles, but they confiscated them and coldly refused to answer her demands that they give them back to her. Like a broken record, the obese customs official at Melbourne Airport kept repeating, It's all down in black and white, lady. Nothing sharp on board.

Do I look like a bloody terrorist? she screamed at them. Sophie pulled her aside. Don't make a scene, she cautioned, and looking up at Colin's grim pale face, the old woman had felt ashamed and she immediately apologised.

—I don't mind. I was just worried that they were going to strip-search us.

Rebecca snorted.

—One finger anywhere near me and I'll show them real terror.

Without her knitting to occupy her, it was an interminable flight to London. She recalled, for the first time in many years, her journey from Europe on the ship. She remembered how that journey too had seemed to last forever.

It was a long, agonising wait to clear customs at Heathrow. She had wanted to insult the stiff-backed young Englishman who carefully scrutinised her passport. The English would never trust her, she knew this from her long years in Australia. But Colin was always standing behind her, his hand on her shoulder, making jokes, attempting to make her laugh—if she had not been here with Colin she knew she would have gone mad; he enabled her to survive the wait. At least, she marvelled, you could smoke in the English airports. She had thought that this country would be exactly like Australia. Only older. But it wasn't. She had known it as soon as the jet had landed. Waiting to dismount, she had looked out the plane's window to the blue-uniformed black men below tossing luggage onto a metal crate. When finally they were out in the Heathrow morning light—the airport was a city itself—they found a taxi, gave instructions to the driver, and made their way to the hospital.

As soon as she saw her son, she knew he was dying. Colin had been the one to break down, and to see this big man cry, to see the depth and ferocity of his grief, had made her determined that she would save her son. Isaac's face had aged and his pallor was that of cigarette ash. His cheekbones stretched the grey skin and his lips were nearly black. It was only his sunken eyes, their almond shape now grotesquely big for his thin face, only his eyes that reminded her of her child.

As soon as she had entered the room she had also seen the other there. His boy's body was curled up beside her son, his thin fingers were stroking Isaac's skin. He would not look at her. She even called out the childhood name she had for him—Angelo, she whispered—but he did not see her, did not hear her. Isaac, however, heard, and the desperate eyes he turned to her were full of pleading. She took her son's hand. Colin was kissing Isaac's face, his mouth, his sweating forehead. She did not cry a tear.

The doctors had nothing reassuring to say. We are sorry, we have done all the necessary blood tests but we don't know what it is that is causing his immune system to mal-function. We are sorry, he is dying. Colin continued to ask endless questions but she did not listen, did not care. Before arriving in England, she had not been able to think straight in her grief: all she could do was cry and lament. But here, in this foreign city, it was as if she and Colin had exchanged roles. It was he who would alternate between haranguing the doctors, falling into tears, pacing, smoking, crying. Isaac's friend Sam had come to London. She recognised Isaac's teacher immediately; like her, he had aged. He had been young and conceited when he taught Isaac, and dismissive of her concerns about her son's scholastic performance. She had felt undermined by him. He had thought her illiterate, and though his manner to her and Lucky had always been cordial and kind, it had also been aloof and patronising. She had felt a perverse pleasure when she had heard about his disgrace. But all this was past now. She hugged him warmly and thanked him for helping her son. He looked confused and frightened. Don't blame yourself, urged Colin, but then with the next breath he would berate Sam with questions. What happened? Who was with him? When did it happen? How the fuck did it happen?

She only half-listened to the man's responses. Her son had been drinking at a hotel in the city Sam lived in. She could not catch its name; it was unfamiliar to her. He had been drinking alone and then had gone off to London. No, Sam did not know who he had gone to London with. It was assumed he had been hitchhiking. The police had found him ranting and screaming in the city. What was he doing? asked Colin. Nothing, nothing, said Sam, all he was doing was screaming. The police had first thought he was drunk. It was then that they had called Sam—fortunately, Isaac still had his phone number in his pocket. By the time Sam had arrived in London, Isaac's health had worsened. He had immediately called Colin. But something else must have happened, urged Colin. Sam had shaken his head. But Colin would not, could not, stop asking questions. Sam tirelessly repeated the story. Rebecca excused herself and went back into her son's room.

Isaac had fallen asleep. His breaths were hoarse and exhausted. The ghoul had his thin arms and long gaunt legs wrapped around her sleeping son. He was kissing him. Rebecca crossed herself but she made no prayer. She knew that it was useless to offer false promises and she knew that more was to be asked of her than prayers and supplication. She walked over to her son. The nurse had not yet come around to collect the food trays. Isaac's lay on the dresser, the meal untouched. The doctors had said he was now unable to feed himself and from the morning they would be feeding him on a drip. Rebecca had made up her mind. She quickly glanced around the room. Two of the other patients were also asleep; a third was watching a television monitor above his bed. She picked up the white plastic knife from the tray and dragged it across her wrist. The serrated edge was blunt but she hacked at her skin until a foam of scarlet blood appeared. She placed her wrist on her son's lips. It was then that the ghoul looked at her. His face was contorted in anger. He had not recognised her. She knew she was just something that came between the demon and her son. The ghoul had always been this way. It was possessive and suspicious and cruel. Now it wanted her son. All that existed for it was her son. She willed her blood to pour, to feed into Isaac. It hurt her, as it had hurt when he first began to suckle from her breasts, a pain that had forced her hour by hour to tears and fury; but she had forced him onto her raw bruised cracked nipples, and she forced him to drink from her now. Isaac coughed and opened his eyes. She rubbed her wound and kissed him on the mouth. The demon had left them. But not for long. Not for long. She kissed her son again. There was much to do.

She was in charge now. Sam had organised a small hotel room across the busy main road from the hospital, and there she prepared meals for herself and the two men. She was shocked at the price of food in England. She told Colin that they were taking Isaac back to Australia immediately. The doctors were initially resistant but they could not deny that Isaac seemed a little better since their arrival, and the truth was that as there was nothing they could do for him, they needed his bed for someone they could help. Rebecca had been appalled by the shoddiness and desperate poverty of the hospital. She had assumed that England would be not only powerful but rich. But from the haggard expressions of the Slav and African cleaners, and the exhausted faces of the nursing and medical staff, she was aware that there was little money, little of anything.

They were to leave in three days and she knew that this offered scant opportunity to see anything of the city, but on her daily walk from the hotel to the hospital she saw enough. This was not Australia. If nothing of the air and the sky and the earth looked like Greece, she recognised the churlishness and the abrupt rudeness of the people: she remembered this toughness. As if visited by a distant memory, she saw that this city was indeed European, by which she meant ancient. Her husband had called Australians unsophisticated, and looked down at them for it, and she finally understood what he had meant. It was nothing to do with education or the class to which you were born. It had everything to do with one's place in the world. She had been born in a remote corner of damaged, destroyed Europe but it had still felt like the centre of the world. As a Greek she knew she was at the centre of the world. She could tell, just in three days, that Londoners too knew that they were at the centre of the universe. She could not help wondering what it would be like to have come here, to have migrated here instead, to have remained in Europe. She would probably not feel that hunger for *something else*, which, for her, was the meaning of being Australian. O *neos kosmos*. The New World. She realised she envied these cold dour Londoners. But she also marvelled at their acceptance of the little that Europe now offered them.

Waiting for a red light on a busy street corner—such a large, anxious swarm of people, such a mob did not exist in Australia—she saw a young Irish girl begging, her child wrapped in a small blanket in her arms. No one noticed her, the girl's smack-blasted eyes, the baby's pallid skin. Rebecca found herself speaking out loud to Lucky. Imagine, husband, all these centuries of being a superpower, of meddling in the world's affairs, of wanting power, and this is what you end up with. She could hear her husband's laughter: oh, how she missed that laugh. She thought then of her son and what she must now do. She must prepare to never hear her husband's laughter again.

Their hotel apartment was tiny but it did not matter, for they spent all their time in the hospital. She got to know the other patients in the room and became friendly with their families. The patients were all suffering from diseases of the blood. The boy in the bed next to Isaac was younger than her son. His family was from Pakistan and she could not help comparing them to her and to her own family and circumstances. The father was large and silent, refusing to betray any emotion. His wife did not leave her son's side except at night when her husband forced her to leave the ward. She and Rebecca would often arrive at the hospital grounds at first light. Rebecca told her of life in Australia, and Azamir told her of life in London. They prayed together for, as Azamir said, it was the same one God.

Rebecca demanded that she be the one to sponge and bathe her son and Colin had asked her if she wanted him to leave the room. This had made her laugh. Why? she had asked him.

If I don't mind you fucking him, why should I mind you seeing me bathe him? The nurse who was marking Isaac's chart, a plump Caribbean woman, giggled on hearing this, and then quickly apologised. She and Rebecca were also to exchange stories of exile. It struck Rebecca that if migrants were to form a nation, they could conquer the earth.

She and Colin would bathe Isaac every morning and once again before they left the ward at night. There were moments when she could not bear to touch the ashen paleness of his skin. More than his distended belly, his swollen feet, the putrid stink of his blackened, hungry mouth, the child-like wrists, it was his skin that terrified her. She was grateful for Colin's calm courage then. Often in the past she had resented his aloofness. It reminded her of the boys and men whom she had lived alongside all her life in Australia; the boys and men who had bullied her and abused her; or worse, for a woman with her pride, who had simply ignored her, remained oblivious to her and her world. She had nicknamed him 'kokkini', the red one, and though it was a term that had become an affectionate nickname, it had initially risen from disdain. She was exacting a small revenge every time she used that name and though Colin had never minded, never seen the spite in it, Isaac and Sophie chided her whenever they heard it.

But now, standing across from him as they each sponged down Isaac's torso, washed his face, as Colin assisted him to shit and to piss and then cleaned up after him, Rebecca silently asked a thousand pardons from the man. Colin, she knew, was convinced that his lover was dying. She now understood that she could not read his grief from his words or tears or cries but from looking into his bewildered eyes, from seeing how his coarse workman's hands shook whenever Isaac gasped and wheezed in his sleep.

Colin wanted to remain in England and allow Isaac to die here. He feared that the shock of the long flight to

Melbourne would only hasten his death. Rebecca had promised him that Isaac would live. She could not help it. She wanted in some way to still his anguish. In this she succeeded, because she saw the flash of fury in his eyes: a red temper indeed. He had said nothing but had left the ward and when he returned she could smell the tobacco on his breath and she could see from his bruised eyes and flushed face that he had been crying.

—I promise you, Colin, he will live.

On the eve of their departure Colin took her for a walk around the city. She had initially refused, not wanting to leave her son to the caresses of the demon, but Colin had been adamant and she had finally acquiesced. She was also curious to see more of the city. She could not quite believe that it was real. It was a city from a fable, at times wondrous, at times malevolent. Colin proved to be an excellent guide. They descended into the great Underground and she marvelled at the swiftness and the extent of the services. Colin explained to her that Londoners were always complaining about their Tube and she retorted that they were English and it was in their nature to always complain. On the train she read the brief notices plastered along-side advertisements which asked passengers to report any suspicious-looking parcel or container. They came up into Piccadilly and it was there that she understood the scale of the city she was in. She felt regret, then, not so much for herself but for what her husband had forgone to be with her. Melbourne and Australia had imprisoned him, he was too big for the cramped Australian cities. It was not a question of space. She knew the moment she stepped out into Heathrow that Australia had more air, more room, more land. But it was, nevertheless, a small country. Population, not geography, made a nation. Her husband needed move-ment and there was little of this in their lives. For him, heroin had been the way he had dealt with the inert weight of life. For her, heroin had been a way to escape the whispers of conscience, which for her were—and could only ever be—the voice of God. But God was eternal. She finally understood this, standing in the middle of London, comprehending the enormity of Europe. He was patient. In a Lebanese cafe in Kensington filled with pictures of Princess Diana, she wept, and Colin silently witnessed her grieving.

That night they packed up Isaac's belongings. Sam had placed all the European photographs and proofsheets in a folio, and Colin and Rebecca had flicked through each clear plastic sheet, looking at the black and white images beneath. With a jolt she recognised her ancestral home and had to bite her palm to stop herself from screaming. She had thought that the day in London had made her reconciled to her estrangement from Europe, but seeing the dirt of her father's earth, the light of her family's sky, the gate and courtyard of Papa Nicholas' church, the shadows of the poplar trees, she had felt a wave of sorrow flow through her. She was cursed. Never to settle, to have roots, to belong.

Colin was shocked by the obscene, ugly reality of the photographs: the landscapes awash as if in blood; the misery on the cadaverous faces of the figures. After the first few he could not bear to see them and had lit a cigarette and stood at the window looking down at the road below. She could see the night sky beyond him and she thought it peculiar that it was only during the day that London seemed a metropolis. At night it was quiet and still. She zipped up the folio.

—What do you think of those photographs? He was gazing down at the world below.

—I think they are true.

—And what truth is that?

His tone was bitter. She wished he would allow her to touch him, to soothe him. She realised that he would be lost without Isaac. Not that she feared that he could not survive tragedy—he had strength—but without Isaac his isolation would become complete and she feared he would never let another touch him again.

—The truth of Europe.

—That's not Europe in those photographs, his words rushed out. Those photographs are Hell. What Hell did Isaac see? What Hell is he in?

—Europe has suffered Hell.

—Fuck Europe. What Hell do they know? The truth of Europe is money. I fucking hate Europe.

—Of course you do, darling. She wished she was better educated, she wished she had her husband's knowledge and his words. He could explain it all. Missed their arguments. You don't understand Europe. You're not from here. You feel trapped here, I understand. That is what I see when I look at Isaac's photographs. Europe scares you. You're Australian, you don't understand Europe.

—I'm as European as you. As European as Isaac.

—No, you are not. She was surprised by the vehemence of her own anger. You are not, Isaac is not. What do you know of Europe? You're children. You're bloody children here and you are bloody children there.

She was experiencing the frustration she always felt when confronted by the petulance and impatience of her son and daughter. They had never gone hungry, never experienced war or exile and yet unceasingly demanded more from this world. Like the grown man at the window, his arms crossed, angry at the world when he knew nothing of it.

The words were about to tumble from her lips: what do you know of suffering? Then she thought of her child, and reminded herself of the man's grief. In grief, she reminded herself, you become adult; you have entered the world. The words she did finally speak were quiet and conciliatory.

—You are fortunate, you are Australian.

—They're the fucking lucky ones, Rebecca. He was not

ready to let go of his anger. The poor child, she thought to herself, and with that her fury vanished. Colin nodded to the world outside the hotel room. They're the ones at the centre of the world. They're the ones with everything, they're the ones making all the decisions.

—They will suffer again. She said this quietly. And as soon as she said it, she knew it to be true. Could he not see it? In just three days she had seen it. The beggars on the streets, the Slav girls who cleaned the toilets in the hotel, the train stations plastered with warnings of terror. Their fear, their anxiety, it suffused the city. Could Colin not see the truth of the photographs? Isaac had not photographed the past, he had captured the future. She could not wait to get home.

Colin had come and sat beside her.

—You never think of returning to Greece?

The poplar trees. The dry hard earth. The cemetery gates. Her home in black and white.

—No, she answered quietly. She would have liked to answer that it was only those from a new world who believed that home was a matter of choice. But she didn't speak because he had taken her hand and was squeezing it tight. His hand was rough, weathered. It was not like her husband's hands; their softness had always taken her by surprise. Isaac had his father's hands. But Colin had rough hands, with calluses, scabs and scars, just like hers.

—No, she finally answered. Why should I return to Europe, to Greece? Europe didn't want me, Greece didn't want me.

Sitting next to her on the bed, Colin began to flick through the photographs again. A man's weary, aged face stared out at her, beckoning her. She gasped, and the world became motionless and hushed. She exhaled, and the world moved again.

—What is it, Rebecca?

—Nothing. That man in the photograph reminded me of someone long ago.

Colin picked up the envelope and stared at the man's face.

—Who?

—A friend from the past. Isaac was named after him.

She stared into the old man's eyes. Yes, they were calling out to her.

—Who was he?

—A good friend, an old comrade of Lucky's. He killed himself, a long time ago.

Colin took the photograph out of the plastic sheath.

—Why did he do it?

—Loneliness. He married a beautiful woman, a Dutch woman, but she could not bear Australia. She could not live without Europe, Australia was slowly killing her. But he could never live in Europe again.

—And Isaac is named after him?

—We called him Gerry. The Australians could never pronounce his real name. But his name means Isaac.

Colin got up off the bed

—We should go to sleep, he said softly, slipping his hand away.

—I will put away the photographs.

She clutched at the photograph of the old man all night. She could not sleep. What odyssey have you been on, Isaac? she murmured to herself. How will I bring you back from the underworld? What am I to sacrifice?

On leaving the hospital, Azamir and Rebecca threw their arms around each other, could not let themselves break the embrace. The men had to ease them apart and they wept as if they were sisters.

When they walked through the sliding doors of Melbourne Airport she felt a gust of biting Antarctic wind and was astonished by its clarity. There was no blood in this wind: it was intoxicating. Her wrists were scarred with fresh raw wounds. On the long journey she had used the plastic aeroplane knife to carve at her arms and to feed Isaac her blood. Colin had watched the bizarre ritual and not said a word. But on returning from the cabin toilets she had found him pricking at the flesh on his finger till it bled. He placed the dripping blood on his lover's lips. From Dubai to Singapore, from Singapore to Sydney, from Sydney to Melbourne, they took turns feeding Isaac.

She had no patience for rest once they reached home. As soon as they had put Isaac to bed, she wrapped her scarf around her head and took Sophie's car keys off the kitchen table. Her daughter implored her to stay. The girl was half-mad with fear for her brother and wanted to know what the doctors had said, whether her brother would survive. Rebecca pushed Sophie off her. I have to go, she explained. Colin will tell you everything. She kissed Colin's brow. It will be over soon, she promised him.

First she drove to her own house, and opened the bottom drawer of her bedroom dresser, and took out a small object wrapped in a black shawl. A small wooden box lay inside the shawl's folds. As she opened it, she realised the wood was chestnut. She remembered that in the grove where her grandmother had always tethered the goats, the air always smelt of chestnut trees. This was one of the few memories she still retained of her childhood in Greece. From the wooden box, Rebecca removed the only necklace that remained, and took out the ring and the brooch. She pushed the jewels into her coat pocket.

Walking through the Jewish section of Springvale Cemetery, Rebecca was humbled by the simplicity of the gravestones. She could see across to the adjacent allotment where extravagant, baroque Catholic angels and saints reached up to the dark, simmering sky.

She remembered that she'd had the same sensation when she was a young woman at Gerry's funeral and had stood at the edge of the small group who had gathered to pay their respects to the man. She had felt foolish and a little afraid, listening to the chorus of men chant their laments in the ancient Hebrew tongue, her handkerchief tied loosely around her hair because she had not known that she was meant to cover herself with a scarf. If Lucky had been with her he would have explained the ceremony to her; she would not have felt alone. But Lucky had not come and she had been glad for it. She had never seen him as drunk, as furious as he had been that morning. His curses at God, at Anika, had been vile and shocking.

My friend did not want to be buried as a Jew, he had screamed at Rebecca. He wanted to come to the burial, to denounce God in his friend's name.

This is for Anika, Rebecca had pleaded with him. What good is your rage? The Hebrew is dead.

He suicided, her husband roared. Will they say that? Or will they lie and say he died in his sleep, will they lie and say that he was a man of God?

They cannot bury a suicide, she had answered. No faith will bury a suicide. Anika does not need that shame.

Then let me bury my friend, he implored her, not the priests or the rabbis. Let me bury my friend.

She had become angry herself then. She could not believe that for all his mocking of God and the Church, it was he, finally, who feared death more than she. You will not shame Anika, she had firmly told him. You will not shame me. And she had had her way. She had attended the burial alone.

She slowly crossed the paths, searching the headstones for his name. Rain began to fall. The stones lay close to the earth, and their markings, in English and in Hebrew, gave the barest details of the dead. She wished this too could be her fate. The cemetery reminded her of the Mohammedans' burial ground. Those people too knew God and their place in His order. She looked around at the grounds that seemed to go on forever, and realised that this earth was to be her home. Lucky was buried there, but not on consecrated ground, as her children had forced her to not betray his wishes. Tassio and Athena were buried there. Gladys and Nina, old Giorgos Atkinas, Sally O'Connor, Manolis Vachis. Kalantzis and the Old Woman, even Eleni was buried here. Her father was buried here, the Hebrew lay here. Soon she would be buried here. This was her home.

The rain was now falling heavily and she despaired of finding the grave. But finally she came across the name. It was in English, and below his name was the date of his birth and the date of his death. He had hung himself, Lucky had told her, and it had made sense to her. His death had to be courageous and virile. Underneath the dates there was the Star of David and Hebrew script. She knelt on the damp earth and stopped herself from making the sign of the Cross. Not because he had been a Jew, but because he had not been a believer. She pulled the jewellery out of her pocket and tossed the pieces onto the earth. The stones gleamed brightly and she pushed them into the earth until they disappeared from view. She looked at his name, at her son's name, and found her resolve. This is what matters, Reveka, she scolded herself, not the jewels. What matters is the promise you are about to make.

If you save my son, Lord, the Devil can have my soul.

She could never understand what brought her to do what she did next. It was as if an ethereal hand had clasped her wrist and forced her to action. Her hand had lifted a rock from the earth and she used it to pound away at the Hebrew's name. The weathered concrete face crumbled easily and before long she had erased his name.

If you save my son, Lord, she repeated, the Devil can have my soul.

As she made her way back to the car, the rain cleared and sun burst through the heavy clouds.

And so the sickness did pass. Its passing was swift. Isaac returned to the world but as he did they all noticed that his appearance had changed forever. He was no longer a young man. He awoke to find his mother and his sister, his lover and his niece and nephew, around him. He knew what he wanted.

—Zach, Isaac had called out, bring me my camera. You know how to work it, don't you?

The little boy nodded.

—Good. Isaac lay back on the pillow. Colin, fully dressed, got into the bed. Sophie lay on the other side of her brother. Rebecca, unsmiling, stayed standing, holding her grand-daughter's hand. Maritha. Sophie had called her daughter, Maritha.

—Take it, Isaac ordered, take the photograph.

The following Sunday Sophie asked her mother to go with her to church. Now that her brother was better, she would be driving home to Canberra the next day. Rebecca tied back her hair, fixed her scarf over her head and walked with her child to church. Once inside she stood in front of an icon of Christ, her God, and looked into his face. It was not the Christ Child but the stern mature face of the Christ Pantocrator. The unforgiving eyes of the creator and judge stared down at her and she bowed her head. At the end of the service the con-gregation began to queue for Holy Communion. The severe Father, still gazing down at her, admonished her as she unthinkingly went to take her place in the queue.

Rebecca pulled away from her daughter, and turned and fled the church. The trees had begun to shed their leaves. She understood now the extent of her punishment. She was never to see the light of the Saviour's face, she would never again taste of His blood, partake of His flesh. She was never again to hear her husband's booming, singing laughter, would never be reunited with her father. She was never to find rest with her family and children. This earth, this earth that smelt of sparse rain and parched ground, this earth and this boundless sky, was Hell.

The old woman leaned against a tree and began to weep. The elderly man selling almond biscuits outside the church rushed to her assistance, but she pushed him away. No. She was to be alone, forever alone.

No, whispered the boy, and his cold lips kissed her face, his stone hands clasped hers. He kissed her again and again, whispering her name, wrapping his slender, icy arms around her.

Not alone, but together. You and I, together, for all of time, for all of eternity.

ACKNoWLEDGEMENTS

This novel was made possible by the encouragement, support, argument and passion of the following people: Jessica Migotto, Jeana Vithoulkas, Angela Savage and Alan Sultan. Thank you.

And thank you to Wayne van der Stelt and Jane Palfreyman for making it all possible.